SHE WAS A MAIL-ORDER BRIDE WITHOUT A GROOM . . .

"Do you need anything in town?" John's brusque question was at odds with his earlier demeanor. Lottie turned her head to look at him.

"Well?" he added. The word was harsh. He felt frustration rise within him as he watched her. This scrap of a woman appealed to him mightily. From her golden hair to the curves beneath her dark dress to the sharp wit that edged every word she spoke, she posed a challenge that he found almost impossible to ignore.

"Why would I want anything in town?" she asked, her brows furrowed in puzzlement.

"Thought you might want to check on your preacher friend or look over the rest of the male population."

Lottie's chin lifted. "The Reverend Bush is not a subject for discussion. He eliminated himself from my list when he disappeared yesterday morning to avoid marrying me."

"How long is that list of yours?" John asked, his voice gently mocking.

She leveled a glare at him, eyes frosty with disdain. "None of your business, Mr. Tillman. Rest assured that your name was not on it."

"Not a chance. Marrying a pig in a poke is pure foolishness, as far as I can see. Never could understand how my brother could get so desperate as to send off a letter asking for a mail-order bride."

"I don't fancy being referred to as a barnyard animal, Mr. Tillman."

"My apologies, ma'am." His eyes fed on her. She'd hold her own in a battle—a worthy opponent. "I'll give you two weeks, and you'll be writing to that preacher in town to come to your rescue."

"We'll just see about that, Mr. Tillman."

TODAY'S HOTTEST READS
ARE TOMORROW'S SUPERSTARS

VICTORY'S WOMAN   (4484, $4.50)
by Gretchen Genet
Andrew—the carefree soldier who sought glory on the battlefield,
and returned a shattered man . . . Niall—the legendary frontiers-
man and a former Shawnee captive, tormented by his past . . .
Roger—the troubled youth, who would rise up to claim a shock-
ing legacy . . . and Clarice—the passionate beauty bound by one
man, and hopelessly in love with another. Set against the back-
drop of the American revolution, three men fight for their
heritage—and one woman is destined to change all their lives forever!

FORBIDDEN   (4488, $4.99)
by Jo Beverley
While fleeing from her brothers, who are attempting to sell her
into a loveless marriage, Serena Riverton accepts a carriage ride
from a stranger—who is the handsomest man she has ever seen.
Lord Middlethorpe, himself, is actually contemplating marriage
to a dull daughter of the aristocracy, when he encounters the
breathtaking Serena. She arouses him as no woman ever has. And
after a night of thrilling intimacy—a forbidden liaison—Serena
must choose between a lady's place and a woman's passion!

WINDS OF DESTINY   (4489, $4.99)
by Victoria Thompson
Becky Tate is a half-breed outcast—branded by her Comanche
heritage. Then she meets a rugged stranger who awakens her
heart to the magic and mystery of passion. Hiding a desperate
past, Texas Ranger Clint Masterson has ridden into cattle country
to bring peace to a divided land. But a greater battle rages inside
him when he dares to desire the beautiful Becky!

WILDEST HEART   (4456, $4.99)
by Virginia Brown
Maggie Malone had come to cattle country to forge her future as
a healer. Now she was faced by Devon Conrad, an outlaw
wounded body and soul by his shadowy past . . . whose eyes
blazed with fury even as his burning caress sent her spiraling with
desire. They came together in a Texas town about to explode in sin
and scandal. Danger was their destiny—and there was nothing
they wouldn't dare for love!

Available wherever paperbacks are sold, or order direct from the
Publisher. Send cover price plus 50¢ per copy for mailing and
handling to Penguin USA, P.O. Box 999, c/o Dept. 17109,
Bergenfield, NJ 07621. Residents of New York and Tennessee
must include sales tax. DO NOT SEND CASH.

CAROLYN DAVIDSON
HOMESPUN BRIDE

ZEBRA BOOKS
KENSINGTON PUBLISHING CORP.

ZEBRA BOOKS are published by

Kensington Publishing Corp.
850 Third Avenue
New York, NY 10022

Second Printing: February, 1995

Printed in the United States of America

To Susan Elizabeth Davidson Niepoth, daughter and friend, whose faith in her mother has been a constant encouragement since the very beginning.

And with special thanks to Dr. Debbie Dove-Kidd DC, for keeping me "straight" and generously sharing with me from her storehouse of knowledge.

But most of all, to Mister Ed, who loves me!

Prologue

The two men were as much a matched pair as the horses that pulled the hay wagon. Brawny, tall and bronzed by the Missouri sun, they were farmers. Their heads were crowned with lush golden hair, almost shoulder-length—they were both in need of a haircut. But cutting hay took precedence over vanity, and since neither of them was burdened by that particular sin anyway, the barbering could wait.

Sweat streaked James Tillman's brow, and he drew his muscular forearm over it in a weary gesture. "Next turn about, we'll stop in the shade for a drink, John," he called out to the man who worked to one side of the heavy, wooden farm wagon.

John looked up at his older brother with a grin. "Tired already, old man?" he asked with mocking humor.

"I'm not too old to take you on, young'un," James retorted from his perch atop the hay. Legs spread wide for balance, he thrust his pitchfork into the rounded stack and leaned on it.

"You'll have to run at a pretty good clip to catch me," John answered with a chuckle, "and I'm not sure you're up to it."

"Pitch hay, boy," James hollered in a voice that would

have made a lesser man cringe. "I've got plans for this evening."

His pitchfork full of fragrant alfalfa, John stopped midway through the thrust that would have sailed it to within inches of where his brother stood. His brow furrowed momentarily, and he clenched his jaw.

"You haven't got your hopes up, have you, James?" he asked quietly. "She may choose the preacher. After all, he sent the money for her fare."

James shook his head in an arrogant gesture that suited his posturing. Like a Viking of old, he lifted his face to the sun. The gleaming gold of his hair caught its rays.

"She'll surely choose a prosperous farmer over that young sprout the bishop sent out last year," he said firmly. "I've already told the reverend I'd repay him what loose change he's invested in her transport."

"What if she's cross-eyed and bow-legged?" John asked slyly, his smile wide as he mentioned the possibility.

"I need a woman to cook and tend the house," his brother retorted with an imperious wave of his hand. "She can do that so long as she has two legs and isn't blind."

"You can always put a sack over her head at bedtime," John teased. "That is, if there's room in your bed for both of you."

James laughed, and the sound rolled from him. "If she's got a bit too much weight on her, I'll work it off," he bragged with masculine pride.

"Mail-order bride . . . who ever would have thought a Tillman would be sending away for a woman." John scratched his neck where bits of hay stuck to the sweaty surface of his skin. "You'd just better hope she's willing to raise those two young'uns Sarah left you with."

James sobered and his mouth firmed as a residue of pain drew furrows in his cheeks. "She said in her letter that she likes children," he said as he met the eyes of his brother. Sarah's name had put a damper on their frivolity, and they both felt it. "I know it's too soon, with Sarah only gone six months," he muttered.

"She'd understand." It was firm and certain. Both of them knew that the woman who had been James's wife would have gladly given her blessing if the choice were hers.

With a rough gesture, James urged his brother on. "If we don't get this hay into the barn, I won't have time to get to town," he said. Pitchfork ready, he watched as John shifted his weight to toss a sheaf in his direction. Spreading it toward the back of the wagon, he once more settled into the rhythm of the chore. One man pitching a forkful from the neat rows that the hay rake had lined up only yesterday, the other packing the loose alfalfa on the wagon.

They had worked as a team for so long that it was automatic. Their muscular arms flexed, their bodies bent and their golden heads gleamed in the noon sunshine. Completing the semicircle around the wagon, John halted and motioned to his brother.

James nodded and reached for the reins which were twisted about an upright stake in the front corner of the flatbed wagon. With a flex of his wrist, he snapped the leather above the horse's backs and let the reins fall to rest upon their broad flanks. Slowly, as if they knew that the journey was short, they walked in unison and were brought to a halt before they had gone six yards.

Wrapping the reins loosely about the stake, James

reached for his pitchfork. So quickly that John later could never be sure how it had happened, the older man slipped, the fork flying from his hand, its tines piercing the hindquarters of one of his patient horses. Rearing in pain, the animal lurched against the harness, frantic to escape. James fell between its flying hooves and the heavily laden wagon.

Before he could reach the head of the team, before his hands pulled on the harness to quiet the snorting animals, John knew. Before he made his way to where his brother lay beneath the wheel, he had felt overwhelming dread seize his chest in a grip that stopped his breathing. And before those blue eyes opened to gaze into his with a look of stunned surprise, John's heart had begun to shatter with grief.

"Ah, James . . ." he moaned. "Why . . . oh, James." His voice broke in anguish.

A trail of bright crimson blood flowed from James's mouth as the grievously wounded man struggled to speak. But the words were lost in the pain of shattered ribs that had pierced a lung and punctured an artery within his chest. Blood flowed in a pulsing stream and, even as he spoke, John knew his words were unheard.

The sun shone, obscenely beautiful upon the scene. It glittered in the river of blood that ended the life of James Tillman in a hayfield just a few miles from Mill Creek, Missouri.

One

Life had never been particularly easy. If Lottie knew anything at all about her chances, it was about to get more difficult.

If it had not been for the jouncing of the hard seat beneath her, she would have long since been tempted to relax and close her eyes against the bright rays of the setting sun. Low in the west, it glared with intensity and she squinted against it. In the near distance a grove of trees caught her attention, and she groaned as a particularly deep hole in the rutted road they traveled reminded her painfully that she'd best not be sightseeing. Surely it can't be much farther, she thought stoically, as she hung on to her high perch with desperate hands and gritted her teeth.

The man who drove the team of horses had ignored her from the beginning. Slouched beside her, he clutched the reins with gnarled fingers, and except for shifting his well-worn boots occasionally, he appeared oblivious to her presence. She had been the object of a slow, critical appraisal as she climbed atop the seat of his wagon in town, and then ignored as the buckboard jerked into motion.

Henry Clawson had made no secret of his dislike for this chore, and had obviously not relished the thought of being responsible for his female passenger and her

meager bundles and bedraggled belongings. Certainly
he lacked the social graces, Lottie had decided, when
with a disgruntled glare, a nod, and a spray of tobacco-
colored spittle, he had reluctantly agreed to cart her
along on his return trip from town.

Lottie shivered as a breeze from the west fluttered
the ribbons that tied her hat, and then hunched her
shoulders against the promise of cooler air. She thought
of her shawl, shoved into one corner of her carpetbag
earlier in the day, and deliberated for a moment. If she
didn't have to hang on so tightly to the seat, and if the
bag in question weren't so far in the rear of this cum-
bersome wagon, it might be worth the venture to search
for it. But, as matters stood, she decided that she was
probably doomed to sit next to this silent example of
manhood and hope that it wouldn't rain before they
arrived.

The wagon rattled on its way for well over an hour.
Ahead, the sun was almost below the horizon, settling
rapidly between two gentle hills that gave relief to the
flatness of the landscape. Off to the right, a line of
trees took shape, offering a welcome respite from the
monotonous view. The green foliage provided a trail of
its own, and the final rays of the sun glittered on the
water that flowed between the clusters of willows and
verdant bushes.

"We're here," came the rough pronouncement from
next to her. Lottie squinted, peering through her lashes,
as white structures loomed in the twilight just beyond
the winding stream.

She bit at her lower lip, clung to the unyielding seat
beneath her, and anxiously surveyed the buildings for
signs of occupancy. The man next to her let loose a

stream of tobacco juice over his side of the wagon, and then turned to face her.

"James'll likely be in the barn, putting up hay," he grunted. His head nodded off to her right toward the largest building, and she squinted in the approaching darkness. She caught sight of a woman's figure, almost indistinguishable in a dark dress that blended into the evening shadows.

Lottie stiffened her spine. Whatever awaited her here could not be worse than what she had left in Boston, she reminded herself firmly. James Tillman was a respectable man, a widower with two young children, and though he was her second choice, he had offered her a new life. He'd offered her his name and a place to live. And according to the sheriff of Mill Creek, Missouri, James Tillman was going to be delighted to find that she was prepared to be his bride after all.

Next to her, her companion gripped the reins in one burly fist and pulled his team to a halt, rising to his feet with a muttered oath, as he glowered at the woman who waited to greet him.

"What you doin' here, Maude?" The question was abrupt, his surprise obvious, and his disapproval apparent.

"James had an accident, Henry," the woman answered and then tilted her head to look up with suspicion at Lottie.

"Who's she?" she asked.

"Miss Lottie O'Malley, according to the sheriff. She needed a ride out here. Sheriff says James will be expecting her."

The tired eyes blinked once and then with a shrug the woman looked up at Lottie. "So, James really did it? Really sent for a woman from back East?"

Lottie nodded slowly. Her tongue touched the center of her top lip and her fingers twisted in her lap as she faced the censure of the older woman who watched her.

"The preacher brought letters from several men in this area who were looking for wives and I chose two who—" Lottie stopped, aware of the silence that had fallen as she spoke.

"Well, I hate to be the one to tell you, but you better hope the other offer still stands, Miss O'Malley," the woman said, her voice flat and without inflection, as if she had long since used up her store of emotion.

"He changed his mind?" Lottie asked in a tight little voice that caught in her throat.

Maude shook her head. "He got run over by the hay wagon this afternoon. His brother John came to get me to watch the children." Her chin lifted and jerked to the right. "They're inside."

Lottie clutched at the folds of her skirt and shivered, as a chill wind blew around the corner of the house. The gathering darkness, the stoic expression of the woman before her, and the silence of the man who stood now on the ground next to his buckboard pressed in on her. She felt a deepening sense of foreboding.

"Is he hurt bad?" she asked softly, her eyes scanning the yard and focusing finally on the barn.

Maude blew out her breath and nodded in a gesture that clutched at Lottie's racing heart.

"About as bad as you can get, Miss. His brother's gettin' ready to take him to town on the wagon."

"To the doctor?" Lottie asked hopefully, even as she saw Maude's head shake.

"He's dead. John's takin' him to the undertaker," she answered flatly.

"You'll need to be getting back home, Maude," Lottie's traveling companion said as he walked around his team of horses and approached his wife. "I'll ride to town with John. You take the wagon on home."

Lottie stood up quickly. Her mind was spinning in a hopeless whirl. Gone were the hopeful dreams of marriage to a good man. In their place was the stark reality of death and darkness and her own bleak situation. Behind her eyelids, hot tears fought for escape, and she bit harder against the soft flesh of her lip as she swallowed against the lump that had formed in her throat.

"What will I do?" she whispered to herself.

"What about her, Maude?" the man asked gruffly as he cast a glance at the girl who stood in his buckboard, her face a pale shadow against the twilight sky.

"Well, she won't lack for something to do," Maude sniffed. "Those children need to be tended to. I thought to take them home, but since she's here, she can look after them."

Lottie sighed. Her smile was weary as she heard the familiar words. "I guess I can, all right," she said as she turned and climbed down from the wagon, taking care not to soil her dress on the wheel. She was wrinkled and dusty, but there was no sense in making it any worse. Taking care of children was old hat. She could do it in her sleep, she thought with resignation. It was what she had been doing for years, after all.

"John will need to stop at the preacher's place, so he can get ready for the burying," Maude reminded her husband briefly, as she prepared to get into the place Lottie had vacated.

"Not much chance of that." Henry shot a sidelong glance at Lottie, as she struggled to lift her bundles from the back of the wagon. "Preacher's gone," he said with distaste. "Ran off this morning."

"He was supposed to marry me," Lottie snapped as she grappled with the last of her shabby assortment.

"Two men sent for you? Were you his intended?" Maude asked with guarded interest.

Lottie nodded. "The Reverend Bush sent money for my traveling expenses, but James—Mr. Tillman wrote that he would marry me, if I decided against the preacher once I got here."

"Where'd he go?" Maude asked, and nodded as Henry shrugged and shook his head. "Cold feet, more than likely," she muttered beneath her breath. "You'd been better off with James, anyhow," she said sagely as she looked down at Lottie.

"Well, it looks like I'm not getting married to anybody," Lottie said briskly, determined to keep the tears at bay until she could find a private hole to crawl into. Not much else could go wrong, she thought in despair. James Tillman's death was the crowning touch to a miserable day. She had been abandoned twice, although, to be honest, James Tillman's departure had certainly not been voluntary.

"Well, get on inside," Maude advised her. "There's enough to do in there to keep you busy till John gets back. Give her a hand with her things, Henry."

Silently, the big man gathered up her boxes and Lottie lifted the bag that held most of her clothing, heading for the shallow porch that fronted the cabin.

The door opened, scraping against the floor inside, and two small figures stood silhouetted, a lantern within the house shining behind them. Dressed in a homespun shift, the small girl was standing on one bare foot, her toes curled against the wooden flooring. Her other foot was drawn up, its sole pressed against her shinbone. She wavered there, clutching her brother's arm with tiny fingers. The boy was older, dressed in overalls that he had almost outgrown, his shirt tucked in haphazardly, his expression defiant. But beneath his lowered eyebrows, Lottie caught sight of the frightened child who was facing his unknown future as best he could.

"I can take care of Sissy," he said in a thin voice that wavered just a little.

"I suspect you can," Lottie agreed quietly. She waited, allowing him a few moments to look her over. "But I have nowhere to go right now. May I come in?" she asked.

Sissy lowered her foot to the floor and shuffled a few inches closer to her brother. "Let her come in," she said in a teary whisper.

Lottie drew in a quick breath, her heart touched by the woebegone expression on the small face. Without hesitation, she stepped onto the porch and dropped to her knees, holding out her arms in an unmistakable gesture.

The flaxen-haired child held back for only seconds, then stepped forward, accepting the comfort offered. Lottie's eyes met those of the boy as he firmed his lips and nodded at her.

"You can come on in," he allowed, his eyes on his sister as she clung to the woman who held her.

"Get these things, boy," Henry called from the edge of the porch, as he dumped Lottie's belongings on the single step.

"Yessir," the boy answered quickly, moving past Lottie and his sister to pick up the bundles and Lottie's ancient carpetbag.

"Can't get past you, ma'am," he said from behind her.

Her face was buried in the slightly sour-smelling hair of the child she held. Lottie struggled to her feet, lifting the girl in her arms and clutching her tightly. Her right foot tripped on a floorboard that was awry, and she barely saved herself and the child she carried from disaster as she aimed for the nearest chair.

With a *whoosh* of air, she sat down, the child straddling her lap and clasping her firmly, her small face buried in the ample curves of Lottie's bosom. The boy struggled with her belongings and made a second trip to the porch before he managed to carry them all inside.

"Ma'am?" Henry called in her direction.

"Yes," she answered over the little girl's head, rocking in the chair as if she would comfort the child by the swaying motion.

From the doorway, he eyed her grimly and wiped one big callused hand across his mouth before he spoke. His tone was more subdued, as though death had softened his demeanor. "Maude here's going on home, and I'm heading for town with James's brother." He jerked his head over his shoulder. Beyond him Lottie could make out another man at the edge of the porch.

"What do you want me to do?" she asked softly, her mind befuddled by the turn of events.

"Who is she?"

At the sound of the words, terse and angry in the darkness, Lottie's eyes narrowed, peering through the shadows to where the tall figure stood. The man separated himself from the night and stepped onto the porch and watched her from behind Henry, his face drawn in harsh lines.

The figures blended for a moment as the homesteader backed from the room, and then the doorway was filled with the man who had snarled the question.

"Who are you?" he asked again, this time directing his query at the young woman who sat in the middle of the cluttered room.

"Lottie O'Malley," she answered evenly, rocking more slowly as she held the whimpering child tightly to her chest.

"I suppose you're the mail-order bride?" His look reeked of scorn as he swept his dark gaze over her. His lips curled in a humorless smile as he allowed his eyes to rest on her bonnet.

From deep within her, a spark of anger ignited. Bedecked with flowers and gilded with ribbon, the navy blue bonnet had been her one extravagance. The one bright spot in her wardrobe, the booster of her flagging spirits during the long, tiresome trip to this miserable dust speck in the middle of the country. And this man, unless she missed her guess, was sneering at it.

"Can you cook something for the children to eat?" he asked her, his expression doubtful as he scanned the length of her slender form.

"I can cook," she allowed, her lips tightening as her tattered emotions began to fray at the edges.

His eyes doubted her claim.

She lifted her chin and rose from the chair, allowing the little girl to slide from her grasp. The child stood next to her, one grimy hand clutching a handful of her skirt.

Lottie had been, by turn, hopeful and disappointed more than once during this long day. She had been bruised by a long, bumpy ride to the middle of nowhere, dumped in a less than graceful manner to cope with two grieving children, and then assailed by this . . .

this man . . . who wanted to know if she could cook. She, who had single-handedly run the kitchen of the New Hope Orphanage for Young Females.

Her chin lifted a fraction higher and her hands clasped defensively at her waistline as she glared her finest frown at the man in the doorway.

"I've been cooking for more years than you can imagine," she said severely, her eyes flashing fire for the first time in days. Her back stiffened before his disbelieving look, then he shrugged, as if the matter were of little account.

"Just don't let them starve before I get back from town," he said stiffly. "I'm taking my brother in to the undertaker."

Lottie closed her eyes against the pain in his voice as he turned away from her. For a moment, she had forgotten. James Tillman was his brother. He had seen him killed, had brought him in from the field, had suffered the loss by himself. And she had snapped at him.

A flush suffused her face. She took one hesitant step to the doorway, in time to see him move away from the porch. He turned back momentarily and their eyes met, his dark and shadowed, the scorn held in abeyance as they sought her face.

"Bar the door when you go to bed," he instructed her. "If I get back tonight, I'll bunk in the barn."

Two

Thomas was the boy's name. Seven years old, headed for seventeen at a fast pace, from what Lottie could tell. She watched him as he carefully added chunks of firewood to the cookstove, conserving the precious commodity as he peered into the coals, gauging the fire's intensity.

"That ought to do it, ma'am," he said finally, wiping his hands against the worn fabric of his overalls. His hair, a combination of tan and golden blond, hung in uneven lengths about his head. One hank draped across his forehead, stuck to the faint mist of perspiration that the heat of the cookstove had brought to the surface. His eyes were solemn as he pronounced his chore completed, and Lottie caught a glimpse of boyish pride in the set of his mouth and the angle of his jaw.

"Thank you, Thomas," she said crisply, her tone defying the wearying fatigue that had beset her. Sitting down with Sissy had been a mistake. All of the joints that the wagon ride had tested so severely were crying for rest. She had been sorely tempted to make her way to the bed that took up one corner of the large room.

But years of conditioning had taught her that food never got cooked and put on the table without someone holding a spoon and stirring the pot. Lottie had been a pot-stirrer since she was able to reach the iron range in the orphanage kitchen. Hungry children had long provided her with incentive enough to keep her busy three times a day, doing her inventive best to fill their stomachs.

"Can you fix oatmeal?" Sissy asked shyly, peering through tangled curls with wistful eyes.

"Is that what you like to eat?" Lottie asked. One look in the rough cupboard had been enough to tell her that food supplies were down to bare essentials, and she had been contemplating corn mush as a last resort. Oatmeal didn't sound much more inspiring, she thought, but if the children were fond of it, she could make a meal of most anything at this point.

"We've got some raisins left to put in it," Thomas suggested from across the room. "I can get you a piece of side pork from the barrel, Miss Lottie, if you want to slice it up."

She shot him a grateful glance and her smile was brilliant. "That sounds like a good idea," she said with enthusiasm. "We'll get some supper going in no time, Thomas."

James Tillman had been a thoughtful husband, Lottie decided, looking around the house. His wife had had to carry water from the pump outside, but she had a sink to put it in. A shiny black cookstove reigned against one wall and a cupboard of sorts stood near it. The shelves held a surprisingly nice assortment of dishes and tableware.

The cabin was large by settler standards, with a loft accessible by a sturdy ladder. The furnishings were sparse, but solid. Two chairs, complete with handmade cushions, sat near the fireplace. A footstool, constructed of small logs, tied together and covered with the same fabric showed the loving hand of the woman James had married and then buried.

She couldn't have been dead very long, Lottie decided as she remembered the half-dozen glass jars of canned goods that reflected the lantern glow from the back of the cupboard shelves. A faint tinge of neglect coated the entire room though, silent witness to the lack of a woman here.

Her chin lifted in an unconscious gesture of determination as she made another survey of her surroundings. Already her busy mind was listing chores to occupy the morning to come as Thomas came through the doorway with a bundle in his hands.

"Here you go, ma'am," he said breathlessly. He must have hurried through the darkness. He offered her the piece of pork, wrapped in a feed sack, and she smiled her approval as she accepted it from his hands.

"Now, if you'll find me a knife, Thomas, I'll slice some of this off and put it to cook while the oatmeal comes to a boil." The battered kettle she had half-filled from the bucket was beginning to steam. She scooped a double handful of oats into the simmering water. The meat smelled fresh, not like some of the moldy pieces she had scraped and cleaned at the orphanage before she could cook them. James Tillman had been a careful farmer.

Once more a pang of sorrow at the twist of fate that had robbed these two young ones of their only parent struck her. Lottie fought back the quick tears that blurred her vision. Bad enough to be motherless. The loss of their father was a crushing blow.

Side pork sizzled in a black iron skillet and oatmeal bubbled gently on the back of the stove. Lottie moved between the stove and cupboard, locating bowls and a plate for the meat as Sissy watched with wide eyes. Her hands clutched a ragged piece of blanket in her lap as she huddled in one of the three chairs that surrounded the table. The fourth side was closest to the stove, leaving a passage for Lottie to travel as she prepared the meal.

Silently and without prompting, Thomas located a jug and disappeared out the door, leaving it partially open as he headed for the small shed halfway to the barn. Reappearing within moments, he carried the jug, brimming with milk, into the kitchen. With one foot, he nudged the door closed behind himself. It scraped on the wooden floor, and he finally leaned his backside against it to close it firmly.

"Do you want me to put the bar across?" he asked as he lifted the jug to the tabletop. "It's full dark out, and I doubt Uncle John will be back for a long time yet," he said. His voice wavered a bit as he spoke the last few words.

Lottie clenched her teeth at the young boy's acceptance of events. Sorrow was written on his countenance, his eyes were dark and shadowed by his grief, but he held within himself the depths of his hurt. The looks he cast in his young sister's direction were frequent. He seemed to monitor her well-being. His eyes often watched Lottie, alert and intent on doing his share of preparation.

"Does your uncle live here, too, Thomas?" Lottie asked as she turned the savory meat in its own grease, careful to stand back so that the splattering would not stain her dress.

"No, ma'am," he replied. "He has a place just a ways from here, toward town."

Lottie frowned, scanning her memory. "I don't recall

seeing another farm building on my way out here, once we left the farms close in to Mill Creek," she said slowly.

Thomas stepped closer to her, his eyes intent on the food that filled the small house with savory smells. "His place is back off the road, built close to the river. The track is about a mile or so and over a rise. Can't see it from the town road," he explained as he pursed his lips and inhaled the scent of his supper.

Lottie smiled at him and shared his simple enjoyment, her nostrils flaring as she sampled the savory odor of the meat. "We're ready to dish up, Thomas. Help your sister to wash her hands, will you?" she asked.

"Yes, ma'am," he answered as he scooped Sissy from her chair and led her to the sink. Dipping a rag that lay on the edge of the wooden cabinet into a pan of water that sat in the sink, he dampened it, then swiped at her tiny fingers. Carefully, he drew the rough cotton fabric across her face, dabbing at the dried runnels where tears had left their marks earlier.

"Oh, Thomas, you make owwies on me," the little girl protested, screwing up her mouth and wrinkling her nose as she backed away from his ministrations.

"I'm being careful, Sissy," he said patiently as he scrubbed gently at a spot on her chin.

Sissy bore up under his touch, her mouth pouting, her eyes squinted shut, and her fists clenched at her sides. Lottie turned away to hide the smile that would not be denied at the sight of the child's forbearance. For a moment, she envisioned what her life might have been like, were James Tillman still alive, if he had claimed her as his wife. Wistfully, she allowed herself to pretend that these children were her own, that this house . . .

She shook her head at her own foolishness. Dreams are a waste of time, Miss Conklin used to say, back in the kitchen of the orphanage. Face up to life and expect the worst . . . that way you won't be disappointed. It was only one of her firm beliefs that had been drummed into a youthful Lottie for years.

The heavy bowls were steaming with hot oatmeal, laced with plump raisins and swimming in fresh milk as the three sat down. Sissy perched on her knees, the better to bend over her bowl. Thomas folded his hands, signaling to his sister as she reached for a spoon from the jar in the center of the table. Belatedly, she settled back on her heels and carefully held her hands together beneath her chin, shutting her eyes tightly while she waited.

"Ma'am?" Thomas prompted.

Lottie bowed her own head and was silent for a moment. What could she say, what words could she speak in this house where happiness was so fragile a commodity? Where death was a reality to two small children . . . and where she was existing on sufferance.

The words came from her memory and she spoke them quietly, repeating by rote the prayer that had been delivered three times a day throughout her childhood. ". . . For what we are about to receive, make us truly thankful. Amen."

Both children repeated her final word and, without hesitation, reached for a spoon. Quietly, Lottie began her own meal, relishing the flavor of the oatmeal, comparing it with a grim memory of the porridge she had eaten as a child. Watery and thin, scantily doused with skim milk, a donation from a local grocer who used the cream to make butter for sale in his establishment . . . the mainstay of orphanage breakfast time.

"I sure like raisins," Sissy breathed, chewing with her eyes shut and savoring the flavor of the tasty fruit.

"Pa got them for a treat when he sold the extra corn crop," Thomas explained. "He even got brown sugar and some tea."

"Did your pa like tea?" Lottie asked, wondering if there was any left to be brewed. Tea had been scarce in her own memory, a rare treat.

"Naw, he liked coffee better. But Ma always liked tea. She used to make it for us sometimes, with milk and sugar." He scooped a spoonful of oatmeal into his mouth and shrugged in a regretful fashion. "It didn't taste the same when Pa made it, though. But we drank it anyway. We didn't want him to feel bad."

"Maybe we can brew some for breakfast, if you like," Lottie suggested, unsure if she would be treading on old memories, better left alone.

"I like tea," Sissy announced firmly. "I'd have some for breakfast."

So much for that, Lottie thought with quiet satisfaction. Sissy was apparently a resilient little soul, able to seek comfort from a stranger, willing to accept whatever came her way.

"You may help in the morning," Lottie promised the girl. "While Thomas does chores, we'll fix breakfast." She glanced up at the boy and lifted her eyebrows.

"What are your chores?" she asked him quietly. "Will you need help?"

"Uncle John will be here," he replied "I just feed the chickens and turn them loose during the day. Pa was just teaching me how to milk Rosie, and I have to carry out the stuff to slop the pigs."

"What stuff?" Lottie wanted to know. Slopping pigs sounded like a messy job to her way of thinking.

"Leftover milk and whatever food scraps we got in the house," Thomas explained glibly.

From the looks of things, there weren't going to be many leftovers for the pigs in the morning, Lottie decided as the children cleaned their bowls and licked the greasy side pork from their fingers. They sat back in their chairs and Sissy sighed deeply.

"I think I can go to bed now," she said with certainty. "I'm real tired, Miss Lottie."

"Considering what you've been through today, I wouldn't be a bit surprised," Lottie whispered under her breath as she cleared the table quickly and deposited the few dishes in the sink. She opened the reservoir on the side of the cookstove and noted with relief that it had been filled, probably early in the morning. With a small pan, she dipped water, carrying it the few steps to the sink, pouring it over the dirty dishes.

"Where do you keep the soap, Thomas?" she asked, bending to poke beneath the sink top.

"In there," he said from behind her, pointing at a glass jar that held the glutenous, gray stuff she was looking for. Scooping out a bit, she swished it through the dishwater, and then dried her hands on a dingy towel that lay across a peg at the end of the sinkboard.

"Let's get you washed up and into bed, Sissy," she said, coaxing the child with wiggling fingers and a tender smile. Small arms lifted and a sleepy face formed a lopsided grin as the girl reached for her. Breathing deeply, Sissy burrowed her nose into the front of Lottie's dress and sighed in a satisfied fashion.

"You smell good," she mumbled as she relaxed against the warmth and comfort that had been offered.

"Soap and water and a little rose sachet," Lottie said with a chuckle.

In a matter of half an hour, the cleaning up had been accomplished, Sissy was tucked into her trundle in the loft and Lottie had refused Thomas's offer of a fire in the fireplace.

"We'll be fine with the cookstove till morning, Thomas," she said firmly. "No sense in using the wood."

The bar had been put up across the door, fitting into wooden arms on either side of the doorway. Thomas yawned widely as he headed for the ladder. "Good night, ma'am," he said. He halted on the second step and looked back at Lottie. "You'll be here tomorrow, won't you?"

Her heart lurched within her chest at his tentative look and hopeful question, and she nodded. "Of course I will. I'll be here as long as your Uncle John needs me to be."

The scent of newly mown hay had risen about John Tillman's weary body through the night like a fine perfume. Even this morning he inhaled it deeply, not immune to the sweet, harvest smell.

For a moment, close upon wakening, he'd forgotten, his mind only aware of his surroundings. Not for the first time, he'd spent the night in his brother's barn, cradled in the loose hay, wrapped in a musty quilt.

But this morning was different. Lifting his head, he heard once again the sound that had roused him, the lowing of a cow past milking time. Rosie, foolish name for a cow, he thought with a scowl. But then, Sarah had given the choice to the children, and Sissy had lisped out the word without hesitation.

Sarah. The fair, unattainable woman who had married his brother. The mother of his brother's children.

Sarah . . . pure of countenance . . . pure of heart . . .
surely pure enough for the angel choir, James had told
the children.

John Tillman rolled from the cocoon of quilt that
surrounded his big body and surged to his feet. The
luxury of dwelling on Sarah's memory was one he rarely
allowed himself. Certainly, this morning, it was sinful
to be remembering her. He'd need to push her over in
his mind, make room for James to be beside her once
more.

He clenched his teeth against the pain, but the ache
in his chest only clutched harder, taking his breath in
its intensity. Eyes closed, he saw it again, heard the
creaking of the hay wagon, the low rumble of his
brother's chuckle in response to the ripe, ribald teasing
that had been tossed between them. He'd watched for
a frozen moment the flight of the pitchfork, James
lurching off balance, then the jolting of the wagon as
the horses bolted, throwing James beneath . . .

A groan escaped his lips, a cry from his depths, and
he threw back his head to release it.

Once more Rosie moved in her stall, and the mundane chores of the morning gave him reason to set aside
his grief. Time enough to mourn when things were put
to rights. For now, it was enough that he prepare the
children for what they must face today. And then, there
was the issue of James's piece of fluff from the East to
deal with.

Flowers and ribbons on her hat. Curls dangling next
to her ears, and that tilted-up little chin that defied him
so pertly. She'd smelled good. Even from four feet away,
he'd caught the scent of her, that faint, flowery woman
scent that made him think of Sarah.

"She's nothing like Sarah," he admitted to himself

under his breath. "Still don't understand what he was thinking of . . . having her come here." He jerked on his boots and stomped them into place, his words huffing out with each breath. "She'd probably never have come if the preacher hadn't offered for her. That'd been a good place for her . . . her bonnet might have to go, though," he said, muttering the words to himself. He propped his foot on a sawhorse and bent to tuck his pant leg down into the leather that rose halfway to his knee. Reversing feet, he repeated the procedure, then shoved his shirt snugly inside his pants, pulling his suspenders into place.

The Reverend Bush wasn't much for frippery, he recalled with a wry twist of his mouth. Plain black and no frills was more his style. Too bad he hadn't stuck around to meet his bride, John thought with disdain. It would have saved me from having to ship her back.

He stood in the wide doorway of the barn and watched as the sun rose in the eastern sky. The clouds were wispy, pink on the edges and too high to bring any rain. He eyed the neat array of buildings that formed his brother's yard. The spring house, the corncrib, the chicken house, where even now the hens were noisily proclaiming their accomplishments. The stone smokehouse was almost empty, he knew, awaiting fall butchering. So much to do and no man on the place.

"You shouldn't have died, James," he groaned in agony. The doorpost provided a resting place for his brow as he breathed his anger and despair.

The voice woke her, then the steady thumping against the door brought Lottie upright in the bed. She watched with horror as Thomas lifted the bar.

"Wait, Thomas," she protested, clutching the quilt to her throat as she sat in the middle of the feather tick mattress.

He glanced at her over his shoulder and lifted the bar with a grunt. "It's only Uncle John," he said reassuringly.

"I'm in bed, Thomas," she said despairingly as the door swung open slowly and the tall man entered, blocking the daylight with his breadth.

His shoulders were wide beneath the blue chambray shirt; dark suspenders held up denim pants. His face was damp, and his hair was slicked back from his forehead. Boots rose halfway to his knees; his trouser legs were tucked into them neatly. Feet apart, he halted just inside the door as his eyes swept the dimness of the cabin.

"It's time to be up," he announced in the same gravelly voice she remembered from last night.

"I'm sorry . . ." she said, her words husky as she began the apology.

"The chores won't wait for lay-a-beds, Miss O'Malley," John Tillman said harshly. "You're only welcome as long as you can make yourself useful here."

Her chin lifted and her eyes flashed with anger. For the second time in less than twelve hours, the man had succeeded in setting off her fuse. She fought the words that flooded her mind. Better to be silent than to be foolish, Miss Conklin used to say. For once Lottie obeyed her better instincts.

"If you'll leave for a few minutes, I'll get up," she said carefully, unwilling to anger him while her position was so unsure.

"I'll turn my back," he said as if that were his final

word. Swiveling toward the doorway and leaning against the uprights on either side, he waited.

"Thomas . . ." she said firmly and, following his uncle's example, the boy joined him, squeezing past him to step onto the porch, careful to keep his back to the woman inside.

Lottie slid from the bed, lurching from the comfort of the feather tick and rising to stand on the braided rug that kept her bare feet from the wooden flooring. Groping in her carpetbag, she pulled out a pale gray dress and clean undergarments, then quickly pulled them on beneath her nightgown. Stepping into her petticoat, she drew it up and tied it at the waist, before she turned her back on the doorway and lifted her gown over her head. She drew on her camisole and tied it between her breasts before she tucked it into the waistline of her petticoat. Next she swept the fullness of her dress into a double handful of material and plunged her upper body into it, sliding her arms into the sleeves and tugging the gathered skirt into place. Her fingers flew to fasten the buttons, and she turned back to glance at the broad back of the man who waited for her to make herself presentable.

"You may turn around now," she said as she bent to locate her hairbrush in the box she had opened late last evening. It held her essentials for grooming. The last thing she had done before retiring had been to brush out her hair. It hung now in a tangled mass, over her shoulders and past her waist, gleaming in a pale cloud as she shook it from her face.

The picture she presented to the man who watched her was enticing. Unknowingly seductive, she lifted her arms to scoop the length of her hair to one side, preparing to tame it with her brush and braid it into submission. The full, lush lines of her breasts formed a tempting curve beneath the coarse cotton fabric of her dress, and he felt a heated coil twist in his groin as his narrowed gaze treasured the gentle rounding of her bosom.

It's been a long dry spell, John Tillman, he acknowledged to himself. When the innocent movements of a young woman could catch him so unawares at six o'clock in the morning, he was in bad shape. Needy, that's what he was, and in no position to do much about it.

His eyes slid down her form, estimating the circumference of her narrow waist and noting the flare of her hips beneath the faded gown. Then he reversed the route his hungry gaze had taken, and found himself looking into startled eyes. From the flush that traced her fine cheekbones, he'd have to guess that Lottie was either mighty embarrassed, or well on her way to being mad as a wet hen.

Good, John thought. He wanted her flustered and off balance. Probably she was used to being given the once-over, and she wouldn't be beyond sashaying her little behind a bit to tempt a prospective husband. Mail-order brides were a mixed lot these days, he reminded himself. Lester, down at the lumber mill, had almost got caught up with a pretty little piece who wrote dandy letters. She'd just conveniently forgotten to tell him about the bundle she carried under her apron. It had turned out all right though, when one of the older farmers took her in and ended up marrying her.

Then, too, there'd been a few who were beyond the usual marrying age, who'd fudged a bit on their number of birthdays. But in the woman-hungry West beyond Mill Creek, they'd nevertheless managed to find a place to land and a nest to feather once they arrived.

This one was a plain little piece—though with no worry about too many years to her credit. Likely she was looking for a place to hide from whatever scandal she had left behind, he decided. His eyes narrowed on her as he considered the overall picture she made.

Wide-eyed and blushing, she looked the very personification of an innocent. Whether that was a fact or not made little difference to him. She'd be out of here before long, either way. She'd probably already laid plans to head into town and scout around for a third candidate to work her wiles on. His mouth twisted into a cynical smile, as he wondered where she had learned those moves, those gestures that proclaimed her femininity. Even as he watched, she began a new ritual.

Lottie finished the rapid motions of her fingers that entwined her hair into a braid, wrapping loose strands from her hairbrush around the tail to hold it from unraveling. Then, rather than take time to put it up in a coronet on her head, she let it hang down the center of her back as she brushed the unruly short ends into place about her face. They curled and waved no matter how hard she tried to tame them, and by day's end they would have formed a frame for her fine features, lying in wispy disarray against her neck and temples and over her forehead. She dropped her brush back into the box and walked briskly to the sink, aware of the heated gaze that followed her steps.

The kettle of water she had put on the back of the stove last night was more than warm, and she lifted a stove lid to check on the fire that had been banked hours ago. It smouldered, red and black intermixed, and the draft from the open lid flared it into live coals.

She bent to the wood box and chose several lengths of kindling, laying them carefully inside the hole, then added two heavier chunks of wood before she closed the lid with the aid of the metal lever.

Lifting the kettle, she placed it over the front lid and went to the sink to wash her hands. A dipperful of water in the pan and a dab of the soap provided her with suds enough to scrub at her face with the pads of her fingers. She bent low to rinse off the sudsy residue, before she groped for the rough towel at the end of the sink.

It was thrust into her hands. She opened her eyes, blinking in surprise. John Tillman stood beside her, his approach silent and unheard.

"Thank you," she said doubtfully as she wiped at her face, drying herself and hanging the towel back in place.

"You're welcome," he answered with a nod of his head. "The funeral will be this afternoon," he said in an undertone, meant for her ears alone. "I'll talk to the children about it after they eat."

Lottie nodded and dropped her head for a moment. The accident had been so quick, so tragic, so final. Life here was different, she thought sadly. Mourning was barely allowed. Survival was the order of the day.

John turned and rested his hip against the cupboard. He crossed his arms against the breadth of his chest. "Are you cooking breakfast this morning?" he asked mockingly. "Or have you decided that we're too primitive out here for your fragile eastern sensibilities?"

She gritted her teeth against his mockery and searched for a bit of patience. "I told you last evening that I can cook, Mr. Tillman, and I don't have any *eastern sensibilities* that I'm aware of," she said primly.

"Show me," he retorted in a gentle voice that mocked her once more, as if he knew how tight a rein she kept on her tongue.

She lowered her eyes, aware that they would flash fire in his direction if she loosed the full force of her chagrin at him. Besides, these children didn't need to hear the adults they were entrusted to—even if temporarily—at each other's throats.

A sound from the loft caught her ear, and she looked up into the dimness to see Sissy peering over the floorboards at her, rubbing one eye with her fist as she frowned her displeasure.

"You woke me up," she said with a pout.

"It's time you were up anyway," her uncle replied, his voice soft and teasing as he approached the ladder and motioned to his niece to make her way down.

Sissy pushed herself up from the floor and clung to the log railing that kept her safe. "I need to get dressed, Uncle John," she said with a yawn.

"Well, hurry up," he advised her. "You don't want to miss breakfast."

"I'm gonna help make tea," she called down to him as she turned away to find her dress.

"Tea?" His tone was disdainful, and his brow rose in disbelief as he glanced at Lottie. "Tea?" he repeated.

"I promised," she said simply with a shrug of her narrow shoulders. She grinned at his expression of distaste.

"Do you know how to make coffee?" he asked after a minute, during which he had made himself comfortable on a chair.

She looked at him over her shoulder, holding the knife still as she halted midway through a thick slice of the side pork that was left from last night.

"I can make the best coffee you ever drank," she said with firm conviction. Her mouth pursed as she sliced in quick, even strokes, and her hands were deft as she filled the black skillet with the meat in neat fashion. The skillet skidded into place next to the kettle. Lottie reached for the coffeepot that sat above the range, even as she turned away for the bucket of water next to the sink.

Her movements were economical and brisk. He leaned back in his chair to watch, feasting on the sway of her skirts and the flash of bare feet as she stepped lightly back and forth.

"Well," he allowed in a lazy drawl that caught her unawares, "Maybe you can at that. Or maybe, I'll be so busy watching the scenery, the coffee won't matter."

Three

The grave was a gaping wound in the earth, with piles of dirt sitting on all sides, waiting for the final words to be spoken.

The coffin was simple. White pine, lined with a piece of yellowed fabric that the storekeeper's wife had found on the back of a shelf and had given to Mrs. Sharp. That lady, married to the undertaker, had spent all morning ruching the material into a fitting frame for the part of James Tillman that was presented to public view.

He was dressed one final time in his dark blue suit, the same clothes he had been married in nine years ago. The coffin was narrow, and his broad shoulders touched both sides. His hair was flaxen, like Sissy's. Lottie resisted the urge to smooth back a wayward strand.

She stood next to the children, a stranger to this community, yet respected as the wife James would have accepted with a joyful heart.

I feel like a fraud, she thought. I'm mourning a man I didn't even know. I'm angry with him because he got killed and left me stranded. The unfairness of her logic brought a flush to Lottie's throat, and she felt the heat creep up her face as she bowed her head even lower. Chin tucked against her chest, she closed her eyes as she listened to the words of the Baptist minister.

James had been well thought of, Lottie was discovering. Although he hadn't attended the Baptist church, its pastor apparently held no grudge against the Methodist he was burying. He'd already guaranteed him a place in heaven by virtue of his hard work and devout patronage of Stephen Bush's ministry.

And that's another thing, Lottie thought, with a sharp exhalation of breath. God had provided her with two wonderful prospects for marriage, and then allowed the best of the two to run off without a word on the very day his bride was to arrive! Somehow, the hand of providence had not been hovering over her as promised, she decided. And Aggie Conklin had been so sure that Lottie's years of service in New Hope were finally being rewarded. A lot she knew, Lottie thought bleakly. Poor Aggie would be most distraught if she could see me now.

A small hand tugged at her index finger. Lottie opened one eye to see Sissy's face screwed up in a most painful scowl. Forming a stern scowl of her own, she shook her head just a bit and pursed her lips.

"Shhh," she whispered, even as Sissy squeezed her eyes shut and wrinkled her nose.

"I gotta *go*, Miss Lottie," she said in a painful, little squeak. One knee was bent, and she was twisting one foot against the other in a silent agony of impatience.

Lottie felt the heat in her face intensify as skirts rustled and half a dozen pairs of eyes swung their way. On her left, the well-worn boots that shod the feet of John Tillman shifted, and his head lowered till it hovered next to her bonnet.

"Do you want me to take her?" he whispered.

The flowers on her hat swayed as she shook her head. He lifted his head quickly, eyeing the colorful mass with a baleful glare. "No, I'll tend to her," Lottie said softly and then bent to press her mouth against Sissy's ear.

"It will only be a few minutes, honey," she said in a coaxing whisper. "Can you wait just a bit longer?"

Sissy's eyes were desperate as she turned her head in a violent motion. Her hair tickled Lottie's nose as the curls swished past, and the child breathed out one frantic word.

"Noooo . . ." The sound was eloquent. Without hesitation, Lottie gripped the small fingers and turned away from the gathering of townsfolk who were forming a huddle about the open grave.

A grove of trees hid the water of Mill Creek from the mourners. It was to that secluded spot that Lottie and her scampering young charge headed. Sissy was clutching the front of her skirt with one hand, and had latched onto Lottie's fingers with equal fervor with the other.

"I'm sorry, Miss Lottie," she said in a mournful undertone. "I just hadda go!"

On the other side of the first cluster of maples was a thicket of blackberry bushes. Beyond them, as far as Lottie could see, there were no observers. She knelt on the hard-packed earth and reached beneath Sissy's dress, skimming the child's underwear down and tucking her skirts out of the way, before she eased her to squat over a windfall of leaves.

The simple task was quickly accomplished, and her hands worked briskly as Lottie restored order to the child's appearance. Quickly she brushed at the rough fabric of Sissy's skirt and straightened her collar.

"There you go, sweetie," she said with a sigh as her fingers tamed the curls that hung in wild abandon about the fragile beauty of the girl. Reaching into her pocket, Lottie drew forth a handkerchief and wiped at a smudge on Sissy's cheek.

"Stick out your tongue," she instructed the child, and dampened the cloth to better clean the offensive spot.

Sissy bore up bravely, apparently no newcomer to spit cleaning, and waited patiently while Lottie looked her over. "Are we goin' back now?" she asked as the handkerchief was returned to its pocket. Her voice was wistful, her question mournful, as if she hoped for an answer that would deliver her from returning to the solemn event that had confused her so mightily.

"This will be the last time you ever see your daddy," Lottie explained as they set off for the group of mourners. Her words were uttered in a low whisper as they made their way between the uneven rows of graves that made up the back part of the cemetery.

"Is he in heaven with my mama?" Sissy asked, dragging her feet against the clumps of grass that struggled to survive in the heat of late summer.

Lottie nodded her head and placed her index finger against her lips in silent admonition. The child's mouth closed tightly as she obeyed.

Before them, the lid of the coffin had been shifted until only James's face lay exposed to view. New nails had been pounded partway into the wood and stood in an elongated diamond shape on the edge of the cover, glittering brightly in the hot sunshine. Flat at both ends, the container was simply built, wide where the shoulders required extra space, narrowing at the foot.

Approaching quietly, Lottie took her place once more beside John Tillman; Thomas looked up with grateful eyes as he fidgeted beside his uncle. This is too much for children to bear, Lottie thought with a burst of indignation. They'll never get over this loss. The unfairness of it all brought quick tears to her eyes, and she chewed on the inside of her cheek as she fought to contain the evidence of her sorrow on the behalf of the children who waited with her.

One by one, the townspeople and farmers who had gathered to pay their last respects walked past the open coffin, until only the four main mourners were left. John offered his arm, and Lottie rested her left hand against the smooth fabric of his coat. It looked to be made from the same bolt of material as James's suit, she thought distractedly as she was led to within a foot of where the coffin lay. The children stood quietly on either side of them, and Lottie waited patiently for John to say his final goodbyes.

Thomas and Sissy were holding up well, Lottie thought, but a smothered whimper from the boy banished that idea. She watched in mute anguish as he finally succumbed to the harsh reality of his father's death. His slender body bent forward, and he brushed at his tears as his eyes fed with greedy need on the beloved face of his parent.

John scooped his arm about the narrow shoulders that shook with sobs the boy tried to suppress, and Thomas turned to him. He buried his face against the stomach of the man who offered rough comfort. John held him tightly, one large hand cradling the back of the boy's head. Then, as if Thomas's sorrow had spurred her own, Sissy burst into tears and howled her distress without caring if anyone liked it or not. Lottie bent low and picked her up, snuggling the curly head against her breast and shoulder. She patted the small back and kissed the damp cheek in sympathy, as she consoled the girl with whispered sounds of consolation.

"There . . . there . . ." she breathed. "It will be all

right." And even as she uttered the platitudes, her sensible mind told her it was a falsehood. Never again would life be the same for the orphans. Her lips compressed and her heart thumped in an uneven rhythm as Lottie recognized that one more bond had been forged in her life. She was irrevocably bound, through the bonds of their loss, to these children. She, who had never known the love of a parent, was the only person here, probably, who could respond to the cry of the young hearts that were torn by grief. Within the circle of sorrow that the four of them formed, Lottie sensed a grafting of spirits. In an automatic gesture, one of her hands went out to lay in gentle caring upon the head of Thomas. Swallowing his tears and lifting his face, he rubbed his fist over the remnants of sorrow that shone in the sunlight against the childish planes of his cheeks.

"I'm all right, Miss Lottie," he said with stubborn assurance.

"Of course, you are," she answered him briskly, knowing that more sympathy at this point would only undermine his pride.

The undertaker's helper had stepped up, hammer in hand, to seal the coffin. John leaned forward to help him align the lid. The shiny nails were sent home with true strokes of the hammer head; the sounds rang out in the air as the assemblage watched silently. Like church bells tolling, Lottie thought as she unconsciously counted them. Beside her, John's hand clutched into a fist, and she watched as his knuckles whitened with the force of his clenching muscles. She placed her fingers once more on his forearm, hoping to offer a semblance of comfort, and felt the long tendon harden and knot as his control spun to a fine edge.

The hammer stopped, the cover was secured, and four more men stepped forward to take their places on either side of the wooden box. John shifted Thomas to stand before Lottie, and moved the final steps that put him at the head. Lifting in unison, the men picked up the pine box and shifted it to where three ropes lay across the open grave. The ends were wrapped about pegs that had been driven into the ground earlier, and the coffin balanced on the ropes. The men carefully loosened the pegs and began the process of lowering James Tillman into his final resting place.

Lottie's gaze was drawn to the man directly before her. She watched as the sun reflected from the straight golden swathe of his hair. His legs were braced, his muscles taut as he slowly fed the rope through his hands, matching the movements of the other men who worked in unison. A fine mist of perspiration from the heat of the afternoon bathed the brows of the solemn workers, and one lifted a gnarled hand to wipe briefly as drops of sweat hung in his eyebrows.

It was Henry Clawson, sedate in dark clothing, clean-shaven and subdued. Lottie finally recognized the stoic farmer who had been her silent companion only yesterday. The job was done; the ropes pulled from beneath the coffin and rolled quickly into neat circles. Henry delivered them to Mr. Sharp, and he in turn handed them to a young man who stood behind him.

They've all done this before, Lottie realized. The whole ritual, the putting to ground a member of their community . . . it was familiar to them. She looked up as Mrs. Sharp stepped forward. A basket of flowers—daisies from the meadows, hollyhocks from gardens in town, and a few choice dahlias—lay on the ground. The woman picked it up and passed it among the mourners.

Lottie watched as each person chose a flower. When it was finally brought to her, she helped Thomas and Sissy select red dahlias, following their lead as they threw the flowers into the open grave.

Before her eyes, the stark bare cover of the pine box took on a gentler look as the colorful display hid the rawness of death. Her own blossom fell in unison with the yellow daisy that John released into the yawning hole. Then they stepped back as two men picked up shovels that had been waiting by the piles of dirt.

The sound of earth falling against the wood sent shudders through her body. She felt the vibrations through the soles of her sturdy shoes. The men worked rapidly, coats discarded and sleeves rolled to their elbows, as the sun beat on their unprotected heads.

As never before in her young life, the finality of death was driven home to Lottie. She shrank from the sense of loss that hovered over the gathering. Then, as if to answer her need, the voice of the Baptist minister rose in a clear tenor as he began a hymn that offered its own comfort.

"In the sweet by and by . . ." he sang, and the second line was lifted with strength by the voices of the group as they followed his lead. ". . . we shall meet on that beautiful shore." Their voices rose in unison. And the music cast a blessing over the gathering that muffled the dreary sound of the burial rite, as James Tillman was given over to the earth that had claimed his mortal body.

"Do you need anything in town?" The brusque question was at odds with his earlier demeanor. Lottie turned to find John frowning at her. They were on the seat of James's wagon, the children sitting on a pile of hay in the back.

Left from the work done yesterday before the accident, the hay had held James's body during the trip to town last night. It made a softer seat than the hard wagon bed, and Thomas had piled it up before he perched Sissy on top of the heap.

"Well?" The word was harsh, and his brows were lowered over the glittering blue orbs that considered her with a look of speculation. He felt frustration rise within him as he watched her. This scrap of a woman appealed to him in a mighty way. That fact had him in a turmoil. From her golden hair atop her head, to the curves that hid beneath her dark dress, to the sharp wit that edged each word she spoke, she posed a challenge he found it almost impossible to ignore.

"Why would I want anything in town?" she asked in a wondering fashion, her own brows furrowing in puzzlement.

"Thought you might want to check on your preacher friend, or look over the rest of the male population before you settle for watching two young'uns." His drawl was low, aware of the two children in the wagon bed who sat in silence behind him.

Lottie's chin lifted in a gesture of prideful determination. "The Reverend Bush is not a subject for discussion. He eliminated himself from my list when he disappeared yesterday morning." She sniffed in a ladylike fashion and lowered her eyes to consider the gloves she had pulled on before the funeral. One finger was patched, two others held neat, tight stitches where she had mended them. Altogether they showed a considerable amount of wear. She tugged at them gently, removing and folding them carefully, aware that another pair would be a long time in coming.

"How long is that list of yours?" John asked, his voice gently mocking.

She leveled a glare in his direction, and her eyes were frosty with disdain. "None of your business, Mr. Tillman. Rest assured that your name was not on it."

"Not a chance," he grunted as he twitched the reins over the horse's backs and turned the wagon in a wide circle. "Marrying a pig in a poke is pure foolishness, as far as I can see," he said firmly. "Never could understand how James could get so desperate as to send off that letter."

"I don't fancy being referred to as a barnyard animal, Mr. Tillman," Lottie retorted with asperity. "And further, I consider it a most respectable method of bringing together two people who are needy of marriage for one reason or another. It was all done with respect and dignity. The Methodist minister who approached me in New Hope assured me of the sincerity of the gentlemen who offered for me."

"That's another thing," John said, considering her outburst with a distinct gleam in his narrowed eyes. "How did you latch on to *two* men? Did you just plan on keeping one in reserve, in case the other didn't work out?"

She shook her head, and the flowers that surrounded the brim of her bonnet caught his eye. The brave colors had seemed out of place at the graveside, but James would have appreciated the touch of color amid the dark and dreary hues that had clothed the mourners. It had been James who turned over the earth for Sarah's flower bed, and James who had plucked the blossoms just months ago to carry to the grave when his wife was buried. Yes, his brother would have approved of the bonnet that perched on Lottie's head, he decided, and unknowingly his gaze softened as he watched her.

Her head lowered, and she made her explanations in a patient, careful voice, hoping that his baleful regard would alter, that he would realize that she was not a flighty creature.

"The Reverend Bush sent money to my minister, to pay for my fare by train and stage to Mill Creek. Your brother knew that my preference was to remain in town and live near the church. I thought I'd be able to use my experience in New Hope to benefit the members of Reverend Bush's congregation."

"What experience?" he asked gruffly. "What did you do in New Hope that would fit you for life out here?" His tone doubted her, dared her to consider herself sturdy enough for anything but the cosseted life of an Easterner.

She turned in the seat and lifted her bared hands for his perusal. Her palms were small, faintly calloused, and reddened from wringing mop rags and pulling weeds in the orphanage garden. Her fingers were slender, but strong, her nails short and neatly trimmed.

"Do these look like the hands of a lady of leisure?" she asked with a measure of pride.

He transferred the reins to his left palm and reached out to her, accepting one of her hands into his own. His fingers traced the tough skin on her palm that told its own story, and then turned to rub his thumb against the softer flesh on the back. "What did you do in New Hope?" he asked again in a neutral tone.

"I lived in an orphanage and ran the kitchen, feeding thirty-seven people, three times a day," she replied with a degree of arrogance that made him smile as he considered her.

"You cooked," he said.

Her head cocked to one side, and a light of battle gleamed for a moment in the depths of her eyes. Green eyes, they were, he decided. Although earlier this morning, he could have sworn they were blue.

"Yes, I cooked and I grew the vegetables and kept the garden. I raised chickens and gathered eggs and scrubbed and cleaned my kitchen every day." Her mouth pursed with indignation on the final word. Then she jerked her hand from his grasp and folded it in her lap with its counterpart.

"All that?" he asked idly, as if he were hard put to credit her with so much ambition.

"Yes, all that," she repeated, and then turned to face the road that stretched out before them.

"Well, you shouldn't have too much trouble tending to the house and two young'uns for a while, should you?" he said, his words more a statement than a question.

"For a while?" she asked, her eyes widening as she wondered at the time span he was suggesting.

He slid a furtive glance at her, and his frown deepened. "Were you planning on settling in at James's place?" he asked, as he lifted one booted foot to rest against the wide plank that fronted the wagon.

She shook her head. "I've learned in my life not to make any plans, Mr. Tillman. I just live from one day to the next. Nineteen years I lived at New Hope, one day just like the others. Until I left there with the promise of marriage from two different men, I had never had much of a choice as to what happened in my life. When I arrived on the stage in Mill Creek and the sheriff told me that Reverend Bush had left town and no one knew where he was, I knew that I had to find my way to your brother. He'd written that if I found the Reverend Bush not to my liking, he would offer me marriage and a home with him and his children."

"I never could figure out what got into him to do such a thing," John mused. "But then, when a man's desperate for a woman in his home, I reckon he'll do about anything to rectify the situation."

"Well, I was desperate enough in my situation to consider either proposal of marriage," Lottie said bluntly. "In Boston, either a woman has prospects of marriage, or she works in another woman's home, or she looks elsewhere for—" She flushed at her own boldness, lifted her head defiantly, and met John's eyes firmly. "I couldn't stand the thought of cleaning up another female's clutter for the rest of my life. But then, putting myself in the position of being some man's . . . well . . . that didn't do much for my soul either. That left marriage, and I did the best I could to bring that about."

Her mouth snapped shut, and she straightened to perch on the edge of the seat, her back stiff and her feet planted firmly on the floorboards.

"My apologies, ma'am," John said, his amusement at her display of ladylike displeasure evident in the smile that creased his cheeks.

"I'll thank you not to laugh at me," she snapped, aware of the undertone of humor in his voice.

"Yes, ma'am," he replied meekly. She shot him a glare that registered her disapproval of his mockery.

"I'll stay with the children and work the place for as long as you need me," she said finally.

His eyes fed on her. The high planes of her cheekbones were rosy, and her eyes sparkled with a mixture of emotions that she made no effort to hide. She was feisty, this child bride from the orphanage, hardly old enough to be out on her own. But, he decided with a full measure of appreciation, she had a backbone that made her a worthy opponent for any man on the lookout for a woman. She'd hold her own in a battle, he wagered, noting the firm set of her jaw and the militant stance she had assumed next to him.

"Then what will you do?" he asked as he eyed her with pure masculine approval.

"Why then I'll find somewhere else to go, Mr. Tillman," she said crisply, as if that were a logical conclusion.

"We'll let it go at that," he agreed. "I'll work both places for a while, at least as long as I can hold things together. James and I had some family in St. Louis. Sarah's people are there, too. Maybe she'd want her folks to take the children to raise."

She glanced over her shoulder, and her voice lowered so that he leaned closer to hear her words. "You'd send them away?" she asked uneasily. "They're your own flesh and blood."

He shrugged his wide shoulders, and his jaw tightened as he considered her. "I don't think that's any of your business, Miss O'Malley. A man does what he has to, and if finding a home for my brother's children means sending them away, then that's what I'll do."

She opened her mouth, closed it, and then, as if she reconsidered, spoke what was on her mind. "You wouldn't want to raise them yourself?"

"Me?" he asked with scorn. "A man alone, with more work to do than he can handle? I know better than to shortchange those two. They need a woman's care, and

I'll see to it that they get it," he said vigorously. "You said you'll stay till I can do better, so let it be."

"Well, you just try to do better than me, Mr. Tillman. You just try!" she said emphatically.

"You'll have to prove all those fancy claims you made, Miss O'Malley," he said with a scornful glance. "I'll give you two weeks and you'll be writing to your preacher in New Hope to come to your rescue."

She folded her arms across her breasts and then, as the wagon hit a deep rut, she gasped and clutched at the seat on either side of herself. Her eyes flashed fire at him as she gritted her teeth and turned her face away from his dark glare.

"We'll just see about that, Mr. Tillman," she promised grimly. "Mrs. Conklin used to say that you never get ahead in life if you're always looking over your shoulder. And I, for one, don't believe in looking back."

Four

Mill Creek Mercantile was a fine store to Lottie's way of thinking. Certainly as well stocked as the establishment that Aggie Conklin had patronized in New Hope. Her early training had taught her to think in terms of fifty-pound sacks of flour and burlap bags full of rice. Today she'd be shopping from a different list, she decided as she approached the long, wooden counter.

The flour in the orphanage kitchen had never been finely milled or of a good grade. She had spent many a tedious half-hour sifting out mealy worms before she could set her dough to rise. Early morning sessions with inferior kitchen supplies were a fact of life in Lottie's background. The delightful notion that she was not limited to second or third quality foodstuffs this morning caused her feet to move quickly across the uneven planks that formed the floor of this establishment.

She inhaled sharply. The scent of spices and leather goods, mixed with the rich smell of apples formed an aroma that pleased her immensely. She drew in another deep breath, and her feet stepped lightly in the plain black boots she wore, one hand reaching to touch with fleeting longing against the fine leather of a pair of shoes that rested on the countertop. Never in her wildest dreams had Lottie thought to be turned loose in a store with an almost unlimited supply of hard cash to spend. And no one to answer to when she walked out the door.

While the buggy rolled briskly over the town road, John Tillman had made it clear that Lottie was on her own.

"I've given you a fair amount of cash for supplies for the kitchen," he announced as he reined in his frisky mare and held her to a trot. His hands were big and well formed, knuckles prominent as his fingers wove the leather straps through his palms.

The sleeves of his blue chambray shirt were rolled to within an inch or so of his elbows and Lottie's eyes were drawn to the muscular expanse revealed. Pale, sun-kissed hair curled over the surface of his forearms and touched the backs of his wide hands. His boots rode firmly about the denim pants he had tucked into them, and the fabric was pulled tightly across the husky thighs that tensed with his movements. She had felt a guilty stain rise from her breasts to settle against the high ridge of her cheekbones, as she had surveyed his frame. Never in all of her years at the Orphanage for Young Females had a man so well endowed set foot inside those rigidly prescribed walls.

"Lottie, are you listening to me?" he'd asked with an impatient growl.

Her eyes widened, and she sat up straighter on the cushioned seat of his racy, black buggy. Her fingers clutched the small reticule she carried. Within it she could feel the weight of the coins he had designated for kitchen supplies.

"Yes, Mr. Tillman, I'm listening," she said primly, aligning her feet and holding her knees precisely together.

His glance was impatient. "Are you sure you know what you're about?" he asked, doubt coloring his words. "It takes a lot of food to keep four people eating well, and there wasn't any garden this year to speak of. James had let things go slack over the past few months," he said more slowly, and his mouth hardened as he allowed his thoughts to stray.

Lottie had stiffened her back, and her tone was equally as firm as the spine that held her upright. "I assure you that I'm most capable, Mr. Tillman. I have my list right here," she said, pressing one hand over her pocket where a sheet of paper rustled at her command.

Now the shelves of the store beckoned her, and she stepped briskly to the counter, unfolding her list to lay it before her on the gleaming walnut that had been polished by years of use. Unconsciously, her fingers cherished the smooth wood, rubbing at its rich surface as she waited.

Harvey Slocum had run his establishment in Mill Creek for over thirty years, but was not too old to allow his masculine gaze an appreciative look at Lottie.

"I reckon you're the bride from back East," he said in a bluff, easygoing manner. "Here to fit out the Tillman kitchen, are you?"

Lottie nodded briefly, taken aback by his recognition. "Yes, I'm Lottie O'Malley, and I'll be caring for Mr. Tillman's youngsters for a while."

A young woman at the end of the long counter turned at Lottie's words and approached. Her long, dark hair hung in precise curls, scooped up with a ribbon that tied at her crown. Her dress was flowered, the material finer than the muslin Lottie wore, and the apron tied about her waist was starched with ruffles over the shoulders.

Lottie glanced at her, with one quick look assessing the dress, the ruffles, the ringlets that hung prettily to form a frame for the piquant face, and then felt her own lips curling in an approving smile.

"Miss O'Malley, I'm Genevieve," the dark-haired vision announced. "This is my daddy, Mr. Slocum," she said, her fingers spread daintily against her father's white shirtsleeve.

"I'm pleased to make your acquaintance," Lottie replied with a nod, gratified to find a friendly face within minutes of her arrival in town.

Dropped off in front of the door, she had felt bereft as she approached the store, sure that she was the subject of inquisitive eyes, unsure of her welcome. The townspeople might not approve of her living in such close proximity to John Tillman, she had already decided. And there was no way she wanted her morals questioned in this small town.

That Genevieve was so openly welcoming was a pleasant surprise, and Lottie's response was genuine. She peeled off her gloves—careful to protect the mended spots—and tucked them neatly into her cloth bag, snapping the metal clasp closed. Then with one slender hand outstretched, she offered her friendship to the storekeeper's daughter.

Genevieve accepted the gesture and clasped Lottie's capable hand, shaking it briskly once before she released it. Her curls bounced as she turned her head to smile broadly at her father's florid face.

"I'll tend to Miss O'Malley, if you like, Daddy," she said in a musical voice that trilled through the room.

Harvey stepped back and his own smile was beneficent, as though he could do no less than give his daughter's request his full approbation. He looked back at Lottie, and his smile remained full and approving.

"Genevieve will see to you, Miss O'Malley," he said with a flourish as he made way for his daughter.

"Now," Genevieve said firmly, as she leaned both palms on the counter and looked down at Lottie's list, "what do you need?"

Lottie turned the piece of paper about, and her finger traced down the items it listed in her fine, rounded script. "Just about everything," she admitted softly. "Mr. Tillman had let his supplies get pretty low, I'm afraid."

The other girl grinned pertly and revealed a double row of perfectly formed, white, even teeth. Her eyes flashed with eagerness as she viewed the orphan before her. The contrast was clearly drawn. Lottie with her dark, plain dress, cut from the very same pattern that each preceding gown had been made from, was like a small, brown hen. Only the bright flowers that rimmed her hat provided any color in her garb, and against the glowing good looks and vibrant clothing of the storekeeper's daughter, she was definitely outclassed.

In response to her honest estimation of their comparative appearance, Lottie lifted her chin and flashed her own smile. She had good teeth, she knew. Strong and sturdy, like the rest of her short, full-bosomed body. That she might ever allow her hair to be coaxed into ringlets or her less-than-elegant body be contained by fine fabrics and starched ruffles, was a moot question.

"We each have to do our best with what the good Lord has given us," Aggie Conklin used to say, and Lottie had done just that. That the good Lord hadn't seen fit to give her dimity and batiste to wear, was a fact. That she wore sensible boots instead of soft, leather shoes that caressed the ankle, was another fact. But the purpose of her visit here, she reminded herself, was not to compare her own capable self to the feminine creature who waited to assist her.

"I need a lot of things." she began, running her finger down the list. "Maybe we'd better start with basics . . . flour, lard, some vegetables to fill in with, and a pound of coffee."

"Make that five pounds of coffee," a masculine voice ordered from behind her, and she felt a flush rise to paint the hollows of her cheeks as John Tillman spoke. "I like good strong coffee," he explained glibly to the smiling Genevieve, "and lots of it."

Lottie turned her head and her voice was low. "I thought you had things to get," she said softly.

"Just checking up on you," he answered gently. "Is everything all right?"

She turned to him and her eyes searched his face wonderingly. His mouth twisted in a strained smile, and he lifted his wide shoulders in a motion that pulled his shirt tightly against the firm muscles beneath.

"I'm fine," she assured him. "Miss Slocum is going to find what we need."

"Genevieve," he said, greeting the dimpled creature behind the counter. He had scooped his hat from his head as he spoke, nodding once.

Her eyes were warm, and her mouth trembled as Genevieve smiled at him. "I didn't get a chance to speak the other day, at the funeral," she said softly. "But I sure felt bad about James, leaving those two children all alone in the world."

"They're not alone," John corrected her with a gentle

smile. "They have me. And for now, they have Lottie. We're doing just fine," he said firmly.

"Yes, well, I can see that," Genevieve replied, her eyes lighting with a speculative glow as she considered the couple before her. She turned from them and reached up to lift a large tin from the shelf, and then looked over her shoulder at Lottie.

"Is five pounds of lard all right?" she asked.

"Fine," Lottie replied. She pointed at a round metal tin just over the other girl's head. "I need baking powder, too," she said "and a bottle of vanilla."

"John, if you'll come back in about fifteen minutes, I'll have all your things gathered up," Genevieve said, as she turned to deposit the foodstuffs on the counter.

"I'll need a box to fill with apples," he said as he stepped back from Lottie. "Will you want to weigh them?" he asked.

"No, Daddy is selling them by the peck," Genevieve answered, bending to locate a bag of sugar on a lower shelf.

"We'll need closer to a bushel," John said, as he picked up one of the large, red fruit and polished it on the front of his shirt. His teeth bit into it, and a fine line of juice trickled down from his mouth as he closed his eyes in appreciation of the tangy flavor.

Lottie's eyes watched in fascination as he chewed, her gaze caught by a drop that settled into the cleft in his firm chin. One hand lifted, and an index finger swiped at the liquid with careless ease, as John felt the bead of moisture move against his skin. His eyes opened and met those of the girl who was watching him with rapt attention.

His jaws moved slowly, his strong teeth chewing at the tart pulp, and then, as she watched, his nostrils flared, just enough so that she caught the faint movement. His eyes narrowed in recognition of her interest.

Deep within her, Lottie sensed a warmth that had nothing to do with the temperature of the room. Neither did it come from the weight of the skirts that hung about her legs, nor the shawl that draped over her shoulders. From the lower depths of her belly, where Miss Aggie had told her that her female parts were centered, came a glowing sensation that spread to encompass all of her inward being. Aware of the unsteady thumping of her heart, she lifted a trembling hand to her throat. Opening her lips, to better catch a breath, she ran her tongue over the edges of her mouth as she watched him.

He couldn't take his eyes off the plain, little baggage who stood before him. From the tips of her dark, sensible boots to the top of her foolish bonnet, she was as ordinary a creature as he'd ever seen. But beneath those heavy clodhoppers she wore, was a pair of dainty, pink-fleshed feet that had caught his attention in great style. And under that flighty, little, flowered creation on her head lay a crown of golden hair that he knew, for a fact, reached below her waist. He'd seen it, curling in a frenzy of wild abandon, when she rose from her bed on one memorable morning. In between was a body he could only guess at, but he sensed, in some deep recess of his soul, that it would fit with precision into his arms, given half a chance.

Her pink, damp tongue was sliding in feminine witchery against the plump flesh of her bottom lip, even as he watched. He met her glance quickly, wondering at the flirtatious gesture. But instead of inborn female knowledge, he found an innocent awareness that rounded her eyes and heightened the color that rode her cheekbones.

Lottie swallowed again against the dryness that had possessed her throat, and lowered her lashes until her vision was narrowed to where her hands clenched together at her waistline. The flutter of her heartbeat in her chest caught her attention, as the steady drumming took flight and missed a beat in its frenzy. John had looked at her so strangely, as though he could sense the hectic direction of her thoughts. Surely he must think her addled—great clumsy girl all openmouthed and staring.

She inhaled sharply, and her wonderment grew as she delighted in his scent . . . the clean combination of leather and sun-kissed skin that clung like a musky perfume. In a welter of confusion, she subdued her wayward thoughts and turned once more to face the counter.

Her gaze focused on the bland, unknowing smile that lifted Genevieve's lips into friendly warmth as she spoke to the man who towered behind Lottie.

"Get yourself a basket from the storeroom, John," she said. "You can bring it back when you come to town next."

He nodded and released his breath in a warm rush that blew its heated draft against Lottie's nape as he stood behind her. He watched as a faint shiver lifted the short hair that curled against her finely pored flesh, and then frowned as he backed away.

His mouth tightened as he made his way to the back room to seek out the basket for apples, and he chastised himself with dark threats. "Silly fool." He mouthed the words as he fumbled to separate two baskets that clung to each other stubbornly. "Asinine jackass," he said beneath his breath, as he straightened and closed his eyes. Too long without a woman, he thought firmly, when a plain little piece like that can turn my manhood into a fencepost without even trying.

Carrying the basket before him, he went back into the store and stoically ignored the two women at the counter, who smiled and spoke in low tones as they gathered the items Lottie had chosen. He sat the basket on the wooden floor and filled it with double handfuls of the apples, placing each carefully, so that they would not bruise with rough handling.

Then he rose and lifted his load, his eyes once more turning to Lottie. "I'll be back in to carry the things out," he said roughly. Before she could turn to him, he was on his way, shouldering the heavy door open as he thumped his way down the wooden steps.

Lottie smiled at Genevieve. "I think John must be in a hurry. He sounds like he's getting a bit impatient with me," she apologized, as she ran her finger down the items listed and mentally checked them off. She glanced at the bolts of fabric on the far wall, and gauged the amount she had spent already.

"If there's enough left, I'd like to choose a piece of calico that would look nice on Sissy," she said in a low tone, opening her bag to spill the coins on the shiny walnut countertop.

Genevieve bent her dark head and began adding up the column of figures that marched in precision on the paper sack she had used to keep track of Lottie's purchases. Her eyes counted up the money that lay between them, and she looked up with approval.

"You've plenty left, Lottie. Let's go over and find something."

They walked on either side of the partition that separated them, until they reached the wall where yard goods were lined up in neat piles. Lottie reached eagerly for a pink-and-white-checked gingham, then pursed her mouth as she fingered the selvage edge. With a sigh that spoke of regret, she lifted her hand with a final caress of the dainty print and moved her fingers slowly to where a darker pattern lay. It was covered with small flowers in shades of blue and green against a tan background, and she firmed her lips as she nodded her head.

"This is a better choice, I think," she said with decision. "It won't show the soil so quickly, and I fear that Sissy is drawn to dirt like fleas to a dog."

Reluctantly, Genevieve agreed with the decision, and quickly cut a length of the calico to Lottie's direction. A spool of thread and a card of buttons was added to the pile. Then, with several practiced moves, it was wrapped in a piece of brown paper from a roll on the counter and tied with a piece of string that dangled from the ceiling.

Lottie tucked the parcel under her arm and thanked the girl who had been so careful to tend to her needs.

"I'll be looking forward to seeing you again, Genevieve," she said politely.

"John usually comes in to church on Sunday," the dark-haired girl said easily. "You'll probably want to attend with him. The children are used to spending a bit of time with their friends."

Lottie hesitated and lowered her voice. "I thought the preacher was gone, had left town," she said quickly, looking about to see if they had an audience. Her cheeks were rosy as she felt the flush of embarrassment flood her at the memory. "Surely you knew that . . ."

Words failed her as she was smitten with the shame of that virtuous man's perfidy.

But with a languid gesture that spoke of sure knowledge, Genevieve considered her fingernails, curling her hand and peering at those well-tended ovals as she answered glibly.

"He came back this morning, didn't you know?"

Lottie swallowed and looked toward the doorway, as if fearing that the gentleman in question might, at any moment, enter upon the scene. "No, I didn't," she said uneasily.

Genevieve's eyes were watchful as she trained them on the newcomer. "Well, he did," she said shortly, and then shoved one of the boxes of groceries across the counter. "John can get that when he comes back in, I'll get this one," she said, picking up a smaller container and changing the subject matter with a toss of her dark curls.

"Why don't you hold the door for me, Lottie?" she asked, as she rounded the end of the counter and headed for the wide, glass-paned portal that opened onto the wooden sidewalk.

Outside, John unceremoniously loaded the buggy, and nodded only briefly at Genevieve before he hoisted Lottie into place. Saying her farewells as the buggy jolted into motion, made them, of necessity, rather brief. Lottie swiveled in the seat and waved a final goodbye, determined to leave a good first impression with the lovely Genevieve.

Turning, she adjusted her clothing and settled herself for the ride back to the farm. Beside her, John flicked the reins and made noises with his tongue that the horse appeared to understand. Lottie was forced to grip the edge of the seat as the mare broke into a quicker gait.

Flustered by the tight-lipped profile of the man next to her and unfamiliar with small talk, Lottie subsided with good grace, deciding that patience was a virtue she might do well to pursue. The wheels rolled smoothly, and the horse trotted briskly as she looked about the countryside. Fields of grain alternated with newly mown areas on both sides of the narrow road. Several times, she caught sight of rutted lanes that traveled from the main thoroughfare. Once she thought to ask John about them, but then held her tongue.

She cast a look behind herself and found the two children huddled together on the second seat, Sissy tucked as close as possible to her brother's side. There was little space available, every square foot of the floor and part of the seat being covered with boxes of food and wrapped parcels.

Finally, the sight of Sissy's wide eyes looking at her with such pensive bewilderment gave her courage. John's reticence had affected the children. Sensitive to every nuance of emotion, they surely were aware of his darkly brooding frown, so she took it upon herself to break the silence he had imposed upon all of them.

"Genevieve made me feel welcome," Lottie ventured with studied assurance.

"Humph," John muttered. She was left to guess at the meaning of that most enigmatic response.

Trying again, she cleared her throat and turned to him with a cheerful smile. "She asked if we would be going to church on Sunday."

His glance flickered, his eyes closing for a moment, and then he looked at her with an impatience he didn't attempt to mask.

"You want to get a good look at that preacher, do you?"

Lottie's eyes widened and her mouth tightened, as the meaning of his cutting remark flayed her tender emotions.

"He left you hanging, Lottie," John said roughly. "Do you really want to go sit in his church and let all those people—"

"No!" The single word burst from her lips, and she felt the flush of shame flood her features. "I didn't think about that, John," she confessed, as she lifted her hands to cool the heated planes of her cheeks.

"Well, I think you'd best steer clear of him," he grated, as he lifted his foot to rest against the front of the buggy. He leaned his forearm against his uplifted knee and held the reins loosely, looking at her with a frowning intensity that softened as he noted her rosy countenance.

She spoke haltingly, in a low voice that excluded the listeners in the back seat. "I just thought the children might do better, if we stuck to their usual schedule."

His shrug lifted the shoulder nearest her, and he considered the idea. "Maybe . . . maybe so," he said, acknowledging her reasoning as sensible. "But the thing of it is . . . you're living at John's farm and—" He cleared his throat and a muscle twitched in his jaw, as he decided to leave that subject for later.

"How did you know he was back in town?" he asked her quietly.

"Genevieve," she answered quickly. "She said—" Lottie frowned and tried to remember. "She said he came back this morning, I think."

"Yeah, that's what I heard at the mill," John drawled.

"Seems his urgent business only took two days to take care of."

Lottie sat up straight, her eyes fixed on the road before them, and her thoughts in a flurry of confusion.

"You knew he was back? When you came in the store, you knew?" she asked softly. "You didn't say anything to me . . . you just loaded us up and headed back home." She bit at her lower lip as she considered the ramifications of this bit of knowledge.

Had John wanted to be rid of her, he could have dumped her at the church. But then, she reasoned silently, what would he have done with the children. For two days, she had cooked and baked, cleaned and mended. Had, in fact, put his brother's house in order, and taken the care of his niece and nephew off his hands.

"You decided I might be useful after all? Was that it?" she asked him tightly.

He frowned at her. "What's all the fuss, Lottie? You had nowhere to go, and I offered you a place to stay. If James—well, if things had been different, you'd have been married already to my brother," he stated firmly.

Her eyes flashed a defiant message as she faced him fully, twisting in the buggy seat and speaking in a deceptively soft tone.

"Well, I'm not married to you, Mister," she said stiffly. "And not likely to be, thank the merciful heavens."

His frown deepened, and his own words were tersely delivered in a harsh whisper.

"In case you haven't noticed, Miss O'Malley, I didn't ask you." His eyes did a rapid survey of her, resting for a moment on the fullness of her breasts beneath the drabness of her muslin dress. He swept his gaze down to where her feet rested on the floor of the buggy, and his mouth curled in derision as he noted the scuffed boots she wore. With a drawl that spoke his scorn, he added to the insult he had already dealt her.

"What makes you think the preacher would want you now, anyway?" he asked politely, his eyes shining with barely subdued frustration. Yet, even as he spoke, he rued the words that left his lips with such devastating results. Blast and damn, the girl had gotten under his skin, and there was no getting around it!

Lottie slumped in the seat as the meaning of his barb hit home. Her face whitened, as she bore the sting of his querulous tongue-lashing. Such a simple question to so fill her with shame. But he was right. She knew it with a certainty. No one would be after her with a wedding ring in hand, when she was living in such close proximity to a young bachelor. Her reputation was probably already in shreds.

Miss Aggie used to say that regrets are useless, they just stand in the way of forward motion. Best to forget your mistakes and move ahead as best you can. Lottie searched her mind for some comfort in the thought and came up empty-handed. Even Miss Aggie would have a hard time aiming her in the right direction now.

The buggy rocked and swayed in a soothing fashion, as Lottie clutched her hands together in her lap. Her feet were tucked beneath the seat, hiding the worn footwear she hated with such a passion. Her toes were crunched in the narrow toes of the leather boots. She tried to ignore the cramping, and instead began concentrating on the moment she would be able to pull them off. Hateful things, she thought with gritted teeth. Miserable secondhand boots, jammed onto feet that were too large for them.

She glanced over her shoulder once more into the

back of the buggy, and flashed a reassuring smile at
Sissy. It was answered with a wavering, watery grin and
a wiggling half-wave of fingertips from tightly clenched
hands. Thomas had eased one thin arm about his sister's shoulders and squeezed her closer. He nodded at
Lottie, smiling with a distinct lack of cheer, his mouth
tight as he exposed the edges of his teeth politely.

Her sigh was silent as she turned her head once more
to face forward, and she closed her eyes against the pain
that had been so evident on the faces of the children.
They were in as much of a bind as she was, she decided
sadly. Left with an uncle who was moody and friendly
by fits and starts, stuck with a stranger who was only
there by default, they were by necessity clinging to each
other like two bits of bark, headed downstream at a fast
pace.

John Tillman was sunk low in his own brand of hell-
fire, shoulders slumped and eyes slitted against the dust
that kicked up from his horse's hooves. He'd gotten all
in an uproar for nothing.

"Big mouth," he grunted in an almost silent accusation. He'd been unduly rough with her, and all because
she'd licked her lip and looked at him like a doe in a
thicket, startled by a hunter at sunrise.

He'd let this little brown hen appeal to his baser
needs, and she wasn't nearly as perky as half the women
in Mill Creek, doe-eyed look and all. She couldn't hold
a candle to Genevieve, and yet . . . He closed his eyes
and pictured the two, side by side. Genevieve with shiny,
dark curls, this mite of a woman with a thick braid that
rounded her head and then some. Superimposed over
that picture, a vision of sunshine blurred his imagery,
and in the midst of that sunlight was the memory of a
round-eyed female with sheets pulled up to her chin,

smack in the middle of his brother's feather tick. Hair of a golden hue that defied description tumbled about her shoulders and down her back, and he tried in vain to subdue it into the plaited hairdo she managed to tame it to every morning.

Genevieve, with her frock of sprigged organdy, flowers running wild in glorious profusion over the yards of fabric, up against the mousy, dark, dust-stained muslin of Lottie . . . there, that was better. Satisfied with this vision, he smiled with approval. Until his mind, that treacherous part of his brain that would not yield to his control, envisioned the lithe, curving body that lay beneath the frowsy dress.

Genevieve has lots of curves, too, I'll wager, he thought defensively. But, his better self argued, can she put together a meal from empty shelves, tame a six-month accumulation of neglect in a house, and scrub up two young'uns till their noses shine like daybreak?

So, she'll make a good farmer's wife, he thought, his defenses in order. But not mine, his stubborn will determined. I'll not be boxed into a convenient arrangement just to see that James and Sarah's children are cared for.

"Are we almost home?" Sissy asked plaintively from the back seat.

"She's wigglin'," Thomas put in bluntly.

John nodded. "See the turnoff, right up ahead, Sissy?"

"I can't see nuthin' from back here," she complained, drawing her legs up until she could hug her knees and rock back and forth. "I just gotta go, is all," she said firmly.

"Bad habit of hers," John muttered under his breath, and Lottie felt a smile twitch at one corner of her mouth.

That this man could destroy all of her righteous indignation with one softly uttered phrase was ridiculous. The flick of his reins told her he was hurrying to accommodate the child, even as he mumbled his complaint. In the same fashion he had pressed coins into her hand, enough to outfit the barren shelves, and given her full sway. He'd not questioned her purchases then . . . only to turn ornery on the way home in the buggy, and snarl his nasty remarks in her direction.

A strange combination, she decided. Must be that being a bachelor had addled his brains. Poor man couldn't make up his mind whether he was nasty or nice, and he surely didn't understand the rules of genteel behavior.

He'd looked at her with such an odd gleam in his eyes back in the general store, and then been ornery as blue blazes all the way home. Definitely could not make up his mind, she thought with a flare of righteous indignation.

The buggy came to a halt. John eased the horse to a stop next to the barn and twisted the reins over the slender upright post next to it. He jumped down and reached past Thomas to lift the willing Sissy from the back seat. With a heartfelt mutter of thanks, she scampered past the corncrib to where the necessary was half-hidden by morning glory vines over a wooden trellis. The door banged shut and Lottie busied herself, reaching for several bundles to carry into the house.

She pulled the bulk of her skirt to one side and slid her legs over the side of the seat, ready to jump to the ground.

"Wait, I'll help you," John commanded her roughly, as he hurried around the head of his mare and came to where she was perched precariously on the edge of the padded seat.

He lifted his hands to her waist and held tight to the narrow firmness, aware of the breath she caught in reaction to his touch. He lowered her easily, slowly, and stopped when their eyes were on a level, her feet dangling almost a foot from the ground.

"I didn't mean to be so hateful," he said tersely.

Lottie's mouth fell open at his rough apology. She'd about decided to let it go and just ignore his ornery mood, and here he was, trying to make amends.

"We'll go to church on Sunday, if you want to," he offered in the silence, while he watched the pink tongue commence its journey across her lower lip again. Confounded woman, didn't she know how that looked?

"We'll talk about it, all right?" she asked haltingly, not sure if the idea held as much appeal as it had when Genevieve suggested it earlier.

John nodded and lowered her pliant body to the ground, where she stood, clutching her wrapped parcels to her breasts. His hands were warm and firm against her waist, and she relished that touch for the few seconds they rested there, aware of the spacing of his fingers against the back of her ribs and the cupping of his palms in the indentation of her waist. His thumbs were riding just beneath the underside of her breasts, and she chewed furtively on the inside of her cheek as those two strong digits flexed and then moved from her.

"I'll fix dinner," she said, picking up her skirt in front and heading for the cabin. Better that she mind her business and earn her keep, she chastised herself firmly. Thinking about John Tillman's hands and craving his regard was leaving her mind open to thoughts of the flesh. And Miss Aggie had impressed upon her, more than once, that an idle mind is the devil's workshop.

Five

"Do I begin with the back two, or the ones in front?" Lottie asked in a puzzled tone. Her dimple flickered into being for a moment as a flighty thought crossed her mind and, daringly, she spoke it aloud.

"Or perhaps I should start catty-corner, Thomas . . . you know, sort of to balance the whole thing out," she explained. Her elusive grin teased him gently, until he allowed the somber expression on his rounded face to be replaced by a smile that recognized her joke.

"Pa never told me if there was a right place to start," he said, squatting by her side as she perched on the milking stool, skirt draped between her knees and hands at the ready. His mouth pursed as he stretched in front of her and placed one small hand on the elongated teat at the front of the cow's udder.

As if to measure it, he fit his fingers about its circumference and grasped it loosely. His head turned to face her and his eyes narrowed as he spoke, demonstrating his scant store of knowledge, like a teacher before a classroom of students.

"See, Miss Lottie, you just hold it like so," he said slowly, and obediently, her eyes moved to watch as his fingers clenched lightly.

"Then you push up against Rosie's udder, sort of with your knuckles of your thumb and pointing finger,

and then when you back off a bit, you squeeze down."
His explanation complete, he released the cow's flesh,
settled back on his heels, and shrugged.

"That's all there is to it," he informed her loftily.
"Now you try it."

She looked at him with doubtful hesitation, then bent
to look searchingly at the full udder that awaited her
attention. With her left hand, she patted the animal's
flank and muttered a few words of admiration.

"She's not a good girl at all, Miss Lottie," Thomas
muttered darkly. "Sometimes she kicks the bucket over,
if you don't do this just right. Pa said she likes a firm
hand and no pinching," he added in an undertone, as
if they might have an audience.

"I was just trying to make her acquaintance and pay
her a compliment, Thomas," Lottie explained, hoping
that her nervousness wasn't nearly as transparent to the
cow as it was to the child who watched her with a frown.

Learning to milk the cow had seemed like a wonderful idea an hour ago. John had said he might be a little
late arriving to help with chores this morning, and
Thomas had suggested at the breakfast table that with
her help, they might have them done before his uncle
got there.

Sissy had looked insulted by the idea and had made
a production of showing Lottie her minute scabs, where
one of the chickens had pecked her hand less than a
week ago.

"I was only tryin' to get her egg, Miss Lottie. She
came at me like a banshee from the dark place, just
peckin' and squawkin' till I—"

"She's too little to be in the hen house," Thomas
interjected, cutting Sissy's explanation off just as she
was getting warmed up.

"Am not," his sister huffed, shooting to her feet to stand upright on the chair she had been kneeling on. Towering over the other two at the table, she placed her hands on her nonexistent hips and bent at the waist to spit her fury in her brother's direction.

"I'm bigger now," she crowed. Her head swung to Lottie, who had been stifling the urge to laugh aloud at the little girl's antics. "I can take a chair out there and reach better than Thomas, Miss Lottie," she cried victoriously as she proved her point, her bare toes seeking to curl about the rounded sides of the wooden seat.

Thomas rolled his eyes and ducked his head over the bowl of oatmeal he had been consuming at a rapid pace. His low undertone traveled across the table and hit its target.

"She'll want gloves to wear next," he muttered. "Silly baby . . ."

Sissy's eyes filled with tears, and her lower lip quivered as she slid with fluid grace to the seat of her chair.

"I'm not," she whispered in a burst of teary emotion. "Pa said I was gettin' to be a big girl, and he let me help him shuck the corn for the chickens. I was goin' to start doin' the dishes pretty soon, too," she stated in a stronger voice, as her chin lifted in defiance of her brother's scorn.

Lottie decided that enough was enough; she cleared her throat and frowned at the pair of them. "I don't think your pa would want you two to be fussing at each other, do you?"

Thomas shook his head and flushed guiltily, while Sissy allowed two tears to escape from her overflowing eyes, her chin wobbling in its effort to hold back her sobs.

"I wish Pa was here," she whimpered as her eyes

squeezed shut and the salty stream flowed down both rosy cheeks.

Lottie moved with haste and scooped the child from her chair in a sweeping movement that had Sissy clinging to her with eager fingers, intent on burying her head in the center of Lottie's abundant bosom.

"Hush, now," Lottie admonished her with gentle firmness. "Your pa can't be here, baby. But he taught you lots of things, and now you have to make him proud of you and take hold with the chores and get along with each other . . . you hear?"

Sissy's head rubbed against the rough fabric of her benefactor's dress as she nodded her agreement. Thomas grunted a reply and reached up to scrub one fist against his eye, and then abruptly left the table to carry his dish to the sink.

"I'm going to need both of you to help me learn the chores," Lottie told them, easing Sissy to her feet and patting her head with a comforting hand. The fact that she had been tending chickens for most of the years of her life, she held in abeyance. Better that Sissy gained back a bit of pride in the showing of her knowledge, she decided.

"I'll show you how to milk Rosie," Thomas offered quickly. Milking had not been nearly as easy as he'd first thought, and his few lessons had gone poorly. His eyes flitted over Lottie, and he nodded his head as he scanned the size of her hands. "I believe you could do it easily, Miss Lottie," he said with approval. "Your fingers are longer than mine, and I suspect that's part of the secret of the whole thing."

Lottie eyed her capable hands, holding them before her and turning them from palm to back. "I guess these two helpers of mine have done harder chores than milking a cow," she allowed with a grin, pleased to put away the solemn moments and anxious to turn the children's thoughts to brighter things.

"I'll find the egg basket," Sissy offered brightly, her tears forgotten as she scampered to the door.

Thomas opened the heavy portal and winced as it scraped against the flooring. "Pa was going to fix that, soon as he had the time," he said, shrugging his shoulders. "Maybe Uncle John will take it off the frame, and I can plane it down a little."

"We'll ask him," Lottie put in quickly. "Now get the milking things together and I'll be in the barn in a few minutes," she'd instructed him briskly, unwilling to let mention of James put a damper on the boy's mood again.

Now she faced the moment of truth, her forehead resting against the side of the brown and white cow, who lifted first one foot, then the other, as if she would urge this process to begin without further hesitation.

"Good old Rosie," Lottie said in an encouraging undertone, ignoring Thomas's opinion of the cow's behavior. "Just let me take hold here and wrap my fingers around your—"

With a frown on her face and hunched shoulders bending her low, she reached for the far set of teats and examined the rough surface with the palms of her hands, gripping firmly along the length of each. She pushed upward gently, feeling the warmth of the cow's udder against the sides of her hands as she pushed into its fullness. Then, as Thomas had instructed her, she tugged downward on the teats and squeezed.

Nothing happened. The cow stomped her left hind foot a bit harder and flipped her tail in a vicious swing that narrowly missed Lottie's head, but other than that, the maneuver was a failure.

"Did I do it right?" Lottie asked, watching the boy.

He scooted closer, his feet rustling in the straw, and poked his head within inches of the field of action. "Try it again, Miss Lottie," he instructed her. "Maybe you didn't push up hard enough."

Heads almost touching, they bent to the task. Rosie tried her best to turn to join the inspection, her neck enclosed by the stanchion that was keeping her from getting too involved.

Once more, Lottie encircled both teats and pushed into the full bag of milk, which by now the cow was only too ready to have emptied. She pulled down, and again the result was fruitless.

"Are you sure I'm doing it right?" she asked in a low voice. Rosie lifted her head and opened her mouth at that moment, with a wailing *Moooo* that tickled a laugh from the man who watched from the doorway.

"I think you have your answer," he said between chuckles.

Lottie sat up and twisted her head to look over her shoulder, her face flushed from her efforts, her hair in curling tendrils about her cheeks and forehead, her eyes wide with surprise as she faced John Tillman's grinning good humor.

"Thomas—" she began.

"Miss Lottie—" Thomas blurted.

John's hands went up, palms outward, and his mouth widened even further, till his white, even teeth gleamed in the shadows of the barn.

"Never mind, the two of you. I can see what you're doing. I just think you need a bit more experienced hand to show you the way of it," he drawled in his easy, teasing fashion.

Lottie stood abruptly and turned to face him, her

skirt falling about her legs and almost concealing her bare feet from his watchful gaze. It was the sight of those two pale, slender objects that brought a frown to his countenance.

"Rule number one, Miss O'Malley," he said firmly. "You never, never come into the barn without shoes on."

She flushed even more and felt the heat rush up from her breasts to suffuse her cheeks as she glanced down at her feet, toes burying themselves in the straw as if they would conceal their presence from the man who watched them so sternly.

"Why ever not?" The words were brave, and she lifted her chin with a trace of defiance, embarrassed to be caught running about barefoot like some hoyden.

"Barns can be dangerous places," John explained. "Not only can you get your toes crushed by one of those feet Rosie keeps shifting about, but you might cut yourself on something and get manure in the wound, and then you'd really be in trouble."

"Ohhh . . ." Lottie breathed as her defiance vanished in unison with the air from her lungs. Her shoulders lifted in a hopeful movement, and her eyes begged for his understanding.

"I've never done this particular chore before," she began slowly.

"Well, if Thomas will run to the house and fetch your boots, I'll give you another lesson, if you like," he offered, touched by her eagerness to learn the homely task that Thomas had endeavored to teach.

"Yes sir," the boy responded, and he was quickly gone, his feet flying as he raced to the door of the cabin.

Lottie didn't know where to look. Her eyes had rested momentarily on John Tillman's face and then slid to his throat, where she watched his Adam's apple rise and fall as he swallowed. Hastily, she had glanced at the width of his shoulders beneath the blue work shirt, and then had allowed her gaze to flutter down the rest of his body until she concentrated on his feet. They were apart, as if to balance the weight of his husky frame, and once more she noted the neatly tucked trouser legs he had placed inside of his boots.

Her eyes were truant, unwilling to focus on such mundane objects as two large, dusty boots. They made the return journey up his narrow-hipped body until she was once more aware of the tight-lipped frown he was wearing.

"You're angry with me," she stated.

"Hmmm . . ." he answered, and she caught the flare of his nostrils as he breathed the syllable.

She looked toward the house and breathed a sigh of relief as she watched Thomas's legs stretch out at a full run, heading for her with boots in hand.

John turned to the boy as he approached and reached for the black leather objects, his eyes taking in the worn soles and the scuffs that Lottie's most diligent polishing could not hide.

"You could use a pair of decent shoes," he said gruffly, as he turned to her with the hated boots in hand. He motioned to the stool. "Sit down," he ordered her, and then watched as she obeyed, her eyes wide with surprise at his tone.

"Give me your foot," he directed, holding out one boot. At her hesitation, he lifted her heel, grasped the ankle, and slid the boot into place. He grunted and shoved the heel, noting her wince as it slid onto the slender length of her foot. Frowning, he performed the same process on the other, looking up in silent surprise as she shivered within the warmth of his broad palm, her foot betraying the shimmer of molten awareness that spun a delicate tracery over her body.

She sucked the fullness of her bottom lip, and her breath caught in her throat as she met his eyes with a look of wondering astonishment. His scent rose to her nostrils and they took it in . . . the same mixture of leather and sun sweat, this time with a dash of horseflesh thrown in to tempt her fancy. He smelled good, she decided. Unlike any other human she had ever been so close to. Very few of them had been male, she reflected silently. Funny how men had a different odor about them than women, she mused as she watched the way his eyes narrowed and his pupils enlarged to almost swallow up the blue rimming them.

"Turn around on your stool, Lottie," he whispered. The air between them was vibrant, and she inhaled the scent of him once more, as if she would store it to consider later.

She turned and faced the cow, who had watched with placid eyes as the humans in her stall carried on their shenanigans. The brown gaze was focused on Lottie as she tugged the stool beneath her and draped her skirt once more over her knees, the better to allow room for the bucket.

Behind Lottie, John dropped to the floor, squatting on his haunches, hat tipped back on his head, and heels almost touching the seat of his trousers. With easy grace, he hovered over her, his shirt brushing against the back of her dress, his arms surrounding her loosely as he held each of her hands in one of his own. He guided her fingers to rest against the cow's teats once more, and covered each digit with his longer ones.

Lottie caught a deep breath and concentrated on the

lesson in progress. She watched as John gripped her hands and pushed them gently, firmly, and easily into the full bag of milk. First with his forefinger and thumb, and gradually with the other three fingers, he stripped down the length of the animal's long nipples.

"It worked!" Lottie whispered, glee and satisfaction mixed in her exclamation.

"Of course, it worked," John agreed, shifting against her back as he balanced himself behind her. His hands repeated the movements, and once more, twin streams of bluish white liquid splashed in the metal bucket and foamed up the sides.

He eased a bit closer to her, aware of the faintly sweaty smell of her skin, the sweet flowery fragrance of her hair, and the softness of the female form that he cradled with his masculine length. Once more he guided her hands, and once more she whispered her approval of their teamwork. Again and again he held her hands captive, demonstrating the procedure, until even to his own mind, he knew she was capable of doing the simple chore under her own steam.

He released his grip on her and nodded. His chin rested on her shoulder, the breath he exhaled lifting the hair that curled in a wispy tendril against her cheek as he spoke. "Go on, you can do it, Lottie," he encouraged her.

I could do it better if you weren't breathing in my ear, she thought, chewing on her lower lip as she gave attention to her newfound skill. Having this great hulk of a man rubbing against her back was certainly not conducive to concentrating on much of anything, except his warmth and nearness. And then there was that hard lump that kept poking against her spine.

Easing back from the tempting woman who had fit

so well within the circle of his arms, John glanced down at the proof of her appeal, shaking his head in mute disgust at his body's betrayal. She smelled good, he argued defensively as he rose to his feet and swiped the hat from his head to hold it protectively before himself. She puts some kind of flowery stuff on her hair and then distracts me with the odor, he told himself firmly. Just a typical woman trick, luring men and gettin' them all—

"Am I doing all right?" Lottie asked eagerly, her fingers applying the necessary pressure and keeping up a steady rhythm.

"Yeah, you're doin' fine," John growled, as he stood over her and frowned at the picture she presented to him. Brown and shapeless, her dress clung to her in only one spot, snug only about the fullness of her bottom as she perched on the milking stool. The material pulled from her shoulders, not even suggesting a hint of waistline as the fabric covered her like a drab shroud.

"Don't you have any decent clothes?" he blurted out, after his eyes had denounced her gown as hopeless.

She twisted her head to peer up at him and lost the cadence her nimble fingers had set into motion. Her mouth fell open in surprise and her hands retreated to her knees as she stared at him.

"Why ever should you care about my clothing, Mr. Tillman?" she asked primly.

"My name is John," he reminded her, and his mouth twisted in a grin as he squashed his hat back on his head. "And if you're going to be staying here and watching these young'uns, I'll be paying you a wage, and I'll expect you to dress so as not to bring shame on me. You look like an orphan of the storm in that getup you're wearin'," he said in a voice that pronounced judgment on her dreariest dress.

She stood abruptly and he stepped back, almost clunking his chin on the crown of her head as she shot up from the stool.

"I'll thank you not to insult my wardrobe, *John*," she said, emphasizing his name with scorn. "And in case you've forgotten, I happen to *be* an orphan, and I feel like I've been in the midst of a storm ever since I got here last week." She spun away from him, and the homely dress draped her body in a nondescript fashion that reinforced his opinion even more fully.

"You sure do get your feathers ruffled in a hurry, Lottie," he mused as she spun once more to face him, her cheeks pinkened and her eyes flashing fire in his direction. "I only said that you need some new clothes. You should have bought enough of that flowered stuff for a dress for you, too, when you got a piece for Sissy the other day."

"I'll get along with what I have," she announced, her nose in the air and her teeth gritted as she defied his suggestion.

He stepped closer to her and was pleased to see the flicker of unease that she was too slow to hide from him. Her eyelids fell to shield herself from his piercing perusal, and he grasped her shoulders within the palms of his hands, holding her in place.

"Lottie . . ." The word was firm and demanded her attention. He repeated it even as her eyelids flickered and then lifted, allowing him access to the dark depths of her shadowed look.

"Lottie, I didn't mean to insult you," he said with a trace of apology. He meant to bargain with her, and there was no point in letting her think he was soft, right off. "I want you to make yourself a couple of dresses to wear, and to get rid of this one. Will you do that?" he asked with firm assurance, as if he didn't doubt her answer for a minute.

"You're ashamed to be seen with me?" she asked bleakly.

His head shook slowly. "No, I'm not." He glanced to where Thomas stood next to the barn doorway, his eyes wide with wonder at the argument that involved his two adult guardians. "We're not ashamed of Miss Lottie, are we, Thomas?" he asked sternly.

"No sir . . . ma'am," the boy answered, floundering as he debated which of them he should defer to.

"I love you, Miss Lottie," Sissy piped up, from her perch on the ladder to the haymow. A silent watcher, she had not stirred once during the whole time of Lottie's milking lesson or the ensuing discussion.

"I love you, too, pigeon," Lottie answered distractedly, wondering how she had ever gotten involved in this discussion.

"Did you hear, Lottie?" he asked. "We're not ashamed of you. We just want you to look nice. In fact," he said with another sour appraisal that took in her appearance and found it wanting, "with a gown that fit you properly and had some color to it, you'd be downright—"

His hesitation spoke volumes, and Lottie broke in before he was committed to speaking a falsehood. "I'll never be pretty, John, and we both know it. There's no sense in gilding a lily, and a lot less sense in trying to make a silk purse out of . . . well, never mind." Her breath caught. "That wasn't quite what I meant to say," she amended quickly.

"You're a good-lookin' woman, Lottie," John insisted.

"And we're going to see to it that you get some pretty things to wear around here."

"You can make a dress like mine," Sissy broke in cheerfully. "We can be twins, Miss Lottie. If we get to go to church next week, we can—"

"Maybe we can," Lottie said quickly, unwilling to discuss the issue. Facing the Reverend Bush was not among her favorite fantasies right now. Indeed, the very thought had managed to keep her awake, as visions of horrible possibilities threatened to form into dreams that would surely ruin her sleep.

A lowing that would not be ignored came from the head of the stall, and John dropped his hands as Rosie caught his attention. He lifted an eyebrow and asked a silent question of the woman before him.

"No." She shook her head emphatically. "I've had enough of a lesson this morning. In fact, my hands are cramped already." She fluttered her fingers in the direction of the milk pail that sat waiting beneath the swollen udder of the patient animal. Several inches of foaming milk testified to her diligence, and she smiled at the man before her with a grin of satisfaction.

"I didn't do too badly for a beginner, did I?" Her question was pert and sassy; he shoved his hands deeply into the pockets of his trousers, tempted to tickle her or shake her or something. Anything to relieve the tension her presence had filled him with.

His answering grin told nothing of the silent battle he fought. "You did fine," he admitted with ease. "You can take over the milking anytime you want to, ma'am," he went on, as he rocked on his heels and winked at Thomas in a mocking gesture that brought a peal of laughter from all three of them.

"I won't be quite so hasty as to agree to that," Lottie

protested. "But I'll go get the cloth to strain it with
and meet you in the springhouse in fifteen minutes. I
can do that much," she avowed firmly.

Turning to the milking stool, John squatted into place
and picked up the chore where their foolishness had
taken over, settling into the steady rhythm with ease.
His eyes caught the swish of her skirt as she turned
away, and he allowed himself one quick glance over his
shoulder as she exited the barn, Sissy in tow. The sunlight formed haloes about the golden hair of the two
females as they headed for the house, Sissy chattering
with abandon as Lottie stepped along lightly on the
path, holding the child's fingers within her grasp.

With a sigh of frustration, he leaned his head against
the soft brown side of Rosie and tried in vain to muster
up a vision of the beautiful Sarah. That elusive beauty
who had chosen to marry his brother and had ever after
been out of his reach. Except in the night hours when
he tortured himself by imagining her in James's bed
and enclosed in the circle of James's arms. Where she
belonged, he reminded himself firmly.

Always, the thought of her serene brow, her gentle
voice, had tempted him. The dark beauty of her
straight, black hair that swept over her ears and was
caught in a fanciful arrangement at the nape of her
neck, had ever caught his eye. Hair he had only seen
hanging about her shoulders once, he remembered.
When, approaching the cabin during the day, he had
watched her combing it out after its weekly washing.
Sarah had been sitting in the sun, while she dreamily
tilted her head back to feel the warmth of spring sunshine upon her face. He remembered that she had
started guiltily when he made his presence known and

had flushed as she hurried to the house, embarrassed to be caught in such a casual state.

The milk filled the pail as he switched to strip the cow's udder, back to the first two teats, making sure that he emptied her bag thoroughly. His movements were automatic, born of long practice, as he repeated the procedure he had learned as a boy.

Milking was a comforting chore, he had long ago decided. It freed the mind for other things. Like planning which field he would plow or when the wheat would be ready for harvest or the corn ready to pick. Or like dreaming about his brother's wife. The admission dropped like a field stone into his mind and hung on the edge of his conscience, scoring a sore spot on that tender, indefinable spot within his breast.

"Thou shalt not covet." The old admonition prodded at him, and he sighed with a silent admission of guilt. Contrary to his upbringing, he had more than once looked upon the lovely Sarah with eyes that coveted her beauty, her tender smile, her warmth.

I wonder that I never really got any farther than that, he thought, pondering on the fact. He'd never been able to imagine himself in bed with her, his brother's wife. When he got to that point in his imaginings, he'd stomp his way from his bed to the doorway, sometimes into the night, where he'd look at the stars and get his lusting under control. I never betrayed you that way, James, he told his absent brother.

His inner eye focused on the last woman he'd been with. A tall, lissome lass from Willow Run, upriver twenty miles or so, a two-bit town with a bar and a general store. Not even big enough to afford a church, the folks thereabouts coming to Mill Creek for Sunday services. But what that town did harbor in its bosom was a two-story house on the edge of its main street that contained a pair of the best-looking females in Missouri. That their talents probably outclassed their beauty was only in their favor, John thought with a lusty grin. They had on several occasions—when he was tighter than a fiddle string and about out of sorts—provided him with a measure of enjoyment that had sent him home smiling.

The thought of Lottie's slender form, hidden beneath the cloak of homespun and moving with a lilting sway toward the house, filled his mind. The memory of her bare feet, moving lightly over the wide planks of the floor in John's house, as she stepped to and fro from table to stove and back again, brought a sensual smile to his lips. And the mass of hair that waved in profusion over her shoulders and down her back, as she sat up in his brother's bed and looked at him in horror on that first morning, brought him to a halt.

The little scamp had him daydreaming, had him, for the second time in one morning, thinking of womanly softness and curves that tempted a man to touch forbidden places. He shook his head to clear the web she had begun to spin, a web, he realized with a start of disbelieving astonishment, that threatened to dislodge Sarah from her long-held place.

Six

Due to the benevolent wishes of Abigail Dunstader, the matriarch of Mill Creek's first family and a staunch supporter of the Mill Creek Methodist Church, an organ had been purchased and delivered from St. Louis at great expense. Its installation in the small white church had been an occasion celebrated with holy enthusiasm by the members of that congregation. The organ itself had been an object of envious glances by the pianist of the Baptist church.

Having been the first church in Mill Creek to have a steeple and bell in place, the Baptists had enjoyed the prestige of announcing Sunday morning services with the ringing of that bell. The Methodist congregation had now been elevated to a more stately level of hymn singing, due to the majestic chords of the organ that accompanied them.

But as the buggy rolled past the Baptist church on Sunday morning, Lottie couldn't help but lend a wistful ear to the resounding voices that were raised in cheerful chorus inside that plain, unpainted structure. Not given to fancy doodads, the Baptists had considered the bell to be about as highfalutin as they wanted to get. They were given to enthusiastic worship. Indeed, Lottie's one experience in New Hope at a Baptist church had impressed her mightily, leaving her with a memory of foot tapping, rhythmic music, and eager participation from the congregation that had found her head swiveling in wide-eyed wonder.

"Ever go there?" she asked John, as the buggy rolled past the wagons and buggies that lined the hitching rails in front of the church.

He glanced at her with one lifted eyebrow measuring his disbelief. "What for? I was born and raised Methodist."

"Oh . . ." she said meekly, glancing back once more as the singing reached a crescendo and then stopped, even as a booming bass voice uttered a fervent "Amen!"

"Weren't you born Methodist?" John asked her, slowing his horse to a more acceptable walk, as they neared their destination.

Lottie tightened her lips and lowered her eyes to where her hands were folded neatly in her lap, her gloves in place, as befitted a lady on Sunday morning. "I have no idea what I was born as, other than an orphan," she said softly.

"You had a mother, didn't you?" John asked in a gentler tone.

She nodded once and then looked away from him, as the buggy neared a large walnut tree, next to the cemetery. "My mother left me on the doorstep of the orphanage, when I was just a few days old," she said tightly. "I was taken to the Methodist church along with the other thirty-odd children at the home . . . so I guess you can say I was almost born a Methodist. Leastwise, I've been one all of my life."

John was silent, his eyes compassionate as he scanned the small figure of Lottie O'Malley. She sure had gumption, he decided, aware of her careful grooming, the shining circle of golden braid that lay beneath the saucy bonnet she wore. Her black boots had been rubbed and scrubbed until they looked almost respectable, and her best dress had been washed and ironed with Sarah's flat irons only yesterday.

He'd come in the house as she picked up one of the irons from the stove and flicked a speck of saliva from her pink tongue at it. She'd nodded her head approvingly at the sizzle it produced. He watched in amusement from the doorway as she worked, her hand protected from the bare handle by a heavy flannel pad. The iron had been almost lost amid the full skirt of her dress, as she pressed her way across the table.

"That sure looks like a lot of work to me," he'd finally said, as she lifted the iron to rearrange the dress, the better to reach a wrinkled portion.

Her glance had been startled, her cheeks pink, and her eyes wide, as she responded to his words.

"You could at least knock or holler or something when you come in," she'd said pertly. And then turned back to her chore, her hands busy at the task.

"I expect you were too busy to hear me," John explained. He approached the table and reached to adjust part of the skirt that had caught on the edge, easing it in place for the hot iron to press.

"Do you need a shirt ironed for church tomorrow?" she asked him as she smoothed the damp fabric.

He shrugged and grinned at her, and her glance caught the warmth in his eyes. "I just spread them out wet and smooth them with my hands," he admitted. "They do up all right for working in the barn, I guess."

"Not good enough to go to church in, I'll warrant," she said with a degree of reprimand.

His shoulders lifted again in a gesture of unwilling agreement. "I haven't gone much lately."

She looked up quickly. "I thought James took the children every Sunday."

"He did," John agreed. "I guess I just kinda swore off religion when the merciful, loving God Sarah thought so much of, took her and left James alone with two young'uns to raise." The lines of his face hardened, his jaw thrust forward in a gesture of stubborn defiance. His eyes dared her to reply to his declaration of heresy.

"Did James feel the same way?" Lottie had asked, holding the cooling iron midair as she waited for his answer.

His shrug was eloquent. Indeed, he had the art of expressing himself with shoulder or eyebrow down to a fine degree, Lottie decided as she watched him. That he was unable to speak his thoughts was no matter, when he was so much a master of unspoken language.

A frown or gentle shake of John's head was enough to halt Thomas in his tracks, when he had been rowdy or thoughtless. A smile or outstretched hand could beckon Sissy from yards away, when her uncle felt the need of warm arms about his neck or the touch of small fingers within his palm. And the warm approval of his glance was rich reward, when Lottie had cooked and sewed and done her best to make order in the small house she had been made mistress of. At least on a temporary basis.

The buggy swayed, disrupting his thoughts, as John brought it to a halt. Lottie's hands firmly gripped the reticule she held, her tension visible in the prim set of her mouth and stiffly held posture on the buggy seat.

With a gentle pressure, John's fingers circled one of her wrists, his touch warming her through the dark, tightly woven fabric of her dress.

"Sit still, Lottie," he said quietly. "I'll come around and get you."

Her nod was quick, and he noted the flare of her nostrils as she breathed in a lungful of air. Her eyes were wide, scanning the group of parishioners who were casting glances in the direction of the newcomers. He stepped down and removed his hat, laying it on the buggy seat before he looped the reins through one of the rings that had been hammered into the tree. With long strides, he approached her, and his hands gripped her waist as he lifted her quickly and easily to the ground.

She smoothed her skirts and adjusted her bonnet, aware of the scrutiny of several more worshippers who had followed their lead and driven their buggies into the shade of the tree. Four vehicles could be accommodated by the area beneath the spreading limbs, and latecomers made use of the space.

Sissy had been lowered to stand beside her, and Lottie felt the tugging of her fingers against her skirt. She fixed a polite smile in place and turned to the child, accepting the small hand that Sissy offered and waiting till John brushed the dust from Thomas's pants. She looked down at her own dark dress and wished, not for the first time, that whoever had donated it to the orphanage last year had been more prone to follow the dictates of fashion. Dark and sturdy seemed to be the byword at the orphanage. Its benefactors delivered bundles of clothing for the inhabitants that lived up to that adage. As a result, never had Lottie worn anything but black, brown, or gray clothing. In fact, her navy blue hat had been the first item in her minuscule wardrobe that bore any trace of frivolity at all.

Now she lifted her chin with a quick motion that set her flowers bobbing, and she set out for the gate that hung open to welcome the Sunday morning congregation. Close behind her, the two males closed ranks, as if they would form an escort for the youthful pair they followed.

Sissy was aglow in her new dress, aware of the crisp cotton that Lottie had formed into a becoming frock, even using extra material to make a ruffle that brushed at the tops of the child's booted ankles. The flowers were bright, but no more cheerful than the smile that lit Sissy's face as she proudly carried the tiny pouched reticule Lottie had formed for her from the last scraps of fabric.

Down the aisle of the small church they went, marching in time to the beat of the organ, as Millie Gordon pounded out the chords of "A Mighty Fortress" as a prelude to the morning service. A pew on the right held only one man, and it was there that John halted, motioning Lottie to enter before him. Then Sissy, followed by Thomas, preceded him. John sat on the aisle, aware of the eyes that watched them over upraised hymnals.

The organ wheezed to a final booming chord, and silence settled over the congregation as they nodded their approval of Millie's efforts. From a doorway on the right, a tall, youthful man entered and approached the pulpit, his black suit emphasizing the lean figure within. Dark hair hung in a shiny mantle to touch the nape of his neck, and brushed at the white collar of his shirt beneath his ears. The collar bespoke his calling, and it glistened in the sunlight that entered through the windows and filled the interior of the church with rays of heavenly beauty.

Someone had bleached that collar to a frazzle and then poured on the starch, Lottie thought absently as she fixed her eyes on it. He was young, his arms long and lanky, and clutched in one hand was a black, leather bible which he lifted to the pulpit as he faced his congregation.

The air was hushed, all eyes on the man who faced them; with an air of humility, he spoke.

". . . For all have sinned and come short of the glory of God," he said in a melodious voice that was strangely incongruous, coming from the mouth of the rather nondescript man of the cloth. "Let us pray," he continued in that same, beautiful, male baritone that almost made music of each word he spoke.

Lottie bent her head as his words poured forth. Then in a willful gesture, she peeked through her eyelashes, aware of her irreverence, but needing to set her gaze on the face of the man who had almost become her husband. He was raw-boned, his features chiseled and harsh, but with a fullness about his lips that bespoke a man of generosity. Her eyes took his measure, and then with a furtive twist of her neck, she turned her head to the side and looked at the large booted feet of John Tillman, who sat just a yard or so down the hard wooden pew from her.

Up the length of his trousers, her gaze moved, past the large, wide hands that lay, palm down, on his muscular thighs. Then with a tilt of her head to the left just a bit more, she lifted her lashes, allowing her scope of vision to encompass his chest. Finally, with a penetrating look, she dared to look higher . . . and found to her combined dismay and surprise, that she was staring directly into his amused blue eyes.

Quickly her lashes lowered, and her head turned to

fix her attention once more on the hands that gripped
each other firmly in her lap. With a breath that shuddered, she considered her embarrassment. He had been
grinning at her like an idiot, she thought with an indignation that crested her cheeks with pink flags. You
shouldn't have been peeking during prayer, she scolded
herself silently. Her groan was held within, and her
chest ached with the weight of it.

John attempted to erase the smile that had been
prompted by Lottie's appraisal of the preacher and then
himself. Making comparisons, were you, Miss O'Malley?
he thought. He lifted a hand to cover his mouth, aware
that his grin was not fading as it should, then cleared
his throat, as if the pursing of his lips would help in
his efforts. She was a scamp, he decided, irreverent, to
say the least, and his merriment increased.

At the booming "Amen" that signaled the end of the
preacher's prayer, the congregation rustled, feet shuffling and bottoms moving in uneasy shifting against the
hard seats. Aware that the morning was only begun and
that it would be high noon before the service was over,
they prepared for the long haul.

A series of hymns, led by the preacher's beautiful
voice, filled the small building, the notes vibrating from
the wooden walls, floor, and ceiling. From around her,
Lottie heard the familiar words and joined in with her
own sweet soprano, unaware of the listening ears that
noted her natural gift, caught up as she was in the har-
mony of the music.

John sang in a rusty monotone, his ear attuned to
Lottie. His own ability was minuscule, but he had
enough musical awareness to recognize a woman with
talent when he heard one. He'd caught a few final notes
of her morning wake-up just yesterday, when she stood

in the middle of the cabin and roused Sissy with a cheerful yodeling serenade that had culminated in a blending of giggles and warm hugs as he crossed the porch and entered the door.

"Did you hear Miss Lottie?" Sissy had wanted to know as she peeked over the shoulder of the woman in question.

"Yeah, punkin, I heard her," he'd answered in a noncommittal fashion, and then had frowned as he considered the two females.

Sissy had sure taken up with the woman in a hurry. Of course, what with Lottie making her a new dress and all, it was to be expected. Then there was all the cuddling and rocking they did at night, before Sissy was sent up the ladder to the loft. Likely, Lottie was setting down roots, getting Sissy attached to her, in case she didn't find somewhere else to go once he'd decided what to do with the children.

He frowned at his thoughts, not sure if they were proper, here in the house of the Lord. After all, the woman couldn't be blamed if she was trying to make a place for herself. Being alone in the world, she had to look out for her own welfare, he reasoned. And then felt better for his benevolence toward her.

The preacher, usually firmly in command of his congregation, was faced with a crowd of eager, expectant faces. Knowing that they were well aware of Lottie's presence, his own countenance was not so eager. But with a valiant effort, he read his sermon, and by dint of much perspiration and a few beneficial tugs at the tight, starched collar he wore, he managed to plow through the hour-long dissertation he had prepared.

After the final hymn was sung and the final "Amen" said in unison by the pews of parishioners the group rose as one and made their way to the back door. In splendid black broadcloth, the Reverend Bush waited for his flock, most of them older than he was, all of them eager to see the byplay that was sure to come to pass as Lottie neared the door.

She had known the moment must come and had dreaded it. Only the presence of John and the children made it possible for her to walk slowly toward the open portal and step into the sunshine that bathed the small porch with noonday radiance.

Then she raised her head and met his eyes and smiled. "Reverend Bush?" she asked politely, her teeth nearly meeting behind the slight opening of her lips, as she allowed a polite smile to lift the edges of her mouth.

He offered her his hand in greeting, and she watched as a slow flush rose from his throat, just above the tight collar, to suffuse the craggy features of his face.

"You are Miss Lottie O'Malley," he said in that deep voice that rose to meet her ears with apology apparent in each tone.

She nodded and waited, unsure of the protocol of the occasion. Should she remove her hand from his and step away, or perhaps comment on his sermon, of which she could not remember one single word at this moment? Her mouth tightened about the smile she had managed to form, and her lower lip quivered as she felt a rush of irritation flood her being.

This man had jilted her! And here she was on display for the whole town to see, in her drab, shapeless dress, looking like a dried-up old maid. With a quick gesture, she took her hand back from his grip and prepared to walk away.

Her nod of farewell was brusque and her words were low, but carried to his ear. "It was unfortunate we didn't meet when I arrived in town last week," she said sweetly. "I'm so sorry to have missed you."

Then, with a presence that would have made Aggie Conklin proud, she lifted the hem of her skirt just a bit and seizing Sissy by the hand, made her way down the two steps to the churchyard. Her eyes dared to meet those of the watching townsfolk, and the message of dignity and pride she exuded opened a path before her as she stepped briskly toward the gate.

"Lottie . . . wait . . ." came a voice from one side, and Genevieve approached, one pale, slender hand holding her bonnet in place as she hurried to catch the woman who moved with such purposeful steps.

Lottie turned, eyes open wide in surprise at the interruption to her grand exit. Genevieve smiled, her dimples flashing a message of goodwill.

"I haven't seen you in town all week," she said in a voice that carried, including John and the children in her greeting.

"That's 'cause we haven't been there," Sissy said brightly, twirling a fold of her skirt and lifting it to catch Genevieve's eye.

The gesture worked. Genevieve looked down and then bent low to run an appraising palm over the new dress, smoothing her fingers down Sissy's arm as she exclaimed her praise for the child's benefit.

Sissy beamed, her pride in the new dress overcoming her natural reticence, and reached to cling to Lottie's fingers with her own.

"Miss Lottie made it," she boasted, and bestowed a wide smile on her benefactor.

"I know she did," the storekeeper's daughter replied with a broad smile. Then her eyes went to the nonde-

script outfit that Lottie had, of necessity, clothed herself
in.

"Miss Lottie," Genevieve began slowly and then got
up a full head of steam as her idea came to fruition
and became a spoken offering. "Do you suppose you
could sew a dress for me, if I paid you and brought
out the material and thread and one of my old ones
for a pattern?" Her eyes sparkled as she made the proposal, and Lottie opened her mouth to answer, her
quick mind already rearranging her schedule to make
time for the task.

But it was not to be. John laid his hand on her arm
and shook his head, the gesture both apologetic, yet
firm. "I'm sorry, Genevieve, but Lottie has her work cut
out for her right now. Maybe some other time," he said
with a touch of arrogant assurance in the final words.

"Well, whenever you can . . ." Genevieve said slowly,
her face showing the disappointment she felt at the re-
jection of her plan.

Lottie rushed to answer. "We'll see . . . after all, I
don't know how long I'll be here," she said, her voice
trailing off as she felt the pressure of John's hand, his
fingers tightening on her wrist.

"We need to be leaving," he said, turning to call to
Thomas, who had seized the opportunity to run off
with several young boys and was even now playing tag
in the road.

Genevieve stood back and watched them leave, taking
refuge from the sun's rays beneath an enormous walnut
tree that grew closer to the church. With the exodus of
the Tillman group, the congregation went their separate
ways, buggies and wagons heading in either direction,
and a few parishioners walking toward their homes in
town.

"Genevieve."

She was not surprised at the sound of her name, nor the voice that called it in such a low, wretched tone. With a look cast over her shoulder, she watched as Stephen Bush took the two steps slowly, his feet hesitant as he approached her. The shade above her was pierced by a beam of sunlight that dappled the leaves and cast its glow on the face of the beautiful young woman. With painful precision, Stephen Bush reached to take her hand and held it within his palm, his fingers tracing her oval nails and slender knuckles.

She tugged to free it from his grasp, but he uttered one word that stilled her movement.

"Please."

"Please, what?" she asked softly, her own pleasant modulation torn with pain. "Please marry me, Genevieve?" she asked quietly. "Or please don't mind if I marry someone else?" She turned half away from him, as if she would flee. "What do you want of me, Stephen?" she asked in a whispering plea.

His groan was harsh in her ears, and she halted her flight, her hand escaping his grip, but clenched into a tight, little fist that buried itself in the folds of her full skirt.

"I'm sorry, Genevieve," he said. "I don't know myself what I want, let alone what I expect of you." His sigh was deep and his voice firmed as he continued, "I only know what I'm expected to do as a man of the cloth. I'm torn between my own desires and the obligations I feel toward my church."

As she turned to face him, her eyes were brimming with unshed tears. "Well, I'm sure that your mail-order bride will just fall right into your arms if you make her another offer, Stephen. Why don't you just get your

buggy and ride right out there to the Tillman place
and do your proposing in person this time. We both
know she fits the image better than I do." Her head
was high as she spoke her piece, and she made a valiant
effort to swallow the tears that threatened to fall.

"You know I would marry you—" Stephen began, but
the dark-haired woman cast him a scornful glance that
was not blunted by her tear-filled eyes.

"Then why did you send for Lottie?" she asked with
asperity, knowing what he would reply.

He shrugged and lifted his hands helplessly. "My
bishop suggested it, and at the time it seemed to be the
best idea." His eyes glistened with moisture of their
own as he looked at her with mute appeal. "That was
before I . . . before you and I spent time together. Before I realized how I felt about you."

"Then why didn't you write back that you'd changed
your mind?" she wanted to know, as if it were not a
question he had already answered.

"I told you last week, Genevieve. It was too late by
then. She was on her way." He stood tall, and in the
freckled sunshine that flickered through the leaves of
the walnut tree, his craggy features took on a resolve
that tore at her heart.

"Then why do you speak to me now?" she asked him,
with agony apparent in each word.

"I wanted you to know something," he said slowly,
each word reluctantly uttered. "I'm going out to see
her, to apologize. I couldn't do that here, but I owe it
to her. And I have to renew the offer, Genevieve. I
spoke to the bishop. He said it was a matter of
honor . . . but I already knew that." His mouth tightened and he took a deep breath. "If she'll have me, I
intend to ask her once more to marry me."

And then he watched as her curls flounced in time to the quick steps she took, as Genevieve Slocum walked away, leaving him alone and bereft.

"Change your dress, Sissy," Lottie said absently, as she followed the child into the house. "Here, let me undo your buttons," she amended before the little girl could begin climbing the ladder to the loft. Her fingers were nimble, operating automatically as her mind flew ahead to dinner preparations.

Amazing, she thought as she washed and cleaned the vegetables for stew . . . amazing how the human mind could focus on one chore, while being occupied on another level, with something entirely different.

For instance, here she was, up to her elbows in potatoes and carrots, while her thoughts were still back in the church in Mill Creek. And even as her knife whacked at the leafy green carrot fronds, her aggravation was taking deep jabs at the tall, raw-boned pastor of that prosperous congregation.

She stood for a moment, eyes closed and hands quiet, as she considered his grave, unjust dereliction of duty. How dare he stand before his congregation with such a blot against his honor? With such a stain on his integrity?

Her imagination placed her in the front pew, for just a moment. Attired in her frumpy dress, with mended gloves and too-small boots, she would make a most unlovely picture, she knew. Yet, that was what and where she would have been this very morning, if the Reverend Bush had lived up to his agreement.

Another picture of John and the children, lined up in the wooden pew halfway to the back of the small church, floated into the forefront of her vision, and her mouth pursed as she considered it. John, husky and yellow-haired, with arms that could lift a hundred-pound bag of feed as easily as they could hoist a four-year-old girl into the air. With the shirt she had ironed for him buttoned up tightly to clutch at his throat, he sat tall over the boy at his side, an uncle filling a father's shoes.

Shoes he wasn't all that keen on occupying, she reminded herself. Although, if the truth be told, he hadn't mentioned sending the children to St. Louis but once, back when she first arrived. Maybe, she thought, maybe he's given up that idea.

Her eyes open now, she scrubbed even more ferociously at the carrot she held, intent on removing every speck of dirt from its indented surface. Maybe a turnip would be good, she thought as she dropped the last of the well-scoured vegetables into a pot of water.

Wiping her hands on the front of the apron she had donned, she headed for the garden, that overgrown, weed-infested area that James had left to fate this year. Unless she had been mightily mistaken, a crop of turnips had propagated themselves from seeds lying dormant beneath the snow, and she headed for the spot she had marked mentally just the other day.

Her eyes lit with satisfaction as she plucked a pair of the ripe specimens from their hiding and shook the dirt from them, breaking off the tops to save for dinner tomorrow. Still green, with no tinges of yellow, they would taste good cooked with a chunk of bacon or ham. A trip to the smokehouse just a few days after her arrival had offered a pleasant surprise. Part of a ham and almost a full slab of bacon were hanging there, more than she had expected at this time of year, when hog-butchering time was almost upon them.

John had told her that next month would find the

smokehouse once more the scene of activity, as the long process of preserving the pork was put into motion. Life in New Hope had done little to prepare Lottie for most of the activity here on the Tillman farm, but when it came to food preparation, she was well versed. Even the orphanage had had a smokehouse, there on the outskirts of Boston, where each fall the pork had been hung and smoked for the use of the orphans. Used with stringent restrictions, she remembered with a grim smile. More than once, she had searched vainly for a scrap of meat in the bowl of soup or stew she had eaten.

Lottie straightened, one hand holding the turnips against her apron, the other clutching the greens. Looking about her, her eyes scanned the near reaches of the prosperous farm that James Tillman had worked so hard to carve from the Missouri soil. Quite the least impressive of his buildings was the cabin they lived in. Like most farmers, he was intent on providing shelter for his livestock, and the number of structures he had built were proof of his prosperity. From the large, two-story barn to the slat-sided corncrib, his whitewashed collection of farm buildings were well kept and sturdy.

She stood in the center of the overgrown garden patch and lifted her face to the sky. That she should find herself here, in the midst of such a place, was surely God's will, she thought. Perhaps the course of events had been formed by an all-knowing, omnipotent hand, and she was only a small piece of the puzzle. Surely she would find her own niche in this tapestry of life that was being woven about her.

"Consider the lilies of the field," Aggie Conklin used to tell her, when she despaired of ever finding a life beyond the walls of the orphanage. Somehow the quotation from Aggie's Bible had not seemed to fit her situation, never having equated herself with such a lovely bloom, but Lottie had drawn a certain amount of comfort from it nevertheless.

Aggie . . . that stalwart figure who had sent her on her way with words of encouragement and blessing. Lottie's eyes filled with tears, thinking of the woman who had been as near to a mother as she'd ever hoped to have. Then, with a brisk shake of her head, as if she would put away her sentimental thoughts, she made her way back to the house, bearing the result of her trip to the garden plot.

She picked up her skirt to step onto the porch, just as Thomas came out to meet her.

"I hate turnips," he said, his lower lip protruding as a frown settled over his face.

"They're good for you," Lottie answered immediately, her mouth forming a coaxing smile.

"Nope," the boy insisted. "Pa said all turnips was good for was the tops of them. The rest was fit for pigs."

"Well, they're not my favorite vegetable," she admitted slowly, with a cheerful smile, "but I hate to have them tossed to the pigs."

"Sounds like a good idea to me." John's deep voice had a definite ring to it, as he agreed wholeheartedly with his nephew. "Pigs need to eat, too, Miss Lottie," he said with firm conviction.

"Yeah," Thomas agreed stoutly, ranging himself on the side of his benefactor. He watched hopefully as Lottie considered the two large root vegetables she held, with her head tipped to one side consideringly.

"I concede," she said finally, bending to deposit them on the porch. "We'll cut them up into the bucket after dinner. I suspect they'll turn into good bacon."

John laughed, and his big hand cupped her elbow as

he stood next to her at the foot of the shallow steps. "We'll be glad to eat turnip greens for dinner, Lottie," he suggested with an approving nod.

The air was still, the sun warm against her head, and somewhere she heard the faint whicker of a horse. A feeling of anticipation gripped her, supplanting the moments of nostalgic loneliness she had felt in the garden.

Against her arm, she felt the brush of his fingers and the heat of his palm as he gripped her. In a slow, searching fashion, her eyes sought his. Surely he felt it, this warmth that his touch brought to her flesh. Certainly he must sense her reaction to the contact of his hand against her skin. The long sleeves of her dress had been rolled almost to her elbows, and his brown fingers were spread, fanlike, over the softness of her forearm, each calloused tip impressing itself upon her blue-veined flesh. Her gaze dropped to fix upon the spread of his long, strong fingers, and she felt a flush of feminine awareness creep up her throat.

John's first intention had been to halt Lottie, his hand reaching to grip her elbow before she could climb the steps to the porch. When Thomas had blurted out his opinion of the hated turnips, John could not help but support the boy's case. Lottie did look so sweetly determined, clutching those confounded things against her apron.

His thought had been to tease her a bit, but the bewilderment in her eyes as she glanced up at him had made him conscious of the hold he had on her arm. His fingers held the tender underside, where the skin was pale and the blood ran just beneath the surface. Soft and shapely, the bare limb looked vulnerable within the span of his hand, and he sensed the pulse that beat there. His eyes lifted to her throat and watched as the rosy hue spread upward from the collar of her dress. She swallowed, and his gaze followed the movement and then traveled up to where her darkened pupils dwelt between long lashes that blinked twice, even as he watched.

The little sprout was trembling, he realized with astonishment as his eyes narrowed in their journey over her face. Her full lower lip was quivering, and he allowed his gaze to focus there. There, where just the edge of her pink tongue made a journey from one side of her wide, expressive mouth to the other, dampening the inside of her lip and luring his thoughts in a wayward fashion. For just a moment, in less time than it took that small, rosy tip to travel the span, he imagined the flavor of her mouth. Imagined the tempting, lush cushion of her lip, if he should press his own mouth against it. If his tongue should taste the slick texture of that plump flesh, would it be sweet? Would Lottie's flavor be like the wildflower scent that followed her with such faithfulness.

He shook his head, as if to rid it of the errant thoughts that flooded his mind. This little Easterner was beguiling him, and her rosy cheeks and pink, tempting mouth were tugging at his needy thoughts and making him feel like a penned-up bull next to a pasture of yearling heifers.

Bewildered by his own thoughts, bewitched by the warm flesh his fingers held within their grip, and confused by the errant desire that had begun to bloom within his body, John stepped back. Dropping her elbow from his grasp and clearing his throat with a loud, rasping sound, he watched her intently, noting the twitch of her eyelids as she glanced away from him.

Beneath the dark garb she wore, her breast lifted as she caught a lungful of air, and then her smile was bright as she flashed it in his direction. "I'll get these washed and ready to cook, if you'll fetch a slice of pork from the smokehouse to put in the kettle with them, John," she said as she headed for the door of the house.

Heart pounding and sweat freckling her forehead, she escaped into the cool dimness of the cabin and halted just inside the door.

"Gracious," she exclaimed under her breath, her lips trembling as she considered the revelation that had been visited upon her. "That man has the warmest hands I've ever met up with, not to mention that smile of his, that could coax a flower to bloom in the middle of winter."

She dropped the greens into the basin that sat in the sink and dipped a pan of water over them, sloshing it with her hands to wash them, rinsing off the dust and dirt from the garden. Biting her lip, she considered her plight.

"Miss Aggie, you didn't tell me about this," she whispered in a wondering fashion. "You told me about not speaking to strangers while I traveled, and you told me about being a good wife and being submissive to my husband. But you never said one time that a woman could feel so warm and fluttery and full of funny wiggles down inside."

"Miss Lottie, are you cookin' yet?" Sissy cried plaintively from the loft. "My tummy is makin' me feel hungry," she complained, as she peeked over the edge of the rough planking that formed the half ceiling over the kitchen end of the cabin.

Lottie shook her head against the emotional turmoil John's nearness had set into motion within her youthful frame and set a smile in place before Sissy could scamper down the ladder.

"How about a piece of bread and butter, Sissy?" she

asked the child coaxingly. "I put the meat on the back of the stove before we went to church this morning, and it will only take a little while for the vegetables to cook up in the broth. We'll be eating before you know it."

Sissy nodded emphatically. "I like your bread, Miss Lottie," she announced. "Pa never could get the hang of it after Ma left us, and he just bought it from Miz Clawson for the last little while." She leaned closer to watch as Lottie sliced a generous piece from the bread that had been wrapped in a dish towel on the shelf.

"Miz Clawson didn't make good light bread like you do," the little girl confided. "Sometimes it was so heavy, Pa would say it was like eatin' the Rock of Gibraltar." Her small brow furrowed, and she rocked back and forth as she considered the puzzle. "Miss Lottie," she asked after a moment. "Pa was just teasin', wasn't he? You can't really eat a rock, can you?" she asked with a chuckle and a hopeful look.

Lottie shook her head as she lifted the lid from the butter dish that sat in the middle of the table. Her hands were deft as she slathered the butter across the bread, and she grinned as she answered the question, filing it in her memory to repeat to John later on.

"No, of course not. Your pa was just joshin' you a bit," she said firmly. And then, as the small fingers accepted the bread from her hands, she sensed, with certain sureness, the clinging tendrils of love for this elfin child that had crept so stealthily and firmly about the contours of her heart.

Seven

She looked like a breath of spring. Genevieve Slocum had not been cut out to be a storekeeper's daughter, John decided silently as he watched her slender, pale fingers measuring and folding a length of rich brown piece goods for her customer. Next to her, Mabel Sharp watched closely, garbed in a fashionable gray dress, the color somber, as befitted the undertaker's wife.

Fitting for undertakers and orphans both . . . thought John with a wry grin, his dark humor surfacing for a moment. Then his lips tightened as he visualized once more the sparseness of Lottie's dreary wardrobe, if it could be called by that name. Mabel Sharp had a choice. Lottie had not. And with a determined look that pulled his brows down and narrowed his eyes, he approached the counter at one end of the mercantile store, where Genevieve was finishing up her task.

"Good morning, John," she chirped, her eyes appreciating his appearance as he tucked his thumbs into the waistband of his trousers and nodded at her.

"Morning, Miz Sharp," John rumbled as that lady turned to acknowledge his presence.

Her eyes alight with curiosity, Mabel pursed her lips and then, indulging the vice, she asked John the question he was sure hovered in the minds of half the population of Mill Creek.

"Miss O'Malley still tending to those young'uns out at your place?" Her brow rose in silent echo of her words, while John suppressed a smile.

"I expect the whole town would know it if she'd left, don't you?" he drawled.

Mabel lifted one shoulder in a shrug, as she picked up the parcel that Genevieve had wrapped in brown paper and tied neatly with string. "Land sakes, boy," she said with a prim tightening of her lips, "I'm just thinking of that poor girl and her circumstances. Seems to me that there should be a family in town that could use an extra hand about the place."

"Well, right now, she's keeping busy," John informed her tightly, his good humor at an end. "And she's not at my place, Miz Sharp. She's living at James's house."

"Won't you be takin' over your brother's land? Workin' it for those children?" she asked. "And what about your horses?"

Genevieve's eyes misted as John flinched at the woman's prying words, her tender heart sensing his pain. Her fingers tightened into a knot at her waist and she caught a deep breath.

"I'm sure John hasn't had much time to make any plans yet, Miz Sharp," she put in before the man before her could speak his mind.

He shot her a grateful glance and cleared his throat, choosing his words carefully, knowing they might be carried all over town before the end of the day.

"I've just sold off my two-year-olds. I'm about done with the haying and getting ready for winter. Truth to tell, by the time I get through a day's work, I can't find enough gumption to do much deciding on anything these days," he vowed with a tightening of his jaw that matched the white-knuckled fists his hands had formed.

Uneasily, he relaxed the fingers that were clutching at his belt line, and allowed his hands to drop to his sides.

"Well, I surely do feel for those poor children," Mrs. Sharp said, as her eyes cast an uncertain look at the man before her. "But I'm sure you'll do what's best, John," she said with an encouraging nod as she prepared to take her leave.

John's nod was curt, and his smile was strained as, skirts flying behind her, Mabel Sharp sailed toward the door.

Genevieve's mouth formed an impish grin as John turned back to face her, and his own lips twisted into an answering smile.

"I didn't mean to sound so gruff, Genevieve," he said with a sigh. "I know she means well, but it's not been an easy time for any of us."

"I was glad to see you all in church yesterday," she said as she straightened up the counter, setting aside the bolt of fabric Mabel Sharp had chosen for her new dress.

"Yeah . . . well, that's partly why I'm here," John said in a low voice, although no other customers were nearby. In fact, the place was empty, but for one small boy whose eyes were glued to a jar of hard candy on the far side of the store.

Genevieve looked puzzled. "Whatever do you mean?" she asked, brushing at the lint that clung to her apron as she restored it to its pristine appearance.

John's eyes slid over the young woman's form with a measuring glance. "That dress you have on, Genevieve," he said musingly. "How much material would it take to make one like that?"

Her eyes widened at his query, and then she looked down at the bright blue checked gingham that her mother had sewn for her only last week. With a purely feminine gesture, she brushed at a ruffle that had turned the wrong way and then considered his question.

"Well . . . maybe seven yards or so," she estimated. "But then, you could make it a bit narrower and use less fabric," she said as she took hold of the side seam and showed him the fullness of her skirt.

"No," he said with a firm shake of his head. "I'm not interested in cutting corners. I want a nice piece of material for Lottie to make up a dress before next Sunday. She spent her spare time on Sissy's last week, and I'll warrant she didn't even think about making one for herself."

"I could just hug you, John Tillman," Genevieve said with fervent glee. "I'll bet it's been a long time since anybody gave Lottie's clothing a second thought."

John flushed at her praise. "I owe her almost two weeks' wages," he explained, as he reached into his pocket for the small leather purse he carried. Along with it he drew out a piece of paper that he carefully unfolded and lay on the counter.

"What's that?" Genevieve asked as she bent over to better see what he had drawn on the scrap he held.

"I traced the outline of her boot," he admitted with a sheepish look. "She's wearin' somebody else's castoffs, and they're too tight."

Genevieve clapped her hands in glee. "Now I really could hug you, John," she chortled. "She'll be so pleased."

"Yeah . . . well, I hope so," he said slowly. "She's kinda unpredictable."

"I think she's kinda nice," the dark-haired girl across the counter from him said softly, as she eyed him with speculation. She turned around and, after a moment's

hesitation, slid a bolt of pink-and-white-checked gingham from the pile.

"She took a shine to this when she was in here picking out Sissy's dress goods last week," Genevieve said,
as she unrolled the bolt one turn and then held up the
bright splash of color against her white apron.

"Would that look good on her?" John asked, his head
tilted to one side as he tried to picture Lottie bedecked
in a pink and white dress.

Her head nodded firmly, and her words added weight
to the gesture. "With that beautiful hair of hers, she'd
look like a princess in this," she said decisively.

John nodded, pleased that the choice had been so
simple to make, and gestured expansively at the crisp
folds of fabric. "Just cut off whatever you think she'll
need," he instructed her, and then, as another thought
made its way into his head, he waved his hand again.
"Oh, and add enough for a dress for Sissy. She told
Lottie she wanted to be twins."

Now that he had the ball rolling, he decided to shoot
the works. Stuffing his hands into his pockets, he rocked
back on his heels, watching Genevieve's deft movements
as she followed his directions. His grin widened as he
thought of Sissy's delight at her good fortune. Two new
dresses at a time would be her idea of heaven, for sure.

"Now . . ." Genevieve said with a flourish as she
wrapped the bundle, complete with a spool of thread
and three cards of pink buttons. "Now, let's take a look
at your other project here." She tucked the package
under her arm and snatched up the paper John had
laid down, leading the way to the other side of the store,
where shoes and boots were displayed on the end of
the walnut countertop.

"What are we looking for?" she asked, lifting a slender shoe that fastened up the side with a row of black shiny buttons. "These are quite the fashion, John," she said with a sigh, her fingers smoothing the soft leather and touching the heel that curved gracefully beneath her touch.

His head shook slowly but deliberately. "No, that won't do," he decided reluctantly. "Pretty as they are, they won't look nearly as nice after a trip to the chicken coop and a tromp through the barn."

"What about on Sunday morning, going to church?" Genevieve asked pertly, her lashes fluttering with purely female instinct.

John laughed. "Don't go flirting with me," he said with a wry grin. "It won't help you sell a pair of shoes."

Her own laughter was easy, and her eyes twinkled at his words. "I've known you too long to waste time flirting, John," she said cheerfully.

"I watched you grow up, Genevieve. You flirt with half the men who come in here." He leaned both hands, palm down, on the counter, and looked directly into her startled blue eyes. "When are you going to settle down and do some serious pickin' and choosin'," he asked with gentle curiosity. "You're pretty, and too genteel to be spending your days in this store. You need to be making a home for a good man."

Her eyes softened and, as he watched, welled up with tears. She blinked rapidly to hold them back from the course they seemed bent on taking, and her smile was rueful. "There's nothing I'd like better, John," she whispered. "Maybe . . . if things ever work out right . . ." Her words were hesitant, and she lifted one slender hand to brush at an errant tear that had escaped and was sliding down her face.

He was thunderstruck. Never in a million years would

he have suspected that her flirtatious manner hid such sadness! His hand brushed against the silken flesh of her cheek. "I didn't mean to make you feel badly," he said urgently. "Can I do anything to help?"

She shook her head and forced a smile, drawing a lace-edged hanky from her apron pocket to swipe once more at her overflowing eyes. "No, I'm fine, really, John. Please, just forget I said anything," she begged quietly.

His mind spun in circles as he reviewed the men who might inspire such feelings from the lovely girl before him. Surely in the general vicinity there must be more than a dozen who would look on the storekeeper's daughter with hungry eyes. But the innate charm and graceful bearing of Genevieve Slocum was far beyond the reach of many of the eligible candidates in the area.

The story of her French mother was old news here in Mill Creek. The woman who lived in the big two-story house, that was surrounded by a white fence—who played for long hours on her piano each day—was a misfit in Mill Creek. Adored by her unpretentious husband and catered to, both by him and the daughter she doted on, Marie Slocum lived like a princess. From the slim, fashionable woman and the stocky storekeeper had come this dark-haired creature who had been captivating the menfolk hereabouts since she was barely in her teens. She'd appeared immune to the admiring glances and had been equally friendly to everyone. But now . . . whoever Genevieve might be enamored by was another puzzle he would have to take out and examine later.

This morning he needed to choose boots for Lottie and make his way back to the farm. He'd left right after breakfast and morning chores, and none of the three of them had been too happy with his abrupt departure, especially when he told them he was heading in to town. Lottie had smoothed and soothed the children's ruffled feathers though, he remembered, as he recalled her bending to hug them closer and instructing them to wave their goodbyes as he left. Reluctantly, they had done so, but he suspected that a licorice whip or a handful of hard candy would not go too far amiss at mending their hurt feelings.

Genevieve had selected another pair of shoes, heavier, but still flexible and certainly more attractive than the sturdy clodhoppers Lottie had been wearing. She held up the paper he had traced the outline on, and looked at it quizzically.

"Did you set the boot on here and trace it?" she asked. "Will this be the right size, if I just measure it to the new ones?"

He cleared his throat and shook his head. "No, you'll have to allow a little," he said. "Hers are too small. They pinch her feet."

Genevieve's eyes flew to meet his, and her dismay was apparent. "However does she walk in them?" she asked. "Don't they hurt?"

"I imagine so," John allowed. "Probably with every step she takes. I guess it's why she goes barefoot whenever she gets a chance."

"Barefoot?" The word was filled with horror. The owner of shoes and boots of every description, Genevieve's own tender toes were well shod, except for when she was in bed. And the thought of owning but a single pair of boots was beyond her comprehension.

"Yeah . . ." His eyes sparkled with a memory that would not be banished from his mind, no matter how he struggled with it. Bare, pink feet that stepped with lively movements across the wooden kitchen floor, that had half-hidden themselves in the straw in the barn . . . that had arched in his hand . . . He shook his head and his smile held secret amusement.

"Yeah," he repeated. "She goes barefoot."

"Well, she won't have to anymore," Genevieve said decisively, as she found another pair of boots beneath the counter and measured them against the outline on the paper. "These will work, I think," she said, carefully brushing off a smudge on the fine leather. "Does she have a button hook?"

John looked blank for a moment, and then shrugged. "I don't suppose she does."

Genevieve removed one from a jar beneath the counter and tucked it into one of the boots. "Don't forget to tell her it's there," she advised him, as she fit the pair into a box and tied string about it.

John looked over his shoulder as two women came in the door and lowered his voice accordingly. "I saw the preacher heading out of town when I drove in earlier," he said. "I wonder where he was off to? Did old Carl Webster take a turn for the worse?"

She shook her head, and a pensive look dulled the shine of her smile. "I haven't heard anything," she said slowly. "Maybe he's just gone to call on someone." Her words were careful—casual and noncommittal—and she turned away from him to find a tin of polish for Lottie's boots.

"She'll need this," she said as she offered it to him a moment later. "Tell her it's a present from me."

"Thank you, Genevieve. Figure up what I owe you, and add in some candy for the sprouts, will you?" John slid the polish into his back pocket and then lifted the lid on the tall glass jar of licorice, selecting several pieces to lay on the counter where Genevieve was adding up his purchases.

His leather purse in hand, he selected the coins and paid her, picked up the candy she had folded and put into a small bag, and with a small salute he left.

She watched him go, her eyes thoughtful, her mind rebellious as she wondered at the information he had left behind. Stephen was out calling this morning, and odds were that he was heading for the Tillman place.

She'd folded her sleeves as high as decency would allow, and they were still getting wet on the lower edges. Lottie set her mouth and redoubled her efforts. Washing was not her favorite task, and even the sunshine and warm breeze were not cheering her up this morning.

John had gone to town, leaving her with two disconsolate children and a few questions of her own. Not that she had any right to quiz him about his comings and goings, but she wouldn't have minded a ride this morning. The washing could have waited, she thought with an impatient look at the tubful of clothing she was scrubbing.

The sheets were already spread over the clothesline she'd strung. John had pointed it out to her, hanging on a nail on the porch, where it had been carefully coiled and left some time ago, if the accumulation of dust and dirt on it were any indication. She'd soaked and cleaned it thoroughly, no mean chore to be sure, before she could drape her laundry over its length. A nail someone had pounded on the outer wall of the corncrib and another on the side of the smokehouse, that Thomas had pointed out, had provided her with a place to stretch out the rope. Then Sissy had remembered the tall, slender pole with another nail driven into the top, that would prop the line in the air, once the heavy, wet sheets were draped across it.

There'd been clothespins to use on washday at the orphanage, but apparently James had not seen fit to purchase them for his wife. She sighed at the lack, unsure if she were secure enough here to ask John to buy some at the mercantile. Somehow, this uncertainty of her position had been brought to the forefront of her mind since yesterday. Since she had finally set eyes on the man who had deserted her. Her position here was tenuous, at best, she decided. At the mercy of a man's whims, Lottie felt the cold finger of uncertainty brush at her nape and shivered in the sunlight.

Distractedly, she brushed with one hand at a lock of hair that insisted on falling across her cheek. And her fingers left a damp spot with a residue of suds there, as she returned to her scrubbing.

"Miss Lottie," Thomas called from the barn door. "I see someone coming down the lane in a buggy," he hollered, hands forming a megaphone about his mouth.

"We got company," Sissy shrieked with fervor, as she craned her neck to see from her perch on the porch step.

"Oh, land sakes," Lottie grumbled. "Just what I needed this morning." Her mouth pursed in a disgruntled fashion, and she exhaled through her nostrils with a muffled snort as the black buggy neared the house.

Garbed in her oldest dress—next to the gardening outfit, which John had deemed too far gone to be worn again—she presented a shabby picture. With futile motions, she brushed at the front of her damp dress, only adding to the problem with new water splotches. Lifting her head, she saw the black, elegantly clad figure of the Reverend Bush emerge from the buggy that had halted only a few feet from where she worked.

"Drat and dickens," she whispered to herself with asperity. Her eyes filled with dismay as they met the kind gaze of the man who had sent for her from the orphanage in New Hope.

"Good morning, Miss O'Malley," he said formally, his hat held before him and his tall figure straight as a bean pole.

She nodded and gulped, as the words she attempted to speak became lodged in her throat. Her hands spread out and she gestured at the wet laundry that surrounded her, the tub and scrub board on a low, wide stool in front of her, and a bench to one side that held a shallow basket of things ready to hang on the line.

"I'm doing the wash," she explained needlessly, and then winced at the absurdity of her words. Any fool could see what she was doing.

"I'm afraid I've come at a bad time," the preacher said apologetically, "but I felt I needed to talk to you, Miss O'Malley."

Lottie nodded in agreement. "Probably so," she said, lifting one hand to shade her eyes as she looked up at him. He was a tall one, for sure, she thought. Not as wide as John, but a couple of inches taller. She'd taken his measure during the sermon in church, but their departure after the service had been a blur.

Up close, he was a good-looking man, she decided, with a generous mouth and a gentle demeanor. And then there was that voice . . . that deep, melodious, beautiful voice.

Hastily, she wiped her hands once more on the front of her water-stained dress and motioned to the house.

"Won't you step inside, Mr. Bush," she asked, remembering her manners, albeit a bit late.

His nod was gracious. "Thank you, ma'am," he said, then with another bow in her direction, waited for her to lead the way.

The house was warm from the heat of the stove, where Lottie was baking bread. She lifted her wrist to wipe the perspiration that broke out on her forehead as she bent to check the progress of her loaves.

They were ready to come out and, as she opened the oven door, the aroma filled the room. Behind her, the preacher sniffed appreciatively, and Sissy spoke her approval aloud.

"That sure smells good, Miss Lottie," she said hopefully.

She was irresistible, the little scamp. Lottie's mouth lifted in a smile that glowed from her whole countenance. So much so that she took on an air of rare beauty in the eyes of the man who sat at the table watching her.

"I'd thought you a rather ordinary young woman, Miss O'Malley," he said in a bemused voice. His gaze was intent on her movements as she deftly handled the hot loaves of bread and then bent to brush at Sissy's small face, her fingers gently caressing.

She looked up at him, startled and somewhat perplexed by his statement. "What do you mean by that?" she asked smartly, unaware of the piquancy of her expression, only conscious of her disheveled appearance and the flush that warmed her cheeks.

Stephen focused on the golden flesh that had soaked up the sun's rays hungrily over the past fortnight. Her face was rosy, her eyes expressive and clear, her nose touched by a scattering of pale freckles, and her hair waved contrarily about the fine lines of her brow.

"You are far from ordinary," he said finally. "You are the epitome of womanhood, Miss O'Malley. Intelligent, strong, and capable. Everything that a woman should be."

Her mouth twisted wryly. "You left out beautiful, Mr. Bush," she said drily.

"No," he denied quickly. "Physical beauty has nothing to do with it. In fact," he began, and his smile became enigmatic. "In fact, beauty can sometimes hide the more important qualities. And then we find ourselves beguiled by the beauty of the physical being and tend to ignore the beauty of the soul."

"Have you done that?" Lottie wanted to know, her mind intent on knowing what sort of man she faced.

"Ah, yes," he admitted. "I've been guilty of that very thing. Much to my distress and to the hurt of others."

It was a statement that required no reply, she thought, and so she turned to the stove to set the kettle over the hottest spot. With a tug at her skirt, Sissy silently asked for her attention and Lottie crouched beside her.

"Can we have tea?" the child asked in a loud whisper.

"Why don't you ask Mr. Bush if he'd like some?" Lottie instructed her with a pat on her back as she turned her in their guest's direction.

Sissy flushed and looked appealingly at her. Unspoken was the plea that shone from her eyes, but Lottie shook her head. "You can do it, Sissy," she whispered against the little girl's ear. "Just say it slowly and nicely."

With a final glance at Lottie that earned her an encouraging smile, Sissy took two steps toward the table and then, curling her fingers into the rough fabric of her dress, she lifted her eyes to meet those of the man who sat before her.

"Sir?" she began hesitantly. "Would you like a cup of tea, sir? Miss Lottie makes it real good," she added with a small degree of confidence and a nod of assurance.

"I'd be delighted to take tea with you, Miss Sissy," Stephen said, his own head bowing as he joined the ceremony Lottie had set into motion.

Sissy whirled about, her fine manners deserting her as she faced Lottie once more. "He said yes!" she whispered loudly, her eyes crinkling in delight as she boasted of her success.

Lottie's own gaze was drawn to seek that of the man who had so pleased the child, and she was wrapped in the warmth of his tenderness as he nodded approvingly at her.

I've misjudged him, she thought with surprise. He's really nice, and I've been certain he was a scalawag, what with leaving town and deserting me the way he did.

"I've come for a purpose, Miss Lottie," Stephen said softly, his eyes still holding hers in thrall.

She stood and brushed her skirts into place, aware of the reason for his visit. The man did have an apology to make, that was for sure, and that thought tensed the lines of her jaw as she allowed her irritation to float a bit closer to the surface. His soft-soaping Sissy and polite manners had almost blinded her to the aggravation he'd caused her, she thought with a tightening of her lips.

"I've done you a grave injustice, ma'am," he said sincerely. "I offered you marriage, and then when you arrived, I was gone out of town, even though I knew the stage was due that afternoon."

Lottie nodded in silent agreement. Let him stew, she

thought with pious satisfaction. I'll not help him through this by being forgiving right off the bat.

Stephen swallowed and felt a faint dewing of sweat cover his forehead. "I went to see my superior," he explained in an earnest manner. "I had some hesitation about the step we were about to take, and I felt the need of his counsel."

"You changed your mind," Lottie said with a narrowing of her eyes that warned him to tread lightly.

"Not exactly," he countered. "I just wasn't sure if what I had committed myself to was the best course for both of us to follow."

"I didn't have much choice at that point, Mr. Bush," Lottie said flatly. "You left me on my own in the middle of town without any warning. If the sheriff hadn't sent me here with a neighbor, I'd still be plopped with all my baggage in the middle of the road."

He allowed a small smile to nip at his sober visage before he shook his head. "No, I knew that James Tillman wanted you badly, Miss Lottie. I was certain that he would be there to greet you, hoping that your choice would turn in his direction."

"You were counting on James to take me off your hands," she accused him bluntly, and then silently rescinded every kind thought she had harbored in his behalf over the past ten minutes.

"I think I've gone about this all wrong," he said wearily, as he felt the sweat trickle into his eyebrows and down his temple.

"Oh, I think you've made yourself very clear," she said brightly, her chin tilted at an arrogant angle as she busied her hands with Sissy's curls, twining them about her fingers.

The child had been turning her head, swiveling it

between the two adults who had spoken so tersely, aware only that Lottie was tugging at her hair, winding it about her fingers and pulling it unconsciously in her aggravation.

"You're makin' owies, Miss Lottie," she said in a plaintive little voice, as she drew her shoulders up and scrunched her neck.

Lottie's eyes widened in dismay. "Now see what I've done," she said, flinging the accusation at Stephen's head as she bent to brush her lips over the offended child's head.

"I've come here for a purpose," Stephen said slowly, doing his best to get on with the sorry task he'd driven out here to accomplish. This wasn't going at all as he had imagined it would, he thought disconsolately. He'd thought that Lottie would leap at the chance to marry him, rather than be nursemaid to two children in a one-room house that was certainly only a few steps above primitive living.

He lifted his hand and waved it imperiously at the chair across the table from where he sat. "Please, Miss Lottie," he said, his words imploring her, yet with a note of command. "Won't you sit down and listen to what I have to suggest?"

Drawn by the invitation, her curiosity piqued by his words, she perched on the edge of the woven seat and pulled Sissy to stand next to her, holding her protectively against her side. Her eyes were wary and her mouth was tightly drawn into a straight line, as she tilted her head to one side and waited for him to continue.

"I'm aware of my shameful behavior." One finger dug beneath his collar, loosening it a bit. He flushed as he bore up under her unforgiving scrutiny. "I've come to offer you marriage," he said bluntly. "I want to apologize for my behavior and make arrangements for you to move into the parsonage as my bride. I'm determined to make amends for my failure to treat you as I should have."

"Well . . ." Lottie breathed softly, as Sissy shrieked out a resounding wail and buried her face in the fullness of Lottie's damp skirt.

Eight

The road home from Mill Creek had never seemed so long, and John flicked the reins impatiently over the back of his mare as he traveled the familiar route. Daisy, the pride of his stable, was a small, dainty chestnut creature, who had long been his pampered darling. She was agreeable to his urging and accordingly stepped up her pace, breaking into a fast trot that caused the harness to jingle in rhythm with her flying hooves.

It was still going to be a long haul, John decided. Too long, considering that, with all likelihood, if his hunch was right, the Reverend Bush was even now sitting in James's house, paying court to Lottie. Why that should be so upsetting to his equilibrium was the question that perplexed him.

This was a prime opportunity to secure a place for Lottie, leaving him free to send the children to St. Louis, where either his own relations or Sarah's folks could raise them in comfort. A pang of distress clutched at his chest at the thought of Thomas and Sissy leaving, but he shook his head, hoping to dislodge the sensation.

"They'd be better off there," he muttered darkly. "That fool girl doesn't even have enough sense to wear shoes in the barnyard. How can she help raise two young'uns way out here? This is the best chance she'll ever have to get married . . . probably be better off in the preacher's house anyway," he grumbled. "I sure won't miss havin' to look after all three of them," he concluded with a grating laugh, and then slumped in the seat as he contemplated the immediate future.

Lottie would no doubt be all fancied up, once she saw company coming. She'll be fixin' her hair and puttin' on a clean apron and hustlin' around to entertain her gentleman friend, John thought as his mind's eye dreamed up the picture. The thought gave him no comfort.

Envisioning peace and quiet, the lack of family responsibilities, the cessation of worry over two small children, somehow did not set right with him, and John shifted in the buggy seat with much mumbling and softly uttered curses. Then there was the mail-order bride herself to consider.

He'd come mighty close to compromising her reputation, what with staying at James's place several nights, even though his bed had been in the haymow. Then, too, buying her dress goods and a pair of shoes in the mercantile might not have been a smart thing to do. Had anyone seen him, it would have been a subject for more gossip. Might be the preacher wouldn't even want to wed her, now that she'd been Tillman property, so to speak, for two weeks.

That thought prompted a grin, and John found himself straightening in the seat, suddenly anxious to find the answers to the conundrum he had been mulling over. As the buggy swung into the long lane that led to his brother's house, he frowned at the sight of the preacher's rig, tied to the corner of the well house.

There was Lottie's washtub and the scrub board, both unmanned and probably all scummed over, the water gone cold, while she dallied about the house with her caller. Bringing Daisy to a halt just outside the barn, John jumped from the buggy and uttered one sharp word.

"Thomas," he called abruptly, and was rewarded as the boy emerged from the shadow of a stall.

"Sir?" he answered, his brow furrowed as he sensed the impatience of his summons.

"Take care of Daisy, son," John said, more slowly, aware of Thomas's look of apprehension. The fool woman had him snapping at the boy now, he thought with an impatient gesture as he handed the reins into Thomas's capable hands.

The walk to the porch was short, and John took it in half the time he normally would have. A low murmur of voices greeted him as he stepped closer to the door, and with a grim countenance, he prepared to enter the house.

The horrified wail of his niece propelled him with unseemly haste through the portal. He was stunned to find the child bent almost double, her face buried in Lottie's lap as she cried out her protests.

"No, you can't leave us . . . Miss Lottie . . . you can't go to . . . you said you'd . . . Oooohhh . . ." she cried in a plaintive, loud refrain that lost none of its volume in the skirts of Lottie's dress. Sissy was a howler, that was for sure, John thought as he stood in the doorway and watched the scene that was being played out before him.

"Sissy—" Lottie said, several times in fact, as she tried to raise the child's head from her lap, all to no avail as the two small hands clutched at her dress while she buried her face against the firm flesh of Lottie's thighs.

Stephen Bush rose in regal confusion, his eyes seeking those of the man in the doorway. A flush of embarrassment painted his cheeks brilliantly. His nod was automatic, a polite recognition of the newcomer to the scene, and he hastened to extend his hand in greeting, speaking above the wailing crescendo of Sissy's grief.

"John, it's good to see you," he said with a hastily scraped-up abundance of enthusiasm, his voice booming in the sudden silence as Lottie managed to cover Sissy's mouth with her hand.

Both heads flew up in amazement at the words. Sissy stilled her protest immediately, spying an ally against the plot that had been unfolded only moments ago. Her feet flew across the floor to where her uncle stood, and in a frantic leap, she flung herself into his arms, almost knocking him against the wall with the momentum.

Stephen released his grip on the other man's hand as the child propelled herself into John's arms. Lottie rose to her feet in silent amazement, aware of the tension that flared like lightning between the two males.

John nodded over Sissy's head, which was lodged in the space between his head and shoulder, his all-encompassing greeting including Lottie.

"Seems like I interrupted something here," he said with slow precision. His big hands were holding Sissy close, one of them patting the narrow expanse of her back, as the other clutched about her knees.

Her little voice mumbled next to his ear, and he shushed her with a gentle admonition. "Hush, Sissy. I want to talk to Miss Lottie now," he said in a low rumble.

Stephen Bush picked up his hat, and his hands were huge against the brim, long-fingered and graceful. "I've come to ask Miss Lottie to wed with me," he announced in a sonorous voice, his words vibrating in the pit of Lottie's stomach as she sensed their import.

"Seems like you already did that once," John drawled. "Sure you know what you're doin' this time?" he asked, as his eyes slid with slow critical appraisal over the tall, narrow figure of the dark-garbed minister.

The flush that had begun to fade from Stephen's cheeks darkened once more to a crimson hue as he gestured toward Lottie with one hand stretched out in appeal.

"I'm sure this conversation should, by all rights, be conducted between Miss Lottie and myself," he said defensively, as his eyes pled with her for understanding.

"Have you asked her?" John wanted to know abruptly, although remembering the wails of Sissy's distress provided him with sufficient answer.

"Yes, I have," Stephen answered, his eyes narrowing as he exuded dignified hostility toward the man who had managed to take a firm hold upon the whole ridiculous situation, simply by entering the house.

"Has she given you an answer?" John asked with stern brevity.

Stephen shook his head once, and his gaze flew back to where Lottie stood in dazed silence by the table.

"No, she hadn't had a chance, before Sissy made a bit of a fuss and distracted us," he replied.

John snorted, unable to contain the explosion of mirth as he recalled the "bit of a fuss" that Sissy was so capable of making.

Lottie glared at him, for a moment distracted by his undignified treatment of her suitor. Her eyes glittered with the aggravation that was slowly creeping up from the depths of her being.

"I think I'm quite capable of speaking, John," she

said with a tilt of her chin, a gesture that was becoming familiar to him after two weeks of dealing with her.

Lottie was getting on her high horse, he thought, his mouth widening in a grin that he refused to hide. "No doubt, you are, ma'am," he replied with a nod. "No doubt about that at all," he repeated, in a tone that suggested his prior knowledge of her moods.

She turned with sudden appeal to Stephen, and her eyes glittered with tears of frustration. "May we continue this conversation at another time?" she asked him tersely. "I think we require a certain degree of privacy, Mr. Bush and," she cast a glance in John's direction as she paused, "we are not likely to get anything approaching privacy this morning."

John shrugged in a manner that disclaimed responsibility for the problem and stepped away from the doorframe, Sissy still clinging to his neck. "I'm sure Mr. Bush can come calling another time, Lottie," he said with good humor, his mood expansive as Stephen made to take his leave.

"You'll be more than welcome," Lottie said firmly, as she blinked back the tears that had threatened to fall. More in charge of the situation now, she yearned to have Stephen gone, anxious to set her hand to the scrub board and vent her wrath upon the clothing of John Tillman. That she was about to lose control of her temper was a fact. That she not lose it in the presence of her suitor was mandatory.

Stephen looked helplessly at the young woman he had come with lagging feet to court. Frustrated that her answer had, of necessity, been postponed, he nodded his farewell. Heading for the door, he brushed past the husky frame of John Tillman as he passed through the portal. His stride lengthened as he headed for his buggy, and his hands dealt quickly with the lead rein he had tied to the well house. Stepping easily into the shiny black vehicle, he turned his mare in the direction of Mill Creek, a final tipping of his hat in Lottie's direction signifying his respectful regard.

"Well, Little Bit," John said cheerfully, sliding Sissy down to the floor and calling her by a pet name he had given her in infancy. "Seems like you howled us right out of our company, didn't you?"

Sissy's lower lip pouched out as she slid her glance toward Lottie. "The preacher wants to make Miss Lottie his bride," the child said, with horror apparent in every word.

"Well, he was first choice with her, you know," John said with a grin. "Too bad he muffed it. She'd have already been cookin' his meals by now, if he hadn't missed his chance." His brow furrowed in mock sorrow, as he pulled his mouth down into a parody of sadness "And then what would we have done for a cook, Little Bit? We'd be eatin' dry bread and turnips."

"Fat chance of that," Thomas said from the porch, hearing the dreaded word.

"Thomas," John called expansively. "Come on in. We're just discussing Lottie's cooking." His mouth quirked into another grin, as he noted Lottie's hands clenched at her sides and the flaring of her nostrils as she gritted her teeth and glared in his direction.

"I'll thank you not to poke fun at me," she said, her fury fueled by his jocular good humor.

He drew his mouth into a prim expression, even while his twinkling eyes belied the effort. "Why ever would I want to do that, Miss Lottie?" he asked. "I'm just reminding the children of how fortunate we are that the Reverend reneged on his first offer to you."

"We'll see how fortunate *you* feel, when suppertime comes and I'm still trying to do the washing," she sniffed, as she headed for the yard and the tub of soaking clothes. "If you expect any hot food today at all, I'd suggest you empty that reservoir into a bucket and bring it out to me, Mr. Tillman," she instructed him tersely.

"Yes, ma'am," he said obligingly, with a wink at Thomas and a grin in Sissy's direction. Snatching the bucket from beneath the sink, he set to work, ladling the steaming water from the container attached to the side of the cookstove that held hot water at the ready, as long as the wood burned and kept the reservoir heated.

"She's really mad, isn't she, Uncle John?" Thomas said in an undertone.

"Naw, she'll get over it," John said, tousling the boy's hair as he headed for the woman who was even now scrubbing vigorously at one of his shirts.

Placing the bucket aside, he lifted one side of the tub and tilted it to allow part of the cooled water to flow onto the ground.

"That's enough," Lottie said shortly, waiting while he settled it once more on the stool and poured the hot water on top of the clothes. She plunged her hands back into the suds that had risen with the pouring of the water, and attacked John's shirt once more.

"If you scrub any harder, you'll make holes in that shirt, Lottie," he said softly from behind her.

She stood up and turned her head, looking back over her shoulder at him. "If you'd like to take over, I'll be glad to step out of the way, Mr. Tillman," she said without a shred of warmth in her tone.

"Now, Lottie," he began, with an engaging smile that

was full proof of his good humor. "I just don't want you to be mad at me this morning."

"You were rude to Mr. Bush," she stated firmly, as she bent back to the scrub board, her hands seeking another garment to work on.

"Not really," he said, ignoring caution as he tucked his thumbs into the suspenders that held his trousers in place. "I just felt like you needed a chance to think things over . . . you know, without any undue pressure. Make up your mind without having to hurry it along."

"I'd already made up my mind about him once," she reminded him as she wrung out a shirt of Thomas's, plopping it into the bucket for rinsing.

John lifted an eyebrow as he considered that fact. He ambled around her and leaned against the wall of the well house, the better to watch her face as they talked.

"Are you sure you can depend on him not to run out on you again, Lottie?" he asked, his expression somber as he posed the question.

She looked up quickly, and for a moment her defenses were down; her shoulders slumped, her eyes frightened as she faced the fact that she was indeed, in a most vulnerable position. With a visible gathering of her reserves, she stiffened, and John was in awe of the strength she exhibited in that moment.

"We all take our chances, don't we, John?" she asked, her formality at an end as she considered his sympathetic gaze.

"Looks to me like you've taken more than your share, Lottie," he said softly. "It's about time someone started lookin' out for you."

"Miss Aggie used to say that we're all responsible for our own happiness," Lottie said briskly. "I can't depend on anybody to provide that for me."

"Maybe not, but at least we can provide you with a place to live and folks who care about you," John vowed with certainty.

Lottie's mouth twisted a bit as she wrung another shirt between her capable hands. "I'm grateful for a place to stay," she said. Her lips softened into a tender pose that hovered on the brink of a smile, as her mind considered the children who had brightened her days during the past weeks. With a sigh, she swiped one hand over her forehead, replacing the fine film of perspiration with a damp trace of soapsuds. Then she met John's eyes with an appealing glance that told him her fit of pique was at an end.

"I've appreciated your friendship, John," she said finally. "I didn't mean to get so upset over that mishmash in there," she muttered, waving her hand in the general direction of the house.

"You had good reason," he allowed. "It's kinda hard to entertain a suitor with Sissy as an audience. Next time the Reverend comes calling, I'll take the kids, and we'll make ourselves scarce."

Lottie glanced down at her wet dress, the hem muddy from the wash water that had sloshed onto the ground. "I'm not much to impress a man like this," she said with chagrin apparent on her mobile features.

"I don't know about that," he replied, his glance encompassing the flushed woman who allowed him to take her measure. She was so vulnerable, he decided, there in her dingy dress. It fit at no particular spot, but clung damply to her breasts, outlining their fullness for his perusal, then draped across her hips to fall in an uneven hemline close to the ground. Her black, muddy boots peeked from beneath the equally muddy hem, and the sight reminded him of his purchases in town earlier.

"Thomas," he called to the boy who had perched on the steps of the porch.

Rising eagerly to answer the summons, the boy raced to his uncle's side. "Yes sir," he said with a wide grin.

John dropped a hand to his shoulder and Thomas's grin expanded, causing his dimples to deepen even more. "Go to the buggy and bring me the packages I brought back from town, will you, son?"

With eager steps, the boy ran to the barn and disappeared within the shadows there.

"We didn't need any food, John," Lottie said quickly. "I've got enough stores to last till the first of the month, easy," she told him as she frowned at him in question.

"I didn't buy any food, Lottie," he said airily. "Oh, except for a couple of licorice whips for the children, for after supper."

Thomas came running, the two packages clutched firmly in his arms, and the small bag that held the candy pinched between two fingers, his eyes alight.

"This smells like licorice, Uncle John," he said with anticipation, waving the bag gleefully.

"Can't imagine why," John teased, his big hands seizing the parcels Genevieve had wrapped so carefully. "Maybe you wouldn't need to wait till suppertime for a taste, Thomas. Why don't you share a piece with your sister now?"

"Yes sir," the boy chortled, heading for the porch where Sissy had plopped herself, chin in hands as she sat cross-legged to view the adults' discussion.

John straightened and offered his arm to Lottie. "Can I persuade you to come to the house with me for a few minutes, Lottie?" he asked gently.

"Let me rinse these things first," she said, pouring fresh water over the pile of clothes that she had scrubbed, and sloshing them in the bucket to rid them of soap residue. Her hands twisted them rapidly, and John watched as she worked, his eyes intent on the strength she exhibited in the task she performed.

Then he watched as she snapped them to rid them of wrinkles, and laid them out, spreading them evenly over the clothesline, lowering it first until she could reach the rope. With a deft movement, she tilted the pole skyward. The heavy line of garments swung in the air as the west wind caught them and caused them to billow most satisfactorily.

"I'll clean this up later," she said, waving her hand at the buckets and tubs. One slender hand rubbed in an unconscious manner at the small of her back as she paced herself to his long-legged stride, and then he took her arm as they went up the steps.

John stood just inside the doorway, and his eyes closed for a moment as he inhaled the aroma of Lottie's baking.

In the months that this home had been without a woman's hand, it had suffered greatly from the lack. Even the children had been victims of neglect, he realized. Oh, James had kept them decent enough, clean clothing every few days, and a bath on Saturday night before church on Sunday. The usual rituals had been observed. But the daily routines had been neglected, John thought sadly. The finer touches that a mother provided were gone . . . the hot meals that tempted a man's palate . . . the luxury of freshly baked bread, the loaves brown and tempting, the smell welcoming.

"John?" Lottie's calling of his name brought him to attention, and he moved quickly toward her, flustered at being caught daydreaming.

His smile was sheepish as he faced her where she

stood next to the table, his face warm from the heat that radiated from the black iron cookstove, his eyes bright with the small measure of happiness he had found in the past few moments.

"I need to thank you, Lottie." His voice was gruff, as if he were filled with an unnamed emotion, and Lottie's head tipped back, the better to see his expression.

It gave her no clue. The blue eyes were fixed on her, their merry teasing glances focused now into a piercing regard that unsettled her. His mouth was soft, the full lips forming a smile that hinted at secret thoughts he was not willing to share. But his words were warmly given, and Lottie received them gladly.

"I only baked bread, John," she said with a lifting of her shoulders and a gesture that fluttered her fingers in the direction of the loaves that cooled on the sink board.

"Yes," he said with a nod of agreement, "and did the washing . . . and cooked the breakfast . . . and helped Sissy with the chickens . . . not to mention giving Thomas a hand with the milking." His fingers enumerated the tasks she had completed today, one long index finger keeping score on his other hand as he named each chore, pausing to meet her eyes with a nod between each one.

She didn't know where to look. Such thanks for so little work had never come her way before. Her eyes darted about the room, her gaze unwilling to accept the abundance of his praise.

"Look at me, Lottie, please," he said softly, his mouth forming the invitation with enticement in each syllable.

It was more than she could resist. He'd been many things in the weeks past, from the man who could not mourn his loss, for all the pressures that surrounded him, to the kindly uncle that had, without hesitation, filled a father's shoes. He'd been gruff and teasing by turn. His frowns had been evidence of the worry that rode his wide shoulders like a specter from the dark place. But never had he been this man, who faced her now, with gentle seduction in his words.

She met his look, her eyes unwavering as she obeyed his gentle command. The words he had spoken—the listing of her morning's activities, each small task given due credit—brought a flush of pleasure to her sun-kissed cheeks and a sparkle to blue eyes that had too often been darkened by daily drudgery.

John lifted a hand to touch her face, shifting the package he held to be clutched against his chest. His fingers brushed at the whitened patch on her forehead, where soapsuds had dried. Then the sensitive pad of his thumb eliminated a trace of flour from her throat, a leftover from her baking. With care, he traced the scattering of pale freckles that crowned her nose and spattered her high cheekbones, his long fingers instilling a warmth to her flesh that brought a more brilliant flush to the skin he touched.

"I brought you something from town," he said musingly, his mind unfocused as he sensed a stirring in his loins that was inappropriate to this occasion. Such a little ragamuffin she was, in her oversized dress, with her hair all braided down her back. Only the fine, wispy ends left to wave about her brow and settle in curling dampness against her cheek. But the fullness, the heated response his body was intent on producing, could not be denied, and he dropped his hand from the youthful innocence that tempted him.

Her mouth is ripe, he thought. Full and pink, it lifted in a smile that tempted him to taste the flavor he knew would be both sweet and tart at once. And then, casti-gating himself for the desire that he was allowing to run rampant in his needy frame, he shook his head and reached for the chair that had so recently been occupied by Stephen Bush.

Pulling it squarely into the middle of the floor, he backed Lottie against it. Her movements were automatic as he nodded in silent command for her to sit down. The packages were bulky, and the fingers on his left hand had gone white from the tension he exerted to keep them in place against the width of his chest. Now he lowered them to her lap, and she touched them in turn, her fingers tentative in their quest, her eyes wide with wonderment.

"Both of these are for *me?*" she asked, awe evident in her words.

"It's only a couple of things you need," he said in an offhand manner. Crouching before her, his hands hung casually between his knees.

She turned the brown wrapped parcels over and pressed inquisitive fingertips against the paper, as if she would savor the anticipation of opening them, her hands shaping the corners and smoothing the layers of string Genevieve had used.

"Go on . . . open them," he said, anxious for her to approve of his choices.

Carefully, her fingers untied the string, and his im-patience rose with each knot she unraveled. His lips compressed as he watched the unhurried movement of her hands, and as the final length of string unwound from the larger package, he filched it from her, poking it into his shirt pocket impatiently.

She unwrapped the paper, one turn at a time, her eyes alight with expectancy as she slid one finger within the final fold of wrapping. Her mouth opened into a soft "Oh" of discovery as the tactile survey bore fruit. And then she bent to peek within the treasure she had uncovered, and the inquisitive finger lifted to rest against her mouth as her eyes widened with amazed pleasure.

"Oh, John," she whispered, and the words fell like heavenly sunshine, matched only by the glory of the smile that lit her face with delight. He grinned widely, reveling in the joy that spilled from her, wrapping himself in the abundance of her happiness.

The paper fell to the floor, as she clutched the folded length of dress fabric. She lifted it, shifted it to catch the light from the window, and tilted her head to better see the prize she held. Then with hands that brushed carefully to smooth a wrinkle, she savored the crisp gingham that had tempted her so mightily a week ago in the store in Mill Creek.

"Do you like it, Lottie?" he asked with barely concealed glee.

"Oh, yes," she breathed. "I've never had anything so fine, John. Never anything so . . . so . . ." Her voice trailed off and she took a deep breath, as if she must assimilate the good fortune that was hers.

"Open the other package now," he urged her, impatient for her reaction to the shoes, caught up in the discovery of her youthful wonder. Her reception of his gift had offered him a glimpse of the child that still lived in this woman, and he shifted with anticipation as he took the material from her to place it on the table.

Once more she fussed over the string, until he thought he would surely wrest it from her hands to speed the process. But some small kernel of knowledge warned him that she was reveling in the unwrapping.

That the unknowing was whetting her pleasure, that each twist and turn of string and paper was drawing her to a fine pitch of expectancy, that was a gift in itself.

The box finally lay bare of covering, and Lottie lifted the lid, carefully tipping it from one side to expose the contents. Her eyes rounded, wide and wondering, as she handed him the lid. Her nostrils flared and her breath caught with an audible sound, a soft sigh that spoke an unwritten language.

"They're so soft," she said finally, as her palm caressed the leather that would hug her ankle with a flexible embrace. Her fingers counted the buttons that marched up the side, then traced the smooth line of the vamp as she leaned to inhale the scent of the leather that rose from the narrow shoe.

"How did you know the size?" she asked, as she tore her gaze from his gift to meet the shining eyes that savored her glee.

"I measured your old boot, traced it on paper, and showed it to Genevieve," he said modestly. "I hope they fit," he said, adding a note of caution. "You better try them on and see."

She shook her head hastily. "Oh, I can't. My feet are dirty," she explained, tucking her scuffed footwear beneath the chair she sat on, as if she would hide the evidence.

John rose quickly and took the box from her hands, sitting it on the floor next to her chair. "That's easily fixed," he boasted with an air of nonchalance. "Just take off those old boots, Lottie, and we'll take a rag and a bit of soap to your toes and—"

"Oh, no," she cried in dismay, her head shaking more firmly. "You can't do that!"

"Want to bet on it?" he asked, his hands already busy

at the sink, wetting one end of the towel that hung there and bringing the basin that was still half-full of water with him as he returned to where she sat.

Over her protests, he tugged at the boots that clutched her feet so snugly and heard the almost inaudible groan she tried to suppress as he slid them from her feet. He worked quickly, doing a fast washing-up that would never stand close inspection, but aware that her modesty was being strained by his action.

Her small foot was cradled in his palm as he dried it, using the other end of the towel. His fingertips noted the red wrinkles in her tender flesh, where the shoes had cramped her toes into submission. A frown creased his brow, and he shook his head with more than a trace of anger that she should have been forced to endure the discomfort for so long.

"I should have gotten you new shoes before this," he growled, as he carefully slid her slender foot into the welcoming, soft kid lining. He held the upper in place and fished about in the other shoe for the button hook that Genevieve had placed there. Holding it, he looked up at her helplessly.

"I'm not sure I'm too good at this," he explained with masculine ineptness, as he fiddled with the metal instrument.

Lottie was stunned. Silent, and without one sensible thought occupying her mind, she basked in the warmth of his touch. The haphazard washing of her feet had filled her with a blend of emotions that were almost beyond description. That John should do this for her was unbelievable. That he should kneel before her and perform the humble task of washing her feet . . . it was more than her heart could hold.

The abundance spilled over in the form of tears that

trickled in random fashion down her cheeks, to settle in damp profusion on the front of her dress. She blinked, and the salty drops shimmered on her lashes, outlining her eyes with a glittering frame that served to enhance the beauty that reflected there.

Without a moment of hesitation, she lifted her hands to place them against the ridge of his cheekbones. Her fingers buried themselves in the lush depths of his golden hair and she bent closer. Her intent was clear, her mouth already forming a pouting invitation to the man who watched her approach with fascination.

Her kiss landed midway between his eyebrow and hairline, and it smacked loudly in the silence. She smiled at him with confusion written on her features, as she sat back in the chair, her fingers lingering against the silky tendrils of hair that lay against his temple.

John drew in a breath that caught in his throat, and his hands left the task they had been performing. He lay aside the button hook, pushed the other shoe aside, then rose high on his knees to reach for her. Clasping her by the fine bones of her shoulders, he drew her slowly and firmly from the chair. One hand scooted it back out of the way, as she fell forward against his body. And then he held her before him, kneeling on the floor, her thighs almost touching his as he hauled her tighter to his hard, muscular frame.

"If you're going to kiss me, Lottie, let's make it worth your while," he muttered beneath his breath. His arms slid about her body, her surprise rendering her pliable and moldable as he fit her carefully against his chest. Then, with narrowed eyes, he surveyed her stunned expression. Slowly, savoring each moment, hovering between the passion that drove him and a voice within that warned him of his folly, he cast caution to the four winds and took possession of her mouth.

It was soft and smooth, warm and damp, all that he had anticipated, and yet more. He had expected the plush softness of her plump lower lip, that enticed his tongue to explore. He'd already noted the faint, sweet scent of her breath, that coaxed him to inhale her freshness. But he had not anticipated the small moan of pleasure that rippled from her throat. He'd not expected the response of her pink tongue that met his with careful, tentative exploration. Certainly he hadn't dreamed that she would slide her strong, slender fingers up his throat to grip tenaciously at the collar of his shirt.

Carefully, his mouth drank in the essence of her sweetness, the fragrance of her delicate freshness. Greedily, he inhaled the lush sensual perfume of her arousal that softened her flesh with the first warming tendrils of desire. Her head fell back against the support of his palm, and the fullness of her breasts formed a cushion that shaped itself to the ungiving structure of his muscular frame. He accepted the unconscious offering she presented, the strong lines of her throat that drew him to taste the vulnerable pulse point beneath the line of her jaw.

There, where the frantic beat of her heart kept pace with his own, he savored the faintly salty flavor of her skin. His mouth formed a smile that lifted his lips and brushed like a fluttering butterfly wing against her sensitive flesh.

"Oh, my . . ." she sighed, in a gasping whisper that widened his smile to a delighted grin. He lifted his head reluctantly and carefully, his mouth lowering in gentle touches, paying homage to her lips one final time.

She opened her eyes and focused wide pupils on him. Dazed and uncertain, suddenly flushed with feelings she could not describe, she scrambled to her feet. Her hands rose to cover the heat that had swept up to dwell on her throat and spread to her cheeks.

"John, I . . . I don't know . . ." she said in a choked whimper, her blue eyes wide, her mouth trembling and her hands shaking, as they pressed against the flaming flesh that betrayed her emotional upheaval.

"Lottie, listen to me," he growled, propelling his big body upward in a smooth motion, grasping her arms as she backed from him. He allowed her no quarter.

She shook her head in jerky movements, frightened by the sensations that had possessed her with such fervor. "I'm sorry . . ." she said faintly. "Please, John . . ."

"I want you, sweetheart," he said bluntly. And then he laughed, the sound ringing hollow in his own ears. "You don't even know what that means," he muttered gruffly, the sound containing all the frustration his inflamed senses abounded with.

"But you will, my girl," he vowed in a whisper that shimmered with promise.

Nine

Snuggled within the depths of Sarah's feather bed, Lottie shivered. Her flesh felt alive with sensation, and her eyes closed tightly as she relived once more the few moments she had spent in John Tillman's embrace. Moments that had caused her fragile innocence to tumble and smash into myriad, glowing particles of awareness that even now caused her to tremble with yearning.

He'd kissed her. Not with the pursed lips of Miss Aggie, nor the damply adoring smooches that Sissy had lately been bestowing upon her cheeks . . . but with a masculine, all-encompassing caress that had plunged her into a taste of worldly pleasure. For surely, such toe-curling, stomach-churning sensation such as John had set loose within her, could not be other than carnal.

Long and hard had Miss Aggie preached the message of denial of carnal desire to Lottie's eager hearing. Just what such desire would produce, she had been rather vague in describing, but to the tender ears of Lottie O'Malley, it had sounded like the last thing she wanted to tangle with.

"Don't let any man touch your body, child," Miss Aggie had been fond of repeating. "Kissing is for married folks, and doing the necessary foolishness to get babies is what drives men to spend their lust on young girls."

Would kissing therefore produce a baby? Her brows

furrowed in abject concentration, as Lottie considered
the thought. How a child could be formed within the
depths of her body was a puzzle she had often considered
in the long night hours. Her questions had met with
flushed reluctance from her mentor, and Miss Aggie had
produced no acceptable responses to her hesitant que-
ries. That babies were born on a regular basis—and some
of them to young women who bore them in shame and
without the sanctity of marriage—was a known fact
within the walls of the orphanage. Many of those female
infants found their way to New Hope, scorned by the
society that frowned on fallen women.

Lottie touched her lips with hesitant fingers, wondering at the sensations John had aroused within those
portions of her flesh. He had opened his mouth over
hers, had touched her closed lips with his tongue. At
the remembrance, she shivered once more and shut her
eyes, the better to recall the memory. The damp, hot
caress had drawn her into an abyss of sensation that
even now flared her nostrils and caused her breath to
catch in her throat.

"I want you," he'd said in that funny, guttural voice
that didn't even sound like the John Tillman she knew.
The gentle, hardworking farmer, who had devoted his
days to working the farm and caring for the orphaned
children of his brother, had become a different man in
that moment. His hands had hardened against her,
holding firmly to her shoulders and then sliding with
careful intent to enclose her within his embrace. The
tender, smiling regard he had bestowed upon her as
she opened his gifts had somehow been transformed to
a grim, narrow-eyed survey of her face, before he'd lowered his mouth to seize her own.

And then, with words of purpose, he'd held her

tightly against his muscular chest, until her breasts had
flattened and molded to fit his frame. Only the smothered sounds of protest that had been born within her
throat had prompted her release from his arms. Her
wiggling to gain freedom had only served to tighten his
hold, and opening her mouth to speak had only allowed
the intrusion of his tongue into the dark secrets therein.
She relived the moment. And then blushed in the darkness as she recalled her own tentative response, when
her mouth was invaded in such cavalier fashion.

She hadn't expected the tingling quivers that had ex-
ploded inside her maiden's body. Hadn't been prepared
for the rush of emotion that had greeted his growling
threat.

He'd said he wanted her, and in some primitive
knowledge that fluttered to life within her, she sensed
a response to his avowal. Maybe Miss Aggie was
right . . . maybe kissing could be part of causing a baby
to grow within her body. At the thought, she laid her
hand, fingers spread wide, against her stomach.

Her sigh was deep, and her eyes closed against the
flickering light from the fireplace. John had laid a huge
log against the back wall of the deep firepit, to better
hold the warmth within the house through the night.
It had promised to be cold, with stars shining in splendor from the darkness, and not a cloud in sight. He'd
been strangely silent throughout the evening, eating
supper with his usual enthusiasm, but answering the
children only in monosyllables, as if he had some great,
weighty problem to consider.

Even now, John was in the haymow, heavy quilts his
protection against the night. Lottie wondered if he was
asleep, cocooned against the cold in Sarah's oldest cov-

erlets. He'd said it was too late to go to his own place after chores were finished.

"I might as well stay in the barn tonight, Lottie," he'd said briefly as she sat before the fire, lowering the hem on Sissy's old Sunday dress. It had been relegated to an everyday gown, now that her new dress held place of honor on the peg in the loft.

"All right," she'd answered softly, casting a quick glance at his somber face.

He'd cleared his throat and scooted his chair a little closer to where she sat. "Thought I'd work on some partitions in the barn tomorrow for my horses," he'd said casually, crossing his ankles as his stocking-covered toes sought the heat from the fireplace.

"Oh?" Her surprise was evident.

He'd glanced at her, and his eyes had held a residue of that strange, heated emotion she could not name. "I'm thinking about wintering here," he'd said carefully. "I'll need to bring my mares over." And then in a casual, yawning manner, he'd taken his leave, quilts under his arm.

Her eyelids grew heavier as Lottie examined the events of the evening. What did he mean? How could he plan on "wintering" here? Surely he'd freeze in the barn in the bitter cold nights that winter promised. She yawned, drawing in a deep breath, perplexed by his enigmatic announcement, but unable to consider it longer. Her eyelashes fluttered against her cheek and her breathing became shallow; she sank into the warmth of the feather tick that enveloped her.

"I'll ask him tomorrow," she whispered to herself, as her eyes closed in well-earned slumber.

* * *

John came to the door, shivering in the chill of early morning, and stood before the cookstove, holding his hands over the heat that rose to warm the room.

"Don't want to get myself kicked off the stool this morning," he said with a sidelong look in Lottie's direction, as she lifted her head from the task of slicing bacon for the skillet. He flexed his long fingers and grinned widely. "Cold hands make for an unhappy cow," he said with dry humor, and then chuckled at her look of disdain.

He watched her closely, intent on her deft movements and the sway of her skirt as she worked between the table and stove. His eyes rested on the neat black shoes she wore, and his grin broadened.

"Like your shoes, Lottie?" he asked gently.

Her head swung quickly in his direction, and her smile was bright. "I've already thanked you for them," she said pertly.

"Ummm . . . yes, you did," he allowed, as his memory replayed the chaste kiss she had bestowed. "But I enjoyed the second kiss more."

Her eyes widened and her mouth pursed briefly. "I've never . . . well, surely you know that . . ." She floundered as words failed her. John certainly must know that such kisses were not what she was accustomed to, she thought as the memory of that meeting of lips brought rosy highlights to her face.

"We need to talk about something, Lottie," he said abruptly, his genial manner subdued suddenly. His hand dug into his pocket, and he drew forth a wrinkled envelope and slid from it a sheet of paper. "I picked this up at the post office yesterday. I read it last night, out in the barn." He paused as he unfolded the single page. "It's from Sarah's folks." Lowering his voice, he cast a glance at the loft, where soft sounds of awakening warned of the impending arrival of two hungry children.

"What does it say? What do they want?" Lottie asked, her eyes darkening with concern as she wiped her hands slowly on her apron.

His words were almost a whisper. "They're talking about coming to get the children. They think Thomas would be better off in St. Louis, going to school and all."

Her mouth formed a soft "Oh" of dismay, and she reached instinctively to squeeze his shoulder in comfort. "What can you do?" she wondered softly, her own eyes straying to where Sissy's face appeared, peering over the edge of the loft.

"That's what I want to talk to you about," he said intently. "When I go to town this morning, I need to send them a letter. I plan on getting lumber at the mill and starting in on the stalls in the barn today. But first I have to write to the Shermans, and that's the hitch."

She shook her head slowly, and her shoulders lifted in a shrug that expressed her puzzlement. "What's the hitch?" she wanted to know, impatient with his dithering.

He rose and faced her across the table, leaning toward her, his eyes narrowed and serious. "I need to be able to make a home for the two of them, Lottie. A real home."

She swept her hand about her, and her words were wondering. "What do you call this?"

His hand lifted in a gesture of frustration "A home usually includes a set of parents," he said in a determined whisper. "I know this is a bad time to be bringing it up, Lottie, but I don't have any time to sweet-talk you into this. I want you to consider marrying me."

Like a bolt from the blue, the words pierced her. She stepped back, brushing against the cookstove, her hand touching the black iron oven door. "Oh, land! Look what you've made me do," she spouted fiercely, as she brought the seared spot to her mouth to put it against her tongue.

He stepped quickly to face her, lifting the injured member and holding it between his as he inspected it for damage. "It's not bad," he said, as he brushed it gently and then brought it to his own mouth to tenderly kiss the weal that had been raised on the edge of her palm.

She tugged to escape his grasp, her eyes flitting to the ladder where Thomas was even now climbing down, intent on greeting his uncle. "Let go, John," she ordered him briskly. "I'm fine."

"No, Lottie," he said, denying her words. "Listen to me." He spoke quickly, his voice low and his words hurried. "I have to have your answer this morning. I don't want to rush you, but this is important."

Her hand tingled, the heat of his palms more noticeable than the stinging pain she had suffered from her carelessness, and she pulled determinedly to rescue her fingers from his grasp. Her movement served only to aggravate the situation, as he moved even closer and slid one long arm about her waist.

"John!" she exclaimed in a shocked whisper that brought heightened color to her cheeks. "The children are watching."

"Then answer me, Lottie," he said, with a narrow-eyed persistence that flustered her even more.

"I don't know what to say," she admitted in a breathless whisper that enticed him to lean even closer. His wide chest was too near, the pale curls that peeked from above his open-necked shirt almost tickling her nose. Her eyes widened once more in dismay as she inhaled the musky scent of his skin. The same helpless yearning his nearness had ignited yesterday swept over her with a wave of heated intensity.

"Do you like me?" he asked, his head bending so that his lips touched her ear. She shivered as the warmth of his breath caressed her, and his arm about her waist tightened.

"Yes," she gulped. "I like you." Probably a whole lot more than what's good for me, she thought giddily.

"Do you want to see these children . . ." his whisper trailed off and he waited, frustrated at the lack of privacy and aggravated at his own stupidity at starting this conversation with an audience.

"No!" Her answer was immediate, her quick mind already leaping to the knowledge his question was attempting to impart. That Sarah's parents would come and take Sissy and Thomas away was not to be considered! It would be the final blow for John, she knew without a doubt. Only the fact that he had the two children to live and work for had kept him going through the past weeks.

"Then do this for them," he said finally, his voice harsh as he inhaled deeply, aware suddenly of the clean scent of the woman he held.

"Uncle John, why are you hugging Miss Lottie? And talkin' in her ear so growly?" Thomas asked, his brow furrowed with concern as he watched with anxious eyes.

John stepped back, his gaze still holding her as he answered his nephew. "We're just having a discussion, Thomas," he said soothingly. His eyes sought the answer he needed, but it was to be denied for the moment, as Lottie flashed a flustered glance to where Sissy climbed from the loft. The child clutched the hem of her nightgown in one hand as she carefully kept it from tangling about her short little legs, lowering herself with deliberation.

"Are we havin' breakfast?" Sissy asked as she reached the floor, dropped the skirt of her nightie, and smoothed it with her plump hands.

"Just like always," Lottie said, holding out a welcoming arm to the child. And then the words she had spoken resounded in her head. It wouldn't be "like always" if these two were taken from this place. They'd be dependent on strangers. Grandparents, but strangers, nonetheless.

"Are we havin' tea?" Sissy asked, rubbing her face against Lottie's apron, her arms stretching to reach as far as she could for the comforting warmth of her morning embrace.

Lottie chuckled as she squeezed the child briefly. "Yes, we can have tea," she conceded easily. "The water's hot." She pushed the girl gently toward the fireplace. "Go get your dress and put it on. I lowered the hem last night."

Sissy scampered to where her everyday dress lay folded on Lottie's chair, and then hurried to the other side of the big bed, where she found relative privacy to slide her nightie over her head. Chilled in the far corner of the cabin, she pulled the dress on and then ran back to where Lottie faced the stove, turning bacon in the skillet.

"Do me up, please," she asked prettily, turning her back and holding her hair up out of the way.

"You need a petticoat on," Lottie said absently, as she laid aside the wooden-handled fork to tend to the child.

"After breakfast?" Sissy asked, her eyes avid as she sniffed the air. "Did you make biscuits, Miss Lottie?" she asked hopefully.

"Biscuits?" Thomas repeated as he dried his hands on the towel.

"Biscuits?" John asked teasingly, as he watched the

byplay between the three people who were fast becoming his whole world.

Lottie's ears caught the tender mockery in his word, and she looked up to find a most vulnerable expression gleaming from his eyes and tugging his mouth into a wistful smile. If I could only hold this one moment, grasp it in my memory and store it forever, she thought as she basked in the center of their attention. Why, she thought with a glimpse of intuitive insight, this is my family. My real family . . . these people who need me.

"Yes, biscuits," she said, reaching for the flannel pot holder to open the oven door. Leaning back from the rush of hot air, she waved the pot holder as her face flushed from the oven's heat.

"Back off now," she told them as she lifted the pan of brown biscuits to the table, sliding a folded towel beneath them and then covering them with another. "The bacon will be burning, if you don't let me be." She turned it quickly with the fork and pulled it off the hottest part of the stove, while she issued orders.

"Set the table, Thomas," she said briskly. "Sissy, wash up now and get the sugar for the oatmeal. John, will you get the milk? I put it outside to keep cool overnight."

They moved to do her bidding and, within moments, breakfast was underway, the pot of oatmeal on the back of the stove having been stirred and ladled into bowls. Lottie split a biscuit and nibbled at it, aware of the man who ate silently and rarely took his eyes from her, as he sat across the table from where she perched on her chair.

I want you to marry me, he'd said, and the words reverberated within her head, echoing until they allowed no other thoughts to intrude. She closed her eyes against the phrase and sucked in a deep breath. And then she saw his face, determined and yet hopeful as he demanded an answer. And in that moment, she acknowledged the yearnings that had engulfed her, put a name to the heated need he was able to arouse within her very being, and admitted that what her hungry heart cried out for was the touch of John Tillman.

Her nostrils flared as her eyes opened once more, resting on the face of the man who watched her. He was all she had ever dreamed of, in those long-ago girlish times, when she had thought about having a husband of her own. He was kind and gentle, generous to a fault, and perhaps that would have been enough. But the fire that had flashed to engulf them in its flames when he'd swallowed her up in his embrace yesterday was only banked, waiting to be blown into existence by his touch. And she was honest enough to admit it to herself. To admit that forbidden desire tempted her, that her mouth craved another of his hot, damp caresses.

"Yes," she said in a voice that wavered. Her throat closed in a swallow, and her chin lifted just a bit as she met his gaze bravely. "Yes."

"You will?" he asked, as if his ears had not heard aright.

She nodded. "I will."

"Will what?" Thomas asked, looking from one to the other, puzzled at the cryptic messages that seemed to flow from them.

"Never mind, Thomas," John said absently. "We'll talk about it later."

Elated, he set to eating his food, eager to write the letter he had only moments ago dreaded the thought of composing. Surely Sarah's parents would understand that the children would be better off here. His mind began forming the words and sentences he would write, and he grinned as he considered the things he would say.

"Lottie and I are getting married," he announced to Genevieve as he approached the counter in the store just hours later.

Her mouth fell open and her curls bounced erratically, as the girl turned to face him, bright spots of color appearing in her cheeks as she considered the news. "When?" she asked quickly.

"Soon as I can get the preacher to say the words over us," John laughed, his spirits high as he tucked his thumbs in the webbing of his suspenders.

"Well, I'll be . . ." Genevieve breathed in wonder. "And here I thought the Reverend Bush was going to press his suit and—"

John frowned as he interrupted her quickly. "He tried, but Lottie belongs on the farm, with the children."

Genevieve tilted her head to one side, and her smile was teasing. "She's marrying you because of the children? Come on now, John. Surely she has more reason than that."

He shrugged and lifted one eyebrow in a rakish manner. "Well, maybe so, but none that I want to discuss with you, Miss Slocum." I don't know about Lottie, he thought with a sense of satisfaction, but I'm sure I'll realize some benefits from this marriage. At the remembrance of her slender body pressed against his, the plush dampness of her mouth as she tentatively answered the pressure of his kiss, he grinned again. "I'll make her happy," he vowed in a low voice, his words spoken so that only Genevieve could hear them.

"I know you will," she said sincerely. "I'm happy for both of you."

"Now," he began, placing both of his palms flat on the counter and bending to peer at the bolts of fabric against the side wall of the store. "I want something pretty, white and flowery kinda. I want Lottie to make a new dress for the wedding." He stood erect as Genevieve quickly selected three different patterns, and pointed at one that had sprays of lilacs scattered against the white background. His heart beat faster as his mind's eye envisioned Lottie's form filling out the fabric, saw the fragile blossoms draped over her generous bosom and cinched about her waist with a sash. Desire caught him broadside, and he almost swayed with the impact. She would be his. That warm, loving little bundle would be sharing his bed, filling his empty arms. His hand brushed against the fine weave of cotton, and he swallowed against the rush of anticipation that flooded him.

"That one will do," he announced, in as offhanded a manner as he could manage. "Cut a length of it for me, will you, Genevieve, and put in all the other stuff she'll need. I have to go to the post office, and then I'll come back to pick it up."

"I have to run an errand, John," she said brightly. "I'll leave it with my daddy, and you can get it from him."

He nodded in agreement, then turning on his heel, he left the store. Genevieve watched him go as a smile of infinite happiness wreathed her face.

"She's marrying John Tillman." The words fell between them, and their importance flashed upon the countenance of the man who heard them spoken.

His pale eyes lit with inner fire, as Stephen Bush reached a hesitant hand out for the woman who had brought him the news. His long fingers encircled her wrist, then slid down to enfold her fingers within his own.

"Are you certain, Genevieve?" he asked, in a voice that begged for affirmation of his hopes. "She told me she would consider my suit, only yesterday." He shook his head in confusion.

"John told me himself," Genevieve said firmly. "He came in the store and bought dress goods for her for a wedding gown, and said he was going to the post office." She looked about the parlor of the small home where Steven lived. "I know I shouldn't have come here, with you alone and all, but I had to tell you, Stephen," she said breathlessly.

"No one saw you come in," he assured her with a quick smile, as his hands slid up her arms to grasp her more firmly as he drew her into a loose embrace. "I want to just hold you for a minute, Genevieve," he whispered against the side of her head. "I thought I'd never be able to do this again."

"Do you think that God answered my prayer?" she asked him humbly. "I didn't know if it was the right thing to do . . . I mean praying that you wouldn't have to go through with marrying her." She closed her eyes and leaned her forehead against his black vest, not having left him a moment to pull on his coat when she'd burst into the house minutes before. She lifted her face to look with pleading eyes into his. "I couldn't have borne it, if you had married Lottie," she cried brokenly.

"God would have strengthened you, if it had been His will for that to happen," Stephen replied with certainty. He hesitated, and then smiled in a way that made him look suddenly youthful. "I have to confess to you that I prayed the prayer of our Lord in the garden myself. Although," he amended hastily, "the circumstances were far less gripping than those of His. I asked that I not have to do this thing that I was committed to, Genevieve." His eyes closed, and his head tipped back as he faced heavenward, there within the small parlor, as if he could sense the Presence beyond the ceiling that blocked his view of the sky above.

Genevieve's dark head lay against his breast, and she inhaled the essence of his stiffly starched shirt and the sharp scent of the soap he had used to wash with. "May I speak my thoughts, Stephen?" she asked with naked emotion apparent in her voice.

"Surely. There's no one here to listen but me," he answered.

"It's you who needs to hear what I say," she whispered. "I was afraid to tell you before, when you came over and studied with me in the parlor and told me about the judges and prophets and everything."

He lifted one long finger, easing beneath her chin so that he could look into the depths of her eyes as she spoke. "Go on, dear one," he urged her. "Tell me what you hold in your heart."

"I love you, Stephen," she admitted softly, her voice breaking as she spoke his name.

"Ah, my sweet." His words of endearment hung in the air, as he dropped gentle kisses on her forehead and temple, his hands resting circumspectly on her shoulders. Then, with daring, he bent lower and meshed his lips firmly against her own, sampling the soft sweetness she offered so willingly.

A knock at the outer door of the house brought his head erect, and he glanced about himself as if he would hide her from the intruder. "You must leave by the back door, Genevieve," he said quickly. "I don't want your reputation to be tarnished, if you should be found here alone with me."

"All right," she agreed, picking up her skirts as she hurried through the hallway to the back of the house. And even as she escaped detection out the wooden-paneled door, she heard the distinctive sound of John Tillman's voice as he came into the front vestibule.

"It's wrong to eavesdrop," she whispered as she hesitated in the doorway. "Mama says you might not like what you hear, when you listen in on other folks' conversations," she reminded herself sternly, even as she slipped back into the kitchen and pulled the outer door almost closed.

Breathless with the shame of what she did, Genevieve hovered next to the doorway that led to the hall and bent her head, the better to listen to the man who spoke.

"Stephen, I hope I haven't caught you in the midst of anything important," John said courteously, with an unaccustomed lilt to his voice.

"No . . . no, of course not." The deep tones that never failed to thrill her, echoed in the hallway, and Genevieve covered her mouth with one hand as she heard the hesitation in his reply.

"I needed to stop by and give you a bit of news this morning, and deliver a message from Lottie while I'm at it." She heard John clear his throat, and then the shuffle of feet against the bare floorboards told her that the two men had moved from their place in front of the door.

Stephen's tones carried well, but she knew they must have gone into the parlor, and Genevieve leaned around the doorway, fearful of missing a single word that fell from their lips. "Is there a problem, John?" he asked with hesitation.

"No . . . I'd say not," was the reply, and then, in a rush, John spoke the words he had earlier said in the store. The short sentence that had so elated Genevieve and sent her on a secret visit to the parsonage. "Lottie and I are getting married," he said with a trace of pride underlining the announcement. "She sent you a note, Stephen, and her apologies for not telling you in person."

"I see," the other man said slowly. With a great clearing of his throat, he managed to cover the jubilation that colored the words he spoke next. "I must offer you my congratulations, John. I hope you and Miss Lottie will be very happy together."

Genevieve heard another session of foot shuffling, and managed to back into the kitchen just as the two men made their way back into the vestibule. She peeked through the crack behind the kitchen door and watched as John offered his hand to the tall man who stood next to him, his face wreathed in a smile that was far from appropriate for a man who had just been scorned.

But John appeared oblivious to that fact as he made his request. "I'd like you to marry Lottie and me. If it won't be too great an imposition, that is," he added, as if he had suddenly considered the circumstances.

Stephen smiled even more broadly, and his handshake was vigorous as he replied with firm, resonant agreement. "I'd be more than pleased to do anything I can for the two of you. Miss Lottie is a fine woman. I'm sure she's made the choice that will make her happiest," he said. His arm pumped John's with an enthusiasm that caused Genevieve to cover her mouth, lest her

amusement burst forth in a fit of giggling laughter that
would expose her for the eavesdropper she was.

The door opened and John was ushered to the stoop,
where he turned back and made his final request. "I
almost forgot, Stephen. I'd like the ceremony to be on
Saturday, if that's no trouble."

Stephen's head nodded purposefully. "No problem
with that, that I can see. Can Miss Lottie be ready so
soon?"

John's smile was almost fatuous, and Genevieve responded to the sight with a giggle she could not suppress. Stephen backed in the door quickly, as if he had
heard the sound that condemned her, and his wave was
distracted, almost closing the door on his fingers as he
leaned against it.

"Genevieve." He called her name with a low, threat-
ening note that brought her from her place of hiding
immediately. "You were listening," he accused her, his
brow drawn into a frown of apparent disapproval.

She flew down the short hallway, her face radiant with
the happiness she could not conceal, and launched herself at him with all of the natural exuberance of youth
that had been suppressed by Stephen's dutiful atten-
dance to honor.

"See," she crowed with delight. "What did I tell you?"

His mouth curved in a reluctant smile, as he enclosed
her tenderly in his arms. "I should scold you for your
misdeeds," he began as he patted her back with one
hand. His head bowed until his face was cheek to cheek
with hers, and his eyes closed as his voice wavered.

"I can't find it in my heart to spoil your pleasure
today, my dear," he said tenderly, "since it is so closely
bound to my own."

Ten

Her fingers clasped tightly together under the lap robe, Lottie consciously loosened the grip she had maintained for the past half hour. The fine tendrils of tension that wrapped about her today were making it difficult for her to catch a deep breath, let alone concentrate on the matters at hand. And those matters definitely needed her full attention.

Against her left thigh, the heated length of John Tillman's right leg pressed firmly. The warmth from his body penetrated her clothing. Surely the fine film of perspiration that was even now making her hands feel so damp and clammy could be laid to his nearness. But being near him had never before brought about so strange a reaction, she thought as she cast a glance at him from beneath her lashes.

His face was in shadow, but the sharp line of his jaw and the straight thrust of his nose lent a strength to his profile that reminded her of one of the busts in the museum in Boston. Miss Aggie had taken a troop of her charges there once. Expeditions such as that had been rare, and Lottie had never forgotten the thrill of that afternoon. The memory of the white marble bust was exactly what John reminded her of now. Somehow, in her mind, that pleasure she had felt when faced by the art treasures of the ages, all at her disposal for a whole afternoon, bore a resemblance to the expectancy that gripped her this minute.

She watched him now without the subterfuge of lowered lashes, turning her head to feast on the masculine beauty she found in his face. His hair, golden and just long enough to curl over the edge of his collar, tempted her fingers. Never before had she felt the need to touch another human being the way she had during the past week.

John's kiss had unleashed a fount of sensation within her that had not found release, and so bubbled close to the surface whenever they chanced to be together. The urge to see him had been satisfied by the daily rituals of their life, but he'd not touched her since that morning when she'd agreed to marry him. In fact, she realized suddenly, he'd gone to great lengths to stay away from her in the past few days.

Her eyes widened in sudden awareness. Perhaps he'd changed his mind, but been too honorable a man to go back on his word. The thought struck her with dismay, and her low sound of protest was audible, breaking the silence that had up until now only been pierced by the sounds of the horse's harness as the buggy moved through the oncoming twilight.

His head turned and his eyes measured her, narrowing as he focused on the confusion that caused her mouth to soften and her tongue to paint its way across her upper lip.

"What is it, Lottie?" he asked in an impatient growl. The girl had been tempting him all week with her long glances and swaying hips. Not to mention those quiet moments when she'd brush her hair before the fireplace, then braid it into a rope that he could have wrapped about his wrist several times, so long did it hang down her back.

He'd done his best to keep his hands off her, waiting until the deed was done and the words spoken that would make her his wife. But the silent temptation she offered had been almost more than he could stand. He cleared his throat against the harshness that had coated his words to her and tried for a softer approach.

"Is something wrong?" he asked softly, bending his head to speak closer to her ear.

She shook her head dumbly. Then, with a show of confidence, smiled brightly at him. "Nothing, John," she said finally. "I just wondered what you'd like to have for supper when we get home. I didn't put anything on the stove before we left."

He grinned unexpectedly, the first sign of levity she'd seen from him all day. The sight lifted her spirits. "You aren't expected to be thinking about cooking on your wedding day, Lottie," he teased.

The easing of the tension between them was welcome. The few minutes spent before the altar in the small church had formed them into a couple, but they had walked down the aisle and back into the sunshine as two separate persons. Her emotions had been under strict control, the excitement of the wedding rigidly confined to a tiny corner of her being.

She'd considered her problem all morning, and there, in the little church, she'd faced the thought that had kept her company for days. *John is marrying me in order to keep the children.* The hard fact of the matter had been enough to almost dim her joy all week. The thrill she'd wanted to feel at the idea of being married had been dulled by the circumstances. But now, the deed was done. He was smiling, and she knew a surge of happiness within that brought an answering lift to her mouth and relaxed the knot of anxiety she'd been toting around in her belly.

"Didn't you get enough to eat at the parsonage?" John asked her, even though he knew better. She hadn't eaten enough to bother with, he remembered. Just slid a few forkfuls of food about on her plate and looked after the children as they'd scooted about excitedly, aware of the festivity surrounding the occasion.

"It was good of Steven to arrange a reception for us, wasn't it?" Actually, she thought it had been very strange behavior for a man who had been scorned only a week ago.

John laughed, his mouth twisting into a smile that crinkled his eyes. "He had a lot of help with it. In fact, I think it was a celebration of sorts for him, too."

Lottie was puzzled. "Why would he want to be celebrating?" Granted, the man hadn't looked to be sorrowing over the fact that his once-intended bride was marrying another man. But then what could he expect, what with leaving her in the lurch and all, she thought with a smug surge of satisfaction. *I got the better of the two anyway*, she decided. Not that there was any contest. John Tillman was rough, without the polish that Stephen Bush's education had provided him with, but the weeks since her arrival in Mill Creek had made Lottie more than aware of the solid goodness that formed the core of the man who rode beside her.

"Did you see Genevieve's face at the wedding?" John asked her softly, aware of the children who were crowded together in the narrow back seat.

Lottie looked puzzled. "She was happy for us, I suppose," she ventured. "Why, she and her mother cooked the food for the most part, and arranged the reception."

"*I'd* say, from the foolish grin on her face, she was halfway to hog heaven," he said dryly as he grinned his widest. "She couldn't take her eyes off the preacher . . . didn't you notice?" Leaning back in the seat, he allowed his arm to drape over the cushioned leather behind Lottie, his fingers clasping her shoulder with casual ease.

Lottie shook her head and frowned. "Whatever are you talking about, John Tillman?" she asked. "Besides, you shouldn't have been noticing another woman at your own wedding," she sniffed, pouting her lips and lowering her lashes teasingly.

"Don't worry, Lottie," he breathed softly against her ear. "I haven't had you out of my mind for a minute all day."

Casting a warm look in her direction, he basked in the anticipation that filled his imagination to overflowing. *I've had a hard time keeping my hands off you, little girl,* he thought. A surge of hunger tensed the long muscles in his thighs and caused a spasm of desire to jolt to life within him. Shifting in his seat, he attempted to guide his attention into safer channels.

"You didn't mind having a few townfolk there, did you, Lottie?" he asked, wishing his randy thoughts would go into hibernation for an hour or so.

"They're your friends, John," she said easily, oblivious to his problem. "I'm glad they came."

His hand gripped her shoulder more tightly. Snuggling her against his side, he felt the fine tension leave her muscles. She's been tighter than a drum all day, he thought. Uneasy, like a barn cat in season. Twitching her tail and mincing about on tiptoes, she'd been, in a manner of speaking. Sassy with him and tense, as if she were wary of what the day would bring. And well she might be, he decided with a wry grin. He'd been storing up for a long time. The night promised to be full of surprises, most of them on Lottie's part, he thought with a flare of satisfaction, if he were any judge of things.

"Are we almost home?" Sissy asked plaintively. Just behind John's shoulder, she had leaned forward to place her pointed little chin against the leather upholstery.

"You can wait, Sissy," Lottie said firmly, knowing what drove the child to ask the question.

Thomas groaned audibly and clicked his tongue. "Girls," he muttered beneath his breath, as if he were a great judge of the species.

Sissy sniffled once and settled back in the seat, but within a few moments she leaned forward again, this time to whisper in Lottie's right ear.

"Miss Lottie, I can't help it," she breathed apologetically.

"I know, sweet," Lottie soothed, then turned her face to brush a kiss against the warm cheek that the child offered. "We'll be home in just a minute, now."

"Quicker than that," John told her as he turned the horse into the lane that led to the farm. The scent of home, the promise of her stall and the portion of oats she would find there, spurred the dainty mare to greater effort. She picked up her pace, lifting her hooves quickly to reach her goal.

"She's getting used to being here," John said, letting the horse have her way. "See, she knows her dinner's waiting in her stall."

Only moments later, he tugged gently on the reins as they approached the two-story barn. Turning from

Lottie, he climbed from the buggy and stretched. With measured movements, he reached to help her down. His fingers were tight about her waist, and his strong arms lifted her easily until she stood on the ground before him. Sissy and Thomas had scrambled out the other side, while Lottie was enclosed in the space John's body allowed her.

Behind her was the black buggy wheel. On either side were his arms, forming a cage that offered her no escape. Before her was the man she had married only hours before, and that thought was enough to bring a flush to her cheeks and an uneven rhythm to the heart-beat that was already pounding against her ribs. It was like the first time he'd lifted her from the buggy, that day when he'd allowed his hands to rest at her waist, lingering longer than necessary and making her all flut-tery inside. I want him to touch me like that again, she thought with wonder. I want him to put his hands on my back and pull me up against him, till I can't get my breath, what with my breasts squeezed tight to his chest and—

She dropped her head, embarrassed by the thoughts that had run rampant in her mind. Even thinking about her bosom that way made it get all swollen-feeling, and she shrank back against the buggy wheel, lest he fulfill her errant yearning. This must be part of the carnal desire Miss Aggie told me about, she thought, with only a lingering sense of shame.

Lifting her head, she found his eyes intent upon her, and with a bravery she had not known she possessed, she whispered the desire of her heart.

"Do you remember how you kissed me that day?" she asked in a breathless whisper.

He nodded, his eyes taking note of the splashes of

high color that painted her cheeks. He watched as her breathing lifted the firm lines of her breasts, saw the beginnings of awareness that added luster to her blue eyes, and then smiled with what he hoped was gentle encouragement. "I remember, Lottie," he said carefully.

"Would you mind doing it again?" she asked, her long lashes coming down to cover the brilliance of her eyes as she waited for him to do her bidding.

His groan was muted by the lushness of her mouth as he took possession without hesitation. His lips parted over hers, and he sipped carefully, but greedily at the sweetness she offered him. Knowing that he would frighten her if he unleashed the full force of his passion, he lifted his hands to encircle her face and then blessed her fragile features with the muted caresses that he fervently hoped would help to ease his tension. From her lips, he moved to her forehead, then to the tender place where her pulse beat at her temple, only to shift once more, seeking pleasure in the soft fragrance of her throat, as he explored the area his hands framed for his delectation.

He inhaled her scent, that flowery, clean essence that he'd come to associate with Lottie. He tested the fullness of her mouth once more, the plushness of her lips that gave with such innocent abandon. And then he moved her away from himself, knowing that his body was set on a path of fulfillment. Only the presence of the two children kept him from lifting his bride and carrying her into the house to make her his wife, in fact.

"Like that?" he asked her, his voice husky in her ear.

She was breathless, wonder and excitement ablaze in her eyes as she opened them to find him watching her with a lazy grin that vied with the rasping tones of the question he'd growled.

She nodded. "Yes, like that," she said with a whisper that spoke of her astonishment. "Why does it make me feel so tingly inside when you kiss me, John?" she asked in that same wispy voice, her innocence making her bold.

He tipped his head back, as if he would gain strength from the first star that glittered just over the edge of the barn roof. The wishing star, that he'd *not* spent his time utilizing in more years than he could count. Now he fervently cast his wish into the heavens, in desperate hope that he could manage to get through the next little while. That he could hold fast to his resolution to keep his needs in check long enough to loose Lottie's maidenly inhibitions and soothe her fears.

"It makes me feel the same way, Lottie," he assured her. "It's just the way kisses are supposed to work, I guess," he said with a tight grin. He stepped back and, with one hand at her back, set her off in the direction of the house.

"I'll just put the horse up and milk Rosie, and then I'll be right in," he told her, as he slid the barn door open and caught at Daisy's bridle, guiding the mare into the dark interior of the stable. Tying her lead to a ring that had been installed for the purpose, he unhitched the buggy and backed it deftly into place beside the first stall. From behind him, he heard the laughter of the children as they chased a loose chicken across the yard, Sissy squealing as the hen turned to harass her pursuers. He smiled as he wiped down the sides of his mare and removed her harness, his hands forming once more the bond between man and beast that gave him such pleasure.

"I got married today, Daisy," he crooned as he slid the halter over her head, clipping it beneath her jaw and then leading her into the stall he had built for her at the back of the barn. In the shadows, he walked with firm purpose, his voice gentle as he put the horse up for the night. He'd helped James build this barn. He knew every inch of it and, in the past few weeks, had come to consider it his own. As it would be until young Thomas was old enough to take his share of the inheritance his father had left.

"She's a pretty thing, Daisy," he said in a low tone as he shook the oat bucket, giving her a generous portion. After checking the amount of hay that lay in the manger, he left the stall, latching the door carefully behind himself.

"I think we'll do well, Lottie and me," he mused as he reached for the barn lantern and lit it, hanging it on a peg near where the cow waited.

"What do you think about that, Rosie?" he asked, and then chuckled at his own foolishness. Approaching the chore with unaccustomed zeal, he lifted the milk pail from its hook and pushed the low stool into place, determined to strip the cow's udder in jig time.

A stop at the springhouse, where he left the milk, covering it carefully against insects, and then filling a pail with fresh water for the house, completed his hasty chores.

"I got the broody hen put up, Uncle John," Thomas called from the door of the henhouse.

"Good job, son," he called, happy that the runaway was penned for the night. Chasing a crazy chicken is not how I'd intended to spend my wedding night, he thought fervently. I've got other things to do after dark.

Lottie looked up when the door opened and made a

show of taking the bucket from John's grip. Careful not to look directly into his eyes, she waved at the chair by the fire where he enjoyed sitting in the evening.

"I'll have a bite to eat ready in a minute," she said breathlessly, as she wiped her hands on the front of her apron once more. "I haven't seemed to get my thoughts together very well," she went on as John watched her closely.

It was true, she thought. She'd come inside and stood by the door for long minutes, trying to still the frantic beating of her heart. Surely such pleasure from mere touching of mouths was not normal. Just thinking about John lately had been more than exciting, she confessed to herself and then, more boldly yet, she admitted to enjoying the nearness of him. Something about the warmth of his flesh, the lift of his mouth as he smiled, the broad expanse of his chest that filled out the shirts she washed for him; all those brought to life a yearning within her that was almost frightening in its intensity.

Her hand fluttered to her breast and rested between the soft curves that had seemed to swell and throb with an emotion of their own. Eyes wide with the wonder of it all, she considered the man who aroused such feelings within her.

"Lottie?" he said, from the chair by the fire.

She shivered and blinked, embarrassed that he should find her daydreaming. He watched her, a puzzled expression drawing his brow down into a frown, one foot freed from his boot, the other across his knee as he levered the heel off.

"I was thinking," she said in a flustered manner, hurrying to the cupboard to lift down the loaf of bread. In moments she had sliced enough for supper and opened a can of peaches from the shelf. A slab of butter, fresh from yesterday's churning, lay beneath its glass cover, a jar of pear conserve sat beside it. Gathering the hasty meal together, she called the children to wash, then sat at the table to prepare their food.

"I'm glad you didn't fuss with supper," John said as he sat across from her.

"I like peaches," Sissy offered, as she sucked one of the slices into her mouth, her tongue appreciating the smooth texture of the fruit.

"Well, eat up, Sunshine," John advised her. "It's been a long day and it's almost time for you to be in bed."

A frown creased her brow, and she wrinkled her nose in silent protest, but a second look at the determined face of her uncle apparently changed her mind. Her small shoulders lifted in a gesture of surrender.

"Me, too?" Thomas asked, as he admired the thick slice of bread he had buttered with lavish care.

"You, too," John said firmly, and then with a teasing grin, he included Lottie in his glance.

Lowering the wick on the kerosene lamp was her final task, and Lottie looked about the cabin before she leaned to twist the knob that would leave the large room in shadow. The fire was banked, and only glowing embers remained to light her way to the bed.

Careful to keep her eyes downcast, she approached him. Somehow, while her back was turned, he'd managed to slide out of his pants, for they were hung on a peg next to the headboard of the bedframe. Now he watched her from where he sat, propped against both pillows, sheet and quilt pulled up to his waist. One glimpse had warned her that his trousers weren't the only thing he'd removed, for an abundance of bare skin gleamed in the faint glow cast by the log that smouldered in the back of the fireplace.

His arms were brown, tanned by the summer sun, in contrast to the pale flesh of his chest and shoulders. A nest of golden curls glistened there, forming a triangle against his skin and drawing her eyes to its plushness. She lifted her gaze to his face, and all of the uneasiness she felt became apparent to him in that one questioning glance.

"Come here, Lottie," he said, barely moving his mouth as the words breathed from his lips. He patted the bed next to where he sat, and as she neared, he reached for her hand and drew her to sit beside him. His fingers traced the small wrinkles on her knuckles, and his touch soothed her as the invitation had not.

"Are you afraid of me?" he asked in a low, gruff voice that carried only to her ears.

She shook her head quickly. "No, of course not, John," she said without hesitation. "I just don't know . . ."

His smile was tender and his hands were firm as they clasped hers tighter, drawing her closer. "Of course, you don't, sweetheart," he said easily. With a tug, he pulled her to rest against himself. Her feet left the floor, as she was caught off balance.

Her mouth formed an *O* of surprise, and she found herself resting against his chest, his arms having eased their way about her, his hands lifting her into his lap. One large palm pressed her head against his shoulder, and then his fingers twined their way into her braid, as he gently rubbed against her scalp with a soothing rhythm.

"Now, this isn't so bad, is it?" he asked her in a whisper, bending to breathe the words against her forehead.

She shook her head, a jerky motion that brought a quick smile to his lips. "No," she admitted on an indrawn breath.

"Why don't I just hold you for a few minutes, Lottie?" he said, with soothing touches that brushed against her shoulder and down her arm, until he found the button that fastened her cuff about her wrist. His fingers slid it from the hole she had formed with tiny stitches, and with deft movements he traced the veins that lay beneath her fragile flesh. His index finger found the frantic pulsing that he'd searched for so casually, and he felt a pang of sympathy for the child-woman who sat within his embrace.

"You're my wife now, Lottie," he said gravely. "Do you know what that means?"

She nodded quickly "Of course, I do," she whispered. Her head tilted back as she met his glance, and hot color rode her cheekbones. "Miss Aggie said I should submit to my husband and be a good wife, and that's what I intend to do."

His eyes twinkled in the faint glow from the fireplace, and his mouth twisted wryly. "Do you now?" he asked as he bent to drop a quick kiss on her pursed lips.

She nodded with firm purpose, and then her eyes fell from his gaze. "I just don't know exactly what I'm supposed to do," she admitted quietly.

"Well," he began slowly, his hand moving to the front of her dress, where his agile fingers began slipping the buttons from their place. "The first thing you must do is take off these clothes and come to bed. Shall I help you, Lottie?" he asked against her ear.

She couldn't think, what with the warmth of his fin-

gers touching her just above the lacy edge of her camisole. One calloused fingertip moved to travel the length
of her collarbone, then returned to press lightly on the
pulse that pounded in her throat. From there it slid
down until it brushed against the very top of her breast,
where the soft flesh rose in plush splendor. She heard
the sigh that breathed from her own lips as he untied
the ribbon that held her camisole, and she closed her
eyes against the shiver that brought gooseflesh to her
bare skin.

Turning her so that she faced him, he held her for
a moment, his eyes searching her face. "I won't hurt
you, Lottie," he whispered, as his hands left her shoulders and concentrated on the opening that gaped wide,
displaying her lushness beneath the white undergar-
ment she wore. He left the treasure he had uncovered
for a moment and released the rest of her buttons, until
the dress fell from her shoulders with ease. He slid it
down her arms, unbuttoned the other cuff, and lifted
her arms free.

Immediately, her hands fluttered to her chest and
spread against the expanse of bare flesh, covering the
cleavage he had exposed to his sight. Her fingers
twitched against the fabric, as if she would pull it back
into place.

"No . . . let me just look at you." he said firmly, as
he clasped her fingers with his own and pulled them
to his mouth, where he sucked the tip of one pink finger within the grip of his teeth. His tongue teased the
flesh he held captive and his eyes feasted on the rise
of her bosom, where the fine batiste hid what he longed
to expose to his view. Holding her fingers within the
palm of one hand, he reached to brush back the edges

that clung to her flesh and felt the delicate trembling that gripped her.

"John?" her whisper quavered as she spoke his name. He leaned forward to brush a quick kiss against the lips that were tempting him.

"It's all right, Lottie," he assured her softly. "Just let me love you a little."

She looked perplexed as she considered his words. Miss Aggie hadn't mentioned allowing a husband to touch the parts of her body that had never been uncovered within sight of another person in all of her short life. At least not within her memory. Dressing and undressing had been done under cover of darkness at the home, and the past few years had allowed Lottie the privacy of her own alcove in which to sleep and perform the task of unclothing at the end of the day. Nothing had prepared her for the touch of John's fingers against her flesh, or the baring of her breasts to his sight. And now he spoke of loving her a little.

"I don't know what you mean, John," she ventured. "Do you love me?" she asked in an unbelieving whisper.

He shook his head. "That's not what I meant, Lottie," he said quickly. "You know I care for you, don't you?"

She nodded slowly. "I think so."

"Loving means different things, sweetheart," he said, choosing his words carefully. "In this case, it means what a husband and wife do together." He looked for understanding in her eyes, but a perplexed stare met his gaze.

"Do you know what happens in the marriage bed, Lottie?" he asked with a sense of despair. *Please say yes,* he prayed silently, but his plea was denied as her head shook slowly and her eyes filled with tears.

"You must think I'm awfully dense," she said in a fragile, little voice that tore at his heart.

"No . . ." He shook his head and his smile was gentle as he bent to lean his forehead against hers. "Just innocent, Lottie." His sigh was deep as he harnessed the desire that had already begun to prepare his body for her taking. "Is your nightgown close at hand?" he asked tenderly, sliding his hands about her back as he removed the camisole from her.

"It was under my pillow," she said in a muffled whisper against his chest. The air was cool on her bare flesh, and she shivered.

"Let me help you slip it on," he suggested, one long arm reaching to locate it amidst the bedclothes. He lifted it over her head, admiring the fragile lines of her neck as she bent against him. John leaned to place an openmouthed kiss at the nape, where short wispy curls clung to her skin. He tucked her hands into the sleeves and straightened the voluminous folds about her, tugging it down to her waist, where he stopped.

"We have to get the rest of your things off, Lottie," he said patiently into her hair, inhaling the sweet scent of it with luxurious pleasure.

She closed her eyes against the sight of his bare chest. Caught in a whirlwind of strange sensations, stunned by the actions of the man she had entrusted her life to, she felt helpless in his hands.

"Let me up for a minute, John," she breathed against his flesh, her mouth almost touching the pale skin of his shoulder.

"Want me to help you?"

"No." She slid from his grasp and stood on the rug next to the bed, her arms beneath the off-white muslin of her gown as she loosened the ties of her petticoat and then slid the remainder of her clothing into a pile that circled her feet. Her underwear was tangled about her ankles, and she lifted one foot, then the other, to free them from the soft cotton fabric. Leaning over, she slid her long stockings down until they dragged about her calves, her garters caught up in the lisle stockings John had bought her at the mercantile in town. She bent to untangle them and carefully pulled the fine hosiery from her feet.

"There . . ." The word was a barely discernible sound as she bent to lift the white stockings, smoothing them with her fingers as she folded them and placed them on the shelf by the bed.

She stepped out of the circle of clothing she had dropped and bent to pick them up, the folds of her gown falling about her like a colorless shroud. Her hands were almost worshipful as she held her new dress before her, shaking the wrinkles from it before she hung it carefully on one of the pegs John had set into the wall for her near the headboard.

I have to get into that bed with him now, she thought as she smoothed the rest of her undergarments and then slowly folded them. As if her hands belonged to someone else, she watched them, making precise movements with fingers that were trembling and cold.

Miss Aggie had not prepared her for this part of it, and her mind hovered over the unknown that faced her as she pulled the pins from her hair and lay them in precise alignment on the shelf. Her fingers pulled the bit of hair from the end of her braid, and she placed it next to the pins.

There was a mystical bond between married people. She had sensed it once . . . in a couple who had come to the orphanage to choose a little girl. Not Lottie, of course, but a small child, barely able to tend to herself. They'd looked at the baby, then at each other, and a silent message had so obviously passed between them, that Lottie had felt an emotion akin to grief.

With agile fingers, she undid the length of her braid and allowed the hair to flow in crinkly waves down her back. That same emotion had assailed her another time, as she'd sensed the same connection between the minister at New Hope and his wife, an elderly couple who sat closely on the sofa, and whose hands touched frequently as they walked together. That she would ever know that same feeling, that sense of belonging with another person, was almost beyond her comprehension. And yet, John was looking at her with a glimmer of yearning, with a gentle glow lighting his eyes that warmed her where she stood, and she drew a deep breath that quivered in her chest at the joy that look set free within her.

He folded back the bedclothes and patted the feather tick beside him. "Come on, Lottie," he said in that husky voice she'd heard once before.

Lifting the skirt of her gown, she placed one knee on the bed and then turned to move into place beside him, sliding her bare feet beneath the covers. Her hands smoothed the folds of her gown about her legs, and she tucked it beneath her calves before she lay down next to him. He slid down, tugging the pillows with him, until he lay inches from her, adjusting the plump feather pillows to his liking beneath his head.

"Don't I get a pillow, too?"

His fist punched once more into the top mound, and then he settled back with a sigh of contentment before he slanted a glance at her.

"No, you get to lay on my shoulder," he said decisively, patting the spot where her head should lie.

"Is this part of being submissive?" Lottie wanted to know with a quick grin, her restless hands smoothing the quilt beneath the rise of her breasts.

He shook his head. "No, that part's still coming," he said with a smile that promised much. "First, we need to practice that kissing you seem to be so fond of, Mrs. Tillman," he whispered as he lifted just a bit to lean over her. His big hand cradled the crown of her head, and he bent to settle his mouth with tender care over the fullness of her lips.

Lottie's eyes closed as she savored the pleasure the contact brought her. It was warm and damp, enfolding her gently in a caress that lured her closer. She spread one hand on his chest, her fingers tangling in the temptation of golden hair that curled crisply beneath her touch. Then his mouth lifted from her and she drew in a breath, inhaling the musky scent of his body, that mysterious odor that assailed her nostrils with its tantalizing flavor.

"You're a good kisser, Mrs. Tillman," he growled against her ear, his tongue venturing forth to touch the lobe and his teeth nipping gently, before he returned to the ripe fullness of her mouth.

"I've never kissed anyone else," she said breathlessly, her head swimming with a strange, heady sensation she could not recognize.

"I'm glad." His whisper was so soft, she almost missed it, but the hearing of those two simple words brought her a measure of joy that warmed her heart. When he dipped again to take possession of her mouth, she opened her lips to taste him and felt the rush of his breath as he released the pent-up store he had held within his lungs. With an audible groan, he responded to the innocent advances, and she withdrew in haste, backing away to put space between their bodies.

"Did I do something wrong?" she asked quickly, but he clasped her more tightly, holding her against his chest as he shook his head and muttered a reply against her mouth.

"Uh uh . . . no," he said harshly. "Let me in . . . let me touch your tongue, Lottie."

A thrill shot from her breast to settle deep within her belly as he applied pressure to her mouth, biting gently against her plush bottom lip, until she granted him entrance. The possession of her mouth was hot and wet, his agile tongue seeking out every hollow, every ridge, every surface, fencing with her own flesh as she entered into the game he had begun.

"John!" Her harsh whisper was a gust of breath, leaving her lungs as she gasped for a fresh supply.

His growl was muffled in the fabric of her gown, as he lowered his head to wrestle with the fabric that covered her bosom. Catching at the rough muslin with his teeth, he captured the crest of her breast within the prison of his mouth and suckled it between his lips.

"Undo the buttons," he said roughly, and her hands came up to do his bidding, her face flushing with a strange, heated response that tingled beneath her skin.

Before she had undone the last of them, he nosed his way to where her flesh lay exposed.

"Lottie." The single word was at once a whisper and a prayer, as he touched the fragrant skin with his mouth. Inhaling the scent of her, that fresh flowery aura that surrounded her, he lifted from her, feasting his eyes on the lush roundness he had uncovered. Tenderly, as if he would discover a priceless treasure, his hand sought the flesh that lay beneath the other side of her gown's bodice, and he closed his eyes as his palm cupped the firm weight.

The quiver of delight that coursed through her was the response he had been waiting for, and it was with a gentle touch that he lifted his body to cover her. Easing his way, he tried in vain to separate her legs with one of his own, but the gown was wrapped tightly about her knees and calves, and she twisted in his grip to forestall his plan.

"What are you doing, John?" Her whisper was frantic as he pushed between her thighs with his knee, and he shook his head in pure frustration.

"Let me pull up your gown, Lottie," he said in a husky murmur against her ear.

"No!" The word rang out in the room. He sat bolt upright as she jerked away from him, brushing frantically at her hair and pulling her gown together to cover her breasts.

Without hesitation, he covered her mouth with his hand, closing his eyes and holding her against himself as she sought to escape his grip. She wriggled and shoved at him, her hands trapped between their bodies, one long arm clutching her in place, the other hand still over her mouth.

"Hush, Lottie, you'll wake the children," he whispered against her hair.

"Then get off of me," she hissed at him angrily. "I like you kissing me, John, but I don't think I like you laying all over the top of me!"

His frustration was mounting, not to mention the state of his arousal, which had responded apace with her wriggling and squirming beneath him.

"This looks like a Mexican standoff, sweetheart," he

muttered darkly. "Seems to me like there's only one thing to do."

He slid from the bed, casting a warning look at her furious countenance as he rose to stand by the bed. Then, as she watched, stunned by the nude masculinity that he displayed with such nonchalance, he tugged his pants on, sliding the suspenders over his shoulders with haste. His hair was tousled and his face was flushed, but the determination in his eyes warned her not to give him an argument as he scooped her into the cradle of his arms, quilt and all, and made his way to the door.

"Where—" she began in a loud whisper.

"Not a word, Lottie," he ground out, as he opened the cabin door and glanced once at the loft before he carried her from the warm room.

Wish You Were Here?

You can be, every month, with Zebra Historical Romance Novels.

YOU ARE CORDIALLY INVITED TO GET SWEPT AWAY INTO NEW WORLDS OF PASSION AND ADVENTURE.

AND IT WON'T COST YOU A PENNY!

Receive 4 Zebra Historical Romances, Absolutely _Free!_
(A $19.96 value)

Now you can have your pick of handsome, noble adventurers with romance in their hearts and you on their minds. Zebra publishes Historical Romances That Burn With The Fire Of History by the world's finest romance authors.

This very special FREE offer entitles you to 4 Zebra novels at absolutely no cost, with no obligation to buy anything, ever. It's an offer designed to excite your most vivid dreams and desires...and save you almost $20!

And that's not all you get...

Your Home Subscription Saves You Money Every Month.

After you've enjoyed your initial FREE package of 4 books, you'll begin to receive monthly shipments of new Zebra titles. These novels are delivered direct to your home as soon as they are published...sometimes even before the bookstores get them! Each monthly shipment of 4 books will be yours to examine for 10 days. Then if you decide to keep the books, you'll pay the preferred subscriber's price of just $4.00 per title. That's $16 for all 4 books...a savings of almost $4 off the publisher's price! (A nominal shipping and handling charge of $1.50 per shipment will be added.)

There Is No Minimum Purchase. And Your Continued Satisfaction Is Guaranteed.

We're so sure that you'll appreciate the money-saving convenience of home delivery that we guarantee your complete satisfaction. You may return any shipment...for any reason...within 10 days and pay nothing that month. And if you want us to stop sending books, just say the word. There is no minimum number of books you must buy.

It's a no-lose proposition, so send for your 4 FREE books today!

YOU'RE GOING TO LOVE GETTING
4 FREE BOOKS

These books worth almost $20, are yours without cost or obligation when you fill out and mail this certificate.

(If the certificate is missing below, write to: Zebra Home Subscription Service, Inc., 120 Brighton Road, P.O. Box 5214, Clifton, New Jersey 07015-5214

Complete and mail this card to receive 4 Free books!

Yes! Please send me 4 Zebra Historical Romances without cost or obligation. I understand that each month thereafter I will be able to preview 4 new Zebra Historical Romances FREE for 10 days. Then, if I should decide to keep them, I will pay the money-saving preferred publisher's price of just $4.00 each...a total of $16. That's almost $4 less than the publisher's price. (A nominal shipping and handling charge of $1.50 per shipment will be added.) I may return any shipment within 10 days and owe nothing, and I may cancel this subscription at any time. The 4 FREE books will be mine to keep in any case.

Name _____

Address _____ Apt. _____

City _____ State _____ Zip _____

Telephone ( ) _____

Signature _____

(If under 18, parent or guardian must sign.)

LP0195

Terms, offer and prices subject to change without notice. Subscription subject to acceptance by Zebra Books. Zebra Books reserves the right to reject any order or cancel any subscription.

TREAT YOURSELF TO A FREE BOOK.

A $19.96
value.
FREE!

No obligation
to buy
anything, ever.

ZEBRA HOME SUBSCRIPTION SERVICE, INC.

120 BRIGHTON ROAD

P.O. BOX 5214

CLIFTON, NEW JERSEY 07015-5214

ll..l..lll....ll.l.l.l..l.l..l.l..ll.l.l..ll.l..l.ll..l

Eleven

"Stand right there while I light this lantern," John ordered her sternly, depositing her in the middle of the aisle that bisected the barn.

Her nod went unnoticed, as she shivered within the folds of the quilt he had draped over her shoulders when he slid her from the shelter of his arms. Eyes wide with the remnants of surprise the quick trip had inspired, she watched him as he lit the wick and then hung the lantern on a nail next to the buggy.

He turned to her, his face in shadow as he moved with quiet purpose to where she stood. Looming over her, he lifted one large hand from his side to brush at a lock of hair that fallen across her cheek. She trembled at the gentle touch of his fingers, so strangely at odds with the darkly enigmatic expression that marked the contours of his face, and she shivered at the contrast.

As if he had mesmerized her, she stared up at him, searching for a trace of the kindness that had marked his behavior only minutes ago . . . and finding none. His eyes were bold, examining her without pretense, his body muscular and taut with a tension that shimmered in his gaze. His beautiful blue eyes glittered with a knowledge that confused her and brought hot color from her throat to bathe the hollows of her cheeks.

Lottie felt the rise of an unknown emotion within

her, a strangely exciting yearning to know this other side of the man who hovered over her. He smiled, a travesty of merriment, pulling his lips tightly against the white perfection of his teeth. As he bent to enfold her within his embrace, she swallowed hard against the anticipation that gripped her.

"Afraid of me now, Lottie?" he asked in that same menacing voice he had used as they left the cabin.

"No . . ." she breathed, shaking her head, a jerky movement that swung the errant lock of hair back over her face, almost concealing her left eye from his view. His right hand slid up from its resting place against her hip to tuck the tress behind her ear, and then made the return trip, finally clasping her firmly, with his fingers at the small of her back.

"Why did you bring me out here?" she asked in a small voice that betrayed her inward trembling.

He smiled again, and the terrible tension that had taken hold of his features eased a bit with the movement of his lips. "I have some things to teach you, Lottie, and we don't need an audience for the occasion," he said in a guttural tone that rasped against her hearing. "I was foolish to begin this night in a bed right under that loft. For the life of me, I don't know how James conducted a marriage just a dozen feet from two youngsters."

"What do you mean?" she whispered, her eyes focused on the expression of dark intent that tautened the skin over his cheekbones.

"You've got me in a state, Lottie. Between us, we almost made a total botch of this job . . . me with my trying to hurry you along . . . and you with your not knowing diddly squat about anything." The fingers that had gripped her so tightly had begun to ease their possession, and instead were rubbing in a comforting fashion against the soft flesh that was generously padded by the quilt she still wore draped about her.

"But what will we do out here?" she asked him, genuinely perplexed by the speedy expedition across the yard and into the barn.

He dipped his head to rest his forehead against hers, and his words were tangled with his laughter as he rocked her within the comfort of his arms. "Lottie, Lottie," he chuckled. "This is going to be a long night, I can see that already."

He turned her within his embrace until his chest was tight against her shoulders, until she was scooped back against the hard firmness of his body, and then his fingers tilted her chin in the direction of the ladder that climbed to the loft, just ahead of them.

"We're going up there, sweetheart," he said in a raspy whisper in her ear. "Go on, up you go," he urged her, his hands unwrapping her from the quilt and pushing her gently across the aisle.

She glanced back at him, her face a pale oval in the lamplight, her eyes wide and wondering, and then she picked up the skirt of her gown and placed her foot on the first step of the sturdy ladder and gripped the slat just above her head.

He watched her climb up the first few slats, his gaze hungry as he admired the muscles that flexed in her calves and the pink toes that curled to grip the squared wooden rungs. His hand itched to smooth its way up that slender leg, and he fought the urge as he flung the quilt over his shoulder and prepared to follow her.

Lottie pulled herself over the edge and onto the floor of the hayloft, scrambling with haste to her feet as John's head appeared in the opening.

"You all right?" he asked as he eased himself up the final steps. Tossing the quilt on a pile of hay, he reached for her hand, and the determined expression that had darkened his features softened in the shadows that surrounded them.

"Yes," she responded tightly, unwilling to admit the presence of the shivering within her breast. She looked at the man she had promised to love and obey, and for a moment wished with fervent zeal that Miss Aggie had been more specific in her instructions. Just how far this submitting was supposed to go was the issue right now. The man who had laid atop her and attempted to force his knee between her own, was also the man who had kissed her so long and lovingly, and she was having a problem placing the two of them in the same mold.

"I just feel kind of scary inside," she admitted finally as he drew her to where the quilt lay over the pile of hay.

He dropped her hand and grasped the heavy patchwork by the hem, flicking it until it sailed out squarely, allowing it to fall on the rounded mass, forming a makeshift bed that would receive their bodies gently. With a strangely courtly air, he eased her to the center of the coverlet and lay down beside her, propping himself up on his elbow, the better to face her directly.

One long arm captured her and he held her firmly, even as his hand slid up and down the curve formed by her ribs and narrow waist. She held her breath as his fingers strayed to brush carefully against the side of her breast, and she felt the flesh firming beneath his touch. The memory of his mouth, in intimate contact with that same flesh, set loose a shiver that flared her nostrils and bowed her back in a primitive response.

She heard his low chuckle in the darkness, and her

eyes narrowed as she sought to see his face in the shadows. But the movement of his hand brought another spasm of delight, and her eyes closed, the better to savor the sensation. He'd brushed against that small telltale bit of flesh that knotted up at his advance, and she shuddered at the quiver of heat that sped its way to the very depths of her belly. Her legs jerked in response, and she made a sound in her throat that brought another chuckle from the man who bent over her.

"Ah, Lottie," he growled against her hair. "You're such a prize. How did I manage to leave you alone for so long?" His mouth brushed against her forehead, even as his fingers loosed the buttons that she had hastily managed to put into place on the bodice of her gown. She was torn between the heat of his breath on her skin and the calloused fingertips that skated across the fragile flesh of her breast.

It was a toss-up. Assailed by the kisses that he dropped with abandon against the slope of her jaw, his mouth open and damp against her cheek, she turned her head to capture his lips with her own, seeking the resumption of the game begun in the feather bed earlier. The invasion of her mouth had been a revelation a week ago, one she had yearned to resume. The waiting had increased the wanting, until she thought she would do anything to feel the probing of that agile tongue once more. Now it was hers to do with as she pleased, and she wound her own about it as she drew that plump member deep into the confines of her throat.

His hands were doing things she had not thought to allow, venturing across her breasts, squeezing and coaxing her flesh between his fingers, brushing over her in a continuous movement that only increased the coiling pressure within her body. Deep in her throat, she groaned, thinking to call a halt to the venturesome travels his hands were taking, but his teeth tugging at her lower lips brought her within reach of a new discovery.

His nipping at the plump flesh caught her attention. She almost flinched at the sensation, just as he began to suckle it tenderly, as if he would ease the bite. Again he chuckled, deep within the confines of his chest, and she answered the sound with a laugh of her own, as she recognized the playful aspect of this game he shared with her.

"You taste good, Lottie," he murmured into the darkness of her open mouth. "Almost as good here as . . ." His mouth strayed in a slowly deliberate manner to the widely spread bodice of her gown, and his final word was almost lost as he muttered it against the firm mound that lifted to meet his caress.

She arched again at the sensation that streaked through her, at the hot yearning that turned her into his seeking mouth, and she was stunned by the low cry that burst from her throat as his hands formed her body against his. Long, lean, and hardened by the desire that tautened his flesh into a driving force, he absorbed the softness of her, molding her against himself, his hands sliding to cup the fullness of her bottom. He drew her with infinite strength, holding her against the flesh that yearned to join their bodies, and his hands began the journey that would end with his goal accomplished.

Her gown was lifted, and for just a moment, he released her from his embrace, only long enough to swoop the soft muslin over her head and toss it to one side. The chill of night air sent her seeking his warmth, and he smiled into the darkness as the chill aided his cause.

Then she was swept away once more, engulfed by the tender wooing of his hands, his mouth, and the covering warmth of his body as he leaned to enclose her in his full embrace. She jerked once as his hand touched her thigh, and his whispering murmur persuaded her to submit to his venturing fingers. The struggle within her was brief. The years of restraint, the memory of admonitions meant to keep her safe and her purity intact, had done their job well. But the man who held her in the darkness had won her heart. And Lottie knew in a moment of truth, there in the dim confines of her bower, that John Tillman held her happiness within his powerful hands.

She writhed beneath his touch, crying his name with abandon as he brought her shivering pleasure that found her sobbing her response.

She urged his possession unknowingly, shifting until she felt the weight of him resting against her, and then spiraling into a paroxysm of joy as his body claimed her in a joining that was pain and pleasure combined. The tight knot within her eased, the waves of intense, shivering fulfillment overwhelming her with a magnificence she could not have imagined.

"John . . ." Her whisper was a gift in his ear. A wondering, fragile response that told him all that he needed to know. She shifted beneath him and he lifted himself on his elbows, but the hay gave him no firm surface to lean against and his endeavor was in vain.

"I'm too heavy for you, sweetheart," he said softly, satisfaction coloring the words as he smiled down at her with a strange, new emotion churning within him. He'd found an elemental pride in the taking of his bride, a sense of worship as he'd recognized the purity of her responses, and with the greatest care he could manage, he'd claimed her innocence. In an act as old as time, but as fresh as tomorrow, he'd given his bride the best he had to offer, the gift of himself. And in the giving, he had received. For the woman who searched his face in the shadows of the loft wore a look of shining splendor about her that stunned him with its glory.

"You're beautiful, Lottie," he breathed. And realized that the words were true. The plain, little orphan who had entered his life only weeks ago, had been transformed by the power of their coming together into a glowing creature whose face was radiant, and whose golden hair lay about her in splendor, even now tempting him with the waves and crinkly curls that surrounded her.

"I'm not beautiful, John," she said, denying his claim in a soft, little voice that sighed on the words, as if she wished fervently that they were true. "But I'm glad you think so," she admitted after a moment, her fingers rising to brush against the firm line of his jaw, and then sliding to bury themselves with possessive strength into the curls at the back of his head.

"You're my wife, Lottie, he said with a pride of ownership that brought new meaning to the word.

"I didn't know . . ." she ventured carefully. "No one ever told me about . . ." She gave up the attempt as he leaned to kiss her, his mouth smacking with satisfactory emphasis against her own, stopping her halting words.

"I knew you were on shaky ground, sweetheart," he said with amusement. "We'd never have made it in the house, with those young'uns overhead. Will you forgive me for scootin' you out of there and bedding you in the haymow?"

Ummm . . ." Her murmur was the answer he sought as she accepted his teasing words of apology. "But I'm getting a little chilly, John. Can we pull the quilt over us a bit?" she asked as she curled against him.

"I thought you were pretty well covered already, honey," he said with an indignant growl. "I'm the one exposed to the cold air, here." His arm reached to flip the edge of the coverlet over himself, and he tugged it across his back, Lottie lending a hand to pull it into place. In a quick motion, he rolled to the side, enclosing her in the cocoon he had formed. He eased her head to rest at the bend of his shoulder, and then his hand lifted and tugged her into place, until she was wrapped about him to his satisfaction.

"Now . . ." he whispered against her ear with a note of promise. "I have something else to show you."

The sun had never shone so brightly, Lottie decided as she climbed into the buggy. John's hands at her waist were warm, his smile radiant, as she turned to meet his gaze. The morning chill was fading, the frost on the ground melting into damp splotches against the dusty yard, as the children sought the warmth of a lap robe in the narrow confines of the seat behind her.

Lottie tugged the shawl about her closely, her fingers tangling in the fine yarn as she admired the crocheted pattern. A gift from Genevieve, pressed into her hands right after the wedding ceremony, it was the finest piece of handwork she had ever seen. And although the day promised warmth, the early hour should have prompted her to don her heavy coat. But Lottie could not bear to drape the new dress with such a dingy cover, so had chosen to wear the shawl.

John climbed in beside her and wrapped a long arm about her shoulders, tugging her closer, sharing his warmth, aware of her decision to be as fashionable as possible this morning. She'd had quite a morning, he decided with a grin. What with waking late—after an early morning jaunt back from the barn—she'd been faced with two children, hungry and wide-eyed at the sight of Lottie and their uncle snuggled together in the feather bed. He'd taken pity on her, all rosy-cheeked and flustered, sliding into his pants and heading for the barn, with Thomas in tow.

By the time the milking was done and the chickens fed, she'd recovered enough to have breakfast ready and herself and Sissy dressed for Sunday morning. Sissy had saved the day, chattering like a magpie and skipping about the cabin as if her exuberance could not be contained. Even walking to the buggy had been an occasion for the child as she grasped the hands of the two adults that made up her world.

"John."

"Hmmm?" He turned to her, and for the first time this morning, she allowed herself to meet his gaze.

"Will everyone know?" she asked meekly.

He looked blank, his forehead finally creasing into a frown as he considered her question. "Know what, Lottie? That we got married?"

She shook her head, and her eyes squeezed shut for a moment as she thought of words that would describe what she meant. "No . . . not that," she said shaking her head once more. "Will they know what we *did?*" It was a quiet little murmur that he had to bend his head to hear, and the hearing of it touched him with an emotion he hesitated to name.

He cleared his throat and stilled the laughter that bubbled within him, knowing that Lottie would be embarrassed by his humor. "All married folks do what we did, Lottie," he said finally in a low whisper that he spoke beneath the brim of her hat, as close to her ear as he could get.

"They *do?*" she squeaked in surprise.

His nod was solemn, but his eyes twinkled, giving away the merriment that hovered just beneath the surface. "Honestly, they do," he vowed firmly.

She settled back on the seat, her mind working furiously, attempting to fit the act of marriage that John had initiated in the haymow, into the lives of the staid and sedate couples who made up the congregation of the Methodist church. It just couldn't be so, she decided after a few minutes of pondering. It had been so intimate, this thing they had done together. This act of loving could not be so commonplace, surely.

But, if it were so, all of those people would certainly be aware of what had transpired, and that thought almost prompted her to suggest that they turn the buggy about and head for home.

"It's all right, Lottie," he assured her quietly. "No one will pay any attention to you."

But he was wrong, and after the first few minutes, she was painfully aware that if not the whole town, at least half of it was waiting expectantly to welcome the bridal couple. The bell on the Baptist church was ringing as the buggy rolled by, and Lottie hoped fervently that the Methodists would be filing into their pews by the time the Tillmans rolled up in front of the small white church. It was not to be.

Scattered in small groups about the churchyard, the women waited expectantly for the newlyweds. Their husbands gathered near Henry Clawson's buckboard, as they exchanged bawdy remarks and slapped each other on the back with rowdy good humor. John groaned deep in his throat, as he recognized the ribbing that faced him.

Ignoring the bold, teasing looks that were aimed at him, he lifted Lottie from the buggy and, with a hand firmly about her elbow, he steered her in the direction of the church.

"John, you're lookin' mighty slick this morning," Harvey Slocum called out cheerfully as they passed within a few feet of him. "Kinda got a shine about you," he added slyly, and then nudged the man who stood next to him, and winked solemnly at his own humor.

"Mornin', Miz Tillman," said Mr. Sharp, whose black broadcloth suit and sober appearance were in direct contrast to the wide grin that split his face.

"Come on, Lottie," John muttered against her hat brim, stepping quickly to hurry her past the circle of men who were intent on making him the center of their jollity.

At the gate they were met by the spearhead of the flock of women, who had been poised for this moment. Mabel Sharp caught Lottie's free hand and tugged her forward.

"Come on, Lottie," she said briskly, slanting a glowering glance at John as she took charge of the new bride. With one last regal look at John's reluctant grin, she towed Lottie into the center of chattering women, where she was engulfed by the welcome of their congratulations.

"If we'd had more notice, we'd have made you a fine reception dinner, Lottie," said Abigail Dunstader as she loomed before her. Her generous bosom rose majestically, swathed in purple taffeta that matched the blossoms on her bonnet, and the ladies that gathered about her nodded their agreement. Mrs. Dunstader was a picture of elegance, to be sure, Lottie thought wistfully.

"I wouldn't have wanted anyone to go to any trouble," she said breathlessly. "As it was, Genevieve and her mama outdid themselves," she told them, with generous praise for the modest reception that had been put together on short notice.

"Well, we just think it's a fine thing that you did, taking on the raising of those two children and helping John out this way," Maude Clawson said bluntly, her homely face warmed by the rare smile that graced it.

Lottie turned to her, her brow wrinkled quizzically. "You're Mr. Clawson's wife," she said as her mind placed the woman she'd met so briefly on the night of her arrival.

"Your neighbor, to tell the truth," Maude said briefly as she backed off, blending into the clutch of women who hovered about.

Lottie's eyes searched for Genevieve, her store of conversation almost exhausted as the women took her measure. They reached admiring fingers to touch the lavender shawl she clutched with anxious fingers and commented on the dress she had sewn with careful stitches, and within minutes had drawn her into the center of their group.

Only the appearance of Stephen Bush on the steps of the little church brought the attention to an end, as he cleared his throat and, by dint of his majestic appearance alone, caught the attention of his flock of parishioners.

Like the parting of the Red Sea, the women moved to either side of her, and Lottie faced her erstwhile suitor. He smiled a welcome and his hand reached out to her, even as John escaped the horde of menfolk who had been burning his ears with bawdy advice and whispered conjectures about his virility. Red-faced and perspiring beneath the starched collar he wore, he hurried forward to clutch at Lottie's arm, heading her in the direction of the preacher.

"Come on," he grunted in her ear. "Let's get inside."

Only too happy to follow his lead, she trotted alongside him and smiled distractedly at Stephen, as he shook John's hand in hasty welcome.

The morning service passed in a blur of sidelong glances and fervent prayer. Hopeful that the welcoming committee would not reform outside the gate, Lottie tilted her chin skyward as the last word of the benediction rang out in the church. The organ boomed out the recessional, and Stephen Bush walked with firm step and determined smile down the aisle to the back door. Once he had passed, each pew became alive with movement as its occupants stood and stretched, their bodies weary of having been formed to the hard wooden seats favored by churchmen.

Too late for escape, she met the advancing group of women, who were eager to induct her into their ranks. Holding firmly to the strings of her reticule, she drew a deep breath, meant to give her a dose of badly needed courage. John cast her a look of resignation as he fled from the eager women who approached, and his eyes held a trace of amusement as he noted the faint pinkening of her cheeks.

"Chin up, Lottie," he whispered, bending low to lend his encouragement before he made a hasty retreat.

Only the sight of Genevieve in the rear guard gave Lottie the courage she sought, and she smiled her brightest as she faced the well-meaning women.

"The missionary women will be having a quilting bee next week, Lottie," Abigail Dunstader announced, as she looked with a critical eye at the young woman who faced her. "From the looks of that dress, you'll do real well on the fine stitching."

They were words of approval, and Lottie recognized them as such. She made noises of disparagement as she smoothed the skirt of her dress, careful not to accept the compliment too readily. Miss Aggie always said that pride goeth before a fall, and Lottie felt herself teetering on the brink as it was. It was best not to get bigheaded over generous words of praise. It was enough that she had allowed John's pretty speech this morning to fill her with a shimmering delight.

"You sure look like a spring bouquet in that dress, Lottie," he'd said, as he worked at buttoning his white shirt. She'd turned quickly to face him and his eyes had been warm and filled with promise. "You sew real well," he'd whispered, as his gaze ran hotly over the slender body within the daintily flowered fabric. "I'll be proud of you, looking so pretty."

Genevieve stepped closer as Mrs. Dunstader moved past. Her hand rested on Lottie's arm and she whispered her encouragement.

"They like you," she said gleefully. "I knew they would."

Lottie lifted grateful eyes. "You're a good friend, Genevieve," she said with a distinct lump in her throat.

"I'll be out one day this week to visit," the other girl promised, as she squeezed Lottie's hand.

The group fluttered about, eyes intent as they gauged Lottie's appearance. Having given her the welcome due a new bride, they parted to allow her passage to the door.

"Doesn't seem any the worse for wear," Maude Clawson allowed in an undertone that met with side long glances and faint, snickering noises.

Abigail sniffed disparagingly, as if she reserved judgment. "The Tillman boys always appeared to be mannerly," she said briefly. "But then, men are men the world over." And on that profound statement, the group dissolved and followed Lottie out the door.

She made her way down the steps, nodding with a sense of reserve at Stephen as he waited to greet the female members of his flock, and hastened to where John waited by the gate. His face was drawn into lines of grave concern as she approached, and she felt a pang of apprehension deep within her chest at his demeanor.

"What is it, John?" she asked uncertainly.

"Man from the telegraph office just brought me a message," he said, turning her to where the buggy was tied beneath the tree.

She felt the grip of his hand against her elbow as they walked, his fingers clutching at her flesh in a silent message. *Hurry* . . . his touch carried the thought as if his mouth had spoken the word, and she hastened to match his step. He lifted her, placed her on the seat, and tucked her skirt inside, his hand gripping her ankle through the fine leather of her shoe in a silent message of reassurance within the confines of the buggy.

The children clambered in the other side, and then John swung easily into place, lifting the reins as he turned the horse toward the road that led out of town.

"John?" She'd waited for several minutes, her smile tight as she waved at Genevieve, then concentrated on settling herself for the ride home. Her impetuous nature would no longer be reined, and she spoke his name, nudging him with a hand against his forearm as she leaned closer.

"Their grandparents are coming," he said beneath his breath, so softly she strained to hear the words.

"When?" she asked on an indrawn breath.

He glanced over his shoulder at the two children, who were oblivious to the tension that surrounded them.

"This week, probably by Wednesday. The telegram said by first available conveyance."

"The stage," she said, remembering the long, dusty ride from St. Louis that had brought her to this place.

John nodded glumly and flicked the reins over the back of Daisy, who obliged by picking up her dainty hooves more quickly.

"I don't know how we stand. Legally, I mean," he said, a frown etching his brow into lines that brought a pang to Lottie's heart.

"Surely they won't take them away from you, John! You're their uncle." Her voice rang with conviction, and only his quick hushing sound at her vehement protest kept her sitting down. She wanted to fly in the face of fate, railing and ranting against the unfairness of it all.

"We'll have to wait and see," he said with patient resignation.

"What did the telegram say?" Surprised at her own bravery, Lottie made the demand.

"We are arriving to assume custody of Sarah's children by first available conveyance."

The words hung between them. Lottie slid a little closer to the man who had done all he could to keep those words from becoming fact.

"Do they know you're married? Did they get your letter?" she asked.

He lifted his shoulders in a gesture of futility and shook his head. "I don't know. Seems like it would have had time to get there inside of a week. Maybe that's why they decided to come so quick . . . they don't want me to get too cozy with the kids here." He sighed deeply. "They always gave Sarah a hard time about the schooling out here. Told her that their grandchildren deserved better than Mill Creek could offer."

"Shouldn't Thomas be in school this year?" Lottie asked.

John shook his head again. "James had decided to wait till next year, when he's eight. He'll have to ride a horse in every day. Sarah was going to teach him his letters this fall . . ." His shrug was eloquent. Thomas's schooling would be the main issue in this struggle, that was for sure.

"I could do that," Lottie proposed slowly, thinking of the books that lay in the bottom of one of her boxes, still unpacked. "Miss Aggie let me have the books I learned from. I brought them with me," she said, mentally going over the volumes that had been her mainstay through the years.

"You're not a teacher, Lottie," he answered tightly.

"Neither was Sarah, was she?" she asked pertly, and was rewarded by a glare from beneath his lowered brows.

"She was their mother," he said briefly, as if that were the final word. If Sarah had said she would teach Thomas his letters and numbers, she could do it, he thought with a sense of righteous indignation. His image of Sarah had faded through the past weeks, but now he remembered her bright intelligence with a sense of wistfulness. She'd been such a lady, her gentility so apparent in this place, where rough behavior and a disregard for the finer things were commonplace.

Sarah's afternoon tea had been the object of much teasing by both the brothers. Her dainty insistence on manners had resulted in dinnertime lectures more than once. In looking back, John sensed that she had been too fine, too fragile for the hard life of a homesteader's wife.

"Sarah was educated," he said, as if that phrase would suffice as an explanation.

"So am I," Lottie replied carefully, aware that John was defending another woman, making her feel chilled and abandoned.

His quick glance at her was questioning. "How's that?" he asked.

"I went to school every day," she said primly. "Miss Aggie believed that women needed as much education as they could get. I have a diploma from New Hope, from the high school."

"Sarah went to St. Louis Academy for Young Ladies," he said, his words clipped and harsh.

"Well, Sarah's not here . . . and I am," Lottie replied with spirit. "I guess you'll have to do with what you've got, Mr. Tillman."

"Have at it, Mrs. Tillman," he answered gruffly, ashamed suddenly that he had slighted her abilities in favor of Sarah's. "But bear in mind that you've only got a few days to work on it. Don't know what you can accomplish by mid-week."

"Well," she said firmly. "I certainly can't start any sooner, can I? We'll get out my books after dinner and Thomas can begin."

A hopeful voice from behind them reminded her of their audience, as Sissy leaned forward. "Can I look at your books, Miss Lottie?" she asked.

"They heard us," Lottie whispered.

His glance was disbelieving. "Well, of course they did, once you hollered at me. What did you expect?"

"I didn't holler," she said, denying his accusation. "I

only spoke loudly. Besides, they'll know all about it in a couple of days anyway."

"Yeah, you're right about that," he agreed.

"Can I, Miss Lottie?" Sissy asked again, this time with a hint of impatience.

"Might as well start you early," Lottie said firmly. "Women need all the help they can get."

"Am I going to school?" Thomas asked, leaning forward to join the conversation.

"Lottie will be teaching you at home for a while," his uncle said, deciding to ignore Lottie's last provocative statement. He looked at her, a sidelong glance that took in the challenge she offered. His mouth twisted in a grin and his spirits lifted as he considered the woman who sat by his side. She was a formidable opponent, he realized. Spunky and quick to rise to the occasion.

"I'm glad you're on my side, Mrs. Tillman," he said as he leaned to press his mouth against her cheek. His nostrils filled with the scent of her as he inhaled, and he offered another caress, unwilling to leave the softness of her finely pored flesh.

"John!" Her whisper was hushed and her mouth was open, as she twisted to protest his forward behavior. Too late, she realized her error as her mouth slid beneath his. And then she was lost in the warmth of his kiss. For just a moment, she savored the damp flavor of his mouth, and then she jerked back, one hand settling her hat more firmly on her head, the other covering her traitorous mouth that had so willingly accepted his kiss.

"Lottie!" he whispered back, mocking her disapproval. Eyes twinkling, lips still shiny from the caress he had stolen, he faced her brazenly. "We'll continue this later," he drawled as his gaze dropped to her mouth. "That's a promise, Mrs. Tillman," he said with firm intent.

Twelve

"The circuit judge won't be back in Mill Creek for two weeks, and Harley Garrison's gone back East for his sister's wedding," John announced with gloomy finality. His trip to town had been fruitless, with the only lawyer Mill Creek boasted away on a trip, and court not in session till the end of November.

"Who did you talk to?" Lottie asked, bringing a cup of hot coffee to the table where he sat.

He closed his eyes and his shoulders slumped, giving him a strangely vulnerable look. "The sheriff. He wasn't much help. Said that if the Shermans have a legal paper from St. Louis, he'll have to enforce it here."

"Are my grandfather and grandmother coming?" Thomas asked from his seat on the other side of the table.

The time for subterfuge was over and John knew it. "Yes," he answered simply, looking with quiet acknowledgement at the boy.

"What will they do?" asked Thomas, his voice fearful, but his head held high as he faced the unknown with youthful bravery.

John cleared his throat and glanced at Lottie, as if he sought comfort. "They want to take you and your sister back to St. Louis with them, son," he said finally.

"They think your mother would have wanted it that way."

Thomas shook his head slowly. "I don't want to do that, Uncle John," he said with a touch of anger.

"Well, I'm not too taken with the idea myself," John replied. "I think your mother made the choice to live here and raise you children here. Seems like that should be the final word on the subject. But we have to wait and see."

Thomas shoved the slate he had been writing on across the table with a violent push, almost upsetting the spoon container. Only Lottie's quick interference halted the forward motion as she picked it up, rescuing the glass jar, top-heavy with spoons, that sat next to the covered butter dish. She made a small noise, fussing at herself as her fingers smudged Thomas's letters. They had marched with precise alignment across the black slate, painfully straight and painstakingly rounded in his careful printing.

"Look how well he's done in only three days, John," she said as she offered the boy's work for inspection.

"He's a bright boy," John conceded with a glance at the practice letters Thomas had been working on so industriously.

"If I write them one more time, can I stop and help Uncle John now?" Thomas asked hopefully, momentarily distracted from the anger that had seized him.

Lottie shook her head. "You need to do your numbers," she said firmly. "And I want you to write the three words you learned yesterday over again."

"I still don't see how those squiggly lines make words, Miss Lottie," said Sissy, twining herself against her uncle's side, her arm draped with familiar ease over his shoulder.

Thomas cast a disparaging glance at his little sister. "You're too young to understand reading and writing yet, Sissy," he announced with dignity.

"Am not," she argued, her lower lip outthrust.

"She'll catch on real quick," Lottie put in, anxious to call a halt to the argument before it began in earnest. "Here, Sissy," she offered. "Come and use this paper to write on." From under the cupboard where she had carefully stashed it, Lottie unfolded a piece of the brown paper that Genevieve had wrapped her purchases in at the store. Her fingers smoothed the creases, as she laid it flat on the surface of the table.

"Fetch a pencil from my box, Sissy," she said brightly. "I'll write some letters for you to copy."

The little girl scampered across the floor, eager to prove her ability, and searched carefully in the box of treasures that Lottie had shown them. There among the dozen or so books she'd brought with her, were pencils, gum erasers, and white lengths of chalk to be used on the slate Thomas was using. Clutching the one she had chosen, Sissy returned to the table where Lottie had arranged her work space.

"Get on your knees, Sissy, so you can see what you're doing," she instructed her. One index finger traced the three letters she had written in large, block form, as Lottie showed the child the path her pencil should take. "Like this, sweetie," she said against the girl's ear, as she bent over the golden head. Her hand covered Sissy's and she painstakingly formed the first three letters of the alphabet, as Sissy struggled to control the wayward pencil.

"My lines aren't as good as yours," she complained, tilting her head to one side as she compared their efforts.

"Just practice," Lottie advised her, "and you'll be caught up to your brother in no time." She winked and wrinkled her nose at Thomas, who had looked up in indignant surprise at the remark, and he subsided gracefully, pleased to be included in the small exaggeration.

John had risen and was at the fireplace, one hand resting against the mantelpiece, the other holding his coffee cup as he gazed with anxious eyes into the blaze. Lottie watched as he drank from the cup and then deposited it on the mantel, his hand returning to shove deeply into his pocket. She moved quietly to where he stood, her own hands yearning to reach for him, restrained only by the rules of behavior she had been imbued with since childhood.

"Keep your hands to yourself, child." Miss Aggie had not been an advocate of touching, for the mere sake of human need. Babies were diapered and held while they ate. Children were dressed until they were able to tend to themselves. Young girls were instructed to remain inviolate, untouched, virginal. To what end was not explained . . . but the basic premise had been imprinted with repetition. And for Lottie, it had been a tough row to hoe. She had cuddled babies unashamedly, hugged little girls with words of affection and praise for their accomplishments and now, watching John in his moment of soul-searching, she felt the need to extend her hand in comfort.

Silently, she approached him. Hesitantly, she laid her hand against his arm and leaned with only a trace of pressure against his side, allowing her head to touch the solid strength of his shoulder, rubbing her cheek against the rough fabric of his shirt.

"John?" Her whisper was low and questioning, and he responded without hesitation, turning to her with a groan that expressed his need. His arms enclosed her, and he drew her against himself, aligning her slender body against his own, taking comfort from the willingness with which she came.

"I can't give them up, Lottie. It would be like turning my back on James, like admitting that his years here were wasted." He rested his cheek against the top of her head and spoke in an undertone, "He wanted to leave something to his children. He wanted to build a life for them *here.*"

"Can you fight them?" she asked, sliding her arms about his waist, lending him silent comfort in the only way she knew.

He shook his head and she felt the movement. "No . . . that's just it," he said roughly. "Without a lawyer and no judge in town, I can't do much but wait till they arrive and see what legal action they've taken."

"Today's Wednesday," she reminded him quietly. "If they left when they said, they should be on the afternoon stage."

His arms tightened about her in silent reply, and then with a final tightening of his embrace, he released her and dropped a kiss against her forehead.

"I've got to move the rest of my stock today, Lottie," he said as he headed for the door. "I heard of a settler who's looking for a place to winter, and I'm going to offer him my cabin to stay in. But I need to bring the rest of my horses here, now that the stalls are ready for them. It'll take me a couple of days to add on to the corral, but once I get my mares in the barn, I can work with them here."

"Am I going to help you, Uncle John?" asked Thomas, from the table where he had been watching the quiet conversation. "I'm done with my printing, Miss Lottie," he said with barely concealed eagerness.

Suddenly the need to keep their daily lives unblemished by concern for the future took second place in Lottie's mind, and only the need for companionship between the boy and his uncle was important today.

"Go along with you, Thomas," she said as she took his slate from the table and patted his shoulder with reassurance. "John needs your help."

"We're gonna make butter today," Sissy announced importantly, aligning herself with Lottie as she lifted her head from the letters she had been carefully drawing on the paper.

"We'll be back for dinner at noontime," John said as he shrugged into his coat and pulled his hat into place. His eyes met Lottie's, and then slid in careful surveillance down her form, only to make the return trip with slow precision as he allowed his gaze to rest for a moment on the fullness of her breasts. His eyes were tender as they lifted once more to her face and took note of the pink stains that rode her cheekbones.

"Got a kiss for me, sweetheart?" he asked as he held out his hands to her.

She made her way to him on legs that had suddenly refused to operate in their usual fashion. His inspection of her person had brought back in detail the events of the night before, when he'd taken her once more to the hayloft and had conducted just such a survey by the muted light of the lantern down below. She'd been indignant at first, and then acquiescent as his knowing touches had coaxed her to bend to his will, finally surrendering to his hot kisses and fervent caresses with all the passion her youthful body knew to offer.

The memory was in the kiss she offered him now,

and the warmth of his response told her that his own thoughts were riding tandem with hers. He grasped her arms and held her against himself, lifting her from the floor for a moment as he settled her against his chest, his head bending to nuzzle against the warmth of her throat. His breath was hot against her flesh, and she shivered with a delightful spasm of need, her newly awakened body aware of his unspoken message.

Then he was gone, taking Thomas with him and leaving her with daily tasks that she was thankful for, knowing they would provide her with enough occupation to keep her mind off the inevitable confrontation that was to come.

Twilight had muted the lines of the barn and outbuildings, when Lottie heard the nickering of horses in the yard. She'd spent anxious minutes looking out the window toward the road, watching for a conveyance to approach, and now it seemed she'd missed the arrival of their expected visitors.

Her feet flew across the floor as she headed for the door, hoping to see John's familiar figure. She drew in a sigh of relief as her eyes caught sight of him, heading from the barn to the surrey that was drawn by a team of horses from the livery stable in town. She watched as he assisted one of the occupants down, his hand reaching to grasp the woman's arm.

She was tall, generous in girth, and her full skirts were voluminous about her as she headed for the cabin with John's courteous escort. Behind them came the tall, spare figure of a man, leading the team to the hitching post that was near the garden gate.

"Lottie." John spoke her name firmly, and his eyes

met hers with a silent message as the light from the cabin enveloped him and the woman he assisted up the steps. They entered the door, and John nodded at the darkly garbed figure.

"This is Mrs. Sherman, Lottie," he said with gentle demeanor. "The children's grandmother." Behind him stood the stooped figure of the man who had followed them to the house, and John turned to include him in the introduction.

"This is Gentry Sherman."

Lottie's insides were churning with fearful pangs. They threatened to reduce her to a trembling creature who would shame John, and so she straightened her posture, determined that he not be ashamed of her. Catching his eye, she smiled grimly, aware of the quivering of her lips as she turned to the woman who watched her intently.

"I'm Lottie Tillman," she said with as firm a voice as she could manage. "I'm sure you're tired from your journey, Mrs. Sherman. Won't you come have a seat?"

It had been done. She'd spoken and her voice had not failed her. With sweeping relief, she drew a deep breath and hurried to the hearth, where she brushed her hand over the back of one of the chairs that waited invitingly. The woman followed her, eyes flitting about the simple home as if she were taking stock of its contents.

"Thank you," she said simply, as she sat gingerly on the seat of the sturdy armchair. The cushion Sarah had made to provide comfort for her weary husband at day's end welcomed the traveler, and she settled herself more comfortably in its depth.

"May I get you something to eat?" Lottie asked. "We had potato soup and fresh corn bread for supper, and there's a good bit left. I made plenty, in case you hadn't eaten," she explained, aware of the concentrated scrutiny of the visitors.

Gentry Sherman moved into the house from his stance in the doorway, and John closed the heavy door behind him. "We don't want to put you to any trouble, Mrs. Tillman," Sarah's father said kindly, as his gaze met that of his wife's, tacitly seeking her wishes.

Lottie spoke hastily. "Oh, it's no trouble at all. I'll just get out some bowls and plates," she said, relieved that she had busy work to do. "Come help me, Sissy," she said quickly, her gaze lifting to where the little girl peered over the edge of the loft. Both children had fled to their sanctuary and now watched with anxious eyes as the four adults shifted positions in the room below.

"Yes, Miss Lottie," the child murmured obediently, moving to the ladder to climb down carefully, mindful of her skirt being smoothed down over her legs.

All eyes were on her as she reached the floor and turned to face the elder couple. Her head bobbed in greeting as she scurried past them to where the dishes were stored in the cupboard.

"Sissy," John said firmly, and waited for her response.

"Yes sir," she answered immediately, turning to face him with a fearful, wide-eyed look.

"You need to say hello to your grandparents," he reminded her gently. And then looked up into the loft to where Thomas watched from the shadows. "You, too, Thomas. Come on down," he instructed firmly.

The boy swung easily onto the ladder, and his feet made short work of the rungs, bringing him into the midst of the group in seconds. He bowed his head in greeting, and his words were spoken in a hurried, but distinct voice.

"Grandmother . . . Grandfather . . . I'm pleased to meet you," he said with breathless obedience.

"Me, too," Sissy whispered, her eyes flitting from one to the other of the grandparents she had never seen.

"Do you think you can give me a hug?" Mrs. Sherman asked, her eyes intent on the little girl.

"Yes ma'am," Sissy said, looking to Lottie for direction as she approached the woman.

Lottie nodded firmly and glanced at Thomas, her hand motioning him to approach in Sissy's wake.

Over the curly head of her granddaughter, Elizabeth Sherman's face underwent a transformation, its stern lines melting into a painful grimace, as if she felt a clutching ache deep within her being. Her eyes filled with tears, and she blinked quickly, lest they fall. Her hands touched the child before her, holding her from herself, the better to view the soft, almost ethereal features of her granddaughter.

"You're a lovely little girl," she managed finally, as she stroked the side of Sissy's face with trembling fingers. Her eyes sought those of her husband. "She resembles Sarah, doesn't she?"

He nodded in response and cleared his throat, his eyes shiny in the lamplight. "Thomas has the look of our Henry about him," he said gently, looking to his wife for confirmation.

She nodded as her attention shifted to the boy who watched silently "Yes . . . he's fairer than Henry, but the features are much alike," she agreed.

"Please, won't you come to the table and have a bite to eat," Lottie asked, more secure now that she had everyday tasks to set her hand to. "I've kept the soup hot on the back of the stove, and the coffee is fresh."

"I'd be pleased," said Mrs. Sherman, standing and

making her way to the table. John hurried to hold her chair and received a look of appreciation from Lottie for his courtesy. By the time she was ready to pour the coffee into their cups, John had managed to seat everyone around the table, Sissy on his knee for lack of chairs, and Thomas on a backless stool he had brought from the hearth.

The soup was tasty, with dried peas and chunks of carrot mixed with the potatoes Lottie had brought from the root cellar. She'd used the last of the ham for soup stock, and the blend was a savory mixture, hearty and thick. The bowl of corn bread, wrapped in a towel, was still warm, having been kept atop the stove, and Lottie uncovered the butter dish which held Sissy's prized accomplishment.

"I helped make the butter today," the child announced from the safety of her uncle's lap, and then flushed as all eyes focused on her.

"I'm sure you're a big help to Lottie," her grandmother said, as she wiped her mouth carefully with her white hanky.

"Do we have napkins, Lottie?" John asked quietly, and was pierced by the stricken look she wore.

"Oh, yes," she said hastily, rising abruptly to correct her lapse. She opened the drawer in the cupboard and brought out two heavy linen napkins, unused since her arrival. Handing them to the visitors, she apologized profusely.

"I'm sorry, I wasn't thinking."

"Quite all right," Mr. Sherman said, accepting the cloth and laying it carefully across his lap. His eyes were warm on the children, and he ate sparingly, his attention caught up in their every movement.

"Will you spend the night?" John asked, shifting Sissy to his other knee and sitting up straighter in his chair.

"We don't like to put you out," Mr. Sherman said slowly with a glance at his wife. "It's a ways back to town though, and if it wouldn't be too much trouble . . ." His gaze moved from the large bed beneath the loft, to the dark corners overhead in the shadowed area where the children had their beds.

"Lottie and I would be glad to let you have our bed," John offered quickly.

"Where will you sleep?" Mrs. Sherman asked quickly, as she glanced at Lottie.

A flush crept up her cheeks as Lottie's eyes flew to John. "We can go out to the hayloft, can't we, John?" she ventured timidly, the hours spent there within the past week still vibrant memories in her mind.

His nod was vigorous. "Certainly. We want you to stay," he affirmed with assurance.

"It will only be for a night," Elizabeth Sherman said quietly. "We have a room in the hotel for tomorrow night, and the stage for St. Louis leaves early on Friday morning."

The words fell with finality into the midst of the group, and Lottie stood abruptly, her eyes wide with confusion as the reality of the situation struck her. They'd really be leaving. The children she had come to love so dearly over the past weeks would be gone from here within a day. Her mouth quivered and she turned her back, making her way to the sink, where she fussed with the soup kettle, pouring the remnants into a bowl to save for tomorrow. She covered it with a cloth and set it on the cupboard shelf, her movements precise and sure.

Then, with uplifted chin and a determined smile on

her lips, she turned back to the silent group. "We'd best be getting these children to bed," she said brightly. At Thomas's frown, she shook her head. "Your Uncle John has things to talk over with your grandfather, Thomas. You and Sissy need to wash up and find your nightclothes."

He nodded reluctantly and stood, looking about himself with uncertainty. "Should I help with chores first?" he asked.

"I just have to do the milking and feed the horses," John said, shaking his head. "Maybe Thomas could show his grandmother the letters he's been working on this week, before he heads for bed," he suggested to Lottie. He nodded at Thomas and was rewarded by the boy's smile of thanks. "Perhaps Mr. Sherman would like to come to the barn with me, while I milk," John proposed, certain of the response he would get.

"Yes, certainly," Gentry Sherman agreed, heading for the door without hesitation. "I'm not much at milking, but I can help with the horses," he offered.

"They have a judge's signature," John said, his voice a rumble beneath her ear.

Lottie lay, her face pressed against his chest, her arm about his waist, and her feet warming against his. "I suspected as much," she whispered, and knew he heard her acceptance of the situation when he squeezed his arms tightly about her.

The moon was full, and John had opened the small door in the loft, allowing its glow to chase the darkness from their haven. The temperature had dropped since early evening, and already heavy clouds had begun to hang low on the horizon.

"Looks like snow coming," John said as he pulled the quilts over them more securely. "I'll have to shut that door before long."

"Why'd you open it?" Her voice was muffled against the flannel nightshirt he'd pulled on against the cold air.

His mouth sought hers, and he grasped the back of her hair to aid in his pursuit, tugging her head gently into position for his tender assault.

"I wanted to see you better, sweetheart," he admitted as he found her lips with his.

"See me?" she asked against the pressure of his mouth, greatly aiding him in his pursuit of her plush lower lip. He quickly and deftly captured it, holding it carefully between his teeth and tasting it with the tip of his tongue. Then, in a bold move that sent hot flames churning within her depths, he surrounded her lips with his own, and set out on an expedition that left no nook or cranny unexplored.

She sensed a desire he'd only hinted at in their previous encounters, a strength that had been controlled on those other nights in this place. He held her with a desperate embrace that brought to life a like need within her, and she clung to him unashamedly, welcoming the foray he had set about with such passionate skill.

He lifted his head, sucking in great breaths of air, and one big hand brushed at her cheek, where a lock of golden hair feathered across in disarray. "I planned on getting a better look at the woman I've been making love to for the past four nights," he said bluntly. "But it's gotten colder than a witch's tittie out there, and I'm gonna settle for blind man's bluff under the covers."

"John!" Lottie sat bolt upright and spat the word at

him in horror. "What a terrible thing to say," she exclaimed primly.

His grin shone in the moonlight, belying the sadness that had brought frown lines to his brow and dimmed the blue brilliance of his eyes for three days. He reached up and snagged her within his arms, drawing her slowly and inexorably to himself, as he growled words of promise.

"You'll probably hear me say worse before the night's over, sweetheart," he muttered in her ear, holding her captive and drawing the quilts over her as he spoke. "I might even tell you how pretty these . . ."

His words were lost in the folds of her gown, as he buried his face against the softness of her breasts, and she shivered with excitement, as his hot breath warmed her through the fabric. She squirmed against him, unerringly guiding him to where she would have him place his mouth, and he sighed his content, as he obliged her silent request. His fingers moved with precision, one-handedly unbuttoning the line of smooth, white buttons that marched up the front of her gown, and with a sense of rare pleasure, he opened it wide to better accommodate his venturing mouth.

"Are you *sure* all married people do this?" she asked in a wispy, little voice that failed to hide her pleasure in his caresses.

He laughed, a low, husky sound that washed over her, bringing a new set of goose bumps to cover her flesh, as she responded to his praise. "Those that don't are downright foolish, sweet," he whispered. " 'Course, not all women are as well endowed or as beautiful as you. I suspect that might make a difference."

Lifting his head, he looked at her with glittering eyes, the terrible sadness held at bay for a time, by the joy he found in her youthful body. "You wouldn't turn me away, would you?" he asked softly, his fingers tender as they traced the roundness of her breasts and stroked the fragile flesh that peaked at his touch.

She shook her head slowly, unable to speak for the pleasure that his nimble fingers brought her. Again she shivered, and again he repeated the caress, pleased at her response.

"I need you tonight, Lottie." Even as he spoke, his hands courted her, coaxing her need to rise to his touch, her desire to surface, as he urged her woman's flesh to arousal. He inhaled her scent and wondered at the sweetness of it, the clean woman-smell that teased him and beguiled his senses. Cleverly, he led her, carefully, he wooed her. With kisses that roused her body to new heights, and caresses that brought her to new levels of pleasure, he satisfied the coiling urgency that drove her to seek his touch. His breath caught as he heard the sounds of her pleasure, and a rush of emotion he could not name suffused his inner heart of hearts. She's given me more satisfaction than I've ever known, he thought with a sense of wonder. And with renewed desire, spurred by her passion, he set aside his own churning needs.

His hands became more tender, his mouth a gentle balm against her skin, as he wooed her once more, careful of the sensitive flesh he explored with fingers and lips. She moaned deep in her throat, and his heart lifted with the simple joy of pleasing her. But the tightened flesh of his loins could no longer be ignored, throbbing with the need for fulfillment.

"Take me, Lottie," he whispered against her ear, pleading with her, begging for her warmth. And with

hands that explored his male flesh in awe and the newness of discovery, she attempted to do his bidding.

He lifted over her, covering her with the lean strength
of his body, and she received him joyfully, giving him
the welcome he sought, twining herself about him, her
softness melding into the hard, driving passion he offered her. And then in the makeshift bed that held
them, burrowed deeply into the mound of hay that
cushioned their bodies, they came together in a primitive blending of male and female, of man and wife, that
was more than John had ever suspected could be his
fortune to enjoy.

For a time they lay quietly, awaiting the slowing of
their heartbeats, the easing of their harsh breathing.
With a groan of fulfillment, John left her warmth and
tugged her gown down about her legs, wrapping her in
the soft muslin. He tucked her carefully beneath the
quilt and rose, allowing his own nightshirt to fall into
place, covering his loins and the hard muscles of his
legs from her sight. He made his way to the window
that was still open to the night air and, with ease, he
swung it shut, closing it with the simple chunk of wood
that swiveled on a nail.

Without the glow of the moon, he made his way back
to where she lay and crawled into the bed he had made
for them atop the pile of hay. She welcomed him, holding the quilts up for him to lie beside her. Gently, with
the familiarity of a lover, he eased their bodies together,
curling about her back, his hand going unerringly to
curve about her breast.

"Clouds are hanging pretty low in the west," he muttered in her ear. "I'll warrant we get snow by tomorrow
morning."

She hesitated, and then said the words that hovered in her mind. "Will it hold the Shermans up any?"

He shook his head. "No, shouldn't be much of a storm, this early in the year." His sigh shuddered against her back. "They'll be leaving come afternoon, Lottie. I've about made up my mind that I can't do anything about it for now. When Harley Garrison gets back to town, I'll go see him and get his mind on the matter."

"I don't want them to go," she whispered sadly into the darkness. "They're the first family I've ever had, John." She twisted her head to look at him over her shoulder. "It makes my heart hurt to think about it."

He groaned against her cheek, and his mouth pressed a kiss on the softness there. "Ah, Lottie . . ." He could say no more.

Thirteen

"Maybe if I put out enough sweat scrubbin' on this floor, I'll stop hurting so bad," Lottie muttered as she wrung out the rag she was using. The bucket was half-full of rinse water, and even to her critical eye, it passed muster. The floor hadn't been dirty enough to scrub, the clear rinse water was mute testimony to the fact. But she'd needed something to do. Something that would take her mind off the ache that was centered in her breast.

She knelt in slump-shouldered defeat, her mourning too deep for tears. "I didn't know I'd get so partial to them, right off," she whispered, lifting one hand to brush the wispy strands of hair from her forehead. She sat back on her heels and raised hot, tearless eyes to the window, where the sun shone in wintry splendor through the wavy glass. It hadn't even snowed enough to keep the surrey from the road, she thought with a burst of petty anger.

Elizabeth Sherman had pooh-poohed the inch or so of white that lay upon the ground, even as Lottie suggested that the storm might increase in volume. Gentry had been quick to inform her that the clouds were lifting, passing quickly to the north, and the day promised to be fine.

"We don't want to miss the stage in the morning,

Miss Lottie," he'd said with a kindly manner. "Now that the children know what our plans are, we need to put things into motion."

They'd known all right, Lottie remembered gloomily. Sissy had sobbed her fears out in great detail, until John had been forced to be downright stern with her. And Thomas had been so quiet, she'd been fearful for him.

"He's had too much on his plate for a little fellow," she grumbled, as she scrubbed in rhythm to her panted complaint. "Even going to a fancy St. Louis school won't make up for missing his uncle."

The door opened, and the glare of winter sunlight blinded her for a moment, as she squinted her eyes against the rays.

"Don't bring that barnyard dirt in here on my clean floor," she said, her frustration finally allowed an outlet as John hesitated on the doorsill.

"The floor wasn't all that dirty to start with, Lottie," he argued, running one hand through his hair, hesitating to enter.

She rocked back on her bare toes, kneeling amid the suds and bucket. "I guess I can be the best judge of that," she retorted, "since I'm the one who has to keep it clean."

"Why don't you have your shoes on? It's foolish to be barefoot in this cold weather," he said, reaching blindly in his own hurt for ammunition in this battle of words.

She glared at him, almost relieved to be venting her anger on a tangible foe. The floor had received her mutterings without giving her the satisfaction of an argument, and the arrival of John and his sniping remarks added fuel to the fire of her resentment.

"I'm using bleaching powder in the scrub water, and

I don't want my shoes ruined, Mr. Tillman," she spouted.

"Well, why bleach the floor anyway?" he asked in a deliberate fashion, as if he would antagonize her with his questioning of her methods.

She gritted her teeth and spoke through them. "Because we always bleached the floors at the orphanage, and that's the way I learned to keep things clean."

He closed the door behind him and left her blinking once more, as the sunshine was cut off, and she was left to glare at him through fluttering lashes.

"You're not at the orphanage anymore, Lottie," he said patronizingly, as if he would remind her of the obvious.

"Well, who knows," she answered loftily. "I may just go back there. Seems like my usefulness here is over, anyway." She swiped at the wet floor with deliberate movements, soaking up the excess scrub water and wringing out the cloth she'd been using.

He took two steps and halted in front of her, and she found herself in the untenable position of kneeling at his feet. Dumping the scrub rag into the water, she hauled herself erect, lifting the bucket with both hands, intent on carrying it to the sink.

"Give me that," he ordered her, his hands covering hers on the handle, halting her with his grip.

"I don't ask anyone to clean up behind me," Lottie informed him haughtily. "If you want to track in all over the floor, just be my guest. Place belongs to you anyway," she muttered, snatching the bucket away from his hands as he hesitated at her words.

He watched in silence as she carried the rinse water to the sink and left it there. She wrung out the rag and hung it over the edge, her movements slow, biding her time until she should have to face him once more.

"Do you want to leave here, Lottie?" he asked carefully, his voice even and softer than the fall of snow on the roof.

She turned, and her eyes were stony with the despair she'd been harboring all morning within her chest. "You married me so you could keep the children, John. I don't see any sense in cluttering up your life, now that they're gone." She'd been careful not to consider that route since yesterday, when the arrival of the Shermans had burst her bubble of happiness. But it seemed the time had come to be honest with herself, and with the man who had married her out of need. What she hadn't expected was the pain of loss she felt, as she considered the consequences of her rash offer. If John was willing to let her go, if she had sealed her fate with her rashness . . . The thought was too hideous to contemplate, she realized with a sense of cold desperation.

He glared at her, his pride at issue. He'd made her his wife and treated her well, he decided virtuously as he reviewed the past several days. He'd given her a home and a bed to sleep in, and at least provided her with decent shoes to wear, he reminded himself as he watched her. And there she stood—barefoot and clad in a gray rag that should have been gracing a scarecrow instead of a woman, with her hair hanging about her face and her mouth all pursed up till she looked like she'd been sucking on a persimmon that hadn't been left on the tree long enough.

"Well, if you want to be my wife, you can stay," he offered magnanimously, sliding his hands into his pockets and rocking back on his heels. "But you'd better think twice before you decide to go trottin' back to the orphanage."

She was appalled by his words, and her chin lifted accordingly. "Well, I sure don't want to be indebted to you, Mr. Tillman. I'll just see that I've earned my keep before I leave." Her eyes flashed sparks that spoke of her anger, and with it brought a vitality to her face that had been smothered under the bitter sorrow she'd been struggling with all morning. Her hair gleamed in the sunlight that shone through the window behind her. Now, what with the mopping at her forehead and the swiping with damp hands at her cheeks as she worked, a considerable amount of short strands had come loose, and they managed to fly in radiant disarray about her, as she flared her temper at him in great style.

He watched her with narrowed eyes, his own hurt just beneath the surface of his anger. She tempted him, he admitted grimly. Even in the shapeless dress that hung from her shoulders in dingy folds. Even with her head tossed back like a shameless hussy and her hands shaping her hips as she glared at him. Even with that riot of unkempt hair about her head and those blue eyes of hers glaring with anger she had no business feeling, he realized as his hands clenched into fists in his pockets.

Especially with that unruly hair and those flashing eyes, he decided as he sensed a thickening in his loins, a hot flash of unwanted desire that brought a fine tension to his muscles and a crimson stain to ride high on his cheekbones. He took two longs steps and was in front of her, rocking her back on her heels as he nudged against her.

It was a mistake. He knew it as soon as he felt her warmth, felt the taut, sizzling vibrations that flared between them, the residue of their passion that had hovered on the brink of his awareness for the past several days. She was too close, too tempting, and he was beyond playing the gentleman with her today. Fed by the frustration of his loss and inability to hold onto what was his, he turned to her. In this, he was still in control. She was his wife, and if she wanted to earn her keep, he'd just see to it that she did, he decided heatedly.

His hands left the confines of his pockets to grasp with the strength of anger. Her arms were tense beneath his fingers, her strong muscles clenched against the pain of his grasp, and she gasped as he lifted her bodily to hold her tightly to his chest.

"John!" The single word was a gasp of surprise. Her eyes widened, and her face paled as she sensed the power of his emotions. "You're hurting my arms," she managed as she fought back tears that surged to fill her eyes. She'd not cried when the children left. She'd not sobbed once as she cleaned up the cabin and set to scrubbing the floor, for lack of another way to vent her fury. She'd not given way to the sadness that filled her almost to overflowing, until now. Now, the tears filled her eyes and slid in rivulets down her cheeks. And to her shame, she began to sob her distress while he watched.

He'd done it again. Until she'd met this man, she'd never cried before another human being in her life. Her pillow had swallowed her sobs, when the cruelties of childhood had overwhelmed her. And then, in her growing up years, she'd learned to subdue the impulse, learned that crying never got her anywhere, never solved a problem . . . and had vowed not to shed another tear. It was unbelievable that the pressure of John's fingers pressing against her flesh should cause pain enough to reduce her to this, she thought with a deep sense of shame.

He released his tight grip, bitterly aware that his actions were unreasonable, his harsh treatment of her inexcusable. His fingers rubbed carefully against her, bringing warmth and tenderness through the rough fabric of her sleeves; and his eyes closed as he shut out the vision of her tearstained face, her woebegone look.

She hung her head, angry at herself, even as she hungered for the comfort of his broad chest. He was only inches away and it might as well be miles, she thought, wishing vainly for the closeness that had bound them only last night. But then, Miss Aggie had warned her that men only wanted women to spend their lust upon. Lottie shook her head at the thought, a mute protest against the truth she could not accept as gospel right now. Anyway, if it had been lust that John spent upon her willing body, she must accept blame for her own participation. She could bear no complaint against him. He'd never given her reason to think he had any great liking for her, only that he was drawn to certain parts of her anatomy. She flushed crimson at her thoughts, sure that an avenging angel would strike her down for dwelling on such carnal desires in the daylight.

John stepped back from her, his regret forbidding him from adding to her pain by forcing himself on her this morning. The need for succor burned within him, warring with the self-derision he was heaping upon his own head for his part in their battle of words. Now, when they should be joining forces to heal the terrible wound the loss of Sissy and Thomas had inflicted on them, they were instead pulling apart. And he felt helpless to mend the gap that loomed between the two of them in this lonely house.

Lottie turned to the side and carefully eased past him, her head averted, brushing at her face with the palms of her hands as she sniffed loudly.

"Want my handkerchief?" he offered.

"No, I'll find my own," she said, her voice muffled against her fist. Bending low over her stack of boxes next to the bed, she slid one hand inside to grope for the flannel squares she kept there. It would be time to use them for their monthly purpose within a few days, but for now, one would do for wiping her tears and dabbing at her nose. A genuine handkerchief was not among Lottie's belongings, Miss Aggie having seen no reason for such fripperies. Gloves were more important for a lady, she'd said as she bestowed her second-best pair on Lottie the morning she'd left the orphanage.

John swung to watch her, his brow furrowed as he considered the best way to mend his fences.

"Lottie," he began, waiting to gain her attention. Then he lifted his head to listen as the unmistakable sound of harness jingling and a horse nickering broke his concentration on her.

"Company," he advised her tersely.

She shot a glance at him, wary of the picture they would present . . . him all bristly and her all teary-eyed and blowsy. But it was too late to do much about it, she decided as John opened the door and stepped out on the porch.

"Afternoon, Genevieve," she heard him say cordially, as he moved down the steps.

"And I'll bet she looks like she just stepped out of a bandbox," Lottie muttered, as she vainly attempted to smooth her hair and brush away the remnants of her bout of tears.

She was halfway to the door to add her welcome to

John's, when she caught sight of him lifting Genevieve from the buggy. Her breath caught as he gripped the dark-haired beauty about the waist and lowered her to the ground. A pang of nameless emotion tore at her belly as she heard his voice speak some foolish thing, and she frowned at the musical lilt of Genevieve's answering laughter.

He should have married her, Lottie thought glumly. She's pretty and lively and all the things I'm not. And she makes him smile.

But the look he cast her over their visitor's head bore no humor as the pair came in the door. "Genevieve came out to talk to you, Lottie," he offered. "I've got things to do in the barn. I'll leave you two to yourselves."

Lottie forced a smile to her lips and hoped they would not tremble with the effort. Her hands lifted in welcome and, without hesitation, Genevieve stepped forward to take both of them within her own. Her grip was firm and her eyes were filled with compassion, as she beheld the bedraggled appearance of the girl before her.

"Oh, Lottie," she whispered in sudden empathy. "You look just like I felt when my grandma died last year." She loosed the hands she held and transferred her embrace to enclose Lottie within her arms, rocking her to and fro as she leaned her head against the golden hair and pressed her cheek against the tearstained one Lottie offered.

"Well, they didn't die, but it feels like they did," Lottie admitted roughly, as she accepted the sympathy so generously offered. Even her flash of resentment at John's welcoming of Genevieve was put to rest by the genuine warmth she felt in the words of comfort.

Genevieve took charge with an authoritative manner Lottie would never have given her credit for, pushing her firmly into a chair and setting the kettle on a hotter place on the stove.

"We'll just have a cup of tea, Lottie, and talk about everything," she said briskly, as she drew a small packet from her pocket. "Daddy got this in, special for Mama, just last week," she informed her. "It's tea from India and very good, I understand. I thought we could make a pot and . . ." She turned slowly to Lottie, her determinedly cheerful facade slipping from place as she clutched the bag of tea leaves.

"I saw them come into town, Lottie," she said softly, "and I knew you must be feeling just terrible, what with having taken such a shine to those children. Why, I don't for the life of me understand what they're thinking of, taking them to St. Louis, when they belong here with you and John."

Lottie lifted her head and attempted a smile. "I'm sure they're only doing what they think is best," she said. "But perhaps John will be able to do something about it, when the lawyer comes back into town." She had clung to that thought all morning, but only now did it seem to offer any real comfort as Genevieve nodded her agreement.

"If Harley Garrison can do anything, he will." The words were firm, accompanied by a fervent nod of her head, and then Genevieve brought herself up short. "We'll never get to drink our tea this way," she said brightly, heading for the cupboard to locate the teapot and cups.

"Here, I'll help you," Lottie offered, rising abruptly. "I can't abide just sitting here in my own house and letting you wait on me. It isn't right."

"We'll do it together," Genevieve said with emphasis. "And then we'll talk. I need to ask your advice, anyway."

They settled themselves at the table, Genevieve stirring her tea for endless moments, before she cleared her throat in a dainty manner. She lifted her finely arched eyebrows, sighed deeply, and took a careful sip of the pale tea.

"I have a little problem," she admitted determinedly, as she placed the cup on the table and licked a drop of tea from her upper lip. "I need to make some changes in my appearance, Lottie, and I thought maybe you could help me."

"Me?" Lottie was stunned as she took in the fashionably dressed, young woman's appearance. "What kind of help could *I* be to *you?*" she asked in wonderment.

Genevieve bent closer, as if sharing a dark secret. "I have to subdue my more *frivolous* nature," she confided in a low voice. She looked about furtively, as if fearful of being overheard, and Lottie found herself glancing over her own shoulder.

Shaking herself, her better judgment nudging her, she fussed at Genevieve. "For pity's sake, there's no one to listen, Genevieve. What on earth is all the secrecy for?"

Her dark head bobbed decisively as Genevieve leaned closer. "I'm not sure how to tell you this, Lottie," she admitted. "But I might as well just spit it out, I guess."

Her mind taken with the distraction offered, Lottie leaned closer, her eyes shining as she watched, ready to do whatever Genevieve asked of her. She waited, breath held in abeyance.

"I'm in love," Genevieve confided softly, glancing over her shoulder once more and then reaching to grasp Lottie's hands firmly.

"In love?" Lottie was surprised, curious, and pleased. But her upbringing had taught her to listen, not ask questions, and she'd already asked her share for the day. She squeezed Genevieve's fingers with her own, silently urging the other girl to explain.

"I don't know how to say this." Genevieve was dithering again. And then, as if she had decided to take the bull by the horns, she took a deep breath and closed her eyes, spouting the words in a rush.

"Stephen Bush wants to marry me, and he's afraid I'm too *flamboyant—*" She spit the word as if it burned her mouth in the saying. Her eyes opened and she peered at Lottie, gauging the effect her words had had on the woman who watched her openmouthed.

"Flamboyant," Lottie repeated. Her brow furrowed and her mouth puckered, as she eyed the bright dress, ruffles and flounces making up the full skirt.

"Don't look at me like that!" Genevieve wailed. "You agree with him, don't you?"

"Well," Lottie drawled. "Not really. I was just thinking that most all the women in town and probably half the county would give their best bonnet and a year of livin' to look like you do. I don't think Stephen Bush knows what he's talkin' about, that's all."

Her sigh was deep as Genevieve cradled her chin on her fingers, elbows propped inelegantly on the table. "He said I didn't look like a proper preacher's wife. I dress too fancy, he said, and my hair curls too much, and my coloring is too vivid. And probably if he didn't love me so much, he wouldn't even want to marry me." she whispered pensively, as a deep flush swept up from her throat, staining her cheeks with brilliant color.

"He loves you?"

Genevieve looked up quickly, her mouth formed a small O and she swallowed.

"He just started loving you? Or did he love you before I got to Mill Creek?"

"That's what I need to talk to you about, Lottie."

"You want me to help you look more dignified, so that the preacher will marry you? The very same preacher that ran out on me when he'd promised to marry me?" Her voice rose with each word, until Lottie was spitting out the syllables like a Gatling gun in motion.

"That's just it," Genevieve said brightly. "You're exactly what a preacher *should* choose to marry, Lottie. So I thought that since you decided to marry John instead of Stephen, you might be willing to help me."

Lottie shook her head slowly and her eyes narrowed dangerously, as she considered the pleading words. "I don't think I've got this straight yet," she said slowly and precisely. "Stephen Bush came out here and offered to marry me, and at the same time he was in love with *you.*"

Genevieve twisted her slender fingers together and her wan smile was beseeching. "Something like that," she said finally.

Lottie stood abruptly, and her nostrils flared as she inhaled deeply. "He didn't really want to marry me at all, did he? He was just making the offer because he *had* to."

"He chose to do the honorable thing, Lottie," Genevieve said sadly. "No matter what his feelings for me were, he had committed himself to marrying you, and he knew he had to make it right."

Lottie sniffed and gritted her teeth against the mixed emotions that tore at her. Chagrin at the news of Stephen's duplicity was uppermost, tearing her fragile pride to ribbons, as she realized she had been second choice. But then, with a silky, sinuous warmth, came the knowledge that she had chosen well. That John's proposal had rescued her from the possibility of making a grave mistake. The thought of allowing Stephen Bush the intimacies of marriage was beyond her imagination, she decided with a shiver of dislike. In truth, she couldn't visualize allowing him to kiss her as John had, and certainly he'd never made her heart pound and her legs go weak. As attractive as life in a parsonage had seemed while she was in Boston and while she was traveling across the country, it had paled in comparison to the simple pleasures she had found here, in this small home with John and the children.

"Well, I'm glad I had the good sense to turn him down," she said finally, sliding back into her chair as she realized her own good fortune. "I'm glad he loves you, Genevieve," she admitted quietly. "I wish John felt that way about me."

"Oh, he does, Lottie. He was so excited about getting you the dress goods and shoes and picking out the material for your wedding. I could tell he cares about you."

Lottie shook her head. "No, he just needed me to look after the children for him. I suspect he never really wanted to marry me at all, but things just worked out that way." Her eyes dulled as she was brought back to this morning's reality with a thud. Her shoulders lifted and then slumped, as she sighed deeply. "The reasons for me being here are on the way to St. Louis anyway," she said, her eyes fastened on her folded hands. "Things are kind of hanging fire right now."

Genevieve's head shook briskly. "I think you're wrong, Lottie," she said firmly. "You'll see. John will surely find a way to get those children back, and he'll need you to help him."

Lottie's smile was twisted. "That's what I mean. I'm handy when help's needed . . ." Her mouth pursed and her chin lifted proudly. "I'd like to be wanted, just once, because of myself. Even if I couldn't do dishes, or cook or tend to children. Even if I was as useless as . . . well, never mind that," she said briskly. "The fact is, I can borrow the money to get back to New Hope, and John can be rid of the responsibility of a wife."

Genevieve groped for a reply, her mouth working vainly as she listened to Lottie's words. "Look . . . well, maybe . . . don't you think . . ." she began in a cautious way. "Just spend a few days with me in town, if you really mean it about leaving," she said finally.

"No, I've been thinking that I really should aim for catching the morning stage," Lottie ventured, not willing to admit that the thought was a new one, and rather distasteful, to boot.

Genevieve was out of her depth and floundering. Her wail was part pretense and part earnest frustration with the situation. "Lottie!" she cried. "Don't you see? If you're what Stephen thinks a preacher's wife should be like, then you're the best person in the world to help me change!"

Lottie shrugged deliberately. "All you have to do is have your mama make you some dark dresses without ruffles, and pull your hair up into a knot, and keep your eyes looking down most of the time."

"That's all?"

"Well, the rest of you can't be changed, and I'm not real sure Stephen would want it any different than it is, anyway," Lottie said decisively.

Genevieve leaned closer. "I'm not sure he'd really change *anything* about me, if it were only him that was to be considered. It's how other folks see me that matters," she said sadly.

"Well, if they like you as the storekeeper's daughter,

they ought to feel the same way about you as the preacher's wife," Lottie said firmly. "But if you really want to look different, just imagine yourself to be like one of those dowdy little hens out in that chicken yard and act accordingly. Or take a good look at Maude Clawson."

Genevieve shuddered and reached out to touch Lottie's clasped hands. "You don't look dowdy," she said softly. "Not lately, anyway," she amended as she took in the water-stained dress that Lottie had worn to scrub the floor.

"Well, I feel dowdy today. No, what I really feel like today, is hopeless, I guess," she decided aloud.

"What did Genevieve want?" John asked as Lottie placed a bowl of stew on the table before him.

"Oh, just to talk, really," she said, turning back to the stove. How to tell John of her half-formed plan to leave had occupied her mind all afternoon, once Genevieve had climbed back into her buggy and headed for town. The thought of leaving the man who was even now eating her cooking was tearing at Lottie's heart like a ripsaw. But I don't know what else to do, she thought despairingly. He doesn't need any extra burden right now, and that's all I am.

Her eyes were fixed on the strong line of his jaw, the long-fingered grasp he had on his spoon, and the breadth of his shoulders as he bent over the bowl that held his supper. He's fine, she decided, her eyes misting as she contemplated the bronzed profile he offered. And that's another thing, she sniffed to herself. He's got me all teary-eyed, just looking at him, and I've spent years keeping my eyes dry. Now, twice in one day, I'm melting like an early snowstorm.

"Aren't you eating, Lottie?" he asked loudly, and she was aware suddenly that it was the second time he had spoken the words. She turned away briskly, her skirt swaying, her bare feet silent as she filled a bowl at the stove for herself.

"I'm not very hungry," she muttered darkly.

"Well, eat anyway," he said, keenly aware of her silence and the gloom that hung so heavily in the room. It was harder on her than he'd thought it would be. She'd gotten real fond of the children, especially Sissy. He watched Lottie as she turned back to the table, wondering at the moisture that glistened on her cheeks in the lamplight. She was washed-out lookin', he decided. Pale and dingy in that old dress, her shoulders looking like they held the weight of the world.

With a critical eye, his mind stripped her of the dark apparel, his lashes lowering to hide the assessing glance. She was rounded in all the right places, he determined, pleased that he knew what was beneath those concealing folds. Her breasts lifted as she inhaled, and then as she leaned to place her bowl on the table, they formed beneath the bodice of her gown and tempted his gaze with their fullness. He cleared his throat, aware of the direction his thoughts were taking him, and reluctant to consider pressing her for his husband's rights when she was feeling so low. But he couldn't deny that she was tempting him, he thought with a sense of growing need.

"We need to talk, Lottie," he said abruptly, changing the direction in which his errant thoughts were heading. "We'll have to go see the lawyer as soon as he comes back, and make some arrangements. I may even have to go to St. Louis."

"Do you really think you stand a chance of getting them back, John?" she asked bleakly, concentrating on the bowl of stew she was mixing slowly with her spoon.

His eyes closed. "I don't know. I just don't know." He leaned back in his chair and lifted his lashes, just far enough to allow him to see her, not far enough to expose the vulnerable hurt he knew he could not hide. "Maybe the Shermans are right. Maybe they'll be better off in the city, where they can get good schooling and sleep in their own bedrooms and sit on fine furniture. Maybe it's wrong to want to keep them here, just because . . ."

"Because Sarah wanted them here?" Lottie finished for him.

"They're all I have left of James and Sarah," he said darkly. "Is it wrong to want to hold onto them?"

"No, I guess not, but you ought to be thinking about getting on with your life. Make up your mind what's best, and then do it. Don't be lookin' back."

"Is that what Miss Aggie says?" he asked dryly.

"It's what I say right now," she snapped. "I'm done with lookin' over my shoulder, John. When I've done all I can do, then I guess it's time to do something different."

He leaned back, enjoying this exchange, listening to Lottie's pert opinions and watching the play of emotions she allowed to wash over her pale face. She was wiped out tonight, but it hadn't melted her into a puddle. She was still spunky and ready to do battle, he decided. And contrary to what his good sense told him, maybe she'd not be too tired to ease the pain that his own heart had absorbed today.

"I've got chores to finish up," he announced as he shoved his bowl away. "I won't be long."

"You might want to check on that broody hen, John," she said as he stood. "She's bound and determined to make a nest out behind the corncrib."

Who'll remind him next week? she thought, as he nodded and pulled on his coat against the night air. The thought stung as she visualized him here alone. He was fine before I got here, and he'll be better off without me when I leave, she thought firmly. He's got enough to do with his own place, let alone keeping this one up. He can sell this piece, send the money to the children, and go back to being a bachelor without a care in the world . . . and that's a fact, she decided with an emphatic shove against the heavy table as she rose to clean the dishes.

She was already snuggled deeply into the feather tick when he made his way back into the house. Her face was a pale oval in the shadows, her eyes dark and hollowed-looking, watching him sit before the fire to tug at his boots. His sigh was deep, as he loosened the heel and pulled the leather free of his foot. He leaned to place his footwear to one side of the hearth, where it would hold some heat till morning. He'd long since learned that pulling on cold boots could put a crimp in the getting-up process. He looked up. She was still watching him, her eyes unblinking, her face solemn.

Without speaking, he stood and lifted his hands to slowly unbutton the shirt he wore, loosening his suspenders to let them fall from his shoulders. His stocking feet were silent as he headed for the bed, his hands making short work of the buttons that held his fly front closed. Then, as he reached his goal, he stopped and slid from the clothing he had loosened.

She'd not taken her gaze from him, he realized. Silent, looking like a baby owl that had just fallen from the nest, she lay there, her hands tucked up under her chin, holding the quilt in place like a shield that would protect her from his marauding eyes. Lot of good it would do her, he decided as he lifted the warm coverlet to slide between the sheets. She can lie over there on her side of the bed, if that's what she wants to do, he thought with a sense of purpose, but she won't lie there alone.

He's going to want to do that again, Lottie thought numbly. She hadn't been able to fit a word or phrase on the act, her mind not able to label such an intimate joining with any word that was in her vocabulary. Enough that it was what married folks do in bed, according to John, and how he knew all that he knew about it was another question that had been running around unanswered in her head.

Somewhere he'd done this before, and as far as she knew, he'd never been married. Maybe he'd done what the well-to-do men in the city were fond of doing . . . finding a woman down on her luck and setting her up in a house to spend their lust upon. That much her mentor had told her, in order to warn her of the perils that waited out there on the streets of Boston, should a young woman be without a home or family.

She mentally shook her head. I can't imagine John doing such a thing. He must have done his learning some other way, she decided. At any rate, he was about to use some of his vast store of knowledge again, if she was any judge of that determined look he wore.

His hair was falling over his forehead, and she

clenched her fists to halt the automatic lifting of her fingers as she yearned to brush it back. And then she watched in wide-eyed anticipation as he lowered himself to lie next to her, felt the warmth of his arm as it snaked across her middle to slide beneath her shoulder and turn her, with measured strength, to face him.

She drew in a deep breath, waiting in hushed silence for the touch of his lips that even now were parting, as if he anticipated the blending that was at hand. Her eyes closed, and she gave herself over to the inevitable. It might be for the last time, given her half-formed decision to rid him of the burden he'd assumed when he'd taken her on. But even that hurtful thought would not rob her of the bittersweet pleasure he offered tonight, she decided, as his mouth closed over hers.

Fourteen

With a sense of wonder, she allowed the warmth to spiral within her. Somehow, knowing what was to come only served to heighten her pleasure, as he swept his palms over her softness.

He was more direct, more rushed tonight, she sensed, as though he were being driven by emotions that forced him to action. His groan was muffled against the curve of her breast, as he lowered his head to taste the lush bounty she offered, and his fingers worked at her buttons blindly.

A sense of triumph filled her, as she sensed the depth of his desire in the trembling haste of his touch. With a sensuality she had not known she possessed, she twisted beneath him, her flesh rising to the heat of his fingers. Languidly, her eyes opened, her lids heavy with desire, and she smiled as she allowed herself the luxury of twining her fingers into the golden swathe of his hair. It slid like silken thread across her palms, and the sensation sent a thrill of discovery through her. That her hands, her fingers, could be so sensitive to him . . . that she could be drawn into his spell so readily, was a wonderment.

The heat that his mouth drew forth from her flesh left a cooling in its wake, and she felt the peaking at the very crest of her breast that his lips and tongue had coaxed into being. A sliver of delight coursed through her, and she opened her mouth to allow the faint sound of pleasure he had beckoned forth to be uttered.

Never had she thought to be so wanton, so free with her body, and a blush of shame flowed to color her flesh. What must he think of her, she wondered, as she lay before him in such naked abandon. And even as she considered her half-clothed condition, with her gown open to the waist and her breasts the object of his close scrutiny, he lifted his head to consider her with half-shuttered eyes.

"I'll not ask for permission tonight, Lottie," he said in a ragged voice that carried pain in its vibrating timbre.

"Permission for what?" she breathed, her words almost inaudible.

His mouth pursed, and his lips touched the bit of flesh that had formed to his liking, and his eyes darkened as they watched the involuntary reaction he had caused.

"To do what I please with you," he answered roughly against her warmth, as his hands drew her gown lower. He lifted her with ease, as he straightened to remove it from her shoulders and arms, and then slid it down her body, until it lay in a ghostly tumble at the foot of the bed.

The sheets had been shoved aside and in the chill of the room, she shivered, more at the dark scrutiny he offered her than for the cold that lingered in the shadows. He was unsmiling, his eyes laden and dark with a sadness that spoke to her heart.

"I didn't know you needed to ask my consent, John. I thought that being my husband gave you full sway over me." Her voice sounded strangely calm, she thought, even as her pulse pounded in an ever-increasing pace.

He nodded solemnly, his eyes steady on hers, and again she sensed a darkness within him that was a stranger to the man who had lain with her other nights. "It does, Lottie," he said. And then his mouth lowered once more to her flesh, and his eyes were hidden from her as he closed them, as if he would hide the pain that surely must be visible to her discerning gaze.

His hands were swift, his calloused palms barely grazing her skin as he stored in his memory the curves and hollows of her flesh, and she allowed him to lift and turn her as he would. Her breath caught as sensations filled her, the residue brimming over and flowing with heated cries of yearning that fell on his ears as a symphony of praise.

He followed the path his hands had taken with all of the hot, scalding pleasures his lips and mouth could offer. And in his giving, he received the homage she paid with indecipherable phrases and whispered murmurings that delighted him with their fervor.

With a knowledge that he'd not known he possessed, he seduced her to his purpose. With hands that lured her to new heights of abandon, he shattered her illusions of modesty. And with lingering caresses and words of encouragement, he brought them both into a newness of being that lifted them above the physical joining that held them as one. Their bodies strained to capture the prize that lured then to completion. Within her soul, Lottie sensed a gift beyond the satisfaction of her body . . . a blending of their spirits that filled her with an ethereal delight.

It was different, he thought. Different than any other time he had taken her beneath him and given her pleasure and then taken his own. More than physical release, more than the enjoyable flush of primitive possession, he realized he had found a depth of emotion with Lottie he'd not known could be reached. His casual, infrequent encounters with the women downriver faded into his past without a murmur, his memory of them dulled by the unexpected joy he'd found with his bride.

This is what it means to be one flesh, he decided in contentment as he rested against her pliant body. This is what the marriage ceremony is all about, the giving and taking that we do here.

She felt his breath against her skin, the slowing of his harsh panting that matched her own, and she held his muscular body with a strength born of her passion. As if she would keep him close, savor the trembling of her limbs and the shuddering spasms of delight his touch had brought her.

I'll remember this forever, she vowed in silent wonder. And her heart stumbled a bit in its beating, as she contemplated her future. John needed me tonight, she acknowledged ruefully. For some reason, he needed my body . . . for comfort perhaps. And from that need, I've taken my own share of comfort. Maybe for the last time, she mourned, they had claimed each other in this act of marriage.

He rocked her beneath him, unwilling to leave the warmth she offered so freely, and with one long arm, he reached to pull the covers over their chilling bodies. Carefully, he tucked the quilts about them, loath to leave the cushion of her flesh.

He dropped kisses that spoke of his pleasure in her. They fell in random, damp homage upon her face, accompanied by his murmur of comfort as he questioned her well-being.

"You're all right? I wasn't too rough?"

She shook her head slowly, and her eyes opened to find his own intent on her. Not a trace of apology gleamed from those blue orbs, only the satisfaction that told her he was well pleased with the results of their loving. She snuggled against him, seeking to draw a final portion of warmth and comfort from his broad chest and lean, agile body.

"No . . ." she said finally, and her smile dissolved into a yawn as she was struck with a weariness that surprised her.

"You're sleepy," he accused her in a growling voice that teased.

She nodded and burrowed her face against his throat, inhaling the musky, salty flavor he wore. She would store it against the future, she thought with a sad little sigh as she savored the scent he bore.

With care to her comfort, he turned them in the bed, until they were both enclosed in the soft, pillowing confines of the feather tick. And then, as the shadows were licked by the glowing embers of the fire, they held tightly to the comfort they had gained in those fleeting moments of passion.

She wasn't sure what had woken her, but as Lottie threw back the quilts and reached for her gown, she found herself listening intently. Perhaps it was the rooster, she thought as she quickly buttoned the bodice, trembling in the chill of the dark room.

"Lottie?" John's voice was muffled beneath the covers, and she turned to him, her eyes softening as he reached one large hand toward her. "Come back to bed, sweetheart," he yawned. "It can't be time to get up yet."

"Something woke me, John," she said in a low, hurried tone. "I wanted to look outside and see if everything is all right. Do you suppose something is bothering the chickens?"

He yawned loudly and stretched his arms wide. "Not likely," he ventured, "but I'll take a look, if it'll make you feel better." He stepped out on the floor, and his grumble brought a smile to Lottie's lips. "How come you get the rug on your side of the bed?" he wanted to know. "This floor's cold."

She was at the window already, pulling aside the heavy curtain to look out in the yard. "Put your clothes on," she said briskly. "At least your nightshirt and pants. You won't be so cold."

"That won't help my feet," he grumbled, as he tugged his suspenders over his shoulders and tucked the tails of his nightshirt in. "I'll put some wood on the fire, . . . warm it up in here," he mumbled as he headed for the fireplace. His hands made tracks through the length of his hair as he made a rough attempt to smooth it, yawning once more as he poked at the embers and coaxed them to glow beneath the log he'd added to the firepit.

Lottie turned to watch as he sat on the low stool to pull on his boots, and then stiffened as a muffled sound caught her ear.

"Did you hear that?" she asked in a whisper.

"Rifle," John grunted, as he stood abruptly and stomped his foot to settle his boot in place. "Get my coat, Lottie."

Without hesitation, she pulled his heavy jacket from the peg and held it for him, watching as he lifted his own gun from over the fireplace. He opened the box where his ammunition was stored and motioned her to come closer. His hands full of shells, he turned to slide them into the wide pockets of his coat, and then, with his back to her, he donned it quickly.

"What is it, John?" she asked in a subdued manner. His tension was visible in the frown he wore, the rapid movements of his hands as he checked the rifle and loaded it.

His head shook briefly. "Hard to say." he said. "Some sort of trouble." His head came up abruptly as the gun fired again, closer this time.

Lottie turned back to the window. "Someone's coming on horseback," she announced. "Looks like the man from the livery stable."

"Probably Young Willy," John said, reaching for his hat as he headed for the door. He slid the bar from its place and looked at her, his eyes shadowed in the dim light. "Stay inside till I find out what's going on, hear?"

She nodded and turned back to the window as John stepped out onto the porch. The rider approached quickly, his horse moving at a lope. Lottie watched as he pulled back on the reins, bringing the large black animal within inches of where John waited.

"Children are missing," he shouted breathlessly, as he shoved his rifle into the empty sleeve behind his saddle.

"What do you mean—*missing?*" John asked angrily.

It was all Lottie needed to hear. Her feet flew to the door, her hands ready to pull it open. Then, looking down at herself, she shook her head before she ran to the bed to lift a quilt about her shoulders. Young Willy would see a sight to behold, if I were to be standing in front of the fireplace and him looking through my nightgown, she thought with a frown.

The sound of the men's voices was muffled, now that

she was away from the window, but her heart beat rapidly as she considered what they had already said. Thomas and Sissy . . . the children . . . who else would they be talking about?

Before she could pull the door open, John was in the house, his expression grave as he faced her. The flickering flames were reflected in his eyes and cast a glow upon his skin. He closed his eyes a moment and shook his head, a look of anguish painting his features as he released his breath.

"The children got out of the hotel some way, Lottie," he said in a tight, harsh voice. "Gentry Sherman sent Willy out to tell us. They've got half the countryside out looking for them."

"Where . . . why?" she stuttered, wide-eyed and unbelieving. "How could they get away from town? Maybe they're still there . . . did they look everywhere?"

He lifted a big hand to halt her speech, shaking his head. "Simmer down, sweetheart," he said, reaching for her suddenly. His arm enclosed her in a close embrace, and her feet left the floor as he lifted her against himself. Cold lips brushed against her cheek and he squeezed her tightly, as if he would give assurance with his touch.

"Stay here, just in case they get this far," he instructed her quickly. "I'm going to saddle one of my mares and head out looking for them. I'll probably go to town first. Should be there in less than an hour, probably by dawn. It's getting gray already."

"There's more snow on the ground, John. They'll be cold. Why? Why would they leave the hotel?" she asked, her arms snaking about his neck as she clung to him unashamedly.

"Don't know, Lottie." His breath was ragged, as he

lowered her to the floor and planted one more kiss on her forehead. "They didn't want to go, but I sure didn't expect them to run off."

"Sissy was crying when they left," she reminded him, and her own tears were close to the surface as she remembered the tearstained face of the little girl.

"I'll be back when I've found them," he promised her as his eyes sought hers. "I'll find them, Lottie."

She nodded, unable to speak as her vivid imagination set to work. Images of Sissy's fragile body covered with a blanket of snow came to life in her mind. Thomas was a sturdy little boy, she knew, but no match for miles of farmland that stretched to the horizon in either direction. She tried to visualize the road to town, putting in place the trees, the river, the trackless fields.

At least the moon is shining, she said to herself as she remembered the glow that had been cast on Young Willy as his horse cantered up the lane. "The sun will be up soon," she whispered, aware that the dawn was already making gray inroads on the darkness. "They'll be all right, I'm sure of it," she promised herself numbly, as she hastily donned her dress and pulled warm stocking up her legs.

She found she could not, for a moment, put the children from her mind. While she milked Rosie, she thought of Thomas's hands showing her the way of it. His small, sturdy hands that were so capable, and yet so vulnerable with their still-soft flesh.

As she scattered feed for the chickens, she recalled the peckish hen that had left numerous small scabs on Sissy. Her lips twisted in a sad smile, as she remembered the day that the child had solemnly shown her the damage and the lessons learned as they gathered eggs together.

The sun was turning the eastern sky a pinkish hue, as she dwelt on thoughts of the children who had filled her life with hours of affection and delight. She visualized Thomas bent over his slate, and Sissy, tongue peeking out from the corner of her mouth as she emulated his attempts. The cabin was filled with memories. Before the sun was well in the sky, she had begun pacing, her steps taking her from one side of the room to the other.

She peered from the window for another glimpse of the lane that led to the road. Perhaps they'd been found, she thought. John might even now be on his way home with them. No . . . they'd be on their way to St. Louis, if they'd been located so soon.

Her hands twisted upon themselves, as she contemplated the emptiness of the rutted lane. "I need to be doing something," she said aloud. "I need to be out looking for them, too."

Her chin lifted and her jaw firmed with the decision she made. "John isn't the only one capable of hunting for them," she announced to the empty house. "If he wants to get mad at me for not staying here waiting . . . well, he'll just have to get glad again," she decided with the telltale tilt of her chin that betrayed her stubborn spirit.

It took her more than a few minutes to figure out the intricacies of the harness, but the plow horses were docile and stood placidly while she reached to lay the leather in place. Hooks and wobbling wooden bars notwithstanding, she managed to attach the harness to the whiffletree, and then checked to be sure all of the buckles were done up. This looks so easy when John does it, she thought as she brushed a wayward lock of hair from her face.

The farm wagon was covered with a layer of snow, a frosting that had fallen sometime after midnight, and she brushed off the seat as she climbed up. A bundle of quilts lay behind her, along with a half-loaf of bread, wrapped in a towel, and a bottle of milk, still warm from this morning's milking. Rich and creamy, it had foamed over the narrow neck, as she poured it hurriedly at the sink.

"I'll wager they're hungry as a couple of newborn pups," she muttered beneath her breath, as she picked up the reins. Her hands were cold, her knuckles red and rough, and she'd pulled her coat sleeves down as far as she could get them to provide some warmth.

"I should have found John's work gloves to wear," she said, and then shrugged her shoulders. It'll take too long to scout them out in the barn, or wherever he's left them, she thought as she slapped the leather against the broad backs of the patient horses who waited to do her bidding. Besides, she decided, they'd only hamper my driving, and heaven knows I need all the help I can get.

Taking the buggy had been her first thought, but the sight of Daisy tossing her head had reminded her how skittish that animal could be so early in the morning. It had seemed the better choice to flounder among the traces and buckles, harnessing up the broad-backed beauties who were more suited to her inexpert driving abilities.

I'll not make much time though, she thought as she shaded her eyes, looking across the fields that lay dormant. The snow had long since melted in the bleak, wintry sunshine, and the remnants of autumn harvest lay exposed and naked. Stubbles of hay and wheat, a field of shorn cornstalks, and then the line of willows where the creek ran. Beyond, a half mile down the road, a large stand of trees formed the boundary line of James's property, a massive wooded area, blending pine and maple and walnut, along with an assortment of smaller trees in a shady, dense forest.

She was braced in the seat, her feet firm against the short plank in front of her, her fingers clutching the reins as if she expected the team of horses to bolt unexpectedly. But they appeared to have no such intention, placidly making their way over the rutted road.

"I don't have the least idea where to look," she admitted in a frightened voice, for the first time this morning doubting her judgment. "Maybe I should have stayed home, like John told me."

But the inborn need to be of use, the inherent desire to help, had driven her to this purpose, and she had only her own intuition to rely upon, she decided.

Down the road, past another wooded area, lay the road leading to John's homestead, and she was drawn to it. The wagon swayed as she turned the team to follow the narrow set of tracks, and she looked ahead eagerly, squinting in the sunlight to where she could barely make out the lines of his cabin and outbuildings. The horses moved at a quicker pace, as she slapped the reins against their backs and made the clicking sound with her teeth clenched that John had shown her. He'd taken great pride in her ability to catch on so quickly, calling her a prize pupil, she remembered, for a moment caught up in the memory.

Then the cabin loomed up before her, drawing her from her thoughts and reminding her of her purpose here. As she lowered herself over the side of the seat and slid to the ground, the heavy plank door opened, and a hulking man stepped into the sunshine.

"Hullo, missus," he said roughly. "You must be John Tillman's wife."

"Yes," she said quickly. "And you're Otto Schrader, aren't you?"

He nodded slowly, approaching her in a diffident manner. "Is there a problem, ma'am?" he asked, his eyes narrowed against the sunshine.

"Did you hear the rifle shots before dawn?" Surely he must have, she thought impatiently. "The men are out looking for our children. John's niece and nephew, that is," she corrected herself. "They've disappeared from the hotel in town."

He shook his head, his manner reticent. "I heard the shots, but I figured they were none of my business," he admitted roughly. "Where I come from, you don't get involved, unless trouble comes to your doorstep. I had enough of that back east, after the war," he announced with finality.

"You haven't seen them, then?" she asked, already knowing the answer she would get. "I had hoped that they might have headed for home and stopped here to get warm."

"They got no business out in the night," he announced firmly. "Kids ought to be taught to do as they're told."

Lottie felt a burst of anger at his stubborn avowal, and turned from him with a muttered sputter that she tried to smother. What a foul thing to say, she thought with indignation.

"Well, if you don't mind, I'll just take a look in John's barn," she called back at him over her shoulder, as she marched to where that building stood, almost two hundred feet from the cabin.

"Suit yerself," he called after her, plunging his hands

into the pockets of his overalls. "Foolish woman," he muttered. "Ought to be home, where she belongs."

Lottie heard the grumbling behind her, aware that he watched her with barely concealed critical looks from beneath his lowered brows. "Wouldn't know a snake if he stepped on it," she whispered as she strode briskly to the barn.

Her hands worked at the latch that held the double doors shut. Lottie opened them up, listening to the creaking sounds as they slid to either side of her. Motes of dust floated in the air, and the silence of an empty building fell upon her ears. She stepped into the scattering of straw that covered the earthen floor of the entryway and peered down the wide passage, aware that John had emptied the stalls of his horses. Harness still hung on the wall, a saddle lay over a sawhorse. From the loft above she heard a rustling that caused a bit of hay to float to the floor.

Mice, she thought with a shudder. They were not unknown to her, having cleaned out their leavings the first day at James's house. He'd not been careful with crumbs, and the house had been a haven for more than one of them.

With a final look down the aisle and a sigh that signified defeat, she turned from the empty barn and left, closing the door slowly.

"This was a wasted trip," she muttered beneath her breath, as she turned to tromp back to where the farm wagon awaited her. A sound caught her ear, and she saw a flash of brown and then the white telltale sign of a cottontail rabbit that scampered across the field, rustling through the dry stalks. For an unknown reason, drawn by a sense she could not explain, she walked in that direction, cornering the barn and facing the open field behind it.

The sun had not yet melted the snow that remained in shadow there; it lay, a fine cover over the scattering of grass and straw. She strained to look, a disarrangement of its white perfection drawing her closer, and then her breath caught in a gasp, and her mind caught the significance of what she saw.

Two sets of footprints made their way across the un-melted, pristine blanket. Two undeniably small pairs of feet had come this way since midnight, and left their message in the snow.

"Sissy . . . Thomas," she breathed, with a sudden knowledge that they were near. Her heart thumped wildly at the discovery, and her eyes were wide with excitement as she turned back to the front of the barn. Her fingers grasped the latch with new strength, and she shoved with eager arms at the heavy set of doors.

Once more the interior of the barn greeted her. Once more she scanned the walls and the open stalls. Once more she gazed upward at the opening in the ceiling where the ladder led to the hayloft, and this time she headed there with unerring purpose.

Her feet sought purchase on the rungs as she climbed, one hand grasping the heavy folds of her skirt, the other clinging to the wooden ladder. She blinked in the dimness of the loft, as her head and shoulders rose from the opening.

"Thomas . . . Sissy!" she called in a low voice. "If you're hiding up here, I want you to come out right now." Her words were firm and demanding, as she attempted to swing herself to sit on one side of the narrow opening.

"We're here, Miss Lottie," a meek voice said from the shadows.

"We runned away," said another, softer whisper from the same direction.

She heaved a sigh of relief and—with a gesture that was her undoing—reached a hand to where they were crouched in a pile of hay.

"Here . . . come on . . ." she began, coaxing them to where she waited. But the tenuous hold she had formed with her feet, and the bulky weight of her dress, twisted about her legs, caught her unawares. The hand that lay flat upon the slippery hay could find nothing to grip, and the one that reached toward the children flailed in the air, as she disappeared from their view with a shriek and landed with a shuddering thud upon the dirt floor at the foot of the ladder.

Fifteen

"We've gone through every building in town, John," the sheriff said with assurance. "There's no sense in making the rounds again."

"Could we have missed anything?" he asked without hope of an affirmative answer.

"No." The older man shook his head. "We even checked all the outhouses. Not that they'd be likely to hide out in one of them," he admitted with a sheepish grin.

"I went through both churches, John," Stephen Bush assured him. "Genevieve opened the store and looked in the back room and all around, just in case they might have found a way to get in there."

Mabel Sharp stood beside her husband, a frown of confusion on her plain face. "I just can't imagine where they'd have gone. We've had everyone out looking and we can't even figure out how they got out of the hotel unnoticed."

"What you managed to do was waste a lot of time here," Elizabeth Sherman announced with regal authority. "If I know those children half as well as I think I do after just two days with them, I'd say they headed back to the farm."

"I told you to stay inside where it's warm," her husband told her gruffly. His hair was ruffled by the breeze, his eyes watery from the sun that shone brightly in the morning sky.

"They're my grandchildren," she huffed. "If we hadn't been careless and had checked on them sooner, they wouldn't be still missing."

John shook his head. "Thomas is a bright boy, ma'am," he said firmly. "He figured a way to get past you and that's a fact. If he was bound and determined to run off, you'd have had to hog-tie him to the bed to stop him."

"Well, I've got a store to open," Harvey Slocum announced to the group gathered on the wide, wooden sidewalk that formed the broad porch he swept each morning.

"I'm headin' back home," Henry Clawson said from behind John. "I'll keep a lookout on both sides of the road."

"Stop and tell Lottie that we're still looking, will you, Henry?" John asked briefly.

"I can do that," his neighbor answered as he headed for his horse.

"I appreciate what you folks have done," John said to the assortment of townfolk who had gathered about him. "I'm going to backtrack myself. I think the children's grandmother is right. They'll probably be tucked into the loft, sound asleep by the time I get there," he said gruffly. But the look in his eyes belied the words he spoke, and he was not surprised when several men joined him as he strode away.

"We'll give you a hand, John," Stephen Bush said at his right elbow, "Genevieve and I will take my buggy and try all the farms between here and your place."

"Thank you, Stephen," he replied quickly, his look a

grateful glance as Genevieve trotted beside him, her hand clutching that of the preacher.

But before he could mount his horse, before the men who had volunteered to help could gather up their own mounts, a buckboard, drawn by a dark, heavily lathered gelding approached, and its driver waved frantically at them.

"It's Otto Schrader," John said needlessly, aware that the town knew he had allowed the settler to winter at his cabin.

"Do you suppose—" Genevieve began, excitement coloring her tones.

"Maybe the children—" Mr. Sharp surmised hopefully, before he was cut off by the newcomer to their midst.

"There's been an accident," Otto Schrader announced to the gathering. "Your woman fell from the hayloft, and she's hurt pretty bad."

" What was she doing in the barn?" John asked, even as he sprinted toward his mare.

"Looking for those young'uns," Otto grunted as he shook his head. "They must have been hiding for most of the night. The boy said they came across the fields. They knew they was almost home, but they were too cold to keep going."

"Where are they?" Elizabeth Sherman asked, drawn to the excitement and holding her skirts above the wet ground as she approached.

"I'm heading there now," John told her briefly, "Have Gentry get a buggy and follow me."

Impatient with the voices that would deter him from his course, he brushed off hands that touched him, glared at the fingers that clung to his coat sleeve, and shook off the words of advice that flowed from the well-meaning townsfolk that gathered about him.

"I'll tell the doctor to come on out," Genevieve said next to him.

"Do that," he said quickly, gathering the reins of his mare as he made to swing into the saddle.

His mind was racing ahead to where Lottie lay. The children would be with her. Thomas and Sissy could not be pried from her side if she were hurt, and that was a fact he'd have bet his life on. How badly she was injured was the question that plagued him now. He urged his horse into a lope that would cover the distance quickly without winding the animal before he got there.

The road had never seemed so long, his impatient mind noted. The farms on either side flowed past with a rapidity he could not appreciate, so frantic was he to reach his goal. Behind him, unable to keep up, a farm wagon followed, and the team of horses that pulled it were being driven with impatience by Young Willy, full of his own importance as he headed for the scene of disaster. Fast on John's heels was the light buggy that Stephen Bush fancied, drawn by a swift mare that delighted in the race.

Ahead of him, he feared the worst would await, conscious of Lottie's fragile bones, the softness of her build, the slender body that would be bruised and battered by such a fall. His heart beat almost in time with the fast-falling hooves of his horse. He faced with bleak eyes a future without the woman who had crept into the corners of his life just weeks ago, to firmly establish herself as the core of his existence in just a few short days.

The long lane that led to his cabin appeared just ahead, and he took a shortcut, moving with vigilant haste across the field, wary of his horse losing her footing in the rough ground. The barn was just ahead, and he slowed his frantic pace, pulling back on the reins as he spoke gently to the horse.

"Whoa . . . girl . . . whoa, there," he called softly, sliding from the saddle as he neared the double doors that opened into his barn.

Within, he saw the shadowed forms of Thomas and Sissy, sitting in silence beside the still form of his wife. He halted in the entrance, feet apart, pushing the hat from his forehead, catching the breath that insisted on escaping his control.

"Thomas?" He spoke the boy's name in a pained whisper.

"Oh, Uncle John," the child cried, stumbling to his feet as he headed for the door. "She fell, right down to the ground. I couldn't help it," he said with tears garbling his words. "Me and Sissy was up in the loft, and when Miss Lottie climbed the ladder, she got all tangled up or something, and she just fell!" The final sentence was almost unintelligible as he buried his face in his uncle's stomach, clutching at him in despair.

John looked with hungry eyes at the still form of the woman on the floor and, in his haste to reach her, set the boy aside roughly. "Come . . . help me here, Thomas," he ordered in a low tone.

Dropping to his knees, he reached a reluctant hand to touch her throat, and closed his eyes in relief as he felt the even pulse there.

"Lottie?" he said gently, bending low to place his face close to hers. His fingers brushed ineffectively at her cheek, hovered for a moment against her forehead, and then he settled back against his heels as he knelt beside her.

"Has she moved?" he asked Thomas.

"No sir." the boy answered quickly.

"Me neither, Uncle John," Sissy whispered. "I've been sitting right here to take care of her. I was holding her hand to make her feel better."

"Well, let me just check her over a little. You both go on out and wait for the buggy that's just a ways down the road," he said firmly. His hands were careful as he straightened her legs, and his fingers lifted her skirt to her waist as soon as the children were outside the barn. He felt her with fingers and palms, up one leg and down the other, lifting her limbs gently as he went, until he was sure that there were no apparent injuries.

Pulling her dress back down, he lifted one arm, then the other, repeating his careful examination, wincing when he saw the torn sleeve and the abrasions beneath the fabric. His hands moved to examine her skull; John was fearful of moving her too much before the doctor arrived, yet anxious to know if there were an obvious reason for her unconscious state.

"John?" Stephen Bush blocked the doorway, Genevieve behind him.

"Get out of the light," John said harshly.

The couple moved with haste to kneel away from the beams of sunlight that lit the scene. They watched as he carefully slid his hands beneath her head and worked his fingers through her hair, his eyes closed, as if he would see the route his fingertips traveled.

"She has a nasty lump back here," he muttered as he discovered an egg-sized area. "It doesn't feel like it's been bleeding though."

"Can we turn her over, John?" Genevieve asked uncertainly.

He shook his head. "No, best wait for Doc Holmes

to get here." He stood on shaky legs and cast a look about the interior. "We need to find something to carry her on. I've got some planks at the end of the aisle, Preacher, if you want to go get a couple of them."

"Certainly," Stephen said, moving with haste into the shadows, apparently pleased to put legs to his good intentions.

"See if there's a hammer and some nails in the tack room, Genevieve," John said, moving to displace the saddle from his sawhorse. He found the second one in the first stall and arranged them quickly.

"Put those boards here, Preacher," he called out, as he searched through a pile of short pieces of wood. Grasping two that suited him, he lay them across either end of the wide planks.

"Got those nails yet?" he called.

"Coming," Genevieve said breathlessly, as she hurried toward him with hammer in hand. She thrust a handful of nails at him, and he smiled with grim humor.

"I only needed a dozen or so," he said. "Here, you hold them and give me one at a time."

Wielding the hammer with harnessed strength, within moments he had fashioned a flat surface that would hold Lottie. "That'll do." he finally said, lifting the makeshift platform and placing it next to her.

"Doc's here, Uncle John," Thomas called importantly from outside the door.

"Thank God," Genevieve said simply, as she knelt next to her friend.

From pale lips that were barely parted, she heard a faint sound and leaned her dark head closer. "Lottie?" she whispered.

"John . . ." The word was barely audible, but he

heard it and turned. His knees hit the ground by her side, and his hand touched her head.

"I'm here, sweetheart," he said, bending to catch the words that her lips were attempting to form.

"Something's wrong, John," she mumbled. "I can't seem to make my legs move."

He bent lower to brush a kiss against her cheek, and his voice was harsh as he whispered his comfort, "Just lie still, Lottie. We'll have you home soon and everything will be all right," he promised, even as he achingly wondered if the words were a lie.

At the last minute, he'd taken the sawhorses along. Doc Holmes had supervised as the men lifted the boards with Lottie in place. She'd been stowed in the back of the wagon, covered with quilts that encompassed the planks she lay on and wrapped about her for warmth.

"I can't do much here, John." The stalwart man had done a cursory examination, much as John himself had performed, and then pronounced Lottie fit to move. "Her neck's not broken," he'd announced with relief apparent in his voice.

Six hands lifted her, just enough to slide the boards beneath her body. Three men had done their best to be gentle, but John had winced more than once as broken murmurs of pain fell from Lottie's lips.

He'd lain next to her in the wagon, his arm across her waist to hold her against the jolting, his own jacket folded about her head for cushioning. The comfort of his body had almost lulled her to sleep. If it had not been for the fears that assailed her and the throbbing in her head, she would have been content to allow his greater strength to form a protective shield about her.

But through the haze of pain—set off each time she attempted to move her head—came the knowledge that, try as she might, she could not move her legs, could not lift her feet.

Now the sawhorses had been placed to one side of the fireplace, and Lottie's makeshift stretcher lay across it. The quilts had been set aside, for the fire blazed brightly, and she was warmed by its flames. Garbed in her heavy clothing, she suspected she was quite a sight to behold, stretched out like a body waiting for its wake to begin.

At the thought a smile twitched at her mouth. I must be out of my mind, she decided, exasperated at the odd meandering of her thoughts. My body feels like it's floating six inches above this board, and my head's about twice the size it should be. I must have a knot back there the size of a goose egg.

"You do, sweetheart," John said, from above her head.

"Do what?" she muttered.

"Have a huge knot on your head. I suspect it's from where you bounced off that keg of nails on your way down from the loft."

"How'd you know what I was thinking?" she wanted to know, irritated that he could read her mind.

"You've been lying here, talking nonsense for a good five minutes," he teased as he hunkered down beside her, one large hand brushing the wisps of hair from her forehead. He leaned closer to inspect a smudge on her cheek, and his fingers brushed at it.

"Just dirt," he said, relieved that it was not another bruise to mar her tender flesh.

"What are all these people doing here, John?" she asked as her eyelids fluttered shut.

"Just helping out, Lottie," he answered softly against her cheek. He brushed a kiss where the dusty spot had been. "Don't go to sleep, sweet," he instructed her gently. "You need to stay awake for a bit."

"Can't," she announced with a deep sigh. "My head hurts."

From the window, Genevieve turned to call softly across the room. "Doc's here, John."

He nodded once. "About time."

Genevieve drew in a quivering breath, barely noticing as another tear slid down her cheek to fall on the bodice of her dress. She'd been there when they lifted Lottie to the wagon. She'd hurried into the house to set a kettle of water on the stove, seeking Thomas's help to build up the fire in the black beauty that James had brought here from St. Louis for his bride. She'd watched as Lottie was deposited carefully on the pair of sawhorses, and it had been her hands that had straightened Lottie's clothing when the quilts were removed.

The only outward sign of her distress had been the tears, and she had decided to ignore them, for they fell whether she liked it or not. Only when she approached the woman who lay so still beside the fireplace, did she dry her face and force her lips into a smile.

"Can I help get her coat off, John?" she asked softly, as Lottie's eyelids flickered at the sound of her voice. "The doctor will need to examine her."

John looked up at her, and his own eyes were painfilled. "There's no privacy in here." He glanced about himself at the large room that held all the essentials of his household, and more visitors than he had seen at one time in this place. "She never even had a bedroom here. Neither James nor I provided any privacy for our brides, did we?"

"We'll just shoo everyone out for a few minutes, John," Genevieve said briskly. "Why don't you find her gown, and the doctor and I will get her into it, as soon as he comes in."

"Do it myself," Lottie grumbled from the makeshift bed.

"Not on a bet, you won't, young lady," said the booming voice of Doc Holmes. "Let's clear everyone out for a while. Must be some chores need doing outside. You get on out, too, John," he said gruffly, his eyes keenly intent as he surveyed the man who hovered protectively over his young bride.

John ran his long fingers through his hair, attempting to smooth the wind-ruffled length of it, and his smile was hesitant as he eyed the doctor who was issuing orders.

"Won't you need me to help lift her?" he asked.

With a firm shake of his head, Doc Holmes took charge once more. "I've got Miss Genevieve here to lend a hand. You get on out and let us do our job, John."

Leaning over her once more, John whispered against Lottie's cheek. "I'll be back in a few minutes . . . hear?"

Her eyes opened languidly, and she peered at him. "Hmmm . . ." And then she groaned, and her brow wrinkled as she shifted her head a bit. "Hurts . . ." she muttered once more.

The sun warmed the porch and cast its rays benevolently on the children, who were huddled next to the door.

"They haven't moved since Doc chased them out of the house," Elizabeth Sherman said to her husband. They stood in the doorway of the springhouse, where John had strained the milk with Gentry's able help. Now they watched as he set up the separator.

"Looks like I'll be churning butter tomorrow," he said with a frown. "Can't let the cream go to waste."

"What do you do with all the milk, John?" Gentry asked.

"Lottie's been sending the extra butter to town with me, along with eggs. Harvey Slocum takes it to sell in the store. The buttermilk gets used for cooking, and I drink it fresh. What's left over goes to the pigs. The skim goes there, too. Kids drink the freshest, once it's cooled."

"They're tucked up against that door like a couple of ticks on a hound dog, aren't they?" Young Willy said, rocking on his heels as he watched the activity. "Did you know the preacher's gathering eggs, John?"

"Good job for him," John muttered, as he wiped his hands on a clean towel and stood up straight. "Hope he knows enough to clean off those shiny shoes of his when he gets done."

"It was good of him to come out here and help," Elizabeth said mildly.

John stepped into the sunshine and shot a glance toward the henhouse. "He's all right," he allowed roughly, as Stephen backed from the narrow doorway that allowed entrance to the coop.

A deep basket hanging from one of his black-clad arms, the preacher stepped gingerly across the chicken yard as he headed for the gate. "You've got a couple of mean old biddies in there, John," he announced as he closed the chicken wire gate. "Pecked me good," he complained, holding up one hand in mute testimony. Three small rivulets of blood ran from the injuries that the Plymouth Rock hens had inflicted.

"They never peck Lottie," John said easily.

"Well, you better hope you don't get egg duty, while she's laid up," Stephen said slyly. "They might not like you either."

"Miss Lottie showed me how to do it so's I don't get pecked, Uncle John, and I'll be here, so I'll gather the eggs while she's hurted," Sissy called from the porch with an authoritative challenge.

"We'll see," John answered as he headed for the children. "We've got things to work out."

Thomas stood and tugged Sissy to her feet next to him. "We already decided, Uncle John. We're stayin' here. Miss Lottie needs us and we're not goin' to leave." His chin poked out belligerently and trembled just a bit as he spoke, but his eyes were fiery with purpose.

"Yeah," Sissy said with vehemence. "Thomas and me are gonna take care of everything."

Like two stalwart defenders, they stood before the door; the sunlight glinted off their golden hair. That it also revealed the havoc the night had wrought upon their clothing and the dusty tearstained face of Sissy, was a mark in their favor. We've taken a stand, was the silent message that radiated from their weary forms.

"Well . . ." John began slowly, not willing to blast their hopes yet. It was enough that they felt responsible for Lottie's injuries, he thought. They didn't need any more punishment than what they had already given themselves.

"Perhaps we can talk about it," Elizabeth said calmly, as she moved past John and sat on the edge of the porch. Sissy edged back, her bottom pressed against the door, her hand clutching Thomas's shirt.

With that, the door opened, and the child almost fell into the house, only saved by the firm hand of Doc Holmes as he stepped out onto the porch. He squinted in the bright sunlight, and his eyes sought John.

As though he were slogging through a quagmire, John approached, his feet dragging and his steps slow, "How is she?" he asked quietly.

"Hard to say," the doctor said with a single shake of his head. "If we were closer to a big city, we'd be able to get another opinion, but out here . . . I'm about all you've got, boy."

"I'll settle for you, Doc," John said firmly. "You've hauled a lot of chestnuts out of the fire around here."

"Well, I'd say that Lottie's going to be laid up for a while with that back. Looks to me like she bruised her spinal cord some, and it's going to have to heal. Then there's that lump she took. Good thing most women are hardheaded. That knock she took probably would have killed some of the soft-skulled men I know hereabouts."

"Will she be all right . . . I mean, will she be able to move her legs and . . ." John hesitated, unwilling to reveal his deepest fears any farther.

Doc looked down at the young farmer, and his eyes were kind. "That head injury is what we need to worry about for a couple of days, John. Let the back heal for now. Just be sure you wake her every couple of hours for the next day, and watch her pupils to see if they're the same size. If you can't wake her up, get a message to me right away, and I'll come out. Otherwise, I'll be back in a couple of days to check her out again."

"You're going to leave?" Elizabeth sounded incredulous.

"I got a whole countryside full of folks to take care of, ma'am," Doc Holmes said flatly. "Right now, there's a baby being born in town and I'll warrant that Mabel Sharp is doing the honors. Don't you worry, I wouldn't be leavin' if I thought Miss Lottie wasn't going to be all right."

"She needs to be in a hospital," Elizabeth said tightly.

"Well, we all need a lot of things we aren't likely to get," Doc said with a shrug, as he slid into his coat and adjusted the collar with one hand. His black bag swinging from the other hand, he stepped past the two children who had been listening intently to the adult conversation, and headed down the steps and toward his buggy.

"You get word to me, if you need me, hear?" he instructed John, as he gathered his reins and turned his horse in a tight circle in the yard.

"I'll be in town to settle with you, soon as I can," John called after him. But his words were ignored, except for the casual wave of the elderly man, who urged his horse on her way with a slap of leather across her rump.

"I hate this," Lottie grumbled, turning her head cautiously to watch the activity at the stove. Maude Clawson was dishing up bowls full of something she called Hell-Fire Stew from a big kettle. At the table, Sissy and Thomas watched, doubtful looks on their faces as they considered their supper.

"Relax, sweetheart," John said softly. "You're feeling better today, aren't you?"

She nodded reluctantly. "My head doesn't hurt much," she admitted. "But I sure don't like lying here on this board."

"I'm going to fix that right after supper," he told her. "I've got an idea that will make it better for you."

Her pout smoothed into a smile. "I'm sorry, John. I don't mean to complain. I'm just not used to letting someone do for me. First Genevieve here cooking yesterday, not to mention Elizabeth Sherman carrying our dirty laundry to town for someone to wash!"

"Quit your frettin', Lottie," he said with a quality of firmness she'd not heard from him before. "If it was someone else laid up, you'd be the first one there to help, and you know it. Just relax and get better, and then we'll give you all the work you can handle."

"Can she sit up at all, John?" Maude asked, as she approached with a bowl of the stew she'd concocted.

"What kind of meat is that?" Lottie asked, looking sideways at the mixture.

"I corned me a slab of beef in brine last time we butchered a steer," Maude said, as she offered John the bowl and stuck a spoon in it. "Makes good stew," she announced with emphasis.

Lottie looked doubtful.

"Let's sit you up just a little," John said, as he deposited the bowl on a low stool and then lifted her just enough to prop two pillows beneath her head.

"That feels good," she groaned, twisting her neck gingerly as she lifted her shoulders and tested the lump for tenderness against the feather pillows. "Do I have to eat it?" she whispered, as John bent low to tempt her with a spoonful.

He grinned. "You and me both, sweet. Come on, you just might like it," he coaxed.

And she did. It was surprisingly good, but after half a dozen spoonfuls, she'd had enough and begged off, shaking her head carefully in refusal of the next bite he offered.

"Can I have a little bread and butter?" she asked, as he frowned down at her.

He conceded defeat. "All right . . . so long as you eat something."

"I'll feel more like it tomorrow," she said agreeably. "I'll tell you how to make corn bread and mix up a mess of ham and beans."

He looked doubtful, but his wide shoulders lifted in a shrug of agreement as he cleaned out the bowl and headed for the table to wield the knife, cutting her a slice of the bread she had baked two days ago. He buttered it lavishly and carried it back, offering it on the palm of his hand.

"Thank you, John," she said politely, eyeing the offering eagerly.

Within the half hour, Maude was gone, her neighborly duty done for the day, headed for her own home just a mile down the road. The buckboard had scarcely left when John was thumping on the door, calling for Thomas to open it.

He shoved long boards across the floor, rumpling the rugs Lottie had strewn about for comfort, and then he disappeared once more.

"Uncle John's making you a secret," Sissy announced, as she plopped down on the stool by Lottie's side. "He says you can't be layin' on those boards much longer."

"Don't need to tell everything you know, Sissy," Thomas scolded. "It won't be a secret, if you keep on runnin' your mouth."

"Won't be a secret much longer anyway," John said, as he entered once more and leaned against the door to close it firmly behind himself. Hands full of tools, he beamed at Lottie, his hat skewed to one side of his head and cheeks reddened from the cold.

"I didn't know you were a carpenter, John," she said, shifting her shoulders on the rough bed she lay on, the better to watch him.

"I don't do fine work, but I manage to get things put together pretty well," he said in an offhand manner. "I built those chairs by the hearth for James and Sarah for their wedding." His eyes were pained for a moment as the memory assailed him, and then he shook it off, unwilling to dampen the mood he had set out to create tonight.

"You made them for Sarah?" Lottie asked, her stomach jerking as John mentioned the name. He always had that funny look when he talked about James's wife, not to mention his bragging about her genteel ways and fancy manners.

"Yeah," he grunted. "James wasn't much to build things. He did all right on the cabin, though. It was just that he didn't have much patience with sanding off rough corners and fitting pieces together nice and neat."

"Well, I'll be pleased to have you make me something, John. Although I can't imagine what I'd have any use for right now." She sounded prim, even to her own ears, and he glanced up at her with narrowed eyes.

"What are you all huffy about?" he asked in a deceptively soft tone, as he came to kneel next to her, waving Sissy away with a casual movement of his hand. "Here I plan on fixing you up a bed that won't be so bulky and hard to get around, and all you can do is

get that snooty look on your face. You know it drives
me up the wall, when you do that," he said curtly.

"Really?" She eyed him furtively, aware of the raw
edges of temper that had been exposed during the past
two days. But beneath the gruff words he'd spoken, she
caught a glimpse of weary concern that drew lines in
his cheeks and furrowed the width of his forehead.

"Yeah, really," he said.

"Well, now I know how to get to you, don't I?" she
teased, her hand lifting to stroke his jaw, as she noted
the whiskers he'd not taken time to shave today. Her
eyes softened, as she took stock of the easing of tension
that her words brought about. "I didn't mean to sound
snooty," she whispered. "I'm so much in your debt already, John. I surely don't want you to do any more for
me than what you have." She closed her eyes for a moment, but her fingers twined their way into his hair,
holding him closer.

"You're my wife, Lottie," he said simply. "I do for
you, because you belong to me."

Her eyes flew open, surprise evident on her features.
"I belong to you."

"We're family now. You and me and the children."
His glance included the two who watched them from
the table. "We stick together, we do things for each
other, and we accept without talking about debts."

"I thought about leaving you, John," she confessed,
her eyes intent on his as she said the words. "I thought
that if the children were gone, you wouldn't need me
anymore and you could go back to being a bachelor."

"You'd still be my wife," he reminded her gently. "I'd
have just come after you."

"Well, I'm here anyway," she said agreeably, as she
tucked that small piece of information away to be con-

sidered later. "I'll be back on my feet in no time, and everything will be all right."

"Doc says to take it easy, Lottie. Don't be getting rambunctious on me."

She shook her head. "No, he told me I'd probably be laid up for a month or so, John. It'll take time for my spine to heal. He thinks my spinal cord is bruised, did he tell you?"

"He told me."

"He thinks I'll be getting feeling back in my legs soon. Did he tell you that?"

John nodded.

"Do you believe him?" she asked carefully, her eyes focused now on a spot on the ceiling.

"The question, Lottie, is do *you* believe him?"

One tear slipped from the corner of her eye and slid down into the hair at her temple. "I'm trying," she whispered. "I've been praying up a storm ever since my head got straight last night. But it's been three days now, and I can't even wiggle my toes." She shuddered and winced at the twinge of pain that sliced through her head. "I don't want to be a burden."

"You're my wife, Lottie," he repeated. "You'll never be a burden." He shifted his weight to his heels and stood up beside her. "Now, I've got a bed to build before this night is over."

Sixteen

"The Shermans felt bad about leaving, you know." Stephen Bush sat in the chair by the fire and crossed one long leg over the other.

"They'll be back," Lottie reminded him gloomily.

Stephen nodded. "But they retreated gracefully for now. Don't borrow trouble, Miss Lottie," he said firmly.

"I think they didn't have it in their hearts to force the children to leave, after I fell," she said. "But they said they'd write and make further arrangements—whatever *that's* supposed to mean."

He lifted a dark eyebrow, and his gaze took in the narrow bed she rested in. "The Lord works in mysterious ways, Miss Lottie," he announced purposefully. "We'll just have to leave the whole thing in His hands. I'm sure things will work out for the best, for the children and for you."

"You sound like Miss Aggie in New Hope," she said sourly. "I thought she was the only one who knew all those wise things to say at all the proper times."

"I learned a lot of profound platitudes at the seminary back east," he told her, leaning forward as he whispered confidentially. "Your Miss Aggie doesn't have a market on wise sayings, you know. We preachers are supposed to know all the right things to say."

She smiled. She couldn't help it. The man who sat

with her had become a friend, and she had never had friends. Now I have two . . . Stephen and Genevieve. And perhaps John, she decided. Although what we have is less and yet more than friendship, she thought wistfully. He'd been so near, so dear . . . and yet his thoughts and memories were seldom revealed.

"Lottie?"

Her eyes focused on the preacher, on the half-smile that tilted his mouth, the uncertain, questioning look that he slanted at her.

"Are you all right?" he asked with concern. "For a moment there, you slipped away from me. Perhaps you're tired. I should leave." He allowed his foot to slip to the floor and slid forward in his chair.

"No," she said quickly, and found the smile that the thoughts of John had erased. "I'm enjoying your visit, Mr. Bush. Please." She gestured with one hand, and he relaxed once more. "I've been regretting all the times in my life that I've wished for a chance to lie down."

"Enforced leisure is sometimes worse then hard labor," he surmised.

"I've been parked in this spot for over a week, you know," she said impatiently. "I can't complain, though. Except that I'm afraid John has been neglecting his horses to care for me. They're his living, you know." Her voice softened as she looked toward the table where the children sat, engrossed with their chalk and slate. Thomas had taken on the task of instructing Sissy today. His fingers guided hers, as he concentrated on the letters she formed.

"I'm not even able to tend to the children," she sighed.

"Then let them have the privilege of looking after you," he advised her gently.

"They've made me feel useful here, and that's a fact."

His dark eyes were kind, and his smile reflected that same virtue. "You care for them deeply," he said, not questioning, but affirming what he already knew.

"Yes." She nodded and was aware that the movement brought no discomfort. Her head moved again, from side to side cautiously, and then she lifted it from the pillow, and her smile was pleased.

"I'm healing," she told him simply. "It's wonderful to move about without reminders of a headache."

"How about the other injury, Lottie?"

"My back?" She drew in a deep breath, and her smile was tremulous. "Doc says I should be patient. He seems to think that rest is the best cure." She looked down to where her feet rested, bare beneath the quilt John had covered her with earlier. "My toes feel prickly when I try to move them. I can lift my—" She flushed, deciding that her bottom parts were not a fit topic for discussion with the preacher. "Anyway . . . I do have feeling back in my upper limbs. Doesn't that sound like something is happening?"

"I'd say so," he agreed.

His gaze left her to sweep about the cabin, resting on the children, hovering momentarily over the double bed beneath the loft, and then sweeping back to concentrate on her. "You are happy here, aren't you?"

"Happy? Right now?" Her tone was incredulous.

"Yes, right now," he repeated.

"I could never be truly happy, so long as I'm a burden," she said softly. "I'm working on being content, Mr. Bush. And even that's a little difficult."

"I don't think your husband considers you a burden."

She pursed her lips briefly, and her eyes fluttered shut. "Trust me in this," she whispered. "I am."

"Well, Miss Lottie." he began, his tone determinedly cheerful, "I have another topic I'd like to discuss with you, if you don't mind." His gaze was distressed, as if he were mindful of the emotional pain her disability had caused her.

"I don't mind." Her eyes opened, and she forced her mind to concentrate on him. Time enough later to feel sorry for myself, she thought. He's come all this way to be neighborly. The least I can do is act polite.

"I'm considering marriage," he said carefully.

"Well, you've done that before," she said slyly, her lashes lowering to hide the amusement she knew must be apparent in her eyes.

He flushed unbecomingly, and she was immediately contrite.

"I didn't mean to be cruel, Mr. Bush," she said quickly. "Please forgive me." Her hand had reached to him in a gesture of pleading, and he took it between his own palms, leaning forward to speak softly.

"On the contrary, I am the one who should be begging forgiveness, Miss Lottie, for I fear I'm being selfish. But you see, my own feelings of happiness are constantly in my mind these days, and I thought only to confide in you."

He patted her hand in a gesture that brought another quick smile to her lips. "Would this have anything to do with Genevieve?" she asked airily.

His eyes widened. "Has she spoken of our relationship to you?"

"Somewhat." The word teased him.

"We are to be married," he said. "Within the month. Before Christmas, in fact."

"Do you consider her suitable to be a preacher's wife?" she asked easily.

"Eminently," he said quickly. "She and I have . . . ah . . . discussed some outward changes that might more suit the vocation . . ."

"She can't help her curls, Mr. Bush," Lottie said dryly. "And she'll always be beautiful. I sincerely hope she'll never lose her cheery manner and her generous spirit."

His face was a mask of horror. "Oh, no! You can't think I want her to assume a different personality. I just thought it would be more seemly for her to be dressed a bit more soberly." He leaned closer, and his earnest countenance was suddenly youthful and endearing.

"It's hard being a man of the cloth sometimes, Miss Lottie. I have as much appreciation for natural beauty as the next man, but for some reason, I'm expected to subdue it. I fear that by marrying me, Miss Genevieve will be subject to a critical eye from the entire congregation, if not the entire town."

"Well, it seems to me," Lottie said with spirit, "that if they like her as the storekeeper's daughter, they ought to like her equally well as the preacher's wife."

"Our marriage will not give you any embarrassment then?" he asked humbly.

"Whyever should it, Mr. Bush?" she said with a tilt to her chin that John would have called sassy. "I turned you down, if you'll recall."

He smiled, recognizing her teasing. "So you did, ma'am . . . so you did."

"Did you have a good visit with the preacher?" His eyes intent on his task, John asked the question that had been in the back of his mind all evening. He placed the basin of warm water on the low stool next to him, and set about propping Lottie up on another pillow.

"I guess so," she answered, as she gripped his neck while he lifted her.

"Let me do the work, Lottie," he instructed her. "You just relax now,"

"Ummm." She groaned, the sound deep in her throat as he carefully lifted her from the padding he'd formed from two quilts.

"All right?" he asked quickly, halting in his movement, his expression hesitant.

"Yes, it just feels good to move. I was getting stiff."

"You should have told me earlier. I'd have changed you around sooner, if I'd known you were uncomfortable," he said, scolding her gently.

She stretched her arms and shifted against the pillows. "No, really . . . I just wish I could do this for myself. I manage to turn my legs a little, but my feet just don't do what I want them to. I'm afraid to use my upper body too much yet. I'll wager I could pull myself up in the bed, if I tried, but the doctor said to wait awhile, before I put too much strain on those muscles."

"Don't even think about it, hear? That's why you've got me around." His look was stern, as he settled back on his heels to watch her.

"Yes sir," she said meekly, watching him as he wet a cloth in the basin of water and rubbed a bar of fine milled soap on it. Her eyes followed his movements, and she was waiting when he handed it to her.

"Smells good, doesn't it?" he asked, while she washed her face and throat.

"Ummm . . . I've never had such wonderfully

scented soap to use," she admitted. "Genevieve can't begin to know how pleased I was with her gift."

"Not any more than I was," he whispered, as he bent closer to inhale the fragrant suds. "I'm not sure who she bought it for, you know. I'm enjoying it as much as you are."

"Behave, John," she scolded, as she handed him the cloth to rinse.

"I'll be back in a few minutes," he said with a sigh, as he readied the cloth for her once more. Then, aware of her need for privacy, he rose and turned away. "When you get the top done, just cover up and wait for me."

He gave her ten minutes before he finished with his chore at the sink, dishes washed and set to drain. "Ready for me, sweet?" he asked.

She nodded, and they resumed the ritual that was becoming familiar. "May I ask you a favor, John?" It was easier to bear the intimacy of his bathing her, if she talked while the task was underway. Somehow the washcloth took on a gentler touch with his hand guiding it, the feel of his hands against her soap-slicked flesh bringing her to an awareness of her newly wakened sensitivity. As usual, she found herself flushed and breathless within minutes as the bath continued, and she groped for a distraction.

Evening had become a special time for him, one he looked forward to. This hour was theirs alone, after the children were safely asleep for the night, when he would lift her legs in gentle exercise, careful to follow the routine Doc had laid out for them. Then, as his own reward for the wearying chores of his day, he accepted the task of bathing her.

Adamantly, she washed as best she could, her face and arms, as much of her body as she could reach without strain. But then, his hands took over, and he relished the luxury of molding her flesh within the grasp of his fingers. Her legs, slender, but well formed . . . her back, a blend of curves and hollows, topped by the fragile nape of her neck, where damp curls tempted his mouth to linger. Her feet, high-arched and finely boned, were a joy to touch, he had long since decided. He washed them carefully, stretching out the task. Rinsing and drying them with the same care, he blew on the bottom to tease her, running his fingernail down the length of the sole to check her feeling, as the doctor had instructed him.

She frowned, her effort concentrated on the foot he held. "Did they move? I thought maybe my toes . . ."

He clasped her ankle within his palm, and then bent to touch his lips to the toes he'd dried with such care. "Don't try to rush it, Lottie." His voice was husky, almost harsh, as he lifted her leg to brush his mouth against the cool flesh once more.

"John?" She whispered his name, reminding him of her request.

His eyebrows lifted in silent query. "Hmmm? What, Lottie?" he asked finally, as she suffered the lingering caress of his fingers. His smile was tender, his eyes dark with the knowledge of his power over her.

He cleared his throat and lowered her foot to the blanket again. "What were you going to ask me?"

Her brow furrowed for a moment, and her request was hesitant. "If I can't walk by the time Mr. Bush marries Genevieve, I want you to take me to the wedding anyway," Lottie said carefully. "I really think I'll be on my feet by then though, don't you?" Her eyes flashed a look of pleading, before she dropped her lashes to cover the vulnerability she sensed she had revealed.

"I hope so, sweet," he said softly, reaching for her other foot.

She watched him closely, her fresh gown drawn up to cover her body, a towel draped across her legs for warmth. He's taken on too much, she thought sadly, as his fingers rubbed her toes, massaging and working them back and forth. His thumbs worked at the arch, and his palm curled around her heel, as he bent it first one way, then the other.

Moving to the side of her bed, his hands were warm and firm against her thighs and calves. Shifting the towel out of his way, he massaged her flesh, palms and fingers lifting and squeezing in a careful rhythm.

"There, that ought to do you for tonight," he said finally, as he rose to help her pull the soft, muslin nightgown over her head. Sliding one of the pillows from beneath her, he lowered her to lie flat. Then, with gentle care, he rolled her from one side to the other, easing the material into place about her. Lifting her, he smoothed it down her body.

"John," she whispered, as he covered her legs with the quilt. "Thank you."

His eyes swept over her length, and his grin was jaunty. "Don't worry, Mrs. Tillman. I'm keeping track. When this is all over, you're going to owe me a lot of pampering."

"If I ever get up and around, I'll be glad to spoil you rotten, Mr. Tillman," she vowed with fervor. She shifted on the narrow bed he'd devised for her, and groaned. "I'd give a lot to sleep in that feather bed, you know."

"Awww, Lottie . . . you know I'd like to have you there, don't you?" He knelt beside her and his hands

framed her face, tilting it to suit his pleasure as he bent
low to place soft, passionless kisses against her skin.
"Doc said you have to be on a firm surface until we
see definite healing. Just look how far you've come,
sweetheart. Pretty soon, you'll be back where you belong, and we can use this makeshift bed for kindling."

"It's not makeshift," she argued stoutly. "You did a
fine job on it." Her eyes filmed with tears and she
looked away. "Sometimes I feel downright ungrateful,
you know," she whispered. "I'm just impatient, John.
Forgive me for complaining, will you?"

"I'll do better than that," he vowed, his eyes glowing
as he brushed his knuckles against her glowing cheek.
"I've been thinking about something special, Lottie girl.
Will you let me give you a gift? I want to make you a
memory."

"A memory?"

"Yeah, I've been thinking for the past little while
here, that you need something to take out and look at
during the day, when you get down in the mouth. You
know, sort of like a treasure that will make you feel
good." His mouth settled against her temple, and his
warm breath brought gooseflesh to life on her arms
and back. With tender care his fingers brushed her hair
and smoothed a lock behind her ear.

"What kind of treasure?" she asked in a wispy, indrawn voice that told him of his effect on her.

"Oh . . . not the usual thing. No gold and silver and
fine jewels for my wife," he whispered against her hair,
as his hand left the lobe of her ear to move with gentle
precision to where her gown buttoned primly to her
throat.

"What are we talking about, John?"

"Hush . . . just close your eyes, and let me tell you

about this memory we're working on," He breathed the words against her throat, as his mouth followed the path his hand had taken.

The buttons gave way easily. "I'm getting better at this, sweetheart," he bragged in a triumphant whisper.

"John, the children," she mumbled, as she lifted her chin to give him better access to the place where her pulse had begun to beat more rapidly.

His mouth lifted for a moment from its intent exploration. "They're asleep, and if you're very quiet, they'll never hear a thing," he said against her warm flesh.

His hand slid beneath the quilt that covered her and made its way beneath the full skirt of her gown, his fingers tenderly paying homage to her lax limbs as he went. He massaged with gentle touches each surface he traveled, his palm and fingers squeezing with tender care.

"When you're alone tomorrow, when I'm out doing chores or working on the new corral, I want you to remember this. I want you to close your eyes and think about my mouth and my hands loving you."

"I can hardly move, John," she whispered distractedly, as a fine mist bedewed her forehead and her fingers clenched in his hair.

"Ahhh . . . that's the best part of this memory," he told her softly. "You don't have to move a muscle. You just have to be still and let me give you pleasure."

"What about—"

"Shhh, no more talk, Lottie. Just close your eyes and let me make you a memory."

She gave herself up to it. She shut her eyes, aware only of his hands against her, of his mouth that wooed her to arousal. She felt the damp, hot movement of his tongue, the brush of his hair, and the drawing of his mouth. She shivered as the swirling mists of desire surrounded her, beguiling her into their midst as she sank into the dream he wove.

It was too much, the slow, careful exploration of her flesh that led her down the path he had chosen. She gasped as sensations of shivering delight burst into being within her. The hot, drawing, coiling pleasure he had first brought to life only weeks ago, now waited to be revived by his touch. And touch her he did . . . with firm, then feathering movements that brushed quivering flesh into awareness.

Small sounds of undiluted pleasure were born in her throat, and as her mouth opened to allow them expression, he came to her once more. Capturing her lips, he tasted the joy she expressed, holding the music of her passion within the confines of his mouth.

"Shhh . . . shhh," he coaxed finally, as her arms held him close in hungry embrace. He cuddled her within the enclosure of his broad chest and the comforting circle of his arms. His mouth whispered nonsense as he garnished her flushed cheeks with damp kisses, and he smiled as he considered the confusion that darkened her eyes.

"John?" High and uncertain, her voice spoke his name.

"Did you like your gift, sweet?"

"Better than anything I've ever received," she whispered.

"Better than the shoes?" His eyes twinkled with the delight he took in her pleasure.

She flushed even deeper. "Oh, yes," she breathed. "Even better than the shoes."

* * *

The wintry sunlight poured in frosty splendor through the window near the door, and Lottie watched the dust motes that swirled within the rays. The sounds of activity around the table had been banished, as Maude declared she could not work with all that foolishness going on between Sissy and Thomas.

They had been sent outdoors, and now silence, except for the shuffle of Maude's well-worn shoes against the floor, reigned.

Lottie dragged her eyes reluctantly from the dancing specks of sunlight, to watch the older woman dourly set about the task of kneading her batch of bread dough. Hair skinned back from her head, mouth pursed in concentration, she slapped the firm mass into submission, then doubled it over upon itself, to once more beat it into an elongated circle.

"I really appreciate you helping out like this, Maude," Lottie ventured.

The woman sniffed and nodded curtly. "Just doing my Christian duty, Lottie. Preacher says we must 'do it unto the least of these,' and I aim to follow the good book." She split the grayish lump into three parts, formed them quickly, then slid them into the bread pans that waited on the table.

"They'll be ready to bake in an hour," she said with satisfaction. Placing them atop the warming oven, where they would rise once more, she covered them with a clean dish towel.

Lottie watched with hopeful interest. If luck were with them, it would be tastier than the last batch the woman had baked for the Tillman family. Sissy was right, she decided silently. Mrs. Clawson's talents did not include making good bread.

Her hands actually itched with the urge to create her

own loaves; shaping and forming them with pride, baking them to golden, crusty perfection, and serving warm, tender slices to her family. Without thinking, she sighed, long and deep, lost in the daydream that lingered in her mind.

"You all right?" Maude asked, lifting her head, frowning as she considered the young woman who watched her.

"Yes," Lottie said quickly. "Just wishing I could be over there, doing for my family."

"Might as well enjoy being tended to while you can," Maude muttered. "Lord knows it's rare when a woman can be a lay-a-bed, except for birthing. Even then, you don't get much resting done, what with havin' to wait on the young'uns you've already got."

"I have to admit, I'm not really enjoying this," Lottie said, thinking that those words were the truest she'd spoken all day. "I'm used to being up and about. Just being parked in front of the fireplace, where I can see all the cobwebs in the corners, is trying my patience no end," she admitted.

Maude looked up at the ceiling, her gaze meandering from one corner to the next, and then her sturdy shoulders lifted in a shrug. "Can't say I've ever bothered to look for trouble. If it's way up there, it can stay there for all I care," she announced. "I always figure that when I open the door in the spring, the breeze will just blow out the worst of it. It's all I can do to take care of what's on the floor, let alone look for dirt that's hangin' around over my head."

Lottie tried to smile. "Well, I certainly appreciate what you're doing here to help out. My cobwebs will be just fine till I'm able to shake my broom at them again, I'm sure."

"You been teachin' those children here at home?" Maude asked, as she swept Thomas's slate to one side of the table. She bent to peer at the letters he'd been practicing.

"Yes, I've been trying. John says Thomas would have begun riding to school next year, but I thought I'd try to give him a head start."

"Too much book learning isn't good for young'uns," Maude said sagely. "Gives them ideas."

"Sometimes," Lottie began carefully, "I think it's good to learn about what's out there in the world, don't you?"

"Nope." The answer was firm and certain. "Just unsettles them, makes 'em get antsy and uppity, if they get too much education. They get to thinking they're too good to stay home and help out."

"Well, the children's mother wanted them to learn all they could," Lottie said bravely. "I feel obliged to do what I can to follow her wishes."

Maude slanted her a dubious glance, as she settled herself with a pan of potatoes to be peeled. "Sarah Tillman was too soft for life in these parts. She was a city girl, born and bred. This life killed her, you know. She'd done better to stay in St. Louis," she offered in a flat voice that pronounced judgment.

"She wanted to be with her husband, I expect," Lottie said diffidently. "She was happy here, wasn't she?"

Maude grimaced. "What's happy got to do with anything?" she muttered. "We weren't put on this earth to be happy. The Bible says men will till the ground and fight a battle with weeds and thistles, and women will suffer to bear their children. Sounds pretty plain to me." She sliced with vengeance at the potato she was peeling, and spread her legs to better cradle the pan between her sturdy thighs.

"Haven't you ever been happy, Maude?" Lottie ventured hopefully. "Not even when you were newly wedded and first loved Mr. Clawson?"

"Humph!" Her head lifted and her look was incredulous. "I had better sense than to expect a bed of roses, when I got married, girl," she spouted, spearing her knife in the air for emphasis. "My Henry needed a passel of sons to help out in the fields, and it was my bounden duty to supply them. Been doing it ever since," she concluded.

"Who's tending the children while you're here?" Lottie asked, in awe of Maude's stoic acceptance of her place in the scheme of things.

"My oldest is a girl, Josie May. She's almost fourteen now. Good girl, can bake pret' near as good as me already. She's keepin' the lot of 'em busy this morning."

"Don't any of them go to school?" Lottie asked carefully.

Maude shrugged her shoulders, as she dropped another peeled potato into the pan of water on the table. "They go when the weather's good, lessen there's field work to be done. Then Henry can't spare a horse to tote them back and forth."

"They could come here if they'd like, when they can't get to school, I mean," Lottie offered timidly. "I'd teach them along with Thomas."

"Would you now?" Maude's hands stilled, and she considered the young woman who watched her. "Well, maybe the boys could stand to learn a little more about figures," she conceded finally. "Maybe I'll bring a couple of them along next time I come by."

Lottie glowed. "Please do, Maude. I'll feel like I'm

doing something to help repay you for helping out here."

"How long does Doc think you'll be laid up anyway?"

Her chin lifted and her look was determined, as Lottie waffled a bit. "Well, he doesn't say for sure, but I know he's really pleased with my progress."

"Can't move those legs yet, can you?"

She shook her head. "Not a lot, but I can lift them and move from one side to the other. I've even got pins and needles all the way down to my toes," she said cheerfully. "That's better than last week."

In truth, she realized she'd almost despaired of achieving any degree of mobility last week, she remembered. Why the night John had bathed her and . . . Her cheeks flushed as she allowed that memory to slip into place. He'd accomplished what he'd set out to do, she admitted to herself. He'd given her a memory.

"You running a fever?" Maude asked, peering at her with squinted eyes. "You're all red-cheeked."

Lottie swallowed the nervous laughter that bubbled within her. "No! Certainly not. I'm probably just too close to the fire this morning," she said, flustered by Maude's scrutiny.

"Well, I'd better get some carrots topped and into this kettle," Maude announced, heaving herself to her feet as she lifted the pan of potato parings. "Want these in with the pig slops?" she asked Lottie.

"Yes, Thomas can carry them out later." She listened intently as she heard a series of sounds from the yard. "What are they doing out there, Maude? Sounds like John's working on the corral, but surely he's too close to the house."

"He's been draggin' wood up from the barn all morning," Maude said. "Must be he's puttin' something together out back."

"He should be finishing the corral for his horses. I'm afraid he's been neglecting them for my sake," Lottie said unhappily. "And then he had to go to the mill yesterday. He must have needed more posts. I meant to ask him about it, but it slipped my mind."

"Probably tell you it was none of your business," Maude offered bluntly.

Lottie held the small seed of happiness within her that had been growing at a steady pace for weeks. "Well, I'll ask him when he comes in," she announced, certain that John would vindicate her trust in him.

But by the time the stew was ready and the children had been fed, John still hadn't come in. Lottie was anxious, aware now that the sounds from the yard had been transferred to the other side of the house, beyond the wall where she lay before the fireplace.

Thomas burst in the door. "Uncle John wants to know, can you send out three bowls of stew? They're hungry out there," he announced.

Maude mumbled a reply and reached for the heavy, round bowls that sat in the cupboard. "Appears to me that they'd take time to eat dinner at the table." She tucked the bowls under her arm, stuck three spoons in her apron pocket, and lifted the kettle from the stove with a heavy flannel about the handle. Grumbling at the summons, she headed for the door.

"Find out what's going on out there," Lottie said quickly, before Maude was through the portal.

Eagerly she listened, waiting for the woman's return, her curiosity piqued by the activity outdoors. But instead of Maude, the next body through the doorway belonged to Thomas. He scooped up the woman's coat from the peg by the door and was gone before Lottie could question him.

"Mrs. Clawson's goin' home now, Miss Lottie. She says Uncle John can put the bread in the oven."

The last of his pronouncement was cut off by the closing of the door. Lottie pleated the quilt with fingers that itched to do her own brand of baking, as she cast a doubtful look toward the pans that waited John's attention.

"Well, if he's going to take care of the bread, that means he'll be in here before long," she announced to the empty room. "Guess I'll have to wait."

By the time he arrived, empty bowls in one hand, the pot dangling from the other, she had a more urgent request for him to handle. Her words were halting and delivered just above a whisper.

"I'm so glad to see you, John. I thought you'd never get back in the house."

He smiled at her, a triumphant grin if she'd ever seen one. "Missed me, huh?"

"No," she answered tartly. "I just miss being able to go to the outhouse, when I need to."

"Oh, Lottie," he said, suddenly contrite. He dumped the dishes into the dishpan in the sink and deposited the kettle on the stove. "I forgot, sweet," he said, his manner penitent as he turned to her. "I need to wash my hands first. They're like two chunks of ice right now."

Hastily he dipped a panful of hot water from the reservoir. Carrying it to the sink, he hastily scrubbed at his hands, warming them and cleaning the morning's soil with a scoop of the soap that Lottie kept there.

"You wouldn't want these cold hands on your soft bottom, now, would you?" he asked, his mouth lifting in a teasing smile.

She was mortified. "John, it's bad enough we have to do it," she burst out. "Do we have to discuss it, too?"

He reached beneath the bed to locate the bedpan Doc Holmes had brought. Rising, he eyed her solemnly. "What I do for you shouldn't be an embarrassment to either of us, Lottie," he scolded her gently.

"I know," she said. "But I hate for you to . . ."

"Stop it right now," he said firmly, pushing the quilt aside as he lifted her. He covered her again and went to the door, sliding the bar in place before he came back to her.

"Before long, this will all be in the past, you know." His words were a promise, and she clung to it.

"Do you really think so, John?"

He dropped to his knees, holding her hands in his, as he bent to kiss her tenderly. "I know so, sweet," he vowed. "I know so."

He was finished in a few minutes, his task complete, having lifted her to a more comfortable position before he smoothed the covers back in place.

"John!" He was almost out the door, and he stuck his head back around hastily.

"What's going on out there? Who's out there with you?" She was impatient with the unknowing.

"Just Otto Schrader and Mr. Sharp giving me a hand," he said blithely.

"Doing what?" she wanted to know, her words impatient.

His smile was pure deviltry, while the gleam in his eye only served to add to the effect. And his reply elicited a snort of aggravation from her, as he uttered the words, "Secrets, Lottie. Secrets."

Seventeen

"You did a fine job on the dresses you made," Mabel Sharp said, as she unloaded her basket of laundry. Piled on the kitchen table, the neatly folded clothing was a testimony to that lady's rigid standards of cleanliness. Boiled, bleached, and scrubbed vigorously on her corrugated board, they looked cleaner, from Lottie's vantage point, than she would have thought possible.

"Thank you," Lottie said humbly. "Miss Aggie always said I had a fine hand at stitching."

"Well, if you ever want to earn a little extra to put by for a rainy day, I'd be glad to give you some sewing to do for me," Mabel said, as she brushed at a minute speck on one of John's shirts.

"I'd be glad to do your mending, while I'm laid up here," Lottie suggested eagerly. "I could use something to occupy my hands."

Mabel looked at her measuringly. "From what I can see, you aren't going to be there much longer, missy. You're sitting up this week . . . probably be walking by Christmas."

Lottie's eyes glowed with eagerness. "Oh, I hope so," she said fervently. "Doc seems to think I'll be fine."

"Well, he's not given to making false promises, but I wouldn't plan on hiking to town for a while yet," Mabel allowed briskly. "Now, tell me where to put these things, and I'll get this washing cleared away," she said as she sorted through the clothes. "I thought to make you some cinnamon rolls today, while I'm frying up a chicken for your dinner."

"I've had my mouth set for fried chicken for days," Lottie admitted. She settled against the pillows that cushioned her back and once more concentrated on the clothing Mabel had washed for her. "Do you have help with your washing, Mrs. Sharp?" she asked.

The woman's eyebrows lifted in surprise. "Land sakes, girl . . . I've been scrubbing clothes for a cow's age. Mr. Sharp wanted to get in help for me when he opened the undertaking parlor in town, but I told him—" She lowered her voice confidentially. "I said, Charles, there's not another woman in town can do up laundry as good as I can." She nodded her head for emphasis. "I do all the burying clothes, you know. Make sure the departed ones are looking up to snuff for the last viewing."

"No, I didn't know," Lottie answered.

"Well," Mabel said carefully, "if you'd seen the condition of James Tillman's shirt when John brought him to us, you'd know what I mean. My word, I just hustled down to Mr. Slocum's store and got him another. Couldn't do a thing with what he had on." Her mouth pursed as she remembered. "John did the best he could and brought in a different one." She shook her head at the memory. "But it wasn't . . ." Her head wagged again, mute testimony against the substandard shirt.

" 'Course, his suit was in good shape, as I recall, but then he'd not worn it much lately. Sarah's been gone a good long time, and these poor young'uns have been scrimping along on their own. It's no wonder they didn't have a decent thing to wear between them all."

Lottie's chin lifted a trifle. "Well, they're clean now.

And bound to stay that way, if I have anything to say about it."

Mabel nodded decisively. "I looked your washing over real good, Lottie. It was all fresh dirt. No old stains that I could see."

"I wasn't real pleased, when Mrs. Sherman and Genevieve first took you the dirty clothes from here, Mrs. Sharp," Lottie admitted. "I hate to be beholden to someone, but the children do not have enough to wear to get along for more than a week or so without getting their things done up."

The older woman held an armful of folded clothing and headed for the corner near the bed. She bent low to place the pile of John's small things on top of Lottie's trunk, and laid a threadbare nightgown next to them.

"You need to get a new nightie," she said, rising with a muffled groan, one hand clamped to her hip. "This one's about to split to pieces."

"I know . . . I'll be getting a length of muslin and sewing one up, when I'm back to taking hold of things around here."

Mabel looked askance, her brows raised in question. "Won't John get you material? He goes into town every week."

Lottie felt the flush warm her cheek, as she shook her head. "I'd rather take the money for it from the eggs and butter that Mr. Slocum sells for us."

Mabel's forehead creased once again. "I've never known John to be a skinflint, Lottie, He does real well with those horses of his. I'll warrant he'd buy you anything you need."

How did I get into this? Lottie thought ruefully. "I don't mean to make John out to be a penny-pincher," she explained, her hands clenched tightly in her lap as she tried to put the words together as best she could. "I just was raised to be responsible for myself, and if I can do something to help out and earn money, then I'll feel more like I deserve the benefits from it."

"Well, one thing's for sure," Mabel said firmly. "You need more than a new nightgown, girlie. You could use a decent cupboard and some sitting furniture in here. Not to mention a bigger house. There's not enough room in here to swing a cat."

"Oh, no," Lottie was quick to reply. "We're doing just fine! I truly don't need anything, Mrs. Sharp. Not anything like that anyway," she said, qualifying her statement. "I just need to be up and about and able to do for my family . . . that's all I'm asking for."

Mabel's head cocked to one side as a sound caught her ear, and she hastened to the window to peer into the yard. "Well, it looks like you're about to get more than you bargained for. Here comes Maude Clawson with three of her boys, all bundled up on the buckboard."

Thankful for a chance to escape the touchy subject she'd been plowing through, Lottie smiled brightly. "I think she's probably brought them for lessons. I told her to let them come down, and I'd teach them along with Thomas."

Mabel shook her head. "I'm afraid you've bitten off more than you can chew, missy," she said glumly. "Those boys can be scamps, you know."

Lottie's grin widened. "But I'm very good at handling scamps, Mrs. Sharp, she said smugly, "I spent years keeping a passel of little girls in line."

The small house was bursting with activity before the day was over, what with Lottie holding court before the fire with four small boys lined up, intent on impressing her with their prowess. In their scant months of schooling, the Clawson children had collected an admirable amount of knowledge, and Lottie feared that Thomas would lag behind dreadfully. But he spoke up frequently, making her aware that his father had taught him unknowingly, his practical knowledge of sums far outweighing his skills on the slate.

"I just don't know how to put it down in numbers sometimes," he explained. "But I know in my head how to figure things out. Like if pa needed corn, he'd tell me how many ears to get for the pigs, or how many to shuck for the chickens, and I could count out how many that was for him." He held up four fingers and waved them at Lottie, "See, Miss Lottie. I know this is four, but I just don't know how to write the figure for it."

Her eyes met those of John, who had just come in the door. His smile was tender as he leaned against the wall. His cheeks were ruddy from the crisp air, his shoulders hunched beneath the heavy jacket he wore. One hand snatched his hat off, and he tossed it with easy grace to swing from a peg on the wall, while the other hand smoothed his hair back in an automatic gesture.

"Hi there, schoolmarm," he teased, as he undid the front of his coat. "Afternoon, ladies," he said, nodding at the two women who were working at the stove.

Not to be moved from her purpose, Mabel had put together a batch of cinnamon buns and was even now preparing to take them from the oven. Opening the door, she waved the flannel cloth to distribute the heat that poured forth and then bent to slide out the flat pan of rolls.

"Hope you didn't put too much cinnamon in those," Maude said dourly. "I like a mite less than what you used," she observed.

"Never had any complaints yet," Mabel announced, as she deposited the pan atop the warming oven. "These'll be just fine," she predicted.

"Sure smells good to me," John said, as he slanted a glance at his wife, "Bet they'll be pretty near as tasty as Lottie's."

She glared at him, aghast at his bad manners. "I'm sure mine aren't nearly so good," she denied quickly. "These look wonderful"

"Are we done, Miss Lottie?" Thomas asked, as he squirmed his bottom on the floor. "My behind is gettin' sore."

"Thomas!" Her gasp was horrified, as he looked about questioningly. "You're in the presence of ladies. You mustn't use words like that."

He leaned forward, puzzlement alive on his mobile features, "Like what, Miss Lottie?" he asked in a whisper. "Alls I said was my behind was gettin' sore, and that's the truth."

She flushed and waved her hand at him, motioning him to come to her. He rose reluctantly, aware that all eyes in the house were upon him. John was smiling broadly, much to Lottie's chagrin. The two women at the stove were torn between amusement at the boy and sympathy for Lottie's attempts at teaching mannerly behavior.

Reaching to draw him near, she dismissed Maude's three, sending them to the kitchen, where their mother took their slates from them for safekeeping. Thomas, she settled next to her, his small bottom resting on the edge of her narrow bed. With gentle fingers, she brushed his hair to neatness and then patted his cheek tenderly.

Her voice was low and carried only to his ears as she

instructed him. "The behind, as you put it, is a body part that we don't speak of in company, Thomas," she said firmly. "It used to be that any part that was covered by clothing was not to be mentioned. Now, good manners allow us to speak of arms, and within the family, we might discuss other parts. Do you know what I'm saying?" she asked."

He nodded hesitantly. "I think so, ma'am. You mean, I can't say my behind hurts, when there's anybody here but you and me and Sissy and Uncle John."

"Well, I guess that's good enough for now. We'll have Uncle John talk to you about it some more, maybe later on," she promised.

Over the child's head, John looked on with a wicked grin, and Lottie pursed her lips into a grim warning as she sent Thomas on his way.

"I think your wife's had enough excitement for today, John," Mabel said decisively. "We're all going to get out of your way and head for home. Mr. Sharp has a liking for his supper on the table at five on the dot." She went to where her cloak hung near the door and tossed it over her shoulders with a practiced gesture.

"I'll let him know you're ready to go now, ma'am," John offered.

"Did you get—" she began and then halted with a quick glance in Lottie's direction.

"Barn's lookin' real good," he said hastily, nodding his head vigorously. "What do you think of Lottie?" he said quickly. "Sitting up there like nobody's business. Really perked up lately, hasn't she?"

"I told her she'll be walking by Christmas. Probably be able to go to the wedding, won't she?"

"We're hoping to get her there," John said, as he held the door open for the warmly clad woman to leave.

"Take care, Lottie," she said with a lift of one hand. "I'll be back out next Tuesday. Send your wash in with Genevieve this Saturday, and I'll do it with mine on Monday."

Lottie nodded, overwhelmed by all the moving to and fro, the bodies that filled the small space about her, and the conversation that had given her pause. Before she could review in her mind just what it was that had caught her attention, John had ushered the rest of their visitors out the door and was heading for where she sat.

"I appreciate all the help we've been getting, but this house isn't big enough to hold that many people for so long," he said bluntly.

Lottie nodded in silent agreement, her eyes on him as he squatted by the edge of her bed. She brushed at his hair, smiling as she realized that Thomas had, in some quirk of heredity, inherited his uncle's stubborn forelock. Her fingers nudged it into place, and she felt a tug of affection for him that mirrored the tender feelings she'd bestowed on the children. He's boy and man combined, she decided, and I love him as both. The admission stunned her for a moment, and her fingers tightened against his scalp as she buried her hand in the silken gold of his hair. Her eyes closed as she savored the discovery, and she longed to gather him close.

Hie eyes feasted on the woman who touched him with gentle fingers. Beneath her caress, John felt a spasm of delight flood his being. A jolt of awareness that urged him to lean nearer to snatch a moment's pleasure. Dropping to his knees, he leaned one long arm across her, bracing himself as he snuggled his face against hers, inhaling the sweetness that was uniquely her own.

The tendrils of hair that had escaped the confinement of her braid teased at his nose, and he blew at them, a breath of air that brought a shiver to the surface of Lottie's sensitive flesh. She quivered beneath him, and he was suddenly, gloriously aware of the woman he had married. The delicate smell of French milled soap blended with her own faint scent and rose to tempt him, bringing him acutely to the edge of desire. He opened his mouth against the tender flesh of her throat.

"You always smell so good, sweet," he murmured, his lips damp as they moved on her skin.

She tilted her head to one side, basking in the warmth of his admiration, her yearning for his touch honed by their hours apart through this long day. "I haven't seen much of you lately," she pouted, allowing her eyelids to lower, savoring these precious moments of privacy.

"Been busy," he mumbled, his head resting now against her shoulder as he relaxed into her softness. He chuckled, the sound vibrating against her as he leaned more heavily. "You feel good," he groaned, rubbing his face against the soft muslin of her gown.

Her fingers lifted to weave once more into the thick lushness of his hair, and she cradled him against herself. "I've heard you hammering and sawing out back for days, John," she said carefully. "When are you going to tell me what you're doing out there?"

He turned his head to nip at the front of her gown, and then worried it between his teeth. "What will you give me, if I share my secret?" he asked teasingly.

Her arms slid about his shoulders and she rocked him with a gentle movement, her face buried against the crown of his head. "Whatever you want, John," she whispered. "But not because I want to hear your secret."

He raised himself, his arms straight on either side of her as he frowned with mock indignation. "All this fussing you've done for days, and now you're telling me you don't want to know what's going on?" He brushed his nose against hers and rested his forehead against her brow, his teasing unable to withstand her nearness.

His voice carried only to her ears, dark with promise. "Before long, Lottie," he growled. "I'll take all you offer . . . soon as it's safe . . . when you've healed."

"I think I'm well enough, if—" she began haltingly.

He shook his head once. "No. Don't tempt me, sweetheart. I'll be alone in that bed for a little while yet."

"When will we know?" The whisper was low. He closed his eyes, knowing she would be flushed and embarrassed at her own boldness.

"Doc will tell me, Lottie."

"Then I don't have anything to bargain with, do I?" Her whisper was coaxing, her breath sweet, as she murmured the words.

He lifted from her, and his eyes feasted on the rosy cheeks and soft mouth that offered him such temptation. "Be careful, my girl," he warned her, his eyes narrowed and gleaming in the light from the fireplace. "There are things I've a notion to teach you, and I might just start tonight."

Her smile was radiant, her delight in the promise he made, apparent. "Is that so?"

As promised, the cinnamon rolls were delicious. The fried chicken that waited on the back of the stove was crispy and still warm, and Maude's kettle of green beans were savory with bits of onion and ham swimming in the juice.

Plate in hand, Lottie eyed the three sitting around the table across the room. "Would you all join me for supper tonight?" she asked wistfully, her gaze focused on John.

"Over there?" he asked.

She nodded, and waved one hand to indicate the space that surrounded her bed. "We could pretend we're on a picnic." The words were hopeful and the response was immediate.

"Can we, Uncle John?" Sissy asked breathlessly. Picnics were for summertime, and rare at that. Her eyes darted from him to fasten with glee on Lottie's smiling face.

"How can you have a picnic in the house?" Thomas asked doubtfully.

"Easy," Lottie assured him. "You just spread a quilt on the floor, and pretend you're under a tree."

"I'm not very good at pretending," Thomas muttered, as he waited for his uncle's word on the matter.

"Well, It's about time you started practicing then," John said, falling in with the game Lottie had begun. Plate in hand, he left the table and snatched a folded quilt from the end of the bed. With one hand, he shook it open. Before he could bend to spread it into place, Sissy was beside him, eager to help.

"There's room for all of us," she sang, her busy hand smoothing it across the floor. She scampered back to the table to retrieve her plate, and then settled down to lean against Lottie's bed. Her eyes glowed as she surveyed her family, coming to rest finally on John. "See, Uncle John, the chicken even tastes better on a picnic."

Her glee was contagious, and Thomas grinned at her nonsense as he waved his drumstick in the air, "Shoo, flies," he said, as he banished the imaginary creatures from his dinner. "I wonder if this is that old broody hen that's been wantin' to set so bad," he mumbled, as he tore a length of dark meat from the crusty piece he held.

"She'd make tough eating, I'm afraid," Lottie said

with a laugh. "This one is the last of the young roosters from spring, I think. Isn't he, John?" she asked,

He nodded and his grin flashed, white and appealing. "You should have seen Mabel chasing him around the chicken yard. I think he knew his time was up."

"Well, he sure makes a fine supper," Thomas said approvingly, licking his fingers and surveying the naked bones on his plate.

Sissy wiggled against the bed and looked over her shoulder at Lottie. "We get to tell you our secret tonight, Miss Lottie," she said with pride. "I've kept it for a lot of days, and Uncle John said that we could tell it tonight."

Lottie's eyes sought John, and her brows raised in inquiry. "Is this the secret I was bargaining for a while ago?" she asked with an arrogant tilt of her chin. "If I'd known it was going to be free, I wouldn't have been so generous with my offer." Her eyes sparkled with the memory of the precious moments they'd shared, and she was rewarded by his look of appreciation.

His shoulders lifted and his grin teased her. "Just thought I'd see what I could get away with," he said slyly.

Thomas rolled his eyes at the antics of the grown-ups, his mind clearly on the revealing of the secret he'd been sworn to conceal. "Who gets to tell her. Uncle John?" he asked eagerly.

John shrugged. "You can, I suppose." His eyes were dancing with amusement, as Lottie wiggled against the firm surface of her bed.

"Well, tell me!" she burst out finally as the three watched her.

"Uncle John's been building us a room," Thomas said proudly. "I got to help him some with it."

"Me, too," Sissy bragged. "I held the nails and sat on the end of the board while he sawed it."

"A room?" Lottie's whisper was awed. Her eyes flitted to the wall behind the fireplace, where so much activity had been going on for three days.

"I got Mr. Sharp and Otto Schrader to help me out," John said. "We seem to have need of more space in here, now that the children are growing so fast."

Sissy leaped to her feet and stood her tallest. "See, Miss Lottie. I'm bigger," she boasted proudly.

"No taller than you were last week," Thomas said prosaically, as he shook his head at her.

"Am, too," she said stubbornly, hands on her hips as she swished her skirt and stamped one small foot.

"You'll be big soon enough," Lottie put in quickly, reaching to tug at the child's dress.

"We probably won't even be here to see the room anyway," Thomas mumbled, his face drawn in lines of sudden distress. "Remember? *They're* comin' back."

Lottie drew in a breath, as she considered the fact they'd all been avoiding so diligently. "We can only live one day at a time, Thomas," she said finally. "Until your grandparents show up on the doorstep, we're a family, and we'll make plans and do things together. It's not good to borrow trouble."

"Well, I'm not leavin'," he said stoutly.

Sissy's lower lip quivered and her eyes began to fill with tears as she turned to Lottie. Her defiance and quick temper doused by Thomas's dour prediction, she sought the refuge of warm arms and cast herself against Lottie's bosom.

"We don't know yet what's going to happen, Thomas," his uncle said gently, aware that he could make no promises. "I've talked to the lawyer in town though. We'll just have to wait and see." He leaned to pick up Sissy's plate and rose, carrying it with his own to the sink. "In the meantime, we've got a big job to do tonight, son."

Thomas rolled quickly to his knees; his face brightened with anticipation, as he remembered the task that lay ahead. "I'll go and get the tools," he offered.

"No, come on out with me, and we'll do this from the other side." John told him, his smile mysterious as Lottie's forehead furrowed in puzzlement.

"Do what?" she asked plaintively.

"You'll see," was the teasing reply she heard, as the two grinning males reached for their coats and headed out the door.

Within an hour, the cutting was complete, and, piece by piece, the logs were removed from the opening John and Thomas had formed in the wall. Beyond them was a shadowy area, lit by the lantern that sat on the floor and cast its glow in the darkness. Amid much laughter and teasing, the work had progressed, with John poking his head between the logs as he removed them, and Thomas chortling in the background as he heard Lottie's cries of amazement and Sissy's delighted giggles.

With long, straight boards, John framed in the opening, his movements deft and sure as he measured and cut the pieces to fit. He nailed them in place, his hammer blows precise. Then, in a gesture of triumph, he lifted a door from the floor of the new room and stood it in the opening, looking to Lottie for approval.

"What do you think?" he asked proudly. "Will that work?"

"It's splendid," she cried, leaning forward on the bed, as if she yearned to be a part of the activity.

"I've got hinges for it, too," he bragged. "Got them

in town the other day." He motioned to Thomas for his help and, between them, they held the door in place. John searched in his pocket for the pencil stub he needed. With a practiced eye, he measured and marked the places where he would attach the hinges.

"That's got it," he breathed with a sigh, and they lowered the door once more to the floor, out of their way. With a chisel and his hammer, he made quick work of it, chipping the wood to make room for the shiny hinges he'd already attached to the door. Within a short while, he was ready to hang it in place.

"Should we have some sort of celebration?" Lottie asked, "I feel like we need a housewarming or something."

"We got cinnamon rolls left over," Sissy said hopefully. "We could have another picnic!"

"No, I think the party's almost over for tonight," her uncle said, as he considered the little girl's bright face. "Tomorrow's another day. Sissy. We'll have lots to do, and you can help. We'll save the rolls for breakfast."

She submitted reluctantly, but with good grace. "If I can help." She repeated his promise firmly.

His nod gave her assurance, and she snuggled her hand into Lottie's as she surveyed the scene. "This is fun, isn't it, Miss Lottie?" she asked.

"Yes . . ." Lottie's eyes misted for a moment, as she considered the child. She'd tried to put the impending visit out of her mind, but the thought of losing the presence of the children from her life intruded abruptly. If they were to go . . . it was not to be considered. They wore John's whole life, and if he had to give them up into their grandparent's custody again, it would break his heart.

She reached to gather Sissy into her arms and leaned

her cheek against the golden hair. "It is time for bed, lovey," she whispered, as she cradled the child against her breast.

Sissy's sigh was heavy, a dramatic gesture that brought a quick lift to Lottie's spirits. "Scoot along now," she said, dusting the girl's skirts with her palm as she sent her on her way. Sissy's feet were sure, climbing the rungs of the ladder. She swung herself easily into the loft, finding her way to the trundle bed where she undressed quickly.

"I'm ready, Miss Lottie," she called down over the railing.

"I'll bet you didn't wash up," Thomas said under his breath, as he made his way into the room, easing past John, who was sanding off a rough spot on the edge of his door.

Sissy made a face at her brother and muttered a dire threat under her breath. "I was just gonna," she said airily, as she turned about to ease her way back down the ladder. Her gown was tucked up out of the way, and her short, sturdy legs made quick work of the descent. "I need to say my prayers, too," she announced, delighted to have thought of another delaying tactic.

"Are you sure you don't want to take a bath, too?" Thomas said, his mouth twitching as he teased her.

"Well . . ." Sissy said, drawing out the word as she considered the idea.

"I was only funnin' you," Thomas said, with a shake of his head that made his sister laugh delightedly.

"I know it," she chortled, as she flashed her best grin.

John looked up from the task he had completed, one hand moving the door in place, as he listened to the antics of the two children. He met Lottie's half smile with a shrug that bespoke his own amusement. Then, with a final testing swing, he nodded and pronounced it complete.

"I have to close up the outside door back here and get the lantern," he told Lottie, as he gathered up his tools. "I think I'll leave everything right where it is till tomorrow."

"How much more has to be done, John?" she asked, attempting to peer past him through the doorway.

"The floor's not finished yet," he said, "and I've got to put pegs up for your clothes."

"My clothes?" she asked, her hopes being fed by the promise implicit in the words.

"This is our new bedroom, Lottie," he said softly. "What did you think it would be?"

Her eyes glittered as she considered the thought. A room that was private, where she could have her things all in order. Perhaps she could finally empty her boxes. Maybe John would even build a small shelf for her books! The possibilities were endless, she decided.

"I didn't think, John," she admitted. "I was just so excited about having more space. With the big bed out of here, we might even have room for a settee. Do you think you might be able to build one?" she asked hopefully. "I think I could make up some cushions for it. There's a big bag of feathers in the loft," she said eagerly.

He was silent, and she sensed the darkness that had settled upon him suddenly. "John?" She spoke his name, and the sound was hesitant.

"James bought those from Clarie Higgins, for Sarah to make into pillows," he said carefully. "I was with him when he brought them home to her."

Sarah. Again the presence of the woman pervaded the room, bringing a halt to the nonsense of the children, dampening the mood of festivity that had prevailed all evening. For a long moment, Lottie fought a sense of resentment that tarnished her happiness. Will I always be afraid of her memory? she thought hopelessly. Was she so perfect that just the sound of her name is enough to make John look lost and alone?

"Well, no matter," she said briskly, stifling her thoughts. "We'll talk about it another time." But the mood was spoiled, and the children were silent as they climbed to the loft and made their way to bed.

Lottie waited patiently, while John washed up and then brought a basin of water for her use. His manner was strained as he handed her a towel and a soft flannel to use for washing. Beneath her bed was the china bowl that held her soap, and she reached carefully to find it.

John's eyes were bleak as he turned from her, and his shoulders slumped as he headed for the door. "I'm going to check on the animals, Lottie," he said shortly. "Will you need help with your gown?"

"No. I'm fine. Go ahead," she answered with soft assurance.

He nodded once more in her direction and then buttoned his coat slowly. "I won't be long," were his final words as he headed into the night.

Eighteen

"Don't let me go." The whispered words held a desperate note that served to tighten his grip an her.

With one calloused palm swallowing her smaller hand, and the other clasped with gentle support to her waist, he held her upright beside himself. "You know I won't let you fall, don't you, Lottie?" he asked with concern.

Her nod was abrupt, her mind already on the chore of persuading her feet to support her. "I thought I would just stand up and walk," she wailed piteously. "It isn't working that way."

He muffled the laughter that fought to escape his broad chest, and his head shook mournfully. "You haven't even tried yet, sweetheart, and already you're crying quit."

"I am not," she returned stoutly, lifting her chin in the familiar gesture that he'd prodded her to affect.

"That's my girl," he murmured, pleased at the response he'd generated with his accusation. "Just let yourself get balanced, and then we'll take it a step at a time."

"My toes are numb. I can't feel them," she complained in an intent whisper, as she looked down at her bare feet.

"Maybe we should have put your shoes on first," he muttered. "They'd probably help you balance."

"No." She shook her head once, the movement sure. "I've walked barefoot most of my life. I can do this," she averred. With an indrawn breath, she moved her left foot and slid it along the smooth wooden floor. Then, with a shifting of her weight, she followed it with the right.

"Not bad," John allowed, as he kept up with her, his hands a gentle support. "This time, don't shuffle. Pick up your feet, Lottie."

"I'm not shuffling," she grumbled, as she lifted her left foot with exaggerated care, placing it firmly against the floor.

"You're doing fine," John encouraged in a whisper. "Now the other one," he coaxed, his hand tightening on hers, as he watched the lift and fall of her small foot and noted the way her toes curled to grip against the plank flooring.

"Do you want to try standing alone?" he asked in a casual manner, at odds with the uneven hammering of his heart. Gently he eased his hand from her waist, holding it ready lest she lose her balance.

It was the moment of truth, and he was concentrated fully on the movements of the woman who had given him her trust. She stood on legs that he'd massaged with tender care for over a month now. His hands knew each muscle; each inch of skin had felt his touch. Her feet had known the caress of his long fingers; her ankles and knees the guidance of his fingers, as he rotated the joints and kept them fluid and ready to hold her weight. But all of his tender care could not do this for her. He could only hold her, support her with the essence of his spirit, as she made the effort it would take to walk once more. Deep within his being, he muttered the unspoken words of supplication that he'd chanted innumerable times lately.

"Please, God, let her walk." From his depths the plea came forth in a broken whisper that barely reached her ear. She hesitated only for a moment, before she stiffened her spine and stepped out with a firmness in her bearing that caused him to blink away the sheen of moisture that covered his eyes.

Three times she stepped forward and lifted her right foot to join the left. Holding firmly to the hand he offered, her fingertips white with the force of her grip, she moved slowly, but steadily, until the flat surface of the kitchen table was before her. She leaned forward, just a little, until her hand spread there, her fingers outstretched, and she turned glowing eyes in his direction.

"I walked all the way across the room," she said proudly. He didn't have the heart to point out that the distance was not nearly as far as that.

One look at the pale features she offered for his view spurred him into action. He pulled a chair from the side of the table, lowering her with care to sit upon the seat. He handled her gently, supporting her weight easily, and then dropped to his knees before her, his smile warm and relieved.

"I knew you could do it," he breathed, as he clasped her hands within his own, squeezing them gently.

She bent to place her brow against his, and her eyes closed as she rested there. "You were praying," she said carefully. "I've never known you to pray, John."

"There's lots of things you don't know about me, sweet," he admitted.

She nodded, her skin brushing his with the gesture,

and her sigh was admission enough, without words that would only agree with his.

"Sometimes, it seems like I don't know you at all, John. And then other times, I feel like I can see inside your heart."

The pause was long, and she had begun to regret the words she spoke, wondering if he had taken offense at her claim. But his gentle query silenced her fear.

"Like when, Lottie? When can you 'see inside my heart' . . . know what I'm feeling?"

She brushed at the nape of his neck with her hand, moving the hair to one side to better expose the vulnerable flesh. Her fingers massaged the line of his spine as it became the hollow of his nape, and she relished the feel of his warm skin. Here, where he was pale, where the fall of his golden hair hid his flesh from the sun's rays, she allowed her hand to give him pleasure, as she soaked up the warmth of their intimacy.

"I've watched you with the children, John," she said finally. "I've watched your face when you touch them, when you give them your love and attention."

He moved against her, shifting his shoulders. She lifted her head, settling him against her breast as she allowed her other hand to join the first, sliding her fingers beneath the collar of his shirt to smooth the warm flesh that filled her palm.

"I've watched you when you bathed me . . . when you rubbed my feet and my legs and took care of me . . . other ways." Her voice faltered as she struggled to complete her thought.

"Other ways?" His low growl was muffled against the soft muslin nightgown she wore.

She flushed at the memory he'd given her two weeks

ago, late at night while the children slept over their heads.

"You cared for me in a lot of ways, John," she said, skirting the issue as best she could, aware of his chuckle against the softness of her breasts. "I feel so fortunate." She clasped his head against herself and bent to brush her cheek where the crown of golden hair swirled.

"I'm the fortunate one, Lottie," he admitted. He fit himself carefully between her thighs, tugging her gown to cover the curve of her calves, lest the children should peek from the loft. He eyed her with care, noting the return of color to her face, the pink flush that rode her cheekbones.

"Feeling strong enough to head back to your bed?" he asked, satisfied that she had not overdone, had not forced herself to strain the unused muscles.

She nodded quickly in agreement, and he stood, levering her to her feet as he did. He lifted her with ease in his arms and, over her muffled protests, carried her back to the bed she had deserted only minutes ago.

"Can't I sleep in the big bed tonight?" she asked coaxingly.

His eyes told her the answer before he spoke. Regret was alive in his gaze, and he shook his head. "No, not yet. Doc Holmes said to give it a few more days. Your back needs the support."

She groaned audibly and stretched out her full length on the narrow cot he had created for her. "Well, at least sit by me for a while," she said petulantly, her lower lip protruding in a pout. "Talk to me about your horses, John," she begged, as she turned to one side, facing the fireplace. Her sigh was deep. "You can't know how good it feels to be able to turn over, when I want to," she avowed.

"It's been a long haul, hasn't it, Lottie?" he asked, as he lowered himself to the floor by her side.

She thought of the past two weeks, the gradual return of feeling in her legs, the long hours of massage John had so patiently given, and the neighbors who had continued to visit almost daily. "I've learned a lot from it," she admitted, as she drew his hand up to rest beneath her chin, her fingers enclosing it within a tight grasp.

"Like what?"

"Oh . . . like letting other people take hold and do things." She wrinkled her nose at him. "That was the hardest thing for me to do, you know."

"I kind of got that idea," he said dryly.

"Well, I'm used to doing for myself and a lot of other people, too," she said candidly. "I was raised to take care of myself, John. I learned early on that if I didn't take hold and do things, a lot of them wouldn't get done." Her look was pensive as she allowed the curling flames to draw her gaze. "I don't like to be beholden to others," she admitted softly.

"Not even me?"

She shook her head. "Even that was hard for me to accept," she said. "But I knew I had to do it, if I ever wanted to get off this bed and walk again." Her chin firmed and her eyes narrowed, as she voiced the vow she had taken weeks ago.

"I'll make it up to you, John. I'll do my best to be a good wife for you, even if I'm not what you would have chosen."

He formed his words carefully. "How do you know you're not *just* what I would have picked out for myself?"

She smiled wearily, and closed her eyes against the

quick tears that sprang into being. "I'm not what you wanted," she whispered. "I'm nothing like Sarah was."

His silence prodded her into blinking quickly, her eyes seeking his face as she held her breath against the panic that struck her. Would he be angry? Would he call her down for the self-pity she had exposed to his hearing?

A somber frown painted his features, and he shook his head slowly. "Sarah's gone, Lottie. She was never mine."

"But you'd have wanted a wife like her, someone who knew about linen napkins and fine dishes. Someone beautiful—" Her voice broke on the final word she spoke.

"You're beautiful, Lottie," he whispered, and with a rush of warmth within his breast, he knew the words were the truth. Here in the firelight, without the blaze of passion to fire her from within, she exuded a rare beauty that warmed him. Her eyes were soft, loving . . . an odd mixture of green and blue that beguiled him. Her small, stubborn chin and her short, straight nose framed a mouth that had opened in wonder at his words. That same mouth that had offered him such pleasure with its tender smile, its words of praise, its warm, lingering kisses in the night hours.

His eyes caressed her, his fingers lacing through the waves of sunlit gold that flowed in abundance to settle against her back. He gathered the length of it in his palm, drew it over her shoulder, and brushed it into submission against the curve of her breast.

"You're pure gold, sweet," he whispered, his voice a tender hymn of praise to her.

"But I can never be like Sarah," she mourned. "She was so genteel. She knew all the right things to do."

Her eyes were dark with pain, as she considered the woman who had preceded her in this house.

He brushed a tear from her cheek, glaring at her as if he dared another to fall. "I don't *want* you to be like Sarah," he said with harsh surety.

"Do you remember, when we had the picnic . . ."

"What about it?" he asked, even as he remembered the sorrow he'd dealt with during the long hours of that night.

"Just the mention of Sarah's name upset you. I could tell that you were missing her and wishing—"

His fingers hushed her, spreading over her lips as he shook his head, denying the accusation she whispered.

"No . . . you're wrong, Lottie," he said gently. "I was remembering a day I spent with James, when we went to Joshua Higgins's place to look at his horses." He moved his fingers from her lips, brushing them with calloused tips that sent a shiver of anticipation through her senses. He settled into place, his hands catching hers and holding them captive in the grip of his large, wide palms.

"Horses?" she prodded.

His smile was reminiscent. "Yeah. He has a stallion that I'd give a bundle to own. I made arrangements to take two of my mares there for breeding. Then Clarie told James that she had goose feathers for sale." He shook his head, and his lips curved in fond memory. "We were both well feathered ourselves by the time we got that sackful bundled up and tied onto the back of James's saddle."

"Feathers stick like glue," Lottie said with a smile that shared his humor.

"Well, anyway, we got them here, and Sarah had a hissy fit over the mess she had to clean up from our clothes! All that down had gotten into our pockets and stuck to everything. And then to top it all off, she told James she didn't fancy making any more pillows. So he stuck the bag in the loft.''

His eyes held a residue of sadness that pierced Lottie's tender heart. She pulled one of her hands from his grip to stroke the short bristles on his chin and jaw. "I thought . . . thought that you were thinking about Sarah, and not wanting me to use her feathers," she said falteringly, as he tipped his head to rest his cheek against her palm.

"No." He shook his head, a slow gesture in denial of her words. "I was remembering the last, totally happy time I spent with my brother." His eyes misted once more and glittered in the firelight. "It was a day to remember," he said with a smile that trembled on his wide mouth. "The sun shone and the air was almost warm. That stud just snorted and tossed his head and pawed the ground, like he was putting on a show just for us. James said he was—" He hesitated and grinned. "Well, never mind what James said. The fact is, I took two of my mares there just a week later, and they're going to drop their foals in a couple of months."

Lottie's eyes widened as she took in the import of his words. "Then Sarah must have . . ."

"She died just a couple of weeks after that day. She took sick with pneumonia and never got out of her bed again. Doc Holmes said she wasn't strong. She'd had lung fever when she was a young girl, and it left her weakened."

"Poor James," Lottie breathed.

"He had almost got over her, you know," John said musingly. "Oh, he'd never have got over the hurt. But the memory had faded, and he was happy about you coming, Lottie."

"But it wasn't a sure thing that I would be coming to him," she protested. "Stephen Bush had sent me the fare and had first call."

John's grin was crooked, and his eyebrow lifted in a cocky gesture. "James was sure you'd pick him over the preacher, once you saw your choices close up."

"And then . . ." Her sigh was deep. "Oh, John . . . that was a terrible day," she said, her eyes focused on the flames that flickered from the charred log. "I'd had such high hopes. Then when the sheriff told me that Stephen had left town and no one knew where he was, I just—" Her shoulders lifted and settled once more in a shrug that spoke of her sense of abandonment.

"I thought you looked like a waif, when I saw you in the house with Sissy on your lap and your hair all bedraggled under that bonnet of yours, and that awful dress you had on," he said with a chuckle.

"I thought you looked like an avenging angel, set on throwing me to the devil," she answered with a sidelong glance.

"I needed you here, and I didn't want to admit it," he said bluntly. "You weren't what I'd dreamed of, Lottie."

"Sarah," she murmured.

"Yeah, I guess so," he admitted. "She was all I'd ever known. James married her when I was too young to be considered as a husband. Besides, she only thought of me as her younger brother." He grinned fondly as he considered the memory. "I spent a lot of restless nights thinking about her."

"But you never . . ."

"She never knew how I felt," he assured her. "But James used to tease me about getting a woman of my own."

"Why didn't you?" she asked, cocking her head and considering his strong features. "You could have found a wife, surely. How about Genevieve?"

He shook his head. "No, pretty as she is, Genevieve wasn't the one. And you've been here long enough to know that women are few and far between, hereabouts."

"Then where did you—" The question died before it was fully born, and Lottie flushed as she considered the rashness of her query.

"Where did I learn about loving?"

She nodded and then closed her eyes against his knowing grin. "Never mind, John. I don't think I want to know."

He knelt beside her, rising to his knees in a smooth motion that allowed him to hover over the bed, one long arm on each side of her as she relaxed on the pillows, facing him.

"It's not important, Lottie. But it was no one you'll ever meet, so don't think you have to worry about that." So quickly he erased the thought of the women upriver from his mind. So easily those few, hasty alliances fled from his memory, as he traced with loving eyes the features of his bride.

"Do you still think of Sarah? I mean, in the night, does she still keep you awake?"

Her plea was quiet, and he answered it in a whisper that fell like manna on her hungry heart.

"When I close my eyes now, I see a golden-haired woman with a heart as big as all outdoors. I see eyes that are neither blue nor green, and a mouth that smiles at me in the mornings and gives me pleasure in the night." He brushed her lips with a tender caress that drew a soft moan from the depths of her being, and his smile was beneficent.

"Sarah was my dream for a lot of years, sweetheart. But you're my life. You've filled this house with sunshine and made me happy. What more could I ask?"

"Have I made you truly happy?" she asked, her hungry heart crying for the reassurance of his smile.

"Happier than I deserve to be," he said solemnly.

"I love you, John," she whispered, drawing him back to her so that her lips could rest against his brow, as if that would seal the vow she made. "I'll be the best wife I can," she promised. "And if we can keep the children, I'll try to do for them the way Sarah would have."

His grip tightened on her, as he considered her words. "We may not be able to, Lottie," he said haltingly. "I've not wanted to talk about it, but Harley Garrison said that the maternal grandparents have rights over and above mine. Unless we can persuade them differently, we'll have to let Sissy and Thomas go with them come Christmas."

"It's not over yet," she whispered fiercely, her brow drawn down and her eyes narrowed as her fingers tightened on his shoulders.

"I'm glad you're on my side, little girl," he said with a strained chuckle. "You'd make a mighty warrior, do you know that?"

"I'd give my life for you, John," she vowed.

"I know that, Lottie mine."

"I've never known what it meant to really love someone before," she said, her voice awed at the enormity of the emotion that gripped her.

"I didn't even know what the word meant till now,"

he said, his mouth twisting in a wry grin as he lifted his head to pierce her with the power of his gaze.

Her breath caught in her throat, and she felt a warmth creep up to engulf her, as he considered her with that knowing look. "And now?" she asked breathlessly, as she exhaled the air she had pent up within her.

"Now . . . there's you, Lottie. How could I help but love you? You've run circles around me from the day you got here. You switched that little fanny at me and lured me on with those pink toes of yours, running around here barefoot."

"I never . . ." Her eyes widened at his words.

"Oh, yes, you did," he affirmed with a grin. "And then you kissed me. Right over there in that chair, you kissed me and—"

"You kissed me back," she accused.

"Yeah . . . I did, didn't I?"

She peered at his wide grin, at the sheen of his golden hair, the delight in his eyes as he teased her, and her heart set a new pace within her breast. *Listen,* it seemed to say. *What you hear now is yours to hold within you for all time.*

"Lottie." He spoke her name with an absorbed sense of lingering tenderness that gave it a new sound in her ears. "Lottie . . ." he repeated it as if he would draw her attention to himself, until she could think of nothing but his voice and his face and his presence. "You're my wife," he said slowly, as if he made a pronouncement that should be graven in stone.

Her nod of acceptance was automatic, and she waited, willing to be whatever he asked of her.

"I love you, Lottie." It was a declaration of fact, yet

a tender promise for the future. "I love you now. I loved you yesterday, and I'll always love you."

Her smile was brilliant; her eyes shone with the happiness that spilled from the depths of her heart, overflowing in the bounty of his declaration. "John." It was all she could manage, all her wavering voice could speak as his mouth descended to claim hers in a kiss of intent, a caress that vowed his primitive possession of her.

With gentle care, he lifted her from her rude bed, his muscles flexing as he lowered her to the floor, a quilt caught up beneath her. Catching up a pillow, he thrust it beneath her head, before he allowed her hair to touch the patchwork. Silently, he drew another coverlet to enclose their bodies in a cave of darkness and warmth, and then eased himself to lie beside her beneath its cloak of privacy.

Her eyes never left his face as he carefully freed her buttons, easing each from the grip of the neatly turned buttonholes in a ritual that brought a smile of anticipation to his mouth.

He spread the bodice of her nightgown to either side of her breasts and lowered his head to brush lingering kisses against the firm mounds that rose with lush beauty from the slender body.

"Someday you'll feed my child from these," he murmured as he suckled gently, taking the sweetness of her within his mouth.

Her shiver of arousal spurred him, her moan of acceptance urged him, and her hands at the back of his head told him of her silent approval.

"My Lottie. My bride." With the words of his claiming, he marked her as his own. With the touch of his hands and the giving of his body, he sealed the vows of love he had spoken. And as he lifted her gown to rise over her in a primitive taking of her flesh, he spoke once more.

"You're mine." His eyes pierced her with their narrowed gaze, searing her with the strength of his need, marking her for all time with the force of his possession.

It was elemental. Without the lengthy caresses she had known on other nights, without the soft whispers in the dark they had shared in the hayloft. Without the long moments of preparation he had spent other times, he took her. Carefully, gently, considerately, but with a power that stunned her, he made her his own.

She lay beneath him, shaken by the emotion that gripped her, the happiness that ran rampant throughout her frame. He'd not allowed her to participate, had held her firmly in place, but had nevertheless given her a searing pleasure that knew no equal. Within her had coiled a needing, a yearning, and a heated desire that could only be eased by his touch. She knew, even as he claimed her flesh, that his taking would do her no harm, that he held himself in check, that he controlled his movements—that his intent was the sealing of their love.

And in all of that, he succeeded.

"Are you sure you're comfortable?"

"You've asked me that three times, John," she said with an exaggerated patience that teased him gently.

He frowned at her, his brow pulling down till his forehead creased beneath the brim of his hat. "I want to know right away, if you're getting bounced around back here," he said sternly, doing his best to ignore her flashing dimples.

With a great show of dignity, she conceded to his concern, and, folding her hands in her lap, she nodded submissively. "I'm sure I'll be just fine, Mr. Tillman," she murmured meekly. "You have me wrapped up in four quilts with half a load of hay under them. I have three pillows behind my back and Sissy ready to hold my hand." She peered up at him from beneath the flower-bedecked hat she wore and waited for his response.

It was slow in coming. He lifted one long finger to tilt the dark felt Stetson from his forehead, and his eyes glittered as they narrowed against the noonday sun. The hard line of his jaw tensed as he jutted it forward, and his nostrils flared as he inhaled the faint scent that wafted from her flesh.

Kneeling beside her in the hay, he was tempted to bend nearer, the better to appreciate the residue of her morning ablutions. He leaned over her, casting his shadow on her slender form. John sensed the rising of her ardor, and suddenly, being on his knees became an advantage he decided to use. Yielding to the temptation she presented, he smiled, a faint lifting of his lips that widened her eyes with apprehension as he hovered above her. With the same finger that had tilted his hat, he lifted her chin. Lottie reached automatically to rescue the hat that threatened to slide from the crown of her head.

"Let it go," he muttered darkly, as his head lowered to nestle next to hers. His mouth fastened with sure purpose against the lobe of her ear, and his breath was hot against the furled flesh that cradled his nose.

"John!" It was a smothered cry that begged for discretion, ignored as she had known it would be.

"No bedridden female has the right to be so tempting," he growled, as he worried the tender piece of flesh he held between his teeth. "But your bedridden days are over, Mrs. Tillman," he reminded her gruffly. "That bed of yours is about to be abandoned."

Her inhaled breath told him she was ready to scold him mightily for his indiscretion. He grinned, releasing his prize with a final suction that allowed it to slide from his possession slowly.

Settling back on his haunches, he eyed her with a glittering gaze filled with unspoken promise. With careful, gentle hands he settled her bonnet once more atop the coiled braid that circled her head and adjusted one of the pink flowers, pushing it into place.

Eyes wide, cheeks flushed, and hands clutching her reticule, she watched him. Beside her, Sissy giggled, and that faint sound broke the spell that had held Lottie in thrall.

"We're going to be late to the wedding, if you don't quit your shenanigans, Mr. Tillman," she said pompously, lifting her chin in an imperious manner.

"Can I have a promise from you, Mrs. Tillman?" he asked smoothly, his voice flowing over her with sultry ease.

He'd at least backed off, she thought as she squinted up at him, the sun blinding her. "What promise?" she asked doubtfully.

"Hmmm . . ." he murmured hesitantly, his eyes flickering toward Sissy's delighted grin. With a shake of his head, he rose, towering over both of his women, and vaulted over the side of the farm wagon, only to lean both forearms against the wooden side as he leaned toward them once more. "We'll just leave it open for now, ma'am," he announced primly, his eyes glowing with a teasing light.

From the seat up front, Thomas sighed deeply, and his uncle sent a glance in his direction. "We've plenty of time, Thomas," he said, swinging up to sit beside the boy. "You'll be able to get your shoes scuffed and your knees all dusty before the wedding, if we hurry."

"He'd better not," Lottie said grimly from the back. "I'll not be ashamed of him, walking into that church for the first time in six weeks."

Thomas groaned. "I won't get dirty, Miss Lottie," he promised. "I just want to see my friends."

"I'll stay with you, Miss Lottie," Sissy promised righteously, as she pursed her small lips into an expression that mirrored her profession of saintly behavior.

"Are you warm enough?" Lottie asked her, as she eyed the child's attire. The dark coat she wore was almost too small, its sleeves shorter than those of the dress beneath it. Tucked under the edges of Lottie's quilts, the child snuggled closer with a sigh of satisfaction.

"I'm fine," she said stoutly. "My nose is cold, but my hands will be warm when I put my mittens on." She lifted them from her lap, soft and blue, knitted by Lottie's impatient hands during the past week. Only one dropped stitch marred their perfection, and their creator eyed them with veiled pride.

"Those are the first mittens I've made in years," she said, as she watched the child don them carefully. "I used to knit them for all the little girls where I lived before I came here. I made then each a pair every year for Christmas," she told Sissy, who listened to this rare scrap of information about Lottie's past.

"How many little girls lived in your house?" Sissy asked, as she smoothed the long cuffs over her dress and coat sleeves.

"Oh, thirty or so," Lottie answered, her voice wistful

as she recalled the faces of children she would never see again.

"It must have been a big house," Sissy decided, settling back against the cushion of Lottie's pillows.

"It was. A big, red-brick building with two long bedrooms upstairs, with rows of cots for the girls to sleep in." She closed her eyes against the bright sunshine, and in her mind's eye, she viewed the only home she'd ever known as a child.

"We had a big kitchen with a table in the middle, where I kneaded my bread every morning. We had an icebox to hold the milk and butter."

"What's an icebox?" Sissy asked curiously.

Lottie smiled, her mind taken up with another memory. "It's a wooden box that holds food and keeps it cold. The iceman comes twice a week, three times a week in the summer. And if they're very good, he lets the little girls have slivers of ice to suck on."

"You, too?" Sissy asked.

The memory of that cold, quickly melting chip against her tongue made Lottie shiver. "Yes, me, too," she said wistfully.

"Was it a fancy house?"

Lottie shook her head. "No . . . far from it," she said sadly. "The icebox was about the only modern thing we had. We did a lot of making do most of the time, what with hand-me-downs and missionary barrels from the Methodist church and whatever folks didn't use from their gardens."

"Didn't you have a garden, too?" Thomas asked from the seat in front. He turned to lean over the low plank back, listening with interest to Lottie's description of life at New Hope.

"Oh, yes," she said heartily, dragging her mind from

the least appealing of her memories. "I planted a lot of potatoes and beets and carrots in my day. Pulled a lot of weeds, too," she said with a grimace at Sissy, who giggled obligingly.

"And you gathered eggs," the child said, prompting her.

Lottie nodded. "Yes, every day. Eggs for noodles and for breakfast sometimes. Most of them we sold at market, though, or traded for milk."

"Didn't you have a cow?" Thomas asked disbelievingly, as if no home could be considered complete without its own milk-giving animal.

Lottie shook her head. "No, we didn't have a barn. Just a henhouse and a garden."

"Who was your mama?" Sissy asked.

"I didn't have a mother," Lottie said quietly. "Only Miss Aggie."

"Well, who was your papa?"

"That's enough now, Sissy," John put in from the front seat, where he'd been listening intently to the reminiscing from his wife. In ten minutes, she'd told the children more than she'd managed to share with him in three months.

Lottie turned her head and spoke to his back, "It's all right, John. I don't mind answering her questions."

With a sigh of remembrance, she straightened her shoulders, lest her bonnet be spoiled by leaning too hard against the pillows. "I didn't have a papa, Sissy," she began. "Miss Aggie got me from a policeman one morning, when I was no bigger than a minute," she said, quoting the words she had heard more than once. "She gave me a bottle with a nipple on it and watered-down milk inside of it, and swaddled me up to keep me warm. The bigger girls took turns feeding me and keeping me clean . . . so I really had a lot of mamas, didn't I?" she asked cheerfully.

"But no papa," Sissy whispered softly, as if the thought were too sad to be borne.

"No, no papa," Lottie agreed.

"Were you an orphan?" Her voice was wispy as she asked the question, and she looked up hopefully at the woman whose warmth she shared.

Lottie nodded. "Yes, I was an orphan, Sissy."

"Same as me?" The words were hopeful.

"Oh, no," Lottie said urgently, denying the claim. "You have your Uncle John, and that's almost as good as having your papa, you know."

"And now we have you, Miss Lottie," the child said firmly.

"Yes, and I have you . . . and Thomas," Lottie told her with assurance.

"And Uncle John."

Lottie's heart expanded with the love that filled it to brimming. "You're all my family now," she said, assurance coloring the words that marked John and these children as her own.

"Tell me some more about where you lived," Sissy commanded her, snuggling with proprietary ease against Lottie's side. And was delighted when her demand was met, listening avidly to tales of small girls and long days in a schoolroom, and the dreary ordinariness of life that Lottie somehow managed to imbue with color for the child's benefit.

The hour sped by, the horses maintaining a steady pace through the scant inches of snow that had fallen early in the day. But the rutted road had taken its toll on Lottie, and she was more than ready to escape from the warmth of her bedding, when the wagon reached the outskirts of town.

Outside the church, small boys ran and romped, and Thomas waited with barely concealed impatience till the horses came to a halt before the gate.

"Good . . . we're early," he breathed, as he jumped down from the seat, his own laughter joining those of the boys who welcomed him into their midst.

"Isn't there anyone else here yet?" Lottie asked as she craned her neck to look about.

"Only two other families, so far," John said, wrapping the reins in place before he went to the head of his team of horses. Attaching a short length of leather strap to their harness, he tied them to the hitching rail that provided a place for several such conveyances in front of the church.

"Sit still, Lottie," he commanded her, as she began to loosen the bundling he had imposed on her earlier. "Let me get you out of there."

He lifted himself easily to the bed of the wagon and knelt once more in the hay by her side. His cheeks were ruddy from the cold wind, and he lowered his head to press one side of his face against hers.

"John, you're half-frozen," she said, her voice accusing. She lifted her hands from the cocoon of quilts and placed them on either side of his face, warming his skin with her fingers and palms pressed tightly against him.

"Ummm . . . feels good," he muttered and then, with a quick movement, turned his head to place a damp kiss against the palm of her hand. His own hands were busy with the quilts, unwrapping her and the child who nestled next to her and brushing bits of hay from their clothing. With glee, Sissy scooted to the tail of the wagon and dropped to the ground, stamping her feet and waiting impatiently for the adults to follow.

"Well, Mrs. Tillman," he said heartily, as he took Lottie's weight against him, lifting her to her feet, "are you ready to go to a wedding?"

Her mouth pursed at his teasing, and she brushed her skirts into place as he jumped to stand below her, arms upheld to lift her down. She stood firm, her legs strong beneath her, only the telltale numbness in her toes to remind her of the weeks of inactivity. Today marks the first day of my recovery, she thought with triumph, as she leaned into John's waiting arms. He swung her gently to the ground and held her firmly about the waist.

"All right?" he asked.

"All right," she assured him, stepping carefully as he turned her in the direction of the small white church. Today will prove me to be whole, she thought with fierce pride as she walked with precision beside him, her hand tucked into the bend of his elbow.

Nineteen

If Stephen Bush had thought to marry a woman who would fit into the mold he had designed and labeled as "Preacher's Wife," he was sorely disappointed by the vision of loveliness who walked in measured tread down the aisle of the Mill Creek Methodist Church. But no one in the congregation could have mistaken the look on his face for anything but delight, as Genevieve Slocum made her way to his side.

Borne on the wings of love, she stepped lightly, her hand graceful and slender on her father's arm. The eyes of her beloved were intent upon her as she approached. She was radiant, clothed in pristine white, with a veil that allowed only a glimpse of her beauty and caused all eyes to peer closely in an attempt to see within the virginal folds.

They met before the altar; the dark-haired daughter of the storekeeper and the tall, slender man who had won her heart. She, who had brought so much turmoil into his life, was finally to be his bride. Hair, long and lustrous, waving and curling in a loose arrangement that hung almost to her waist—glowing features that shone with an inner radiance—slender lines that curved voluptuously beneath the concealment of her gown—a girl on the verge of womanhood.

"It would be a crime to cover her up with dark dresses

and pin all that hair up in a knot, wouldn't it?" Lottie whispered in John's ear, as the music swelled in volume. Millie Gordon was at her best, her feet pumping vigorously at the pedals, while her agile fingers pulled magnificent chords from the organ. With a final satisfied nod, she lifted her hands in dramatic emphasis from the keys and ceased working the pedals as the song came to an end. Her head nodded once as she approved her own performance, and then gazed with satisfaction at the bride and groom she had managed to bring together with her fine rendition.

"She's not any prettier than you," John murmured back, as his eyes roved over the woman at his side. Much to his delight, she blushed and cast her eyes down, as she shook her head in silent denial of his words. He snuck his hand into her lap and twined his fingers with hers, claiming his prize with an air of nonchalance.

"John!" she hissed at him, in as quiet a rebuke as she could manage.

He frowned at her in mock reproof and turned his eyes forward as the wedding ceremony began. His hand was warm against hers, and the message was clear. He would place his stamp of ownership upon her, no matter what.

A frisson of joy sent a shiver over Lottie's frame, a thrill of belonging such as she had never known lifted her spirits. A love she could not contain lit her whole being with a radiance that rivaled that of the bride.

"Who giveth this woman?" the Baptist preacher intoned with his booming voice.

Harvey Slocum lifted Genevieve's hand from his forearm, and deposited it into that of Stephen Bush, as he made the correct response. Backing away, he lifted his

white handkerchief to dab with surreptitious care at a
tear that had betrayed his emotional state. Then he sidled into the pew where his dainty French wife sat, her
own hanky already sopping wet.

Lottie felt a pang of pity for the couple who were
giving up their only child into the tender care of the
man she had chosen and for a moment mourned her
own lack of parentage. Was there, somewhere in the
world, a mother who thought of her tow-headed infant,
so long ago abandoned into the arms of a Boston policeman?

"Do you take this woman to be your lawful wedded
wife . . ." The words vibrated in his ears, as John
glanced down at Lottie's profile. Beneath the brim of
her bonnet, her cheek was rosy, her eyelids fluttering,
as she listened and watched. He tightened his grip on
her fingers, and she tilted her head ever so slightly,
casting him a questioning look.

He met it with a warm grin and a nod of his head
that seconded the spoken words of Stephen Bush at the
altar.

"I do," rang out the resonant, deep baritone.

"I do," whispered John Tillman in the ear of his
wife.

Before them, the sun cast brilliant rays across the
gathering of supplicants. A cousin from St. Joseph had
arrived to fill the place of honor maid, and a minister
friend from Stephen's seminary days had come in on
the Friday morning stage to stand by his side. Clothed
in emerald-green velvet, the cousin was a perfect foil
for the bridal white of Genevieve's flowing gown.
Stephen and his friend were resplendent in dark suits
with stiff collars and carefully draped ties, their hair

combed with enough pomade to hold it in place for
the whole day and then some.

Lottie scooted with casual movements until she was
pressed tightly to John's side, her thigh only separated
from his by the layers of clothing they wore. Her mind
was following the words of the ceremony, and somehow
she needed to be as close as possible to the man who
made them real to her.

". . . To love, honor, and obey," Genevieve said, her
voice surprisingly clear as she gave herself into safekeeping.

"I like that 'obey' part," John murmured, bending low
to speak almost soundlessly against her ear, and Lottie
glared at him in reprimand. In silent good humor, he
winked, and she was hard put to remain somber.

"You may salute your bride," the preacher said with
great joy, as Stephen lifted the filmy veil from Genevieve's face and planted a kiss directly on her waiting
lips. A titter from the back of the small church brought
a grim glare of remonstrance from Abigail Dunstader,
as she tilted her chin and sniffed reprovingly.

Then it was over. The organ once more pealed out
joyful chords in a march tempo that granted the newlyweds a hasty departure from the church. Following close
on their heels came the witnesses, who had been properly solemn as long as the occasion demanded, but who
now wore faces wreathed with smiles, as they plunged
arm in arm past the waiting guests.

"Well," Lottie sighed, as the emerald gown flew past
her with a lingering whiff of an elegant perfume in its
wake. "It sure doesn't take long, does it?" she asked,
as John leaned past her to tap Thomas on the shoulder,
reminding him of his manners.

"The wedding is short, but the marriage is forever,

sweetheart," he murmured against her ear, as he allowed his long arm to drape over the back of the pew.

"People are watching us, John," she scolded him sweetly, her smile a mockery as she gritted her teeth and flushed a becoming rosy hue.

"Aw . . . they're just glad to see you out and about, Lottie. Nobody cares if we canoodle a little. Most everybody is out giving the glad hand to Stephen anyway." He settled back in the pew and crossed one ankle over his knee, his shining boots a salute to his wife's diligence. "How long has it been?" he asked her idly.

"How long since what?" she asked, her brow furrowed as she glanced over her shoulder at the rapidly emptying church. Only a few laggards remained in the vestibule, anxious for their turn to greet the newlyweds, who waited in the churchyard.

"Since we stood up there in front of that altar," he said softly.

She turned to face him. "Regrets already, John?"

"No . . . just thinking about all that's happened since then."

"Two months," Lottie reminded him. "Just a bit over."

"We've already faced our share of trials, haven't we?"

"Somehow, I don't think this marriage of ours is ever going to be trouble-free," she said dryly.

He cocked his head, and his grin was filled with approval as he looked her over with narrowed eyes. "I doubt I'll ever find you boring, Lottie," he murmured, his low voice vibrating with subdued humor.

She pursed her mouth and sat up straight, her back stiff and unbending. Her hands were folded primly in her lap, the mended gloves snug against her fingers. Her feet were lined up precisely, the toes of her black calfskin shoes gleaming beneath the hem of her wedding dress. She allowed her eyes to slide in his direction, as she tilted her chin in the familiar gesture he had learned to watch for. He was ready for the warning she issued with precisely chosen words.

"I'm not much on the obey thing, you know. I'll do my best, John, but I'm sure not going to make any guarantees. I had to toe the mark for nineteen years at New Hope, and I'd like to think I've come far enough to make a few choices on my own."

"Yes, ma'am," he said meekly, his eyes dancing at her warning.

"Are you making fun of me?" she asked sharply.

"No, ma'am," he countered with a cocky grin.

"Can't we go now?" Sissy begged, weary of the adult discussion.

"Everybody's outside already," Thomas put in impatiently.

John rose and offered his hand to Lottie. "Up you go," he said, as he assisted her gently to her feet.

She winced as she stood, then shifted for a moment, before she sidled to the aisle and then toward the door, her palm resting on his forearm. Ahead of them the children walked as demurely as they could manage, only to hasten down the steps and set off to join the young folks who were gathered by the gate.

"She must be cold," Lottie said, a worried frown creasing her forehead as she saw Genevieve standing beside the narrow walk. Beside her, Stephen was bending low over the hand of Mabel Sharp, his eyes glowing with good humor.

"She'll be warm soon enough," was John's laconic reply, as he offered her his other hand for added support as she came down the steps.

"Lottie!" The word was warm with welcome, and Genevieve's smile was brilliant as she held both arms open to her friend. With careful steps, Lottie approached her and they embraced, the bride careful and cautious, lest she squeeze too hard.

"You're beautiful, Genevieve." It was a tribute given gladly, and the words caught the ear of Stephen Bush. His measuring eye scanned the two women, who were still holding tight to each other, and he turned to John with an amiable grin.

"Bring back memories?" he asked jovially.

"More than you know," was the enigmatic reply, as John's smile focused on his own bride.

"Congratulations, Stephen," Lottie said, stepping from Genevieve to clasp the hand of the groom. "I know you'll be happy with Genevieve. She'll make a dandy preacher's wife, you know." She bent closer and her voice lowered. "Just forget the dark dresses," she advised him. "She'll be putting her hair up now, anyway. That ought to please the nitpickers."

His voice was deep and solemn and rang with sincerity, as he replied, "I love her just as she is, Miss Lottie. After our talk, I decided to allow her to be herself."

From her other side, Lottie heard a faint whisper as the bride bent closer. "He didn't have a lot of choice," she breathed with a giggle. "I told him I look terrible in black."

John tugged at her sleeve as Lottie laughed delightedly, turning to hug her friend one last time.

"We're being descended upon," he said dryly, motioning at the guests who were bent on speaking to the woman who had become the town heroine only weeks ago.

"Everyone's heard about how brave you were, Lottie,"

Maude said in an undertone as she approached. "Let them see a heroine up close."

Lottie flushed darkly and cast a glance of annoyance at John. "I wasn't brave at all," she sputtered. "Just fortunate that I didn't break my neck."

"Well, you went out looking for two lost children all alone and found them to boot," he said flatly. "That sounds pretty courageous to most of these folks."

Her protestations were in vain as the group gathered about her, and Lottie valiantly faced them with a smile. She was surveyed from all directions as they noted her ability to be out and about. More than one housewife had sent out stews or cakes or bowls of pudding to the household where the young wife had been bedridden for so long. Now they were more than delighted to take their share of the credit for her recovery.

"That Mexican chili of mine will put legs under anyone, my Fred says," said Lulu Wanaker. "I knew it would give you strength."

Lottie smiled with effort. That particular dish had sent John and the children to moaning with a belly ache for the whole evening, and she'd been thankful that she had the good sense to bypass it herself.

"Well, my Hellfire Stew was the first thing she was able to put away," Maude averred. "Got her headed for good health in a hurry."

The voices were raised in friendly rivalry, as Lottie was surrounded by the admiring folks who were eager to welcome her back to their midst. But she had begun to sag. Her legs wobbled beneath her, and her feet felt more numb by the minute, as she cast a searching look about her.

"I'm here," he said from over her left shoulder, his arm firm and warm against her back.

"Miss Lottie's had enough for now, folks," he said with good humor. "We'll be at the Slocums for a bit, but I think she needs to get to the wagon this minute."

He guided her with a slow step and then, just outside the gate, he lifted her in his arms and deposited her on the back of the wagon. Scooting her back on the hay, he patted one knee gently.

"Hold tight, sweet," he said. "We'll only be there for a few minutes. I want to get you home."

Her nod told him that the weary look in her eyes was only the tip of the iceberg, and he hastened to turn the team of horses from the hitching post and down the road to the large home where the bride and groom were already taking their places behind the punch bowl.

The snow began to fall in earnest, as the wagon turned into the long lane that led to the Tillman farm. Cuddled beneath the quilts, her voice rising in a contented singsong manner, Sissy shared Lottie's warmth. They'd pulled the coverlet behind them up over the tops of their heads, and Lottie's bonnet was askew. Only the tips of their noses and the sparkle of Sissy's eyes could be seen, but the air of camaraderie was apparent to the man who listened with amusement to the female chatter.

Although, if the truth be told, it was Sissy who was managing the conversation. With observations of the wedding and plans for Christmas and the almost unending litany of off-tune songs, she had regaled Lottie all the way home.

Not one word about having to run to the outhouse, John thought with a dry chuckle. Probably too cold out to make the idea appealing, he decided. But his observation was blown to smithereens, as the wagon pulled up by the porch and the quilts were thrown back with a flourish.

"I gotta go," the child said in matter-of-fact terms. Off the back of the wagon and toward the corncrib she ran, holding her skirts high about her knees, sturdy legs pumping.

Thomas shook his head, his reaction one of acceptance at his sister's behavior. Then he turned to his uncle. He'd been quiet for too long, John decided as the boy chewed on the inside of his cheek. His hands were restless, fingering the edge of the lap robe that had provided cover against the wind.

"Bundy Guthrie said his pa had a telegram for you," he said finally. He squinted through the fast-falling snow to meet John's own narrowed gaze.

"Yeah, he did."

"Was it from St. Louis?" the boy asked diffidently.

His nod was answer enough. Thomas slid from the seat to the ground, making his way, shoulders hunched, toward the cabin.

"Thomas?" Lottie called after him.

"Leave him go," John said from the side of the wagon.

Her eyes were wide and, beneath the calm assurance she attempted to portray, he sensed a flare of dismay. He reached over the plank side and unwrapped the rest of the quilts that Sissy had left in a jumble with her hasty departure.

"Come on, Lottie," he said glumly. "Let me help you off the wagon."

She was silent, as if words would only put wings on the fear that huddled in her breast. She bent to him, hands on his shoulders, and he lifted her with ease to stand on the ground before him. With tender care, he straightened her hat, tugged at her coat, allowing it to fall about her in dismal array, and then turned her toward the house.

His arm was her support, his hand tight against her waist through the layers of clothing, and she leaned into his strength. The steps were slick with a feathering of snow, and she lifted one foot to place it gingerly on the first one. With a movement she wasn't expecting, John scooped her up in his arms. His heavy boots bit against the covering of white to carry her safely to the porch and into the house.

"It's a good thing those two filled up at the party," he observed, as he removed her coat and untied her bonnet. "You're not about to do anything but head for your bed," he decreed in tones that she knew would brook no disagreement.

He hung the coat, brushed at the few flakes of snow that lingered on her perky flowers, and then placed the hat on a second peg.

She watched him silently and was not surprised when he gathered her within the circle of his embrace and held her against the broad expanse of his chest. A shuddering breath was expelled from beneath her cheek, and she reached to enclose his waist with her arms, holding him tightly.

Across the room, Thomas squatted by the fireside, poking with a stick at the banked fire, ready to lay a log against the glowing remnants of this morning's blaze. He looks so small, Lottie thought as she rested her body against John's lean frame . . . so forlorn.

"What did it say, Uncle John?" the boy asked, his eyes intent on the embers that promised to burst into flame momentarily. The dry bark on the freshly added log caught fire and flared in a brilliant path down the length of wood. Still Thomas prodded, his movements automatic as he waited.

"They're coming," was the reply he'd so obviously dreaded hearing, and his shrug was matter-of-fact.

"I thought so."

"Maybe they just want to spend Christmas with us," Lottie burst out hopefully.

John shook his head. "I doubt it," he muttered. "It'd be foolish to wander around the countryside in December, unless you had good reason."

"They're gonna take us away again," Thomas growled as he tossed the stick he'd held into the firepit. He rose and headed for the door, his eyes averted and his coat pulled tightly about his slim body.

"Thomas." It was a softly spoken word of warning.

"Sir?"

"Not a word to your sister, hear?"

"Yes, sir, I hear," the boy muttered, as he jerked open the door and closed it as hard as he dared behind himself.

"John?" Her own plea was for the child who was even now mourning his loss, headed for the barn probably, where he could shed tears that would only serve to unman him before his elders.

"I'll talk to him later, Lottie," her husband said firmly. "Right now, I want you flat on your back with your shoes off and your hair down."

"My hair down?" She leaned back and stared at him with perplexity. "Whatever for?"

His chin jutted stubbornly, and his eyes were flat with an emotion he held tightly to himself. But his hand was gentle, as it eased into the golden crown of plaited hair that circled her head.

"Because I need to see some beauty to ease me right now. And your hair, free and loose about you, always draws my eyes and gives me pleasure." His gaze was steady upon her face, as his fingers pulled the pins from her carefully arranged braids. He gathered them in his hand and then transferred them in a tidy little clump to her own palm, closing her fingers over them with tender care.

He led her to the bed that still held place of honor before the hearth and settled her on it, only to kneel before her and insinuate himself between her thighs. She allowed the intimacy, spreading her legs to accommodate his hips, and then lowered her eyelids as his big hands worked at the task he relished.

With care, he stripped off the circle of hair she had used to bind the end of her braid, placing it in the same palm that held her pins. His calloused fingertips separated the three plump strands she had woven together and coaxed them to lay with heavy abandon about her shoulders. At the beginning of the braid, where her fragile neck disappeared beneath the bones of her skull, he rubbed his fingers.

Tilting her head forward, she rested it against his shoulder and sighed deeply. "Uhhmmm . . ." It was luxury, pure and simple, this massage that he'd begun. She buried her face in his shirt, beneath the coat he still wore, his scent alive in her nostrils. "I love you, John." It was all she could say. And it was all he needed to hear.

"I know." Harsh against her ear, his voice reflected the frustration he held so tightly within.

Relishing the touch of his gentle hands, yet yearning for the child who had made his lonely way from the house, she was torn. Her better instincts won out, and she lifted her head to face him.

Her voice was brisk as she put a stop to their mutual comfort. "Thomas needs you, John. I'll be just fine here . . . in fact, I hear Sissy coming now. She'll tend to me. You go on out and take care of chores and see to Thomas."

His grin was lopsided as he twirled a length of gold about his index finger. "Kinda bossy, aren't you, woman?" he asked in a raw voice.

"Kinda," she replied slowly, her own hands rising to enclose his face. Leaning forward, she claimed his lips in a kiss that left no doubt of its intent. Warm, soft, and giving, her mouth lent him the strength of her love, offered him comfort in a passionless embrace that brought him bittersweet happiness.

"I love you, too," he whispered, one ear attuned to the opening of the door as Sissy made her way into the house. He rose quickly from the spot he had taken as his own, and Lottie closed her legs, brushing her skirts in place with casual touches.

She faced the fireplace, holding her hands out to the flames that were now climbing the back wall of the pit, reflecting warm waves of heat into the room.

"Miss Lottie." Sissy was on tiptoes, lifting a pan of warm water from the reservoir at the side of the stove. "I'm gonna wash up and then fix us some tea. What do you think about that?" the child asked, intent on carrying the small pan to the sink.

"Sounds fine to me."

"I can't reach the teapot." She was scrubbing at her fingers now, her head bent as she scrutinized her chore.

"Get the water on the stove, and we'll cuddle while we wait for your uncle to come back in, Sissy. He'll have to build up the fire a bit, so the water will boil." She lifted her feet to the bed and shifted herself against the pillows. "Maybe we can talk about Christmas."

As if she had already found a well-filled stocking, Sissy's eyes lit with pleasure. She carefully filled the kettle from the reservoir and set it atop the warmest spot she could reach. Then, brushing her hands together, she approached Lottie.

"Will we have candy?" she asked, wide-eyed with anticipation.

"Perhaps," Lottie allowed, thinking of the licorice whips and pieces of fruit-flavored hard candy she had hidden inside a jar in one of her boxes. John had brought home everything on her list from the general store, Genevieve checking off each item as they filled the order.

New store-bought stockings for both children had found her oohing and aahing with delight, as she handled the finely fashioned cotton. A coat for Sissy would be made with the worsted alpaca she'd chosen to use. Tightly woven, it would keep the cold air from the child, and lined with soft woolen fabric, it would offer warmth through the rest of the winter.

Thomas would be delighted with the new overalls and wool flannel shirts his uncle had purchased for him, ready-made. His small things, Lottie could make from grain sacking. No sense in wasting good material, Miss Aggie always used to say. The girls at the orphanage had been resplendent in pantaloons and petticoats with New Hope Granary, in bright blue print, decorating their underwear.

Lottie spared a moment to consider the children she had left behind. Would Louisa Becker have found time to knit the mittens this year? Would Miss Aggie remember to crack plenty of hickory nuts for the fruitcake? Would they miss their Lottie, those homeless waifs who had made up her family for so long?

Her shoulders lifted in a gesture of weariness, as a deep sigh escaped from her lungs. Beside her, her small bottom wiggling to make room, Sissy plopped herself to bask in the heat of the fireside and the warmth of Lottie's arm about her waist.

"We had candy last year. I remember," Sissy said hopefully. "I was little then," she admitted, "but I still remember how Mama made special bread, and we had cookies. On Christmas we hung our stockings at the end of the fireplace. Pa said they'd catch fire if we hung them in the middle." She peered at Lottie intently. "Do you think he was funnin' us?"

"Did he tease you a lot?" she asked carefully, eager to hear the memories the child was dredging up from her pitiful supply.

"Not much," was the sad answer. "I can't remember a lot of things, anyway," she said with a practical shrug of her narrow shoulders. "Thomas tells me things, and then I don't know if *I* remember them or if *he* does."

"Well, this will be a fine Christmas, Sissy," Lottie promised. And as she said the words, she prayed that they would prove to be true.

Twenty

Torn between wanting her new bedroom completed and the knowledge that John's horses were desperately in need of having the corral finished, Lottie fussed at herself.

It was a relief to be fretting about something other than the impending visit, she decided with a wry grin. She considered the empty room that awaited completion, where she'd spent busy hours for the past days. Otto Schrader was coming on a daily basis, and Mr. Sharp, whose expertise had been limited for years to the construction of coffins, had made the trip twice weekly of late. Both of them were knee deep in the dual building chores John had set for himself.

The sounds of hammers pounding in unison was a daily melody in Lottie's ear. It accompanied her as she assigned lessons to Thomas, and today to the Clawson boys. It had rung in her ears as she sewed furtively on Sissy's coat in the chill of the unfinished bedroom. The fireplace was not completed, having been put in third place until the horses were tended to. Wrapped snugly in her own winter coat, Lottie had curled in a chair out of Sissy's eyesight and sewed for an hour or so during two mornings.

The evening hours found her intent on the completion of the garment. Within two days, she had managed to have it almost ready for wrapping. John had watched idly as she sewed, stretched out on a quilt before the fire, whittling on a whistle he'd decided to make for Thomas and a small horse that was taking shape to be put in Sissy's stocking.

They ignored the issue of the Shermans' visit by mutual consent, both wary of the subject. Thomas had been, by turns, glum with apprehension and buoyed up by the lumpy packages that had been stashed beside Lottie's collection of boxes.

Sissy was ecstatic, having been allowed to help in the baking, her face bedecked with flour and her apron generously decorated with bits of dough and splashes of milk and egg. She had talked nonstop today, until Mabel Sharp had spoken with guarded reprimand and chased the child outdoors to play in the several inches of snow that had fallen overnight.

"Is today the day?" she asked Lottie, speaking of the advent of the grandparents, a subject that had not been far from their minds.

"Yes," Lottie told her with a grimace. "On the afternoon stage."

"They staying long?" Mabel wondered aloud. She stirred the soup with a long-handled spoon and lifted a ladleful, allowing the thick mixture to pour in savory splendor back into the bubbling kettle.

"Looks good, Mrs. Sharp," Lottie said, sniffing the aroma of vegetables and chicken stock. "Yes, they'll be here for a couple of days, according to the telegram." Her fingers were flying as she manipulated the yarn and needles that she was working with. A scarf for John was what she'd decided on as she brushed the fine blue wool against her cheek. Bought from the remnant she had held in her cache—butter and egg money from October—

she'd been careful to keep it from John's sight. Now, while he worked near the barn, she knit with furious intensity to complete the gift.

Lengths of red ribbon had been formed into bows that decorated the fireplace, along with a bough from a barren maple tree, that Lottie had covered with paper snowflakes. Hanging from the branches, tied with blue yarn, the white, carefully cut-out patterns had delighted the children. As much as she was able, she'd prepared her home for the celebration that promised to be bittersweet at best.

The buggy carrying Mr. Sharp and his wife had barely left the farm, when John lifted his head from the bowl of soup he was consuming with deliberate pleasure.

"Bells," he said briefly, his eyes on the window where snowflakes still fell sporadically.

"It's them," Thomas predicted with dreary precision.

"Bet they got a sleigh from the livery stable. Just listen to those bells," John said brightly, putting all of the cheer he could manage into the words. He pushed aside his bowl of soup and headed for the door, reaching for his coat as he passed the peg where it hung.

Lottie followed him, eyes anxious as she peered into the yard from the doorway. The muffled and draped couple in the sleigh were alive with animation, as they unwrapped the robe that covered them. She fought for a smile of greeting as she watched them approach the porch, and then stepped back to welcome them into her home.

"We're so glad to be here," Elizabeth Sherman bubbled. "We've missed all of you." Her eyes focused on the young woman who greeted her, and the warmth in them brought a flush of shame to Lottie's cheeks. "You're up and around. I'm so glad," Elizabeth said with fervor. "We've been concerned about you, but I knew that between John and those grandchildren of ours, they'd take good care of you."

"I'm fine," Lottie allowed briefly. "I'm walking and able to do most everything."

"Well, while I'm here, you won't have to lay a hand to anything," Elizabeth vowed. "You can just sit down there and tell me what to do."

Lottie's eyes were wide with amazement. The last visit had been so tense, so filled with apprehension, and so fraught with pain on her part at the end, that she was stunned by this new vision of Sarah's mother.

The door opened once more, and John appeared, arms filled with bundles that he carried carefully. "I'll put these in the other room," he said, looking about for a bare surface and finding none.

Gentry Sherman came in behind him, lugging a huge carpetbag and stamping his feet, lest he carry snow past the doorway. "Lottie," he boomed in a cheerful voice. "You're looking pret' near as good as new."

Such cheer was almost beyond Lottie's comprehension, so hard had she been trying to elevate the spirits of her household for the past four days. And it did not end there. During the next hour, Elizabeth praised the decorations, adding a few glass ornaments she had brought with her to the snowflake-covered maple branch.

Sissy was enraptured by the colors that reflected the firelight, and the glow of the lantern that hung from the center of the room. She was even more thrilled by the fruitcake Gentry unwrapped from layers of newspaper and placed in the center of the table.

Lottie was greedy for the sight of a real issue of the St. Louis newspaper that the elder couple treated with such casual disdain. It had been months since she'd laid eyes on newsprint such as this. Filled with advertisements and articles on fashion and society, not to mention the state of the country, she found it fascinating and had abandoned her company manners to become engrossed in it.

John was deep in a discussion of his horses and the prospects for spring foals with Gentry, who proved to be more than knowledgeable in the subject, and Elizabeth basked in the atmosphere of warmth the small house offered.

Only Thomas sat on the outskirts of the group, sober and taciturn as he rubbed two sticks together, peeling the bark and making a mess on the floor.

"Isn't it almost bedtime?" Elizabeth asked Sissy. "It's fully dark outside."

Looking to Lottie for confirmation, Sissy accepted the nod she had expected in answer to her silent query. "Will we read the Christmas story?" she asked, ready to bring forth the heavy Bible that was almost more than she could carry.

"Certainly," John said. "Then we'll hang the stockings."

"Maybe I'll just go on to bed," Thomas said, with indifference rife in his voice.

"Maybe you won't," Lottie admonished him gently. "This is Christmas, Thomas."

Elizabeth Sherman lifted her head to meet the eyes of her husband across the room. His nod gave her tacit permission to speak the words that were already about to leap from her mouth.

"We might as well get this out in the open," she said,

with a gust of breath that powered her words forth in a mighty burst. "Children, I want you to come here. Both of you."

Thomas glowered, his feet moving as if they begrudged every step, and Lottie's heart yearned to comfort him. Sissy's eyes were wide with question, as she sensed the heightened anxiety in the room. Lottie felt a burst of anger within her that was on the verge of overcoming her good sense.

She tightened her lips, felt the flaring of her nostrils, and heard the thumping of her heart, as the fury built in a storm that threatened to explode.

John's eyes were upon her, his face anxious as he sensed her state of irate tension, and he rose from the table to stand behind her. She sat upright on her bed, which had been in use as a settee during the days of late. Within the folds of her skirt, her hands twisted together, and she concentrated on the kindly woman who held Sissy within the crook of her arm.

"You know that your grandfather and I wanted to take you to St. Louis the last time we were here," she said with a smile of persuasion.

"We didn't want to go," Sissy said decisively.

"Still don't," Thomas put in.

The smile faded just a bit, but the glow in her eyes held firm as Elizabeth continued. "We love both of you, and we want you to have the very best things in life."

"We got Miss Lottie and Uncle John," Sissy piped up.

"Well, yes . . ." Elizabeth shot a quick look of apology toward the couple that watched her closely. "I know that, but I mean other things. Like good schooling and libraries and fine—"

"We're doin' just fine here," Thomas interrupted stubbornly.

"Thomas!" his uncle said, reprimanding him with firm resolve.

"Yes, sir." The boy dropped his eyes, and his shoulders slumped as he acknowledged defeat.

Lottie knew a moment of pure panic, as she realized that the children who meant more to her than she'd ever imagined possible, were on the verge of being taken from her grasp.

"Wait—" she gasped. "Wait a minute, Mrs. Sherman." John's fingers gripped her shoulders in warning, but she twisted from his grasp and rose to pace the floor with long strides that belied the injury that had befallen her just weeks ago.

All eyes were on her, John's amazed, the children's filled with a hope that could not be missed by any who cared to look.

"I may not be their mother, but I think I know what Sarah would have wanted for these two," Lottie said slowly. Her voice trembled with the effort she was making to keep her volume under control. She clutched her fingers tightly at her waist, holding the queasiness at bay that threatened to overwhelm her.

"James and Sarah wanted their children to be raised here. Here, where they can be strong and grow up to earn their own way in the world. They're bright and healthy, and they're learning to take pride in what they do." She waved her hand at Sissy, and her chin tilted as she paid the child her due.

"Sissy is just five years old. She has manners, she can wash dishes, gather eggs, and feed the chickens. She knows her colors and can speak her letters, well, a little at least." Her eyes went to Thomas, who was watching openmouthed and in awe of the woman who had taken on the task of defending him.

"Thomas can milk a cow and plant corn and care for the horses. He's doing well with his letters and numbers, and he can read some words already. As soon as we can send for some books, he'll be well on his way to reading." Lottie looked about herself at the audience of silent listeners.

"St. Louis can offer these children a fine life. I'll be the first to admit that. But I'm not sure it's what their mother wanted for them. If she had, she wouldn't have chosen to live here herself. But she did choose that, and if you take them from here now, you'll be going against what she wanted for them."

She turned to John, and her eyes filled with tears. As if she had been deflated, she crumpled, her arms reaching for him. He picked her up against himself and comforted her, turning his back to protect her from the watching eyes that were stunned by her words of protest.

"Now see here," Gentry Sherman began roughly.

As if they had been released from a spell, both children ran to John and Lottie and clutched at them with eager hands.

"Miss Lottie," Sissy cried, burying her face in the folds of Lottie's dress.

Thomas gulped and turned about, leaning against the solid form of his uncle. "We don't want to go away," he affirmed.

"Now see here," Gentry repeated, rubbing his hand over the top of his head and frowning intently as he looked across at his wife.

"I'm afraid you've all misunderstood me," Elizabeth said gently. "Gentry and I . . . we've come to a decision that I hope will be mutually agreeable to all of us." Her eyes were damp with unshed tears, as she viewed the four people who clung to each other. She waved her hand at the bed and the chairs and her beckoning finger coaxed Sissy to come to her. "Please, won't you sit down and just listen for a moment?"

Lottie gave the little girl a gentle nudge and Sissy followed her unspoken instruction, moving with hesitant steps to stand beside the grandmother she had only begun to know. Thomas stayed beside his uncle, unwilling to change his stance.

"I'm sorry, Elizabeth," Lottie managed, her face flushed with embarrassment as she apologized for her outburst.

"Don't be," the older woman said briskly. "I'm pleased that you care so much for my grandchildren. That makes what I have to say much easier."

"Speak up, mother," Gentry urged her gruffly.

"We—Gentry and I—want to offer a proposition for your consideration," Elizabeth said. "We'd like to offer our home and all the financial consideration necessary for Thomas and Sissy, when the time comes for them to go on to college."

"College?" Lottie squeaked. "That's years away."

Gentry shook his head. "No, not from our viewpoint. Time manages to fly by, when your hair starts to turn white and the calendar changes too quickly."

"We have a lot of good years left in us," Elizabeth said with good humor. "But we know that the children will be better off with young parents. That's why we've decided to leave them here with you. We only ask that you send them to us, or better yet, *bring* them to visit. Maybe during the summers sometime. Certainly once every year or so. In fact, in a few years, when the railroad comes through, they'll be old enough to make the trip on their own."

"On a train?" Thomas asked in a stunned voice.

"Alone?" Sissy breathed, with sheer horror alive in the word.

"I can take care of you, Sissy," her brother said as he cast a look of scorn in her direction.

"You'll leave them here?" John asked softly, for the first time in four days feeling a ray of hope for his immediate future.

"Yes . . . that's what I was trying to tell you," Elizabeth said firmly. "If you'll agree to share them with us, allow us to be real grandparents, we'll tear up the paper that grants us custody."

Lottie rose and went to the woman who had just given her the best Christmas present she could have imagined. Arms outstretched, she embraced Elizabeth, her thanks muffled against the fine organdy of the ruffled collar that adorned the woman's dress.

"I feel just like Christmas," Sissy said.

"It's almost here," Gentry allowed, snapping open his pocket watch to check the time. "Just a couple of hours till midnight."

"Can we read the story now?" Sissy wheedled. "Then we can go to bed, so Christmas can come for real."

Thomas made haste to get the family Bible and laid it carefully in John's lap. His small, capable hand rubbed for a moment at the gold inlaid printing on the cover, and then he opened it carefully.

"This was my pa's Bible," he said stoically. "He used to read it to us, sometimes. But not much since our ma went away."

"Well, I'll read it tonight," John told him, making

room for the boy beside him, as they shared the long bed before the fire.

The light spread its rays from the lantern, glistening on the glass bulbs that had cone direct from St. Louis, then sparkling against the brooch that Elizabeth Sherman wore at her throat. But nothing in the room shone more brilliantly than the expectant faces of those who were gathered before the fireplace. Unless it was the tears that begged to be shed in the eyes of Gentry and Elizabeth Sherman.

"We get raisins in our oatmeal," Sissy bragged, as she sat in the place of honor between her grandparents. The table was crowded, but the children ate quickly, determined to earn the privilege of emptying their stockings.

Chores complete, they had only to finish breakfast, and the moment they had anticipated for days would be upon them.

"I'm done," Thomas announced as he scraped the bottom of his bowl, and with that, he peered anxiously at the food yet to be eaten by the adults.

"Maybe we could just finish this later," Gentry suggested, his eyes bright as he watched his grandson.

"John?" Lottie asked with eagerness alive in her breathy tone.

His smile expansive, John rose from the table. "It's Christmas," he said, as if that pronouncement was all that need be said.

For almost an hour, the air was filled with exclamations of pleasure, as the children emptied their stockings and then opened the gifts their grandparents had brought. John and Lottie watched from their vantage point near the door, as Sissy and Thomas investigated the presents that had been stored in the corner. Thomas's eyes widened as he held up the new overalls and then brushed his fingers with awe over the fine nap of his flannel shirts.

Sissy could hardly be persuaded to remove the new coat. Only the promise of wearing it to church on Sunday convinced her to take it off and hang it on a peg. She stood next to it and patted the fine lining for a few minutes, brushing it with her fingertips and against the side of her face.

When it seemed that all had been examined and praised accordingly, John cocked his head to one side and turned to the window. "Someone's coming," he announced with surprise. "Who would be out on Christmas Day?"

Gentry's mouth twitched in amusement. "Probably someone who wanted to earn a tidy sum," he said smugly.

John stood at the window and watched as a large wagon lumbered up the lane, drawn by two draft horses and driven by Young Willy from the livery stable.

"What on earth is he bringing here?" he muttered under his breath, even as he cast a questioning look at Gentry Sherman, who wore a look of innocent enjoyment.

"Can't imagine!" the older man answered jovially.

Lottie peered past John, Sissy tugging at her skirt. "Let me see, too," she begged, wiggling impatiently.

"Why don't we open the door and see what the gentleman has on his wagon?" Elizabeth suggested from the table.

"A splendid idea," her husband agreed, as he swung

the door wide, allowing a blast of cold air to fill the room.

"Hey there, folks," Young Willy called from the high seat where he held court. "Looky what I got for you, Miss Lottie. And you, too, Mr. Tillman." A broad smile wreathed his face, as he gloried in his good fortune. Obviously, not too often did visitors hire him for such a task, willing to pay such an extravagant wage for a morning's work.

"What does he have on that wagon?" Lottie asked impatiently, nudging John out onto the porch.

"Come here, Lottie," Elizabeth said, summoning her quietly from her place at the table.

Reluctantly, but remembering her good manners, Lottie backed away from the open door and turned to face the older woman.

"Let me tell you about it," Elizabeth suggested with a sad, little smile that brought Lottie closer. "Sit down with me," she said, patting the chair that sat empty next to her.

"All right," Lottie agreed, her curiosity piqued by the woman's strange mood.

"We knew we wanted you to be the children's mother, before we came this time, Lottie," Elizabeth began. "So we thought, as long as you were taking Sarah's place with them, you deserved to have some of Sarah's things. Then, one day, when you have no more use for them, they'll go to Sissy." She paused and drew a deep breath. "That's what's on the wagon," she said after a moment. "We brought you Sarah's bed, with a fine, new, cotton-padded mattress, so that your back will have good support. The chest of drawers was made in Chicago. We had it shipped to St. Louis for Sarah's wedding gift, but she and James didn't have room on the wagonload of things they brought here. There are a few other things, too, that we thought you could use." Her eyes begged for Lottie's words of agreement. "We so want to give you what we can . . . to help out a little."

"But why did you wait so long to bring these things?" Lottie asked bluntly. "It's too late now for them—"

"We had some hard feelings," Elizabeth admitted with a pained look that tore at Lottie's generous heart. "We wanted better than this for our daughter," she whispered, as she waved one hand to include the room they sat in. "But she wanted James Tillman. I truly believe," she said with a quiver in her voice, "that he made her happy. You know, Lottie, it almost broke my heart to know that I had grandchildren here, and still it took my daughter's death to open my eyes to all the time I had wasted." Her mouth firmed as she glanced at Lottie with anxious eyes.

"I vowed to know these children, but I was afraid to approach James. He had some bitter feelings," she said without rancor. "But when he died, too, we determined to take the children back to St. Louis. That was before we met you."

She smiled at Lottie, her sadness held in abeyance by the commotion that was taking place just beyond the doorway. "I think you must come with me now, Lottie, and inspect the furniture we've brought for your new bedroom."

Pandemonium reigned in the yard, as Thomas and Sissy ran from one side of the wagon to the other, alternately inspecting its contents and then joyfully describing the furniture it held in jubilant tones.

Lottie shivered in the cold air, unwilling to miss a moment of the hubbub that filled her vision. Her smile was benevolent as she watched the children's antics. Gentry Sherman stood with thumbs in his suspenders, satisfaction alive on his round face.

Then, from several yards away, a pair of blue eyes caught and held hers, and Lottie was once more in thrall to the spell of John Tillman. Windblown and tousled, his golden hair shone in the wintry sunlight. Wide and gloriously happy, his gleaming grin pierced her heart with a shard of happiness that caught at her breathing.

Tall, broad-shouldered, deep of chest, and hardy as the land that had molded him, he faced her. With promise in his eyes, with love abundant in his glowing smile . . . and with her future in his arms.

Epilogue

"I like the feather tick better." She rolled to settle above him, her leg draped over his thigh, and her cheek nestled where his heart beat at a slow, steady pace.

His hand ceased the soothing movement he had been applying to her lower back, as he considered the whispered complaint. Then, with a chuckle, he resumed his nightly chore, one he relished.

"How long do you suppose Doc Holmes will make you do this, John?" She yawned, stretching the muscles he'd been massaging.

His shrug was eloquent. "Maybe forever," he mourned in a doleful grumble.

"Surely not!" Her whisper was louder, but muffled against his chest.

"Hmmm . . ." His hand drifted a bit and then, with firm purpose, cupped the plush roundness of her bottom.

"That's not the right spot," she muttered, wiggling against his grip.

"I think so," he growled.

"Hmm . . . maybe so." Her smile was content as she burrowed against the warmth of him.

"Lottie."

"Ummm . . ."

"Are you going to sleep?"

"No, just thinking."

"Yeah, me, too." He slowed the movement of his hand as his thoughts traveled to an idea he'd been nursing for days.

"John." She paused and lifted her head from his chest, the better to see his face in the dim light. "You know I unpacked my boxes today."

"Yeah." His smile widened as he considered her worried expression.

"Well, I have these flannel pieces that I have to use once in a while."

"Hmmm."

"Do you know what I'm talking about, John?" Her tone was filled with frustration, as she hoped for his understanding without having to spell out the problem she'd been considering all evening.

"Maybe," he answered in a low, husky rumble.

"I haven't used them but once since we got married, John," she admitted quietly.

"I know," he answered.

"How do you know?" Her query was indignant.

"Who took care of you for almost six weeks, Lottie?" She buried her nose in the patch of hair that centered his broad chest, and sighed deeply. "You did."

"We didn't have to dig out any of those flannel pieces for the whole six weeks, did we?"

"No," she said meekly.

"Do you know what that means, sweetheart?" His low growl was fraught with delight.

"Is it all right?" Her whisper was wispy, as if she groped for comfort.

"It's the most all right thing I can think of," he assured her with a hug that took into account the injury she had suffered, and then rolled her to her back with a gentle movement that protected her carefully. "The question is—is it all right with you, Lottie?"

"Oh, yes," she breathed, with a joyful tension in her whisper that told him what he needed to know.

"Mid-July, do you think?" he asked, his mouth against her throat, as he tasted the sweet scent that was the very essence of Lottie O'Malley Tillman.

"Ummm . . . I guess so." She tipped her head to one side, enjoying his attention. "Do you think Miss Aggie will be surprised?"

"Somehow, sweet, I don't think your Miss Aggie would be surprised by anything you do."

"At least I followed her advice," Lottie said airily.

"What is that?" he mumbled, as he worked at the buttons on her new nightgown.

Her sigh was one of pure satisfaction, as she held him in place while she gave him the benefit of Aggie Conklin's wisdom.

"Miss Aggie always said that if anything was worth doing, it was worth doing well, and if we did our best, reward was sure to follow."

He was past the barrier of buttons and had managed to locate the prize he sought. His voice was muffled against her lush flesh, as he chuckled at her prim recitation.

"Don't you think I've done well?" she asked indignantly, her giggle almost smothered against his hair.

"Well," he drawled in his growly voice that sent tingles down her spine. "I don't know if you've done your best *yet*, sweet, but I'll sure let you keep practicin'. My daddy used to say that practice makes perfect, and I'm thinking it may take fifty years or so to get this just right."

About the Author

Coming from Michigan to South Carolina several years ago, Carolyn Davidson decided to fulfill a lifelong ambition—writing romance novels. As wife, mother, and grandmother, she works in a new/used bookstore and copes with a busy schedule. All this with the help of her husband Ed, her childhood sweetheart, the most romantic man she's ever met!